The Dead Wh
The Red Hatchets
and Evil Eye

THREE HARD-BOILED ADVENTURES OF

The
WHISPERER

by Laurence Donovan and Alan Hathway
writing as Clifford Goodrich

plus

"Norgil—Magician" by Walter B. Gibson
writing as Maxwell Grant

with New Historical Essays by
Will Murray and Anthony Tollin

SANCTUM BOOKS

The Whisperer Volume 1 copyright © 2009 by Sanctum Books.

This Sanctum Books edition is an unabridged republication of the text and illustrations of two stories from *The Whisperer,* as originally published by Street & Smith Publications, Inc., N.Y.: *The Dead Who Talked* from the October 1936 issue, and *The Red Hatchets* from the April 1937 issue, plus "Evil Eye" from the May 1, 1938 issue of *The Shadow Magazine* and "Norgil—Magician" from the November 1937 issue of *Crime Busters*. This is a work of its time. Consequently, the text is reprinted intact in its original historical form, including occasional out-of-date ethnic and cultural stereotyping. Typographical errors have been tacitly corrected in this edition.

International Standard Book Number:
978-0-9822033-5-4

First printing: May 2009

Series editor/publisher: Anthony Tollin
anthonytollin@shadowsanctum.com

Consulting editor: Will Murray

Associate editor and interior graphic production: Tom Roberts
www.tomrobertsstudio.net

Copy editor: Joseph Wrzos

Cover and photo restoration: Michael Piper

The editors gratefully acknowledge the assistance of Randy Vanderbeek, Donald Ramlow and Mark Luebker in the preparation of this volume.

Published by Sanctum Books
P.O. Box 761474, San Antonio, TX 78245-1474

Visit The Whisperer at www.shadowsanctum.com.

THREE
AMAZING
ADVENTURES OF
THE GRAY WRAITH

The
WHISPERER

Volume 1

Thrilling Tales and Features

**Front cover art by Tom Lovell.
Back cover art by John Newton Howitt and Tom Lovell.
Interior illustrations by Paul Orban and R. Doremus.**

THE DEAD WHO TALKED
by Clifford Goodrich

"I will not be home, for I am dead."—words of death that spread terror over the city. Then another warning—and The Whisperer strikes!

CHAPTER I

THE WHISPERER STRIKES

"DUKE" DOLANO was putting on a show. He had just beaten a tough "rap." The Duke had beaten other raps, many of them. But this was a murder rap. It was extra special. So Duke was putting on an extra special show.

A pretty, blond manicurist was doing his long nails. A wizened, black-eyed shoe-shiner was polishing his shoes. A Negro orchestra was playing

The sound that came could hardly be called a shot. Not even with a silencer. If it was, it was continuous. A hissing like the slow escape of steam or air under great pressure.

jazz. Duke's show was public, or rather it was semi-public.

A hundred or more citizens were watching Duke's display of conceit. Perhaps half of these were good citizens. Some of the others might not even have been citizens. At least they were not qualified to vote, having lost their citizenry by confinement in various prisons.

Duke's egotistical exhibition was only partly public because it was taking place in his own fourth floor establishment. This fourth floor was devoted to a variety of games. The games were illegal, for the most part. So Duke's resort had no public or legal recognition.

The games were devoted to taking money from the visitors. In this they were impartial as to who

were good citizens and who were not. They took money from anyone who had it. Some of Duke's employees were making books on everything from horse races to wrestling matches. Others got the money by whirling wheels and having the little balls stop at numbers they controlled by various unlawful devices.

Duke Dolano had a white-toothed grin for all who had money to lose. The grin was wider, more benevolent tonight. For Duke had again made monkeys of the police. He had done that so often, he had come to believe the police were monkeys.

Sparti and Saffern sat near Duke. They reflected his grin. They copied nearly everything Duke did. They were wearing the slickest of evening clothes, like Duke's.

Sparti and Saffern felt that they were a part of this show. They had been taken to court with Duke Dolano, and they also had beaten the murder rap at the preliminary hearing. The police had failed to produce evidence to hold them.

THE MURDER charge had been made because of the death of Sam Markleson, a well-known gambler. Markleson had stepped in front of a speeding automobile. Some witnesses had said, at first, that Markleson had been pushed in front of that car.

Not all of these witnesses had appeared at the preliminary hearing. Those who did failed to remember saying Markleson had been shoved to his death. And some who, at first, had declared Duke Dolano was at the wheel of the death car, had suffered a serious lapse of memory

The police had produced the glass from a broken headlight. It had been presented as coming from Duke Dolano's car. But the police were forced to admit that this car, when found the next day, had two undamaged headlights.

That had been about all of the testimony. So the presiding judge had not held Duke or his body-guarding companions, Sparti and Saffern. No one, not even the judge, but believed Duke Dolano had been driving the death car. But you cannot hold or indict any man for murder on what people believe, even on what a judge believes.

So Duke Dolano's shoes were being polished until they glistened. His small ears were being surfeited with orchestral harmony. Duke basked in what he believed to be the admiration of his gambling house customers. There was an undertone of comment in the place, directed at Duke

This murmur of voices suddenly hushed. Two men had walked through the door leading from the front elevator. One was plainly dressed in a gray suit. Here the quietness of his clothes ended.

This first man wore a broad-brimmed hat that might have seen service in the army. His necktie was violently red. It matched a flaming carnation in the buttonhole of the gray suit.

Nearly everyone in the room knew the man as Police Inspector James Gordon. He was slightly less than average height, but many present were aware he was widely known as "Wildcat" Gordon. Those who didn't would only have to look once into his Texas eyes to suspect why Inspector Jim Gordon had earned the name of Wildcat.

These eyes, now fixed directly upon Duke Dolano, might have been either blue or gray. Texas eyes. Quiet, straight-seeing eyes that no man would want to see behind the barrel of a .45. The eyes that predominated among law enforcement officers in the State of Texas, from the days of the Texas Rangers down to this time.

Inspector Gordon walked straight to where Duke was enthroned in his chair. The inspector had a whimsical smile for the pretty, blond manicurist. He also smiled at Duke Dolano, but that was only from one corner of his firm, tight-drawn mouth.

"Nice to be seeing you, Inspector!" spoke Duke Dolano in a boisterous tone that all in the room could hear. "Nice of you to drop in! Always glad to see one of the boys!"

Duke's boastful speech no doubt was justified. If he had made monkeys of the rest of the police, he had made a monkey especially of Inspector Gordon. The Markleson murder had been handled by Gordon personally.

Inspector Gordon said calmly, "There's only one place it would be nice to see you, Duke. That would be a chair with straps attached. Someday you will get a manicure in one, and it will be permanent."

Duke Dolano threw back his head and laughed as if this were a great joke. The eyes of his companions, Sparti and Saffern held sudden sparks. There was another murder in them. Inspector Gordon possibly saw more than that.

Sparti and Saffern could not take it like Duke did. There was a hint of twitching fear in their faces. They were not so sure yet that Wildcat Gordon had fallen down on this murder case. He had been on other racket homicides. This would be the first where he had failed.

When he had laughed, Duke Dolano said, "You'll always have your little joke, Inspector! Anyway, I'm glad you dropped in! You can have a look around and see how everybody's enjoying themselves!"

"I'll do that," said Wildcat Gordon.
I like to see folks having a good time."

INSPECTOR GORDON had already looked around. Of the hundred or so in the place, he had swiftly classified every man. Yes, some were good citizens. The orchestra blared again. Gordon went over and spoke to a middle-aged fellow sitting at a table.

This man said, spreading his hands, "You would catch up with me in a dump like this, Gordon. It's a weakness of mine to flirt with chance once in a while."

"Gets a man's mind off his troubles, and I imagine you have plenty of them," said Gordon pleasantly.

He knew the middle-aged man as Homer Rand, a noted electrical engineer. Gordon recalled that Rand had been getting considerable publicity recently. Rand had invented a dynamo that was due to make him famous and a new power company immensely profitable.

The man who had entered with Inspector Gordon had not accompanied him when he had spoken to Duke. This man was far along in years. He wore a hard Derby hat pulled down over a bald head. His eyebrows had the bushiness of birds' nests. He peered nearsightedly at everyone. This might have been deliberately deceptive, for he had a habit of seeing and remembering much more than he was supposed to have seen.

The older man was Dick Traeger. He was well along in his sixties. For thirty years, he had been in the department. When he had been retired, much to his disgust, he had been deputy commissioner of police. In his later years on the force, Dick Traeger had become known as "Quick Trigger." This quickness with a gun may have had something to do with his early retirement on pension.

Dick Traeger often trailed with Inspector Gordon. He liked to pass his old-age holidays in close touch with what the force might be doing. For many years, even before Jim Gordon had served a hitch in the army and become an officer, Dick Traeger had been almost a father to him. Now he fathered Gordon's police career.

Old Quick Trigger now watched Gordon talking with Homer Rand, the electrical engineer. He glanced occasionally at the cocky and confident Duke Dolano and said, "The damn braggin' scut!" under his breath.

Some of Dolano's gambling customers showed signs of uneasiness. A few good citizens did not like the idea of being seen here by the police. Several of the other type liked the idea even less. In a few minutes there was a movement of some toward the exit.

Inspector Gordon talked with Homer Rand perhaps five minutes. Possibly it was only by chance that Gordon observed the wall clock and noticed it was 11:45, almost on the second, when the lights in the place went out.

When this darkness came suddenly, the orchestra had just ceased playing. The shoe shiner had finished with Duke Dolano's shoes. The pretty manicurist was folding up her appurtenances. The manicurist uttered a delicious little scream of shock.

This small scream was instantly succeeded by the hush that comes upon any crowd in a moment of emergency, like lights going out. Duke Dolano was first to break it.

"What the hell?" he said. "Sparti—the other switch! Maybe it's a fuse blown out!"

Other voices might have broken forth then, but over and through the room came a whispering. In the confusing darkness, it did not seen to emanate from any particular spot. Rather, it filled all of the room with startling, clearness, a sibilancy that penetrated to every ear and left no doubt of the words or meaning.

"All of you, stay where you are! It's a holdup!"

THE CROWD'S BREATH was suddenly expelled at that. A few growled oaths in undertones. Duke Dolano spoke blusteringly.

"Holdup? What's the joke? What's the joke? Sparti—them lights!"

"Quiet, Dolano! Sparti, stay where you are!"

The ear-filling whisper again. And because of its hissing, the words gave no hint of what manner of voice might be speaking. Only from Sparti, or perhaps Saffern near him, came the exclamation:

"Duke! The Whisperer!"

"Right!" instantly came the high whisper. "And keep away from the money table! The first man to touch the cash will die!"

While the darkness was intense for the first few seconds, a dim light made itself apparent from the windows at the rear of the room in the next minute. These windows were covered with light, iron grillwork. They opened on the fire escape. Street lamps outside made them vaguely apparent.

Against this poor light the persons in the room showed only as stiff shadows. Though it was dark, some had their hands thrust into the air. Whoever had first spoken the name, "The Whisperer" had caused an icy chill to permeate the well-warmed gambling room.

The Whisperer!

None in the darkness there but had read of the exploits of The Whisperer. Like tonight, this fantastic, whispering voice had recently visited other places. In three of six recorded holdups there had been deaths. Perhaps the newspapers exaggerated, but it had been reported these killings had been as sudden and as silent as this sibilant hissing of The Whisperer himself.

Those who had died apparently had resisted. It was marked only that in each killing the victim had shortly before that time beaten a murder rap. The six holdups had been of little profit to the mysterious Whisperer, though each had been staged in some gambling or other mob resort where considerable loot had been available.

Tonight now, in Duke Dolano's place, several thousand dollars lay on the table where the dealers and customers cashed their chips or tickets. This money was close to the chair where Duke Dolano had been sitting for his little show of bravado.

So The Whisperer's name passed from tongue to tongue in the room. Only those uttering the words kept them more silent than The Whisperer himself. There was a rustling, as if the money on the cashing table was being swept up.

The electrical engineer, Homer Rand, said in an undertone, "Here's your chance, Gordon."

Inspector Gordon had been standing beside Rand in the moment before the lights went out. But Gordon did not reply to Rand. The electrical engineer put out his hand. Inspector Gordon had moved from where he had been standing

Homer Rand instinctively slipped as low as possible at the table where he was sitting. No doubt he could envision the movements of Wildcat Gordon across the room. It had been accomplished so noiselessly that Rand had not heard the inspector move away. But Rand expected a gun to flame at any second. Wildcat Gordon must be creeping up on The Whisperer.

Now Duke Dolano swore heavily, saying, "No damn punk gets away with that! So, it's your last bluff!"

IN DUKE'S HAND a cigarette lighter flared. For a brief three or four seconds it flashed a circle of uncertain radiance. Everyone in the room saw the vague outline of a face. It seemed almost to be floating in the air.

There was no doubt but that it was the face of The Whisperer. Nor was this the first time it had been seen. Each time, in some such indefinite detail. An outthrust lower jaw and a queerly long upper lip. From these, all eyes jumped to the colorless blur of the smooth hair above the face. There was no time for other details.

The sound that came could hardly be called a shot. Not even with a silencer. If it was, it was continuous. A hissing like the slow escape of steam or air under great pressure.

Duke Dolano cried out, "Why damn you!"

The face of The Whisperer vanished. The cigarette lighter in Duke's hand snapped over among some of the coins on the money table and went out. None saw where Duke Dolano had been hit, but he was groaning and his thrashing around overturned the money table.

Into that disturbance cane a crashing shot. This was from no silenced weapon. It came from a revolver that perhaps had no need for a silencer. Anyway, Homer Rand, the engineer, was sure it did.

Rand grinned in the darkness and said, "Attaboy, Gordon. I thought you'd be on him!"

A man's voice cried out, but it was more than a whisper. A body thumped on the floor. The man who had been hit did not die quickly. He could be heard moving convulsively.

CHAPTER II
"FOR I AM DEAD."

THOUGH ONE SHOT had crashed with devastating effect upon the ears and nerves of those under the spell and the possible weapon of The Whisperer, it was the second sound of slow hissing, like air under pressure, which sent men dropping flat all over the room.

"Stay where you are! No other man will be hurt!"

This was the commanding whisper. It caused Homer Rand to swear under his breath. What had happened to Inspector Gordon? Why hadn't he got the holdup man?

Duke Dolano must then have judged he was protected from more bullets. He had rolled behind the overturned money table. His right hand had been hit and was bloody.

"Lights! Saffern!" he bawled. "He's got Sparti! Lights!"

The Whisperer must have feared the lights would be switched on suddenly. For again the awe-inspiring whisper commanded.

"Stay where you are!"

The Whisperer had moved. Those in the room could tell he was closer to the windows on the fire escape. Immediately glass crashed. There was the sound of the light grillwork being ripped loose by hands that must have had tremendous strength. A shadowy figure was outlined for an instant, then it was gone.

The Whisperer could not have passed down more than the first ladder of the fire escape when the chilled voice of Inspector Gordon broke from beside the window.

"Stop! Or I'm letting you have it!"

Then Gordon let him have it. A police positive cracked twice in his hand. Lead spun from the fire escape outside and whined over to an opposite wall.

Duke Dolano had gotten hold of a gun with his left hand. He had taken it from the limp hand of his bodyguard, Sparti. Duke now made a brave dash for the smashed window, the gun in his hand.

Inspector Gordon was on the fire escape. The revolver he had just fired was in his hand. He pushed back through the twisted iron grillwork.

"No use, Dolano!" he snapped. "The Whisperer may be hit! He fell partway, but he found his feet in the alley! He got over into that nest of shacks below Fortieth Street! You said Sparti was hit? How bad is it?"

Duke Dolano swore at Gordon. He was swearing when someone got to the light switch.

"Too damn careful of yourself to go all the way after him!" Duke sneered. "Let him get away! And them talking of you being the new commissioner! Like hell you'll ever see that easy chair!"

INSPECTOR GORDON holstered his gun and grinned at Dolano from a corner of his mouth. His Texas eyes took in the overturned money table, Sparti lying near it with blood oozing into his white shirt, and old Quick Trigger coming out from one of the telephone booths at the side of the room. Quick Trigger had called for a squad.

"Boys coming, Trigger?" said Gordon, ignoring Dolano's mouthing. "Everybody stay as you are until the squad's through up here!"

The inspector darted a quick glance around the room. He saw that all there remained in positions relative to where they had been when the lights went out. Homer Rand, the engineer, pulled himself from where he had partly slid under the table. He gave Gordon a sheepish look.

"It only takes one bullet, Inspector," he grinned. "So I was being careful not to stop that one."

Old Quick Trigger was standing close beside the fallen Sparti. Dolano's bodyguard was still alive. He moved and gulped for air. Old Quick Trigger's phone call had caught a squad car close by. A number of uniformed men and two detectives poured in from the elevator.

Duke Dolano still had Sparti's gun in his hand. He was standing near old Quick Trigger, looking down at his wounded henchman. As the other police moved in, Inspector Gordon bent quickly over Sparti.

Only old Quick Trigger heard what Gordon was saying.

"Too bad, Sparti, Duke Dolano got you a one-way ticket. He was afraid you'd squawk. He thought he'd get you in the mix-up, and he said some rats were better dead!"

Sparti's body quivered with pain. The bullet had snapped his collarbone. When he tried to move, the bone gritted. Pain blurred his vision, but he saw Duke standing there with the gun still in his hand.

"Duke?" gasped Sparti. "He done it? He couldn't—why, he—"

"Dolano said you'd squawk, if you lived!" snapped Gordon. And this time the words slapped on the ears of Duke. "So you're going out, Sparti, before you get a chance to talk!"

"What's this? Why, you lying cop, you!" yelled Dolano. "Sparti, keep your mouth shut! Keep it shut, or I'll—"

"No, Duke! No!"

The words squealed from Sparti's fear-filled lips. Duke Dolano was no fool. He instantly understood the clever trick Inspector Gordon was using. No doubt, he also knew the yellow spirit of the wounded Sparti.

Duke Dolano lost his head for an instant. He whipped Sparti's own gun down upon him. Then it was that Gordon demonstrated the aptness of the sobriquet, Wildcat.

He came up with the speed of a striking snake. His fist exploded on Duke's chin. The gun in Duke's hand likewise exploded, but the bullet went into the floor.

"Wrap him up!" Gordon tersely commanded the nearest squad man, again bending over Sparti. "Now you may have a slim chance to live," he told the bodyguard. "But you won't if you don't help put Dolano away. Come clean on that Markleson rubout."

The squad man wrapped Dolano up, in knots. It might have been noted they were especially eager to obey the orders of Inspector Gordon. The coppers had their good reason for this. For, as Duke Dolano had intimated, there was strong probability that Wildcat Gordon would soon be moving into the commissioner's office.

INSPECTOR GORDON had not misjudged the furtive fear he had first seen in the faces of Sparti and Saffern. For Sparti talked. Talked first because he had been told he was dying. Then talked more because of his fear that if he survived, Duke Dolano would surely terminate his career.

"I reckon, Wildcat, that was fast thinking on your part," observed old Quick Trigger, after Sparti had gasped out one piece of evidence that possibly would strap Duke Dolano in the chair.

This was the manner in which the broken headlight on the death car had been changed. Also, the whereabouts of the broken light.

The squad men had the bracelets on Dolano and Saffern now.

"You're what I call a born opportunist, Inspector," said a voice at his shoulder. "If you don't get that commissionership, it won't be because you don't use your head."

Wildcat Gordon grinned a little and rubbed his blunt fingers over the vivid red carnation in his buttonhole. It was Homer Rand, the engineer, who had spoken. The man seemed to be a firm admirer of the inspector's.

"You ought to sign up The Whisperer if you do get that commissionership," stated Rand. "Seems to me I remember one other time the police cleaned up a case after he held up a mob hangout."

Another truculent voice broke in. It came from a captain of the squad detail.

"Yeah! That Whisperer! Inspector Gordon, we got orders today to go gunning for him! We're to get him, dead or alive!"

Wildcat Gordon smiled. "And when you get him," he said, "I believe you'll find a bullet broke his left arm. I put my mark on him as he went off the fire escape, but I had my mind on what this Sparti might be induced to tell, so I didn't follow up."

The frothing Duke Dolano and Saffern were being led from the room where Homer Rand, the engineer, pulled out his watch.

"Mind if I fade out, Inspector?" he said. "I like my occasional game, but the wife always expects me before midnight."

Inspector Gordon said it was all right for all to go. Rand said in parting, "Well, I'll be seeing you, Commissioner," and was the first to go down in the elevator.

Old Quick Trigger at this moment saw a foot protruding from a partly opened door of one of the bookies' booths. The old man walked over and pulled the door open. From inside came jabbering hisses.

Inspector Gordon saw old Quick Trigger pull the youth who had been shining Duke Dolano's shoes to his feet. Quick Trigger looked disgusted, then put his hand in his pocket and produced a dollar.

"Hiding out on the rough stuff, eh, Johnny?" said Wildcat Gordon good-humoredly; then he immediately translated his own speech into rapid signs with his hands. This went on for a period of five minutes.

Gordon had known the little shoe shiner for a long time. He was a deaf-mute by the name of Johnny Clatori. Johnny apparently had crawled into one of the bookies' booths when The Whisperer appeared. And he had remained there, even after the bullets had ceased flying.

The deaf-mute grinned from ear to ear over the dollar old Quick Trigger gave him. He slung his shining-box strap over his shoulder and scurried for the door.

"Just goes to show how soft you are, Trigger," stated Gordon. "That Johnny can't hear and he can't talk, but I'll wager he collects more than any other bootblack in town."

"I reckon I've got more money than I'll ever spend," growled old Quick Trigger. "Anyway, Wildcat, even the high-toned mayor can't keep you out of that commissioner's job now. He'll be—"

Trigger's speech was interrupted. Two detectives came up in the elevator, fresh from headquarters. They saw Inspector Gordon.

"We heard what happened—The Whisperer again, Inspector," said one of the men. "And we saw the boys taking Dolano out. But that isn't what brought us over. We're looking for a fellow by the

name of Rand, Homer Rand. Seen him here tonight, Inspector?"

"Rand? Surely." Gordon glanced at his watch. "I would say he left here not more than five minutes ago. He'd been here since we came in."

"Left here?" blurted the detective. "You mean he was all right, Inspector? Why, his wife said he was dead! She got a call from here and he said he wouldn't be home because he was dead! She fainted, and the operator at the apartment traced the call to Duke Delano's place, one of the booths!"

Wildcat Gordon blinked a little. Old Trigger said, "Now I reckon that's something! Said he wouldn't be home because he was dead? Wouldja mind just saying all that over again?"

The two detectives scratched their heads in unison.

"Well, that's the headquarters report, anyway," said one. "I've got it right here. At 11:45 P.M. by the apartment operator's watch, Homer Rand called his apartment, and the operator listened in. He said, according to the operator, 'This is good-bye, Star Dust'—I don't know why the hell he'd call his wife 'Star Dust,' but it seems he did—'this is good-by, 'Star Dust'—I will not return home—for I am dead.' And then his wife fainted, so the operator called headquarters, and we came right over."

"Well, I reckon any man's wife would faint," said old Trigger. "Now that's my idea of one helluva joke for a man to play on his wife, or anybody else for that."

"Wait a minute, Trigger," interrupted Wildcat Gordon. "You're sure that call was at 11:45?"

The detectives verified the telephone operator's report. Gordon glanced up at the wall clock in Dolano's place. He checked it with his own wrist-watch. The time matched to the second.

"You checked your watches with the operator's own time?" said Gordon to the detectives.

Both said they had. The time had been correct, at least to within the quarter minute

"Rand didn't call his home from here or any other place at 11:45," stated Gordon. "I was talking with him at that exact time. And it was just then the lights went out and the Whisperer appeared. I saw Rand, just after the lights came on, and I'm ready to swear he did not leave the spot where I talked with him until five minutes ago. This may have been a joke, or somebody's idea of one."

The detectives insisted the telephone operator and Mrs. Rand had identified the voice. And one of the detectives said, "Mrs. Rand told us no one ever called her 'Star Dust' but her husband. I wouldn't think any one would."

Wildcat Gordon walked over toward the row of phone booths. He studied the position of the table where Homer Rand had been sitting. When he came back, he said, "Rand didn't make that call. There's been some cross-up. It couldn't have come from here then, for no one could have entered a booth while The Whisperer was in here."

"It's somebody's idea of a damn poor joke," repeated Quick Trigger.

THOUGH WILDCAT GORDON was convinced Homer Rand could not have called his home at 11:45, the reported call had been received at that exact minute in the apartment home of Homer Rand.

Mrs. Rand, a frail, pretty woman, perhaps ten years her notable husband's junior, was seated in a reading chair close to the telephone when it rang. She was alone and apparently waiting up for her husband.

Now Homer Rand had told Wildcat Gordon he always made it a point to return home before midnight, even if he did like his little game of chance. So that, no doubt, was the reason that pretty Mrs. Rand glanced at her watch as she took the call.

She had removed the receiver. For the space of perhaps ten seconds there was nothing but the usual buzzing on the wire. She said, "Hello," the third time before she received a reply.

When the words came, they were spoken slowly, as if with some slight effort. And yet they came with the impact of a thunderbolt, a fantastic stroke that for a full minute could hardly be believed.

"This is good-bye, Star Dust—I will not return home—for I am dead."

"Homer! Homer! Please! What are you saying?" the woman cried out.

And the only reply was the faint clicking of a receiver at the other end of the wire, as if it had been replaced softly, almost stealthily. Mrs. Rand must have jiggled the receiver without results before she screamed hysterically and mercifully fainted.

Now the girl on the apartment house switchboard was having a dull time of it. The Rands, she knew, were devotedly in love with each other. She listened in on their conversations when she had the chance. Perhaps she was encouraged in some love affair of her own to know there was such happiness in the world.

But tonight the chewing gum popped out of her mouth when she heard the voice of Mr. Rand. No. She could not be mistaken! It was the same, slightly humorous tone Rand always took with his wife.

And Mr. Rand was the only one who had ever called Mrs. Rand "Star Dust." The operator always sighed over that and wondered if anyone would ever call her such a foolish pet name.

The operator's mouth remained open as Rand said, "I will not return home—for I am dead."

Mrs. Rand's following scream caused the operator to jerk off her headset. But she was smart, quick-witted. If she was about to be let in on some

tragic mystery of unsuspected domestic discord, then she was going to know more about it.

The girl checked back instantly with the central operator. It was luck the call had not come in over a direct dial to the Rand apartment. There had been the interconnection to be made. The apartment house operator learned that the call had been made from Duke Dolano's gambling room.

This information alone had been enough to impel the girl to call the police before she had hurried up to Mrs. Rand's apartment. At that time, Mrs. Rand had been slowly recovering consciousness.

"Oh, what is it? What can have happened to Homer?" the pretty wife had sobbed on the girl's shoulder. "He's dead—I know he must be dead! He said he was dead!"

Mrs. Rand was quite hysterical about it.

MRS. RAND was still unable to think or talk coherently when Inspector Gordon got another telephone connection to her apartment immediately after the two detectives had reported at Dolano's. Only Gordon quickly ascertained that Homer Rand had not yet reached home.

Gordon checked again on the time. He led the others downstairs. The Rand apartment was only a few minutes away by taxicab or Rand's own car, if he had taken either.

"Mr. Rand, yes," said the street doorman of the Dolano establishment. "He left here seven or eight minutes ago. He had me call a taxi, and I remember it because there was one standing at the corner. It ain't a regular stand, but there was one there waiting."

"He has not reached home," gritted Gordon. "You fellows can go back upstairs and see if you can find out anything," he said to the two detectives. "Come on, Trigger, we'll go on over to the Rand place and check up there. All this may be some kind of a joke, but that's too grisly a trick for any friend to play."

Wildcat Gordon seemed almost to lift his own fast roadster from its parking space. His manner of driving always sent old Trigger bending low in the seat beside him and hoping for the best.

Wildcat took the first corner on squealing rubber. He was following the route a taxicab would most likely go from Dolano's to the vicinity of Homer Rand's apartment house. He recalled it would be a distance of perhaps fourteen blocks.

But Gordon's roadster pulled up with screaming brakes when it was only six blocks on the way. Wildcat was driving under elevated tracks on this street. A midnight crowd blocked several cars between him and the intersection ahead.

Wildcat left his roadster. Trigger puffed along on his heels. They saw the high cab of a large truck jammed into an elevated pillar. Between the truck and one of the steel columns were the colorful sides of what had been a taxicab. It was now about as useful as a cracker box smashed with a huge hammer.

"And I tell you," a bystander was saying loudly to a patrolman, "the taxi stalled there, an' the driver climbed out an' jumped just as that truck come out of the side street. He kept right on runnin', an' the truck driver rolled off, an' I thought he was chasin' the taxi guy."

"Well! Well! Where are they?" was the patrolman's demand.

"Now how'd I know that, Copper?" said the bystander sarcastically.

Homer Rand was in the crushed taxicab. He was dead, horribly so. There was the look on his face that comes to a man when he sees death rushing upon him and cannot avert it.

Rand's watch had been smashed. The hands had stopped at exactly 12:20 a.m. Thirty-five minutes after his wife had heard his voice calling her by his own exclusive pet name, telling her he would not return because he was dead; he had died.

And there was in the death no element that could possibly contribute to a theory of suicide. Apparently a truck had come speeding from the side street and accidentally caught the taxicab in a pinch against the elevated pillar.

"I reckon it's a mighty strange coincidence," said old Trigger in his mild voice. "One of the things fate arranges, just to show us how little us humans count in the scheme of things."

WILDCAT GORDON was not a strong believer in fate. His Texas eyes had taken on an unusual coldness. He first attempted to establish some mental connection between this "accident" and the trapping of Duke Dolano. But he could see no connection.

With the taxicab and truck license numbers, he got on the nearest call box telephone. Five minutes later, Gordon stared bleakly at old Trigger.

"There isn't any Dearborn Wholesale Pharmacy—the name on that truck—and its license plates were reported stolen a week ago from a transfer company," he stated. "Also, that taxicab was stolen from its regular stand about two hours ago. There has been a report out on it ever since."

Old Trigger pulled his hard Derby down over his bald pate. He tugged at his bushy eyebrows.

"Maybe we ain't doing so good," he muttered. "I thought when you made that quick cleanup after The Whisperer was there tonight, it would be easy sailin' for you, right into the commissioner's chair."

"Forget it!" advised Wildcat Gordon tersely. "There's going to be hell to pay over The Whisperer showing up again! Get along home, Trigger! I've a call or two to make, so don't do any sitting up!"

Old Trigger departed, grumbling. Gordon got his roadster out of the traffic jam. Then he went into the nearest all-night drugstore and thumbed through the telephone directory. He found a number. He was surprised to receive an immediate reply.

"This is Jones, J. Grover Jones," said the voice at the other end of the wire. "It's an odd hour to be calling."

Wildcat apologized for the hour. It was an odd time to be calling a man of the importance of J. Grover Jones. For this Jones was the reputed multimillionaire, and more lately mentioned as the president of a huge corporation known as the Black Mountain Power Co.

"Would you know of any reason, Mr. Jones, why anyone should wish an accident to happen to Homer Rand, your chief engineer?" said Wildcat.

The immediate reply of J. Grover Jones was much like the gulping effort of a drowning man to find his breath.

Then he said, "Rand? You mean Homer Rand? Good grief, man! Has anything happened to him?"

"Unfortunately, yes," stated Wildcat. "He has met with a fatal accident. An automobile collision."

Wildcat's ear was glued to the receiver. He had expected to hear some expression of the shock this must bring to J. Grover Jones. But it was more than to be expected from a reputed cold-blooded financier.

Wildcat could have sworn the great man had almost sobbed.

CHAPTER III
AN ATTACK OF MYSTERY

WILDCAT GORDON was convinced that J. Grover Jones had been affected by something more than the news of Homer Rand's death. The financier's tone, from the first, had indicated he was under some great stress.

Wildcat said, "If there's something the police should know, it's only a ten-minute drive; I'll come right out to Belvidere."

He was aware that J. Grover Jones occupied a house in Belvidere. His only immediate relative and companion was his motherless daughter, Nellie, who was always in the society columns.

But Jones said quickly, "No! No! This is a terrible thing, Inspector Gordon! But not tonight! Do not come out! I'll—wait a minute."

While Wildcat waited, there was a murmur of voices. There was certainly the undertone of a woman's cry. The murmur continued for perhaps two minutes.

Wildcat checked on his watch. It was now close to 2:00 o'clock in the morning. He smiled grimly. A woman? Well, J. Grover Jones was a widower and wealthy. Probably a party had been in progress.

The financier would be informing the others of his message. That would account for the woman's shocked outcry.

J. Grover Jones returned to the telephone. He spoke in a clipped, strained tone. It was as if he were attempting to keep his voice from reaching others nearby.

"Don't come out, Inspector Gordon," he said, tensely. "I'll come to you in about one hour from now. I can't make it before then. There's—something—well, I must see you!"

"At headquarters, then?" said Wildcat. "In an hour?"

"No! No!" said Jones. "Not headquarters! Your home address? What is it? I'll meet you there! I'll have to ask you to make this confidential! Mr. Thurston, Rand's assistant, has been here with me. He probably will accompany me to your home!"

This was an unusual procedure. But Wildcat considered that perhaps he was getting a break. He knew the reform element had demanded that he succeed the retiring police commissioner. At the same time, Mayor Van Royston, the new reform mayor, was not in favor of that appointment. The mayor was being forced into it by his own party.

"There'll be hell to pay over this Whisperer again," said Wildcat in a musing tone as he hung up the phone. "The mayor will hardly be giving three cheers for the stiff way we broke this Duke Dolano case. He'll figure something like that may get his kid gloves dirty."

Wildcat grinned over Mayor Van Royston's kid gloves and his almost perpetual high silk hat. The new mayor was a great fellow for the limelight, for public receptions. Wildcat knew the mayor would like to have a police commissioner attached to a string, so he could be pulled this way and that.

No living man had ever had James Wildcat Gordon on a string. Since he had quit the army and come into the department, he had come up fast. He took the toughest cases; he made his own rules, and he broke the cases. Just as he had broken this Duke Dolano affair.

WILDCAT HAD AN HOUR to kill. For several years, he had resided with old Dick Traeger, the retired deputy commissioner. This was down in an unsavory neighborhood, but the Traeger home was different from its surroundings.

It was an elaborate penthouse. But it was located on top of a ten-story warehouse in the waterfront and loft district. When he had retired, Quick Trigger had some funds. He owned the warehouse, so he built his home on its roof.

Quick Trigger's pretty granddaughter acted as his housekeeper. No matter what the hour, there was always a cold snack waiting for Wildcat when he got home. Quick Trigger might have been retired, but he seemed never to sleep.

Wildcat now called his home. He informed Quick Trigger he was expecting company in about an hour. It would have to be private. So they would have to wait until later to discuss the events of the night.

Wildcat got in touch with headquarters. The old commissioner had been retired on permanent vacation. The harsh voice of the present deputy commissioner replied. He was Henry Bolton, and Wildcat knew he was a favorite of Mayor Van Royston. The mayor would have made him commissioner, if he could have had it all his own way.

"There's the devil and all to pay, Inspector Gordon!" snapped Bolton's voice. "Why haven't you reported in on this crazy Homer Rand murder? I hear you think you shot The Whisperer! Well, why didn't you get him, Gordon?"

Wildcat smiled to himself. Though he was on the verge of becoming commissioner, he was still directly under Bolton's command.

"I thought it best to follow through on the Dolano case," said Wildcat. "And it worked out fairly well."

"Yes? Yes?" shouted Bolton. "That's what you think! Now you listen to me, Gordon! They brought Saffern in with Dolano, and now Saffern's dead! He killed himself! The mayor has been informed! Dolano's mouthpiece is going after you for using brutal third-degree methods on Sparti when he was dying! Now he's dead, too!"

"You might slip Duke Dolano a gun, and that would save the State the expense of all three rats," cheerfully suggested Wildcat. "I would like to know as much about the Homer Rand killing as I did about the murder of Markleson."

Deputy Bolton spat an oath over the wire.

"A sweet mess you've made of tonight, Gordon! With Sparti dead, we can't make the Dolano rap stick! As for that Rand affair, it's open and shut! Mrs. Rand stands to come in for quite a fortune. It's a phony, that call she says she got! I'm having her sweated some!"

Wildcat softly hung up the receiver.

"The lunkhead would do that," he muttered; then he considered. "Well, perhaps that's just as well for the present. I'll bet he didn't even think of Homer Rand's connections or J. Grover Jones!"

SHORTLY BEFORE an hour had passed, Wildcat sent his roadster into the warehouse district. He drove along gloomy, deserted streets. Fog was rolling in from the river. Its grayness made Wildcat think of The Whisperer.

The Whisperer, as he had been briefly glimpsed, had on most occasions appeared with a fog. Wildcat recalled how those who had these passing glimpses of The Whisperer declared he seemed to be a gray figure blending with the fog.

"That's a good point to keep in mind," murmured Wildcat, sending his roadster around a corner near Quick Trigger's warehouse.

Then he abruptly swung the little car to one side and parked it. He had hoped J. Grover Jones would have arrived. Well, there had been more than one arrival, if Wildcat was any judge in this thick fog. He made out the vague outlines of two automobiles.

Wildcat moved swiftly along the sidewalk, keeping close to the buildings. His shoes were equipped with ground-gripping rubber soles. He moved noiselessly. His feet were always set for trouble.

The presence of the two automobiles did not arouse any great suspicion. J. Grover Jones was a notable person. He would be extremely cautious making a visit in the early morning hours. Perhaps Rand's assistant, Thurston, mentioned by Jones, had come along in his own car.

Wildcat passed the first automobile, a black sedan. He made sure he was not observed, but the precaution was wasted. No one was in the sedan. Wildcat touched the radiator. It was hot. The car had been there only a short time.

The other car was close to Quick Trigger's warehouse. Wildcat suddenly froze to the side of the nearest building. He heard a woman's muffled voice. The tone was husky but vehement.

Wildcat caught only, "I'm going to him, I tell you—"

The words ended on a little cry. There was scuffling in the darkness. Wildcat's compact body moved with the quickness of a bounding cat. Two shadowy men were holding a woman, who showed only as a long rubbery coat and a white face in the fog.

Wildcat's feet left the sidewalk and he hurtled out of the fog. He did not risk using a weapon. One fist, then the other lashed out, almost as one blow. Two men with hats pulled over their faces were jolted loose from their hold on the woman before they realized Wildcat was on the scene.

Wildcat whirled the girl behind him, against the warehouse wall. As he did, he was close enough to identify her. None in town would ever mistake the much publicized face of Nellie Jones, daughter of J. Grover Jones. She was sobbing, staring at him in the fog.

Wildcat was aware she would not recognize him as Inspector Gordon. His own face was not prominent enough in the newspapers. The girl gasped, "Whoever you are, help me!"

One of the girl's attackers was scrambling to his feet. Wildcat helped Nellie Jones with a most unethical kick with a hard toe under the man's chin.

The other man had rolled over.

The man who had been kicked was getting a gun from his pocket. The other man, to Gordon's amazement, shouted, "Don't do that! It's Gordon himself! I'll take him!"

Not many men could make that boast and get away with it. But this slouch-hatted fellow, recovering from the surprise blow that had knocked him down, was something of a tough customer. Perhaps he had been a wrestler.

WILDCAT had set himself to put the man with the gun out of business more permanently, when the other man hit him with an unexpected dive. Because he had expected a fist blow, the man's hard head drove into his stomach.

Wildcat had an uneasy sensation that some of his ribs had cracked. He locked a tight arm around the fellow's neck and went down with him.

Wildcat was all wire, muscle and bone. But he was best at open fighting. His opponent butted him under the chin with his head and got a hard knee into his stomach. Wildcat went sick. If this kept up, it would be his gun or pass out.

Now the other man had moved close to Nellie Jones, who still stayed close to the building wall. Wildcat could hear him muttering hoarse words to the girl. He could not hear these, but Nellie Jones gasped, "Oh, you couldn't! You couldn't!"

The back of one of her hands clamped against her teeth.

Wildcat was twisting his head free from a locking arm. The knee in his stomach had made him weaken temporarily. But he got in one effective blow that rattled the other man's teeth.

Rolling to one side, freeing himself, Wildcat was getting groggily to his feet. Then he heard the girl cry out! "Ranny! How did you get here? Ranny!"

Wildcat saw the third man. He had come rushing along the sidewalk. He was a tall, young fellow, but it was too foggy to get a clear view of his face.

"You little fool!" grated this young man called Ranny. "I told you what would happen if you didn't keep out of this!"

"But, Ranny—"

That was all Wildcat heard. For the man he had cleared was getting up. Wildcat judged it was about time to whip a gun into play. His thought was to do a bit of expert shooting that would leave at least one wounded man in his hands. He had no desire to kill any of these men until he knew more of what had brought them here, and brought Nellie Jones.

Wildcat thought he was clear. He was an adept at keeping away from swinging fists. But the blow that now caught him, sent him groggily to his knees, then to his face on the wet sidewalk, was a thrown gun. The compact automatic, hurled from one man's hand, struck him under one ear.

There was not a moment when Wildcat did not know what was happening; or at least he imagined he was conscious all the time. The fellow called Ranny had a grip on Nellie Jones. And the girl was walking away with him.

Wildcat could do nothing about this. The shock of the blow under his ear had paralyzed nerve centers for perhaps half a minute. Or his senses may have blinked out for something like that interval.

Two cars were going away on whining second

. . . One fist, then the other lashed out, almost as one blow . . .

speed when he weaved to his feet. Already they were only dim shapes in the fog. But one car remained. It stood close by the entrance to Quick Trigger's warehouse.

Wildcat realized the uselessness of attempting a pursuit in that fog. He flashed a light. The remaining car was a roadster. It bore the monogram "J. G. J." It must have been the car in which the daughter of J. Grover Jones had arrived.

Wildcat shot up in the elevator to the penthouse telephone.

CHAPTER IV
THE FUNNY MR. JONES

OLD QUICK TRIGGER was at Wildcat's elbow when he got on the telephone. "No, J. Grover Jones had not been here and there had been no call," Quick Trigger had supplied.

There was some delay before Wildcat got the financier at his home. The inspector was not giving out information. He was looking for it. So he said nothing of the strange attack, or of the visit of Nellie Jones.

"I've been waiting for you, Mr. Jones," he said into the phone. "Has something happened to delay you?"

Where the voice of J. Grover Jones had been emotional and filled with some uncertainty a little more than an hour before, it was now cold, decisive.

"I was expecting your call, Inspector Gordon," he said. "I have decided there is nothing which I know that would be valuable in the apparently accidental death of Mr. Rand. It is clearly a case for the police alone."

Wildcat debated swiftly. Something had happened to J. Grover Jones in the past hour. Evidently the financier did not know his daughter had apparently made an effort to reach the inspector. Wildcat let him have it.

"Your daughter has just left here, Mr. Jones. You know, of course, what she came to tell me?"

Another surprising dash of cold water on the idea he might put the financier on the defensive, started him talking.

"Yes, I know she was there, but she had nothing to tell," said Jones. "She was a little hysterical and started out to see you without thinking it over. I have heard from her. I think, Inspector, there is nothing more to be said. Sorry if you have been inconvenienced. Good night."

Then Jones knew the girl had failed to talk to him.

The phone connection at the home of J. Grover Jones clicked definitely. Wildcat stared a few seconds at the instrument.

"I reckon I haven't been doing so good tonight," said old Quick Trigger. "Maybe I'm wrong, but I heard Jones, and I know him. When he sews up his tongue, he sews it up. You need a rum toddy, Wildcat, and a cold pack under that ear. A little higher with that bump and you wouldn't be here."

Wildcat could read the retired deputy commissioner like a book. He knew Quick Trigger was telling him in his own way to stop thinking about the Homer Rand case for a little while. That was old Trigger's way. He always said when he ran up against a wall, he quit tiring his brain and after that the wall wouldn't seem so high.

WILDCAT was all for action. He would have gone at once to the home of J. Grover Jones, against Quick Trigger's advice. He swiftly pieced together the newspaper knowledge of the relations of the financier and Homer Rand, the dead engineer.

J. Grover Jones was president of the Black Mountain Power Co. His harnessing of mountain-river power had been given widest publicity. Others had accomplished the same thing, but this power company promised to cut electrical power rates in half for all of the metropolitan area.

That promise had hinged directly upon the new dynamos invented by Homer Rand. It was stated that these would double or triple the amount of power produced from a given source. Existing power companies had made bids for Homer Rand's services. Rand had remained loyal to J. Grover Jones and his board of directors.

That much was public knowledge. In what manner would the removal of Homer Rand affect the affairs of the Black Mountain Power Co.? Why had J. Grover Jones been so agitated, at first, then so icily cold on the whole subject in the matter of an hour later?

Who were the men following Nellie Jones to Inspector Gordon's penthouse home? Plainly they must have known what the girl had come to tell. They had halted her to prevent it. The young fellow called Ranny had said she was "a little fool!" And her father knew the girl had been stopped before reaching Gordon.

Wildcat Gordon could assure himself of only one thing. Sometime today, he was due to be notified of his appointment as police commissioner. And if that appointment came through, he was going into the commissioner's office with considerable of a mess on his hands.

The Duke Dolano case had not turned out so well, with Saffern a suicide in his cell, and Sparti, who had squawked, dead of his wound. Dolano might still beat the rap on the Markleson murder.

Opening with that cryptic, unbelievable telephone call to his home, the Homer Rand murder now had assumed complications that involved

J. Grover Jones, one of the city's foremost figures.

Wildcat only added to his trouble ahead by suddenly recalling that J. Grover Jones was a leader in the reform party and a personal friend of Mayor Van Royston.

"I believe I'll have some coffee and sleep on it," remarked Wildcat wearily. "I have a feeling this is going to be a big day."

"I'll say it's going to be a big day, and you keeping us up until all hours!" exclaimed a bright, flippant voice from the doorway. "I've had coffee and the cake I baked waiting for hours. How about coming and getting it? I suppose now, seeing you're to be the commissioner, I'll have to start calling you 'mister.'"

"TINY" TRAEGER stood there with a dancing light in each brown eye. Wildcat called them dancing little devils. Tiny was a small girl, and though Wildcat was but five feet, five inches in his stocking feet, the diminutive girl came only to his shoulder.

She looked up at him impishly and said, "Well, how about it, Mr. Commissioner? Do you eat that cake I've been keeping fresh all night?"

"Up all night!" snapped Wildcat Gordon. "You ought to be spanked, and for two cents I'd give it to you! You've no business living in the same house with a policeman, and if Trigger doesn't send you away to school, I'm going to move!"

Tiny was pretty, with a tanned, elfin face that made her seem more of a child than she was. Her hair fluffed in curls, and that did not add to her apparent age. She was convinced Wildcat never would realize she was twenty-one and a grown woman.

"Come and get the cake and coffee, and I hope you do move," the girl said, deliberately sticking out her tongue. "I baked the cake when the telegram came, Mr. Commissioner."

Old Trigger rubbed a hand over his bald head. His eyes twinkled under their bushy brows.

"Yes, Wildcat," he said. "I was saving it for a celebration tonight. But so many things have happened, it kind of went over. The news of Duke Dolano's pinch got around fast. His honor the mayor must have stayed up all night. You've had a wire and a phone message. At ten o'clock this morning you are taking over the duties of police commissioner. Now, let's celebrate."

Wildcat Gordon uttered a deep groan. His fathomless Texas eyes held a sudden gleam.

"Commissioner?" he said slowly. "Ex-army officer, police dick, inspector, and now commissioner? Trigger, old boy, we're in the army!"

"Yes, you're in the army. And look, maybe now this may not be the right thing, but don't you think you had better take it easy? You know, being a commissioner is different than being an inspector. You've got to watch—"

"Trigger, you can't tell me it's any different! It's the same thing! I'm going to get crooks, one way or another! I'm sick and tired of all these trick rules and regulations that we've got to pamper criminals with! I'll knock 'em cold when and if I have to!" Wildcat's eyes flared up even more than before.

Old Quick Trigger knew better than to say more. He shook his head at the fighting man whom he had practically fathered through his whole career.

JAMES WILDCAT GORDON was paying little attention to Mayor Van Royston's nervous pacing up and down in his carpeted office, the office of the police commissioner. Wildcat at the moment was thinking of the suspicious moisture that had been in old Quick Trigger's eyes as he had announced the news of his appointment.

Though it was not yet noon after the night of Homer Rand's murder, Mayor Van Royston had on his yellow kid gloves and his tall, silk hat. He wore gray spats and a suit to match, or perhaps it was the other way around. He was a youngish-old man with a chin none too prominent, which he made up for by stiff-backed dignity.

The attire was for some reception at the noon hour. The reform mayor was great on speechmaking and passing out the key of the city. At this moment, he was alone in the office with Wildcat Gordon.

"Let's not misunderstand each other, Gordon," the mayor said primly. "You would not have been my personal selection for commissioner. Perhaps others will learn of their mistake soon enough, but that's up to you."

Wildcat was wearing the army slouch hat with its broad brim. A fresh red carnation was in his buttonhole. A vivid red tie stood out like a marker against his sober gray suit.

"Yes," he assented slowly, "I guess it's up to me. This town has needed a cleaning up for considerable time."

"Sure! Sure!" agreed the mayor hastily. "The city must be cleaned up. But now that you're commissioner, the violent tactics, such as were employed last night, must cease. As the mayor, I will not countenance the kind of third-degree methods used in this Duke Dolano case. Forcing a dying man to confess! Why, it makes it look like the police were actually taking advantage of the infamous outlawry of this fellow they call The Whisperer!"

Wildcat rubbed a blunt finger along his blue, shaved chin. He had the feeling that this same chin was about to be pushed out where it would have to take it.

"One of my first orders, Mayor, was to all the

boys to bring in The Whisperer," he said, quietly.

A tall, angular figure walked into the office without the preliminary of announcement. His nose was thin and his mouth was small and too tight. His forehead retreated at the top of more than six feet of body.

"And we'll get The Whisperer, your honor," Bolton added to Wildcat's words. "Gord—er, the commissioner put a bullet in one of his arms in that mix-up last night."

THE ANGULAR FELLOW was Henry Bolton, deputy commissioner. His small mouth always screwed up in disapproval of those around him. But his manner toward the mayor was subservient enough.

"You will put The Whisperer ahead of every other matter," said Mayor Van Royston. "We are going to have trouble over that Duke Dolano confession of Sparti before he died, and I advise that Dolano be released when his attorney appears with a writ. He will be in, for I have talked to him."

Mayor Van Royston clearly was talking directly to Bolton, the deputy commissioner. Bolton nodded agreement, with a twisting side smile for Wildcat Gordon. Very apparently this was a time to show the new commissioner where he stood.

Wildcat said nothing for the moment. The colorless Texas eyes were apparently fixed on a bird in a tree outside one window. But the orbs might have been seen to darken, if either the mayor or Bolton had noticed.

"Now about that Rand woman, Mayor," went on Deputy Bolton. "We haven't got anything yet, but I've ordered the boys to bring her in. That story about hearing her husband's voice saying he was dead is too screwy on the face of it. We'll get at the truth."

Wildcat Gordon's feet shifted a little. He picked up the interoffice phone.

"Detective division," he said calmly. The mayor and Bolton exchanged quick glances, with a little smile between them. Apparently the newly appointed commissioner was taking Bolton's little demonstration of where the authority lay very tamely.

"Detective division?" said Wildcat.

"We will drop the matter of any special effort to round up the man known as The Whisperer for the present. I want Duke Dolano removed from the headquarters jail immediately. See that he is well ironed and send four men with him in a car. Take him for a long, long ride into the country.

"You will have the men with Dolano communicate with me at midnight tonight. They are not to bring him back into the city until I give a direct, personal order. Commissioner Gordon speaking. Got that?"

Mayor Van Royston's thin chest was puffing out.

His small chin retreated so far it seemed he had swallowed it. The tall Henry Bolton had his mouth pulled into a tight knot from which an oath was being pushed.

Wildcat swung away from the telephone.

"There is another order I could have given," he said, quietly. "But I'm giving you that order, Deputy Bolton. You can tell your men that Mrs. Homer Rand is not to be further molested or annoyed in any manner. Instead of that, you can put out a general order for the arrest of Miss Nellie Jones, daughter of J. Grover Jones of Belvidere, and a tall, blond man known as Ranny Howard with whom she probably will be found."

"What? What?" gasped Mayor Van Royston. "This is unthinkable, Gordon! You cannot remove Duke Dolano from jurisdiction! The Whisperer comes first and—"

The mayor turned red and white.

"This department must not, cannot in any way do such a crazy thing as offending J. Grover Jones! Why, he's the biggest supporter of the Reform Party and—"

Wildcat Gordon came to his feet, all of his five foot five.

"By gravy!" he roared. "I'm commissioner of police! If I'm in this office but one day, I'll run this department! Get Duke Dolano out on a habeas? Well, let 'em try and do it, but first they'll find Duke Dolano!

"If I find it necessary to bring in J. Grover Jones himself, I'll personally throw him into a cell! Bolton, you see that Nellie Jones and this Ranny Howard are brought in! You nor any other man in this department is taking orders from any man but myself! You get it!"

WILDCAT'S hard fist banged down on his desk. The inkstand jumped and so did Mayor Van Royston. The mayor swallowed hard, and his chin almost went with the lump in his throat. Wildcat swung directly upon him, Texas eyes boring in, one fist now thumping in his open hand.

"This city has been and is dirty, and it's had a police department as soft as mush!" roared Wildcat. "Softened up by a political ladle! Politics are out! I'll personally heave a few of these shyster mouthpieces out of the window if they come around! I cracked the Duke Dolano case, and now I'll personally crack this Rand murder!

"When you have orders to give, Mr. Mayor, you hand them to me! Bolton, you're too damned dumb to see through a piece of cellophane! Unless I'm cockeyed, this Rand murder is only the beginning and there'll be more! Now, Bolton, get out!"

The small-mouthed deputy commissioner was looking toward Mayor Van Royston for some support.

But even the mayor's tall silk hat was shaking. He was saying, "Why—why—Commissioner Gordon, you can't—you're only the commissioner—I'm—well, I'm the mayor—"

Then the commissioner's door was pushed open.

"Did I hear someone say he thought the Rand murder was only the beginning?" inquired a swarthy-faced young man with intense black eyes. "I was not eavesdropping. I just overheard, and I came on in because I agree with that. You are Commissioner Gordon? Will you have a look at this?"

The swarthy young man pushed out a quick, slender hand. This hand held a square piece of white cardboard. There was printing on the card in blue ink.

Wildcat Gordon glanced at the lines. He looked at the black-eyed young man.

"So you're Jack Thurston? You were engineering assistant to Homer Rand?"

"I'm Thurston, yes. I was at the Jones residence when you called last night, Commissioner Gordon. I learned only this morning you had become commissioner. So I thought I would bring this directly to you. You are right. Poor Rand's murder may be only the beginning."

Wildcat Gordon read:

JOHN THURSTON—Unless you want to keep company with Homer Rand, you will sever your connection with the Black Mountain Power Co. at once. We recommend a long ocean voyage, for which funds will be sent you anonymously.

If you fail to do this, you will find yourself in the odd position of calling some friend and telling them you are dead.

This is the only notice you will receive.
THE WHISPERER

None there saw the sudden, inscrutable light leap into Wildcat's eyes. He turned the card over in his hand.

"You received this when?"

"My mail this morning," said Thurston. "Have the police any line on this man called The Whisperer?"

"None," said Wildcat. "But we may have in a short time. You were at the home of J. Grover Jones last night? Were you there when Nellie Jones left the house?"

"Yes, but did not know she was gone," said Thurston. "We—I thought she had gone to her room. Her father called me this morning. He thinks she is meeting Ranny Howard. The old man is furious. Howard is a common draftsman. He has been ordered to stay away from the Jones home. The old man thinks he's a fortune hunter."

Wildcat Gordon was thinking fast. Mostly, he was concentrating on a single fact. The death threat to Jack Thurston had been signed, "The Whisperer."

Wildcat made a clucking noise in his throat. Henry Bolton was lingering in the office. Wildcat turned upon him.

"I've changed my mind about The Whisperer," he said. "Get him, if you can, Bolton. Now, Thurston, tell me: would there be any other person who might—"

Thurston interrupted, "I know what you mean, Commissioner. No. I am the only other man alive who knows the secret of the Rand dynamos. Or, at least, I believe I am. It was a great break for me when Rand took me in with him on the dynamo's construction."

MAYOR VAN ROYSTON was reaching for his dignity. He adjusted his kid gloves and smiled authoritatively.

"Well, well!" he exclaimed. "Commissioner Gordon, this must be cleaned up quickly! This young man must have protection! I will have to see Mr. Jones at once! This must be a terrible ordeal for him! Commissioner, you have my order to clean up this Rand murder and get The Whisperer! But there must be nothing high-handed!"

No doubt, the silk-hatted mayor was anxious to impress the visitor with his position. He was smiling, as if there had been no dissension before the arrival of Jack Thurston.

"It will be cleaned up!" snapped Wildcat Gordon. "And don't forget, I happen to be the head of this special army! High-handed or low-handed, I'll make my own orders!"

A slow grin spread over Jack Thurston's dark face. He looked more directly at the commissioner. Thurston himself stood above six feet.

"You think no other person would be in danger?" said Wildcat.

"I can think of none but myself," said Jack Thurston.

CHAPTER V
"I WILL NOT RETURN."

A BIG clock was striking the hour of noon as Jack Thurston said he could think of no other person being threatened. Now a sunny-haired girl of possibly fifteen or sixteen glanced at her small kitchen clock as the telephone rang. She saw that it was exactly noon.

The girl was wearing a kitchen apron. Her sleeves were short. Her rounded arms had marks of flour where she had been baking. She had been working and singing.

The young woman hastily wiped the flour from her hands and answered the telephone. She was alone in the small cottage. The house was in the suburb of the city. Not faraway were the new, steel towers over which the current of the Black Mountain Power Co. was soon to flow.

"Hello, I'll bet that's you, Daddy!"

The girl exclaimed this quickly. Apparently, she was accustomed to having her father call her at the noon hour. There was a winning smile on her pretty face.

This smile abruptly changed to a look of amazement. Then it became horror. Gasping horror that caused her to cling convulsively to the telephone receiver. She cried out, "No! Daddy! What are you saying?"

For the voice in the phone had indeed been that of her own father. More, her daddy called her "Roses," and no other person ever had.

The voice said, solemnly, slowly, "Roses! I am saying good-bye—you'll be a good girl—I'll not be home—for I am dead!"

The girl's terrified words merged into a scream. She was swaying before the phone, but for a little while she fought against the black sickness sweeping over her. She had read in the morning paper of the strange death of Homer Rand. She had been more interested than thousands of others.

For the girl was May Travis, and her father, Charles Travis, had been employed directly by Homer Rand. Travis was one of the lesser construction engineers on the Black Mountain Power Co. project. He now was stationed in one of the company's uncompleted substations, about a mile from the Travis cottage.

May Travis did not stare long at the telephone. Frantically, she jiggled the receiver's hook. She got the central operator of the small suburb. Then she repeated the phone number of the substation in which her father was working. She urged speed.

Surely, this must be some horrible mistake. Her father was the best in the world. He could not have said the thing she had heard. There must be some mistake. And she was convinced for a second or so that this was true when she heard the substation telephone ringing.

Then there was an interruption. It came with the explosiveness of a shot in the girl's ear, almost deafening her. A man's hoarse scream rang over the wire. Then there was the sudden silence that might come with a wire being snipped off.

Again and again the girl's trembling hand jiggled the hook. The central girl at last replied.

"Something has happened to the number you are calling," the central girl said. "I am trying to ring, but I am getting no reply."

For so young a person, May Travis kept her head amazingly. She resisted the impulse to start running, to fly bareheaded through the streets toward her father's side. She gasped out a request for the central girl to trace the call she had received.

After a minute or two the central operator called back.

"Your call did not come from the number you rang," said the operator. "It was made from a public booth in a drugstore on Van Buren Avenue in the city."

May Travis steadied herself. She tried to think if her father had been in the city. He must have been, for he had called her "Roses," and she could not be mistaken in his voice.

But there was an empty sensation around her heart. That was what little Mrs. Rand had said. She had heard her husband's voice saying he was dead. All of it had been in the morning newspaper. The police, the paper said, did not believe it. But it was there.

May Travis called police headquarters in the city. And when the operator got the nature of the call, it went directly through to the office of the new police commissioner, Wildcat Gordon.

The huffy mayor and Jack Thurston, the threatened engineer, were just leaving the office. Wildcat took part of May Travis's message; then he recalled Jack Thurston.

Mayor Van Royston went on to his kid-gloved reception; Wildcat refrained from further ruining the mayor's day.

WILDCAT GORDON'S own high-powered roadster roared ahead of the police squad car screaming its way through the suburb. Thurston sat beside Wildcat.

"I can't understand it," Thurston was saying. "Charley Travis! Why, he was comparatively a nobody! There couldn't be any object in killing him! It must be some mistake!"

The black knot of men around the electrical substation proved it was no mistake. They were awaiting the police. Only the grief-stricken May Travis had been inside, and a workman had prevented her from touching her father's body.

Charles Travis, a man of gray hair, had apparently been alone in the substation. No electrical wires had yet been strung to the small plant where a step-up dynamo was being installed.

Nevertheless, Charles Travis had been electrocuted.

The dead man was still gripping the receiver of the telephone. The skin of one hand had been marked as if by fire. The face was twisted into the contortions caused by the shock of an electrical current.

Wildcat Gordon made a quick inspection. Whatever the source of the deadly juice, it had been removed, or the contact had created a short circuit and blown a fuse. The voltage had been so high that the phone wires were burned out.

No doubt this was the explosion heard by May

Travis. The pretty girl, the flour of her baking still on her bare arms, was crouching in a chair.

"He said he was dead—he said he was dead," she kept murmuring monotonously.

Wildcat put a hand on her shoulder. May Travis was little. She reminded him of Marian Traeger. Wildcat sometimes called Marian "Tiny." He decided he would call Marian as soon as he could and have her look after this stricken girl.

While squad men prowled about, Jack Thurston had gone outside. His sharp black eyes now seemed to hold some fear. He beckoned to Wildcat Gordon and started tracing the makeshift telephone line along the power project's right of way. The phone line had been temporarily attached to small poles, but in some places it ran along the ground.

Within the first hundred yards of the substation the wires had not been tampered with. Here the power towers were placed on the pitch of a steep hill. A highway ran along the creek valley below. Another road ran along the ridge, perhaps two hundred feet above.

Jack Thurston was an active young man. He had the habit of going bareheaded. His hair shone black and sleek in the sun. At a bend in the hill Thurston was fifty yards ahead of Wildcat Gordon.

Wildcat was examining a spot where the insulation had been rubbed off an electrical wire that supplied temporary power for construction work.

Thurston's voice cried, "Gordon, look out! Commissioner!"

THERE WAS sudden rumbling thunder. Wildcat looked, but Thurston was just around the shoulder of the hill. Rocks bounded outward beyond the shoulder and plummeted on down into the valley. One big boulder, the size of a truck's body, scored a path among small trees.

The weight of the largest rock carried the telephone line away. There was a crackle of fire. The electrical line nearby was snapped. Wildcat reached the shoulder of the hill with quick bounds.

Jack Thurston's dark face had turned gray. He was clinging to a broken tree. Blood trickled from a red welt across his forehead. He weaved on his feet.

"Great shakes, Commissioner!" he gulped. "That almost got me!"

The big boulder had missed Thurston. A smaller stone had cut his head. The rumble of the small avalanche died out. From above came the purring of an automobile. Wildcat glanced up. He saw a red coupé gliding along the upper road.

Getting a gun into his hand, Wildcat attempted the steep ascent. Fifty feet from the top, he was blocked. The hillside became a blank wall with not so much as a finger or toehold. The red coupé showed only once more. It was being driven recklessly away.

Wildcat sucked in his breath. He had been given no more than a camera flash of two faces in the coupé's window before it disappeared. One was the nearly round face of a young man with lightest of blond hair. It was a face that Wildcat had seen only once before, but under conditions that had imprinted it upon his brain.

The man driving the coupé was Ranny Howard. The face of the girl beside Ranny Howard was also distinct for the second. It was the white countenance of Nellie Jones, the daughter of J. Grover Jones.

Wildcat slid down the hill. Thurston was wiping the blood from his face.

"Did you see him, Commissioner?" said the engineer. "I'd have sworn I had a glimpse of Ranny Howard, just as that big rock rolled off the edge."

"I saw him," assented Wildcat. "You're lucky you missed the big one. I have an idea it tore away whatever connection there may have been between the wires."

"You think so?" gritted Jack Thurston. "I've another idea, Commissioner! That rock was intended to rub me out! Howard has had it in for me for a long time! You see, well, there was a time when I thought Nellie Jones was a very good friend!"

Wildcat Gordon appraised Jack Thurston briefly. The engineer was darkly handsome. He was much better-looking than the blond, round-faced Ranny Howard. He had a shrewdness, a penetration about his black eyes that marked him as a young man who might go far.

"I get your thought," said Wildcat, crisply. "We'll get back."

A car had roared up carrying Deputy Henry Bolton. The angular official was standing in the substation, his small mouth pursed into an appearance of deep thinking.

Wildcat Gordon surveyed the deputy with unblinking eyes.

"Did you put out an order to pick up Ranny Howard and the daughter of J. Grover Jones?" inquired Wildcat, quietly.

"Why—well—" Deputy Bolton squirmed uncomfortably. He finished by making his voice snappish.

"No, I didn't give the order! The mayor wouldn't stand for it, and you know it, Commissioner!"

Half a dozen detectives and squad men were investigating the interior of the substation. Their muttered conversation instantly ceased. Eyes were bent on Wildcat Gordon and the deputy commissioner. Some word of the altercation in the commissioner's office that morning had gotten around.

"So the mayor wouldn't stand for it?" said Wildcat slowly. "Bolton, you will drop this Travis case. Until you have brought in Howard and Nellie Jones, you need not report at headquarters. The charge will be suspicion of murder! Now get going!"

Breaths were drawn in and let out. Henry Bolton's mouth was like a knot in his thin face. He was a head taller than Wildcat Gordon. He looked once into the now-gray Texas eyes, and he turned and went out.

JACK THURSTON was eager to be helpful. He got Wildcat Gordon to one side. There appeared no more to be done in the matter of the Travis murder until a checkup had been made of the mysterious call from a phone on Van Buren Avenue.

Thurston said there were some things that now would have to be told. He declared he had been holding them back, because of his loyalty to J. Grover Jones and to his daughter.

"But you know the old man had Ranny Howard kicked off the job where he was working as a draftsman," stated Thurston. "And last night I became aware that someone is threatening J. Grover Jones. He called me to his house last night, about ten o'clock. He kept me there until after you had called about Rand's death. First, he seemed to want to make sure I knew all about the new dynamos."

Wildcat studied the engineer. He looked like a young man who would know all about anything he tackled.

Then Thurston said there were at least two other men with J. Grover Jones in his library. But he had not been permitted to meet these men. He said he had never seen J. Grover Jones so upset, so change-able in his decisions.

"Even before we heard of it," declared Thurston, "you would have thought the old man had heard some threat against Rand, or in some way knew what was about to happen. He asked me three different times about what plans were on paper for the new dynamos."

"Those dynamos pretty well control the future of the Black Mountain Power Co.?" questioned Wildcat.

"Altogether," said Thurston. "Well, last night the old man wanted me to consent to instruct other engineers. I mean, after he heard of Rand's murder. He said that left the whole weight of the power company's success on my shoulders and—well, he intimated he had a reason for believing something might happen to me."

"And you refused to pass along the plans," stated Wildcat with a slow grin.

"I refused," said Thurston frankly. "I have the rare chance to hold a lifetime job at a high salary. There are plans for the dynamos on paper. I have them. When all this happened, and when I got that threatening note from The Whisperer this morning, I put those papers in a safety deposit box where no one but myself will know where they are."

"That was smart, very smart," commented Wildcat. "I can't say I can criticize your position. As you say, it's a lifetime job."

Thurston looked pleased that Commissioner Gordon understood.

"You think I took the right position, Commissioner?" said Thurston, as if he somewhat doubted the ethics of his own behavior.

Wildcat said it was what he would have done. So J. Grover Jones had been threatened directly? That might clear up the matter of the millionaire's sudden change of attitude concerning the Rand case.

Thurston had said there were at least two men with J. Grover Jones the night before, at the time of the Rand murder. Those two, then, could not have been responsible for the killing. Wildcat wondered where Ranny Howard had been at that time.

He said to Thurston, "Come along. We'll check on this Travis phone call on Van Buren Avenue. Then we'll run along out to Belvidere and call on J. Grover Jones. I imagine he may be induced to talk, especially as it is likely his only daughter may be requiring his signature on a bail bond before night."

Thurston was a little gloomy about the matter of Nellie Jones.

"I'll gladly go with you to Belvidere," he said gloomily, "but I don't believe the girl is consciously doing anything wrong."

Wildcat liked the engineer for taking that atti-tude, even though at the moment he was thinking it might be well if some other person possessed the key to Thurston's deposit box.

The plans for the dynamos were valuable papers. Thurston would have been amazed to know that Commissioner Gordon had determined to get them into his own hands.

ON VAN BUREN AVENUE, Wildcat found the detectives who had already checked on the mysterious Travis murder call. The checkup had netted exactly nothing.

The telephone booths, a pair of them, were in a corner of the drugstore. At all times there were persons waiting to use them. The clerks could neither fix the time of the murder call nor any possible description of the person who might have made it.

These phones were not of the dial variety. It had been necessary to call the central operator, who in turn had called the suburban exchange to ring the Travis home.

There was only one certainty. For the second time, a man's own voice had been used to announce that he was dead. Then that man had died after the call had been made.

"I think J. Grover Jones will be about ready to

talk now," said Wildcat Gordon grimly. "We'll go on out there."

CHAPTER VI
A MILLIONAIRE SHOOTS

HAD COMMISSIONER GORDON and Jack Thurston, the engineer, arrived at the Belvidere residence of J. Grover Jones ten minutes before they did, they might have been in time to have heard the shooting. However, it was all over when they did arrive.

At the time Charles Travis stepped to his substation telephone and received his death shock, J. Grover Jones was seated in his library. The residence was small to be that of a millionaire. For J. Grover Jones kept only two servants. He held very much aloof from the public.

The financier suffered with a malignant growth that covered one side of his pouchy face. It gave him the appearance of seeing only with one eye. He was extremely sensitive of his affliction and seldom had guests.

Now he had sent both servants out shortly before noon. His reason appeared to be to avoid their meeting with two visitors. These men might have been business associates, only their features were too heavy and their eyes too cunning.

Today one of these men had a strip bandage plastered over one ear. His chin bore a bruised mark. He had said to J. Grover Jones, "Yes, we met Inspector Gordon, who today is the new commissioner. He knows exactly as much as he did before your crazy daughter tried to get to him. That's all he ever will know."

J. Grover Jones constantly rubbed a hand through his sparse, gray hair. He kept the marred side of his face averted. The eye turned toward his visitors was deep-set and at this moment it held a calculating light.

"I'll admit you've got me sewed up," stated J. Grover Jones wearily. "My daughter's safety is more important than my own life. I owe it to my directors to save the company. But your demands are exorbitant, impossible to meet!"

"You'll meet them O.K.," said one of the men cheerfully, his long leg swinging over his chair arm. "We're not going into any of that again. You'll pay, in immediate cash and give your oath of silence. And that holds in the future. Let the police get any of this, and your phone will ring the same as Rand's."

J. Grover Jones was slumped in his chair. His desk telephone buzzed before he could reply. The two men sat up straight and kept keen eyes on the power magnate as he lifted the receiver.

They heard a voice mumbling over the wire.

The expression on the millionaire's face became as fixed as a gray mask. His hand replaced the receiver slowly but his whole body suddenly came out of his chair.

J. Grover Jones croaked hoarsely: "You knew this was going to happen. You came here knowing it, waiting for it! Another one of my men is dead. He called his home, like Homer Rand, and then they found him dead! That ends all of the deal—all of—"

One of his visitors cut in incisively.

"Well, we couldn't be suspected of having anything to do with it, any more than this Rand being bumped off last night," he said mockingly. "You'll have to admit we were here when Rand died, and we are here now. Ain't it a big break for us that we happen to be talking to J. Grover Jones himself? So this stays strictly a deal between gentlemen!"

J. Grover Jones was shouting. One heavy leg kicked his own chair aside.

"Murderers! A deal between gentlemen! A demand for twelve million dollars! Well, we'll settle all of this right now!"

There was no doubt but that J. Grover Jones was a desperate man. It was equally plain that his two visitors were conscienceless crooks. Crooks who somehow held it in their power to destroy his dreams of a lifetime.

None but a man driven to desperation would have done what J. Grover Jones attempted.

"I'll kill you both!" he shouted. "It's you or me and—"

The millionaire's knee had pushed a button. A drawer shot from his desk directly beneath his hand. A heavy automatic pistol almost jumped into his fingers. Death hung on the air.

ONE OF HIS VISITORS laughed, harshly, confidently. From this man's side pocket came a crackling shot, hardly muffled by the cloth. The coat burned briefly with the powder. The man had not taken the time to bring the pistol into view. But his aim was nevertheless perfect.

J. Grover Jones threw up the hand that held his automatic. The weapon slammed to the floor. The millionaire stood looking at his fingers as if they were not on his own hand. The ends of three and part of his thumb were only bloody stumps.

"Now," said the gunman, never removing his pistol from his pocket, "you have come to the end of time for thinking it over! The money will be produced within the next twenty-four hours, or this time there will be two accidents!

"Your own man, Thurston, will meet with one! It might be your sweet society daughter will call you on the phone and tell you she is dead! That will happen if you do any talking!"

J. Grover Jones sat down in his chair. His lips

worked together. They were so dry they rasped each other. He stared at his crippled hand. One of his visitors walked over and picked up his automatic.

"You met with an accident while fooling with your own gun, Jones," he said easily. "That's what you will tell!"

He fired one bullet from the automatic through the open window into the wide garden. He wiped the weapon and brought it over to the desk.

From this man's pocket came a crackling shot, hardly muffled by the cloth . . .

"Grip this in your hand, your good hand!" he commanded, tersely.

J. Grover Jones took hold of his automatic like a man in a dream.

"If your man Thurston meets with an accident," said his tormentor, "we will take over the Black Mountain Power Co. in our own way. We know Thurston has paper plans. They will be good enough, and he will be all sweetened up to hand them over before he passes out."

J. Grover Jones looked dully from his one good eye at the gun in his left hand. Blood dripped from his severed fingers on the desk blotter. He muttered and nodded.

"And you'll tell anyone who wants to know that you was fooling with your gun and shot yourself accidentally," he was told. "You'll have twelve million dollars ready in cash by this hour tomorrow."

The power magnate did not move when the visitors slid from his library. Their footsteps echoed going out. They crossed the garden afoot, for their car was parked some distance away.

They had no more than disappeared when the police roadster with Wildcat Gordon at the wheel came into the driveway.

Jack Thurston pushed the doorbell. Its buzzing sounded, but he pushed it the fourth time before slow steps came down the stairs. J. Grover Jones himself opened the door with awkward fumbling.

The millionaire was handicapped by one hand being useless and the other still holding the automatic pistol. Wildcat and Thurston stared at him, exclaiming.

"For Heaven's sake, J. G.," came from Thurston, "what happened? What've you done? Who's been here?"

Wildcat stepped quickly in and took the automatic from the man's nerveless fingers. He glanced quickly at the other wounded hand.

"I—well, I shot myself," stated J. Grover Jones. "I—it had a shell in the firing chamber, and the safety was off. It was an accident."

Wildcat Gordon said, "Fix up that hand and we'll talk, Mr. Jones. That's a funny accident to have. And it's the third one in a few hours happening to some one connected with Black Mountain Power Co. You didn't happen to call a friend and tell him you were dead?"

J. GROVER JONES had not built up his fortune with the kind of a brain that could be tricked so easily. A smile came to the side of his face that he kept turned to his visitors.

"I know what you're thinking, Commissioner Gordon, but this was an accident," he said, coolly. "Let me congratulate you on the new job. You

should do a lot toward cleaning up the rottenness in this city."

"Thanks," said Wildcat shortly, "but I think we'll stick to the subject. Who shot you, Mr. Jones? And why? We'll get off evading here and now. I know you are being threatened, probably blackmailed. You were afraid to talk last night. Now that we have that out of the way, let's have some names?"

J. Grover Jones had resumed his cold, calculating manner. His gray head shook slowly.

"Whether you are right or wrong, Commissioner Gordon, I have nothing whatever to say. If I had visitors last night, or even today before this accident, that is strictly my business. It has no connection whatever with the murder of Homer Rand, the killing of Charles Travis today."

There are times when any man may know another is deliberately lying. Wildcat Gordon was convinced J. Grover Jones was determined upon keeping his secret. Behind the millionaire's cool assertion, Wildcat was sure he could read the limit of fear. Fear, no doubt, for his own life.

Thurston said, "I've been threatened myself, J. G. It comes from this mysterious bandit they call The Whisperer. My own life seems to be at stake, so I'd advise you to tell the commissioner here all about it."

Thurston's tone was persuasive. He put one hand affectionately on the millionaire's shoulder. Wildcat could see J. Grover Jones had a high regard for the engineer. But J. Grover Jones was not talking.

"Business is business, Jack," he said to Thurston. "I don't believe anything will happen to you. In fact, I am sure the deal on which I am engaged will make both your life and your position secure."

Wildcat saw this was getting nowhere. He recalled old Trigger saying when Jones sewed up his tongue, he sewed it up. The power magnate must have a deep, compelling reason for his fear.

Wildcat had one more card up his sleeve. He was so sure that it would bring the millionaire around that he used it with a grim smile.

"I regret then, Mr. Jones, to have to tell you we have your daughter under arrest on suspicion of murder. She has been taken in company with a former draftsman with your company, Ranny Howard."

But J. Grover Jones reacted to this statement in a surprising manner. Here was the cool financier who never let any emergency shake him. He was not the same man who a short time before had been driven to the desperate attempt to kill blackmailing visitors.

"My daughter? Suspicion of murder?" he said. "You mean in these killings, Rand and Travis?"

"The Travis killing directly," stated Wildcat. "Your daughter was on the scene with Howard. They apparently attempted to kill Thurston here, or perhaps they were only trying to destroy evidence of how Travis was murdered."

Anger blazed in the eyes of the power magnate. He suddenly arose, began pacing the room.

"That damned Howard!" he shouted. "I've told her to keep away from him! So she's locked up now! Locked up in a jail! Well, that's good! That's very good! I don't know of a better place for her, and I would not put out one penny of my money to get her out!"

Then J. Grover Jones just as suddenly became calm.

"But all this makes no difference," he stated. "I've nothing to discuss with regard to my business dealings."

TEN MINUTES LATER, Wildcat Gordon judged J. Grover Jones had spoken his last word on the subject. While he indicated clearly he did not believe his daughter was in any way involved in the murders, he persisted in declaring he would make no move to get her out of jail.

Wildcat dropped that subject abruptly. Nellie Jones and Ranny Howard still had their freedom so far as he knew. The bluff had failed to elicit any information.

Wildcat arose to leave. He turned back and said, "You are like many other citizens, Mr. Jones. I am convinced you could help us put our hands upon these killers. You are afraid. Perhaps you know, too, the identity of this Whisperer?"

"I don't want to be discourteous," said the millionaire, "but I am not discussing the subject further."

Jack Thurston lost his temper momentarily.

"That means, knowing you have to depend on me, you'll leave me on the spot! All right, J. G., I'm going to do all I can to help the police get The Whisperer."

Thurston had no means of knowing he was to have the opportunity to meet the mysterious Whisperer.

CHAPTER VII
UNDER THE GRAY FOG

JACK THURSTON, the engineer, went to his duplex apartment through a thin, gray fog of the late evening. His sleek, black hair glistened with moisture. His keen eyes were shining with some hint of amusement.

Thurston was aware that two men were following him. Two others also kept an even pace ahead, perhaps just half a block. These four had appeared when Thurston had left his garage, a block from his rooms.

Before he had put up his car, Thurston knew two plain autos had always been staying in the same block with him. It had been that way all afternoon, ever since he had left Wildcat Gordon.

The police commissioner had said he would furnish protection. The order had been never to permit the engineer to get out of sight of this group of shadows. The detectives knew their business.

Everywhere he had gone, Thurston knew Commissioner Gordon's men were nearby. If the mysterious Whisperer had any thought of making contact with the engineer, he had little chance.

Thurston's apartment was the upper half of a duplex house. He was acquainted with the family on the lower floor. There were no lights below tonight. So no other person was in the house.

Thurston might not have felt so comfortable had he known the family downstairs had that afternoon been furnished special tickets to a midnight preview at the neighborhood theater. The tickets had come to the family mysteriously, but they were acceptable.

Before he entered his stairway door, Thurston glanced along the street. Two men moved in the gray fog near the corner. Two others were walking slowly toward the rear of his residence.

"Not much chance for The Whisperer tonight," Thurston murmured to himself. Then he emitted an odd little laugh. "Anyway, it's the first time I've ever rated a bodyguard. Now if they haven't got Ranny Howard, and he comes along, he'll walk right into something!"

Thurston frowned at his last words. It was apparent he had some real fear of Ranny Howard. Perhaps more than for the elusive Whisperer.

THE ENGINEER used a key on his door at the top of the stairs. Across his wide living room, he could see the stark branches of a huge oak tree. They were like huge, skeleton-like arms creating patterns of street light on the double French window.

This double window opened on a second floor gallery with an iron railing. One side had been left partly open for air. The duplex was in a quiet, law-abiding neighborhood.

Thurston closed his door and fumbled for the light button. He punched it. Nothing happened. Except for the vague, gray light from the window, the room remained in darkness.

"Damn!" said Thurston. "Now I suppose a fuse has gone out!"

He pushed the light button again. Then the ghostly, penetrating whisper filled the room. It seemed to come from no particular spot. Though it was a whisper without heavy tone, yet it was clear and grated harshly on Thurston's nerves.

"There is no light, Thurston! Sit down in that chair beside you! Don't touch the gun you've got in your pocket!"

"Great shakes!" muttered Thurston. "It *is* The Whisperer!"

"Why?" came the sibilant sound. "Didn't you really expect I would come?"

"What do you want?" demanded Thurston. "What made you come here?"

"But you got my little note, didn't you, Thurston?" spoke The Whisperer.

"Why—yes, the note!" grunted Thurston. "But you didn't—"

"I know when my name is used, Thurston!" said The Whisperer strangely. "I won't waste words! The time is short! You will take the card and key for your safety deposit box from your pocket and toss it toward the window!"

"I'll do no such damn—"

Then Thurston saw the silhouette of The Whisperer between him and the window. It was only the profile. An outthrust chin, a queer, long upper

The Whisperer

lip. Above this a blur of hair. For the rest of him, The Whisperer's body was only a part of the gray fog coming in wisps through the window.

Thurston broke off his speech. Surely The Whisperer had ordinary eyes. He could not see the engineer in the darkness. Thurston had no means of knowing The Whisperer had developed ears far beyond the human range. It was one of the reasons he worked in the darkness.

The Whisperer heard the light scrape of Thurston's fingernails on the cloth of his coat. He knew the engineer was reaching into his pocket. Now the engineer might have been seeking the key to his deposit box, but his words had not indicated it.

The Whisperer had been only an outline by the window. In one hand he held a strange gun. It might have been called the pistol of the hissing death. For it was the weapon that had been heard in the gambling house of Duke Dolano. It really was an automatic with a newly devised air-cylinder silencer.

The Whisperer did not use the gun. His shadow left the window. The Whisperer became real when hard bone and muscle drove into the body of Thurston. The engineer had snatched for an automatic he carried under one arm.

The hard materiality of The Whisperer became apparent when a flesh-cutting fist sliced across Thurston's cheek and staggered him to the wall. The Whisperer had the first advantage. But this Thurston had been a college boxer in his day. He had used a sudden crouch and an upward lift of one shoulder.

The Whisperer was jolted into the wall by the collision. The engineer was two hundred pounds of bone and muscle. He followed up his advantage with rights and lefts to his mysterious visitor's body. He heard the breath oozing out of The Whisperer.

Thurston succeeded in dragging out his gun. He used it as a bludgeon. The Whisperer grunted and fell to the floor. Again the butt of the heavy automatic hammered on his skull. Thurston's hard knee bored into his spine.

The Whisperer evidently had been greatly surprised. He fought to break the crushing hold of the man he had apparently come to rob. An oath hissed from his lips. It was in the high whisper that had given him his name

Thurston raised his automatic high in the air. In another second the heavy weapon would have finished The Whisperer. Two things happened at once.

A piercing ray of light flashed in from the gallery beyond the French windows. Simultaneously an honest-to-goodness shot cracked out with benefit of a silencer. A hand had pointed a pistol rigidly.

THURSTON LET OUT a groan. His automatic fell and struck The Whisperer a glancing blow in the face. The man on the outside gallery had vanished, but within five seconds police positives started barking.

The Whisperer got to his feet. Thurston lay on his face with blood seeping from a wound at the back, high up on his shoulder. The Whisperer staunched the flow of blood. Thurston was not seriously wounded. He groaned and started to roll over.

Perhaps it was a blackjack The Whisperer employed. It made a thick, dull sound. Thurston's head flopped sidewise. He would be asleep for considerable time.

The Whisperer worked swiftly. He used a pencil flashlight. He took a small card and a safety deposit box key from Thurston's pocket. Inspection showed this had not been issued in the name of Jack Thurston

The Whisperer chuckled in a ghostly fashion. The card gave the address of a small bank. The use of the phony name made it clear that Thurston had employed a bank where he was not known. A good idea for the safety of the dynamo plans, if they were in that box.

In the small yard outside, heavy voices of policemen were talking. They must have gotten the man who had fired the shot into Thurston from the window. The Whisperer went to the window and glanced down.

A detective had a light playing on the face of a man they had brought down with their bullets. It was the round face of Ranny Howard with his mop of blond hair.

A voice growled, "Bring that dame over here! You other fellows get upstairs and see what happened!"

For five seconds, The Whisperer clung to his position. He was a small figure. His body merged with the shadows in the room. Into the circle of flashlights below, a tall, trembling girl was led.

"She was waiting in her bus!" grunted one of the detectives. "Had the motor running for a getaway!"

"Oh, Ranny! Ranny!" the girl cried out.

She tore herself free from restraining hands and threw herself beside the man on the ground. The Whisperer heard Ranny Howard say, "I'll be all right. I got him, Nellie."

Feet were pounding on the stairs. Two detectives came into the room. The Whisperer slipped into a closet. He heard one of the dicks swear when the lights failed to work. A flashlight was used.

"Well, he bumped him!" said one of the men. "No! He's still breathin'! Hell! Look here! This is a funny one. That guy never got off that gallery outside, for I was watching him, but this fellow's been shot and pretty well smacked over the head!"

"I'll have a look around," growled the other detective, getting his revolver ready.

He crossed the room, using his flashlight. The door of the closet drew his attention. The Whisperer had left it open a crack. Holding his revolver steadily on that crack, the detective started opening the door slowly.

TWO HANDS, like steel pincers, darted from inside the closet. One fastened on the detective's wrist. The other closed on his windpipe. He was snatched into the closet so quickly it hardly made a sound.

Almost instantly the closet door opened. A figure emerged behind the flashlight. The light was extended so the face and the figure were not revealed.

The other detective was turning Thurston over, poking a flask at the unconscious man's lips.

"Hey, Joe!" he called out. "See anything?"

"There was nothing," came a sibilant whisper that raised both the detective's hair and his body.

At the same time, an instrument like a padded blackjack slapped upon the detective's skull. The officer fell over and went to sleep. The Whisperer saw that Thurston would be a long time out. He deftly bandaged the bullet wound in the shoulder.

Then The Whisperer went back to a desk near a bed. There were papers there. One that appeared to be a letter in Thurston's own writing was poked into The Whisperer's pocket.

None of the other men had come up the stairs. There had been only four dicks on the shadow detail. They had called for a squad car. The Whisperer got to a telephone in the lower hallway. He did a queer thing then. He used the telephone for nearly two minutes. But when a police squad car arrived, The Whisperer had faded into the fog through the unguarded back entrance to the lower duplex.

A motorcycle cop came hurtling after the squad car. An ambulance had been summoned from the nearest hospital.

"Hold up on that!" said the motorcycle cop. "This fellow Thurston, if that's him, is to go to the headquarters emergency hospital along with the man shot outside! Guards are to be put over both of them, special! It's the commissioner's direct order!"

"The commissioner?" snapped one of the detectives. "Don't tell me Wildcat Gordon knows that much about this blowoff? Hell, we didn't do anything but call for a squad and the hospital bus! We didn't have any time to explain!"

The motorcycle cop grinned.

"That's a telephoned order directly from the commissioner's own house, brother! And he said especially this Thurston was to be kept under close guard at the headquarters hospital for his own protection! Also, Gordon said that was good shooting that got Ranny Howard in the garden, and you could see that the girl was locked up and not permitted to talk to anybody until he sees her!"

The detectives who had been shadowing Jack Thurston looked at each other dazedly. One suggested they get upstairs and see how Joe and his partner were coming along.

"Now what the blazes?" yelled one of the first men up into Thurston's room.

The detective, called Joe, was crawling from a closet on his hands and knees, shaking his head. His bulky partner lay stretched out beside the wounded Thurston.

Only Thurston was coming to his senses.

"The Whisperer," he mumbled. "Did you fellows get him? He went—"

Thurston was fumbling in his pocket.

His safety deposit card and key were missing.

CHAPTER VIII
THE GIRL WON'T TALK

GRAY FOG ALSO shrouded the warehouse district. It wreathed upward, wrapping ghostly fingers around the penthouse of Dick Traeger.

The piquant, childlike face of Tiny Traeger was bathed by its dampness as she peered from an open window.

The elevator from below had come up with a soft whining of its gears. This lift cage did not enter the inside of the penthouse. The roof door had been placed outside the residence. Old Trigger and Wildcat Gordon had planned this for a purpose of their own.

Any person coming up in the elevator must afterward seek admittance to the penthouse.

Now Marian Traeger saw a shadowy figure step from the elevator. There was something familiar about the shadow, but the tiny girl could not identify it in the gray fog. The man moved with the crouching noiselessness of a stalking cat.

The entrance light picked out the face. It was an odd face. The chin was outthrust. The upper lip was too long. The bared head was a blur of hair brushed straight back. All of the man's clothing seemed to be of indeterminate gray.

The shadowy figure moved directly toward the door that gave separate entrance to Wildcat Gordon's rooms. The man seemed to have some sort of weapon in his hand.

Tiny Traeger was a very small girl, as has been stated. She tipped the scales at an even hundred pounds. Ninety-nine out of a hundred of her sex would have immediately cried out, screamed for help.

But Tiny was the granddaughter of a copper. If the truth must be known, she was in love with another copper with every one of her less than sixty inches. That other copper was Wildcat Gordon. And now she saw a sinister, threatening intruder stealthily moving toward Wildcat Gordon's door.

The tiny girl uttered no sound. She knew her grandfather was napping. She had been keeping coffee hot for the late return of Wildcat, the new commissioner of police. Perhaps she hoped that becoming commissioner might open his eyes to some other things. The devotion of little Tiny Traeger, to be specific.

Old Quick Trigger dozed on as Tiny snatched one of his old police positives from its holster. The girl went silently into the corridor. She could hear the intruder on the roof, fumbling with the lock of Wildcat's door. The door pushed open and the gray fog poured in.

The shadowy figure with the queer face seemed to float in on the fog. Tiny's voice may have been shaky, but the big revolver she held in both hands was not.

"Stick 'em up!" she commanded, pushing the weapon against the intruder's breast. "Don't move until Granddad gets here, or I'll—I'll shoot!"

The Whisperer, for it was none other, slowly elevated his hands. He did not speak. He just stood there, feeling the pressure of the revolver upon his wishbone and the trembling of the girl's body through the weapon.

The Whisperer had no doubt but that Tiny Traeger would shoot. Yet he was chuckling deep in his throat, giving vent to a hissing laugh. The girl called out. Old Quick Trigger came scrambling into the corridor. It was gloomy in there.

Quick Trigger found a light switch. Illumination flooded the corridor.

Old Trigger had not become a deputy commissioner by slow thinking. Now he saw The Whisperer. He could not miss seeing his pretty granddaughter holding a big revolver with both hands pushed into The Whisperer's breastbone. But something like a stomach laugh shook the old man.

"Well, Dunk Smith!" exclaimed old Trigger. "When I told you to come up, I didn't think you'd run head-on into the artillery! Tiny, meet Dunk Smith an old friend of mine, and of Wildcat's! I forgot to tell you he was coming up to see me!"

TINY REMOVED the threat of the revolver. "Dunk" Smith put down his hands. He grinned a little at the girl and at old Trigger. His queerly shaped chin and mouth made the smile ghastly. Tiny shivered.

Dunk Smith acknowledged the introduction by a slight bow. He did not speak. His eyes seemed to have no color and his face was much like that of a dead man. He wore a dirty gray suit with a dirty gray tie to match. Dunk Smith did not look like much.

Still old Trigger seemed vastly pleased to see

"Tiny" Traeger

him. Tiny was sent to bring coffee. Then The Whisperer talked. His speech was a high hissing, as if he lacked vocal cords.

"Dang it all!" said old Trigger. "Maybe I didn't do so good a job on them plates! I'll have to try it again!"

"You couldn't make them better," came the whispering voice. "Don't you see, Trigger, this has made me The Whisperer? That's a reputation I don't want to lose. Things happened tonight!"

"Yes, and they've been happening down at headquarters," said old Trigger. "But that can wait. What in time are we going to do about Tiny? You wouldn't want her to know?"

"No," said The Whisperer. "I'm your friend, Dunk Smith. Make it strong and let it go at that. Don't you see, that will explain me if something like this happens again?"

"Still, I could've made better dental plates," insisted Trigger.

For years, Trigger had experimented with making simple disguises. As a policeman, he had never used them. It had been his hobby only. So it was a simple pair of dental plates that were responsible for The Whisperer, for his appearance, for his speech.

Tiny came with coffee. She gave quick, furtive glances at Trigger's strange friend, Dunk Smith.

Dunk Smith said, in his whispering voice, "And so I came to you, Trigger. Because of my throat trouble and everything, I'm afraid I'm going to be mistaken for this Whisperer the police are after. I thought maybe you could advise me."

"You're in a tough spot, Dunk," said old Trigger with a glint in his eyes. "But I'll stand by you. I've always known you to talk like that, like you hadn't any vocal cords. And you've always been law-abiding, so far as I know."

Tiny served the coffee. Her brown eyes were as bright as those of a bird. She had a woman's instant sympathy for an unfortunate, this Dunk Smith with such a strange impediment in his speech.

Five minutes later, the glint increased in Trigger's eye. He got up and walked out of the room. He did not seem to see The Whisperer's frantic signals that he should not leave him alone with the girl.

"So you're a friend of Wildcat Gordon?" said Tiny instantly.

"Yes, to be sure," whispered Dunk Smith. "I've known him a long time. Quite a long time."

"That's nice," said Tiny softly. "We like Wildcat, only he keeps me busy answering the telephone."

The Whisperer started a little.

"Answering the telephone?" he whispered, hoarsely. "So he calls up often, or is it his business?"

"Well, not exactly," stated Tiny. "Don't you ever tell him, but it's women. Loads and loads of women.

They're always calling up. Do you think, Mr. Smith, that Wildcat takes any of them seriously?"

The homely Dunk Smith looked as if he were about to choke over his own long lip.

"Certainly not—that is—well, I don't know about Wildcat's women," he got out in his husky whisper. "I think—if you'll call your grandfather, Trigger, I'll be going along."

The girl said, "Well, you'll come up often, Mr. Smith. I want to talk with someone who has known Wildcat a long time. He's so smart about some things and so awfully dumb about things that count."

Dunk Smith got out without drinking his coffee. At the door, he said, "Trigger, I'm going to pull your ears off for that. Now keep Tiny out of the way while I get to my room."

Old Trigger smiled benevolently. "She might as well get used to my friend, Dunk Smith. Now you'd better get on that headquarters telephone. I think his honor, the mayor, is waiting up. I know there's a call from upstate from some of your dicks who have Duke Dolano out for an airing."

APPARENTLY this Dunk Smith of the whispering voice went down in the elevator. But a minute later, he was in Wildcat Gordon's rooms. From his upper and lower jaws came two oddly fashioned dental plates. Powder that had lightened his darkish-red hair was brushed off.

With his bright-red necktie restored, and a vivid scarlet carnation in his buttonhole, Wildcat Gordon surveyed himself in the mirror.

Though the police business at this moment was in considerable of a jam, Wildcat grinned and said, "So loads and loads of women are calling me up, huh? That Tiny is due for a spanking and she's going to get it!"

Wildcat Gordon put The Whisperer in a loose coat pocket. Or rather he placed the odd dental plates there. Old Trigger had been steadily apologizing for this poor disguise. He had made it for Wildcat Gordon when Wildcat had been on a hot case.

Because of some twist in the dental plates, Wildcat had discovered he could only whisper. But it was a high, penetrating whisper that demanded instant attention. It had inspired fear. It had been old Trigger who had pulled out the lights at Duke Dolano's place.

Now Wildcat got on the telephone. First there were the detectives sticking by a telephone upstate. It was after midnight. Duke Dolano, handcuffed in their car, was threatening all sorts of action when he got back. The dicks were tired. There were four of them.

"Take Duke on up to Grass Lake!" ordered Wildcat. "Make camp on the north shore! No one will ever find you there! Buy provisions for a few days and stake Duke out to a tree!"

When the phone was cleared, there came a ring and the voice of Mayor Van Royston.

"Where have you been, Commissioner Gordon? Get down to headquarters at once! Great Scott, man! There's the devil and all to pay! Attorney Hempel's been here for hours with a writ for Duke Dolano! He's threatening to have us hauled into court!"

Wildcat grinned broadly. "Tell that shyster Hempel to run along home and change his shirt. He can shave, too. For I'm not seeing him until around noon."

"What? What? Commissioner Gordon, you are to get down here at once! Do you know The Whisperer has struck again? He nearly killed two of your men! He beat up and shot that fellow Thurston whom he threatened in his note! Another man, Ranny Howard, was shot trying to rescue Thurston and—listen, Commissioner! I have the daughter of J. Grover Jones here in the office! They tell me she was brought in by your order! What is this? What is—"

Wildcat stretched his free arm and yawned widely.

"Yes, yes, Mayor. Now you had better go home and go to bed. That's what I'm going to do."

Mayor Van Royston almost choked to death. Wildcat could see his scanty chin bobbing in and out.

"You can't do that! You can't do that!" shouted the mayor. "If you don't get down here and fix up these matters, I shall put Deputy Bolton in full charge! I'll have everybody turned loose! I'll have my friend, J. Grover Jones, down here and fix up this thing about his daughter! Don't you know J. Grover Jones can make or break us?"

Wildcat smiled to himself. He was betting J. Grover Jones would not even answer his telephone now. And in this he was correct. That was one of the angles adding to the agitation of Mayor Van Royston.

And at this juncture, Wildcat softly set down the telephone receiver. He inserted a broken match behind the bell so it could not so much as buzz. Ten minutes later, Wildcat was snoring gently.

He did not dream of the silk-hatted mayor pacing his office, or even of the mysterious power company murders. He did dream of many women calling him on the telephone.

POLICE COMMISSIONER GORDON did not reach his headquarters' office until nearly the noon hour. Before he opened the door, he could hear excited voices. These hushed instantly as he walked in.

"Good morning!" greeted Wildcat cheerfully.

A fresh carnation glowed in his buttonhole. His vivid red tie was new. His broad-brimmed army hat was set jauntily to one side. His whole manner was that of a man who had rested well.

None of those in the office appeared to have slept at all. Mayor Van Royston's high silk hat careened drunkenly. His retreating chin was in need of a shave. Another fellow with bloodshot eyes and a heavy jaw was also in need of a shave. This was Attorney Hempel.

Attorney Hempel was one of that clique of criminal lawyers who make life a burden for the police. He jumped in front of Commissioner Gordon now and waved a paper.

"There you are! There you are!" he shouted. "Where's Duke Dolano? I demand my client instantly! I've got a writ for him! The judge has heard of this! You produce Duke Dolano, or I'll summon all of you! I'll have you put—"

"You'll have me put where?" came the voice of Wildcat Gordon, much like steel being rubbed across ice. "Get out, Hempel! And stay out! The judge who issued that writ is going to hear of some other things! I've already got men at your office, Hempel, with orders to take possession of every paper and record they can find!"

The bloodshot eyes of Attorney Hempel almost jumped from their sockets.

"You've got what? You've dared—you've—why where do you think you are? In the army yet? No low-lifed buzzard that thinks he's a cop is going to—"

This was a very unfortunate speech for Attorney Hempel. Wildcat Gordon bounded from his chair. One, two, three, four times his flat hands resounded across the unshaved jaws of the shyster lawyer. Then Wildcat's strong hands caught and held, and heaved.

The broad glass in the upper section of the corridor door was not shatterproof. If it had been, the lawyer would have had his neck

"Wildcat" Gordon

broken. Luckily for him, he went on through. Apparently he was not seriously hurt, for he could be heard scrambling away outside.

Mayor Van Royston stood with his mouth open. That looked funny with his silk hat. Then there was a laugh, a little, musical laugh.

"Oh, my gracious!" bubbled a voice, but when Wildcat whirled around the girl who owned it had made her face solemn.

Nellie Jones was sitting to one side. Apparently her position had not prevented her using lipstick. Miss Nellie Jones, despite the undoubted seriousness of her position, did not seem greatly worried.

"You're Miss Jones," stated Wildcat. "I've met you once before, or perhaps you don't remember?"

The girl's face instantly hardened. Her eyes became wary.

"I don't remember," she said, quietly. "I have asked them to lock me up with Ranny Howard. They have refused. You think I'm all wrong, Commissioner Gordon, and perhaps I am. Still I have nothing to remember."

MAYOR VAN ROYSTON had found his voice. He strode over to Wildcat.

"I needn't tell you that unless all of this is explained, you are finished as commissioner almost before you've begun," he said with dignity. "You will immediately have Miss Jones sent to her home. I have been unable to get her father, which is unfortunate."

"Most unfortunate," said Wildcat calmly. "Miss Jones, I am now having you sent to the women's quarters. You are being detained as a material witness, and that may perhaps become suspicion of murder."

"Murder? Murder?" said the girl, a little shaken. "Why, Mr. Thurston isn't dead—they told me—"

"Exactly," interrupted Wildcat. "But Homer Rand and Charles Travis are dead. Now what is it you know about it? What did you come to tell me the other night?"

Mayor Van Royston stared blankly at Wildcat. Except for her reddened mouth, Nellie Jones's face was pale.

"I did not come to tell you anything, Commissioner Gordon. I have nothing to tell, and I never will. They tell me Ranny may die. Even then, understand, I won't talk."

But Wildcat said, "Before long, Miss Jones, I think you will talk. Yes, I believe you'll be glad to speak."

Wildcat was not so sure. Miss Nellie Jones looked like a girl who had plenty of willpower. He ordered her taken to a cell. Mayor Van Royston stood there with his lower jaw sagging.

CHAPTER IX
A JOLT FOR MR. BOLTON

MAYOR VAN ROYSTON sat down. For minutes, he seemed unable to do more than stare at his new commissioner. No doubt he was speculating on when and how he could rid himself of this Wildcat Gordon.

Commissioner Gordon sat silent during those minutes. Deputy Commissioner Bolton had been in and gone out. Wildcat mentally added up a few items.

So Nellie Jones would not talk? That young woman was much more than the society darling of the newspapers. She had accompanied Ranny Howard on at least two occasions when it had undoubtedly been that fellow's cold intention to kill Jack Thurston.

And Ranny Howard was a discharged employee of the Black Mountain Power Co. As a draftsman, he might know considerable about the secret dynamos. And as the unwelcome suitor for the hand of Nellie Jones, he must have had far from a friendly feeling for J. Grover Jones. Moreover, Ranny Howard's chief handicap was his lack of money.

There was no doubt but that J. Grover Jones had been threatened. The murder of Homer Rand removed his strongest reliance in making his power company a success. Then there was the murder of Charles Travis. Thurston was the key man left to J. Grover Jones.

Those mysterious telephone calls. The dead who seemed to talk. That could be for the purpose of terrorizing J. Grover Jones. Then someone had shot the millionaire, wounded him.

Ranny Howard could have had plenty of time to do that after leaving the scene of the Travis murder, where he had attempted to crush Thurston with a rock.

Perhaps Nellie Jones also hated her father? Or, strangely enough, it could be her affection, her fear for her father's life that was keeping her silent. Being locked up on suspicion of murder had not perturbed that remarkable young woman as much as it should.

Again, there was the attitude of J. Grover Jones toward his daughter. He had said he wouldn't spend a penny to keep her out of jail. If there was hatred, it might be mutual.

NOW MAYOR VAN ROYSTON was talking again. He had found speech and one subject that rankled. The mayor was wanting to know why the police could not seem to catch up with The Whisperer. He was rambling on about what had happened the night before. The attempted killing of Jack Thurston, the engineer.

Wildcat said nothing. He had seen Thurston before he came to his office. The engineer was not seriously wounded. So Wildcat had issued strict orders concerning protection for Thurston.

Also, Wildcat had talked briefly with Ranny Howard. This blond young man had not been badly hurt. But he had been tight as a clam. He had given Wildcat no reply to any of his questions. It seemed there was a well-established conspiracy of silence between Ranny Howard and Nellie Jones.

Wildcat did not like to think it true, but Nellie Jones could be involved in some conspiracy to extract money from her father. It had been done before by society daughters infatuated with men who lacked funds.

Mayor Van Royston was still talking.

"Right under the noses of the police this Whisperer almost killed Engineer Thurston," he was saying. "Then I understand, it was by your order that Thurston was brought to jail, instead of being sent to a regular hospital."

"That was my order, Mayor," said Wildcat quietly. "I have my own reasons for wanting to protect Thurston. His life isn't worth a plugged dime outside."

"Just the same," interrupted the unpleasant voice of Deputy Henry Bolton who came in, "I have just issued instructions for Mr. Thurston to be discharged at once. Mr. Jones, his employer, called and insisted upon it. He said that Mr. Thurston must not be detained."

"What—well, what did he say about his daughter?" exploded Mayor Van Royston. "He knows about her, of course! It's in all the papers!"

Deputy Bolton's small mouth screwed into a funny knot.

"Well, Mayor, your honor, he just wanted Thurston so he could get back on the job. I know it sounds funny, but he said about Miss Jones, that she—that—well, dammit, your honor, 'she had made her own bed and now she could lie in it!'"

"Why, that's impossible—impossible!" gasped Mayor Van Royston.

Wildcat Gordon had cocked both feet on his desk. This morning he was wearing bright-yellow shoes. He regarded them with silent contemplation.

"It's all right, then, Mayor, about discharging Thurston, as Mr. Jones asked?" said Deputy Bolton.

"Yes—yes, certainly, if Mr. Jones wants that!" exclaimed the mayor. "You did just the right thing, Deputy Bolton!"

The telephone on Wildcat's desk rang. Wildcat replied, then extended the instrument to Deputy Bolton, saying, "It's for you, Henry."

Words mumbled in Deputy Bolton's ear. He clapped the phone back on the desk, glaring at Wildcat Gordon.

"Thurston!" he rapped out. "He's gone! He was gone when my order got there to have him discharged! The interne said he was removed by your order, Gord—Commissioner!"

"That's right, Henry," drawled Wildcat in a mild tone. "Thurston was removed elsewhere at my order. I imagined an effort would be made to have him discharged. But for the present, he will remain under my protection."

Deputy Bolton's small mouth became a round, hissing hole.

"Why didn't you tell me that?" he squealed. "Mr. Jones and the mayor have said Thurston is to be discharged! By jimminy! Even if you are commissioner, you're not making a fool out've me! You sent him to one of the precinct emergencies, and I'll have him out of there in five minutes!"

Deputy Bolton grabbed at the telephone on Wildcat's desk. Wildcat made no attempt to interfere. Bolton made four calls, one after the other. After the fourth call, he slapped the instrument down.

"So," he bawled at Wildcat, "you've issued orders that I am to be told nothing about Thurston! Made a fool of me, huh! Mayor Van Royston, I won't stand for this! I'll find Thurston and have him out in the next—"

Wildcat's yellow shoes clicked to the floor. His short body came upright with the snap of a rubber band. One hard right hand shot straight out. The fist hit Deputy Henry Bolton directly under the left ear.

DEPUTY BOLTON was a big man. He outweighed Wildcat by perhaps fifty pounds. That extra poundage only seemed to get in his way. He made two or three ineffective swipes at the commissioner, and each time he missed, the same right fist got him in the same spot, under the left ear.

The last time, Deputy Bolton sat down hard.

"Now get up, and get out!" snapped Wildcat Gordon. "And you, Mayor Van Royston, might as well get this! Henry here is no longer a deputy commissioner! He is hereby suspended until further orders! Sergeant Tom Thorsen is taking his place as deputy in this office! I may not be commissioner longer than tomorrow, or the next day, but by damn, while I'm here I'm running this army!"

Sergeant Tom Thorsen responded to a call. He walked in solemnly. His eyes never flickered as he glanced at Deputy Bolton slowly getting up from the floor.

Sergeant Thorsen had what might be called a wooden face. And that wood might have come from a battleship. His eyes were slatey gray. He looked a little stupid. Perhaps just enough so to obey orders.

Sergeant Thorsen said, "Yes, sir," and clicked

his heels together. His right hand snapped to his eyebrow. "What is it, sir?"

"You will take up the duties of acting deputy commissioner, as instructed this morning, Sergeant Thorsen," stated Wildcat. "You will follow the orders I gave you. See nothing, tell nothing, until you have the word."

"Yes, sir!" said Sergeant Thorsen. "I learned that in the army, sir!"

"And that's exactly why you're here, Deputy Thorsen," grinned Wildcat. "Mayor Van Royston, I shall be absent for some hours. I am looking into the failure of the boys to get The Whisperer."

WHEN COMMISSIONER Wildcat Gordon swung from his office, he still sported his red necktie, his carnation, his army hat, and his bright-yellow shoes. But when he emerged from a taxicab in a street on the far side of town, these outward symbols of flashy attire had disappeared

His suit now was a soiled gray. For this occasion, he was wearing a hat that was a little large. It was the same hat Jack Thurston had been wearing the previous day. He had estimated the hour when Thurston had said he deposited the plans of the secret dynamo in a safety vault.

Now Wildcat was sure the guard who had been on duty would be at his luncheon. Anyway, a hat would be recalled where a face seen only once would not. And from one of Thurston's letters, Wildcat had been able to write a name with a flourish.

The name was not that of Thurston. It was the alias he had used in renting the deposit box. Thurston had not then known how easy he was making it for some other person.

When Wildcat entered the small bank, he had become The Whisperer. As commissioner, he had learned several things from Jack Thurston. Thurston, in the headquarters hospital, had told a straight story about how he had been attacked in his room. He had demanded to be discharged.

But Thurston had refrained from mentioning that his deposit box card and key had been taken by The Whisperer. Thurston did not seem to want to trust even the police with that fact. Wildcat, as The Whisperer, wondered a little about that as he passed into the bank.

Excusing his hoarse, whispering speech as the result of a sudden cold, The Whisperer had little trouble with the card and key in gaining access to Jack Thurston's deposit box. Two minutes later, parchments covered with blueprinted symbols were placed in an inside pocket.

The Whisperer had signed the book with the bogus name Thurston had used. This had been compared with another signature and it had passed. The confiscation of the secret plans of the Black Mountain Power Co. had apparently gone off without a hitch.

The Whisperer emerged into the narrow street. He had wisely dismissed the taxicab in which he had arrived. Now he noticed another taxi standing near the corner, and he hailed it.

The Whisperer saw nothing unusual in the thin street crowd as he entered the taxi. It was his intention to change his identity somewhere en route, then dismiss this driver. He glanced into the rearview mirror as the taxi started and he changed his mind.

Two men, with caps pulled low over their eyes, were hurrying into a car parked around the corner. The car was being swung back into the street taken by the taxicab.

The Whisperer studied the back of his own driver's head. The taxi driver had one cauliflower ear. And the driver had narrowed eyes also fixed upon his rearview mirror. He was watching that car containing the two men.

The Whisperer knew then the taxicab had been deliberately planted. He had walked into it. The two men in that trailing car must have known his mission in the small bank.

The Whisperer condemned himself, at first, for not thinking of that. He had been given no reason to suspect others would know where the cautious Thurston had hidden the dynamo plans

Yet he had been watched, possibly by some man who had been inside the bank lobby. And now, he was being trailed. Moreover, the driver of his taxicab was in league with the two shadows.

The Whisperer had given an address near the heart of town, not far from police headquarters. Now he permitted the taxicab to proceed several blocks. The car containing the two shadows stuck in the rearview mirror.

The taxi driver even held up on a traffic light he might have beaten. The Whisperer grinned at that. He could see the driver's small eyes were watching him in the mirror.

SUDDENLY, The Whisperer fumbled in his pockets. He had decided that while he was in a tight spot, he could not have had a better break. He had for some time believed those threatening J. Grover Jones were operating as a clever blackmail gang, a murder mob.

Ranny Howard might be only a tool, or he might even be the leader. Anyway, these men had known where Thurston hid his plans. And The Whisperer could understand how those plans might be used, if Thurston were out of the way.

The Whisperer continued fumbling in his pockets. Then he tapped the driver's shoulder. He asked him to pull up at a small drugstore, saying he had to have cigarettes. The driver glanced at the rearview mirror, apparently made sure his confederates were at hand, then nodded. He pulled over to the curb.

The Whisperer seemed in no hurry. His strange, whispering voice had one peculiar quality. Dogs were attracted by it. He paused to pat a mongrel's head, just before he entered the drugstore.

Now it could be seen by the taxicab driver that this small, busy store had only one entrance and exit. It was jammed between other buildings. Any person entering the front door must come out by the same door.

The car following was parked behind the taxicab. Its two occupants got out and strolled nonchalantly toward the drugstore. From the display window, they could see it was impossible for their quarry to get out. They took up their positions before the window.

"That's the guy," said one, pointing at the short man pushing through the crowd toward the cigar counter. "You couldn't miss him."

The pair kept their eyes on the man as he went to the counter. The Whisperer did not make the mistake of entering a telephone booth. He stayed in the midst of the crowd. He was not there for more than thirty seconds.

"Hell!" grunted one of the men outside suddenly. "That wasn't him you was watching! He's over there by the soda fountain! Say! You was looking at the new police commissioner! That's Wildcat Gordon! Now what the hell would he be doing down here?"

The question was unanswered. Police Commissioner Wildcat Gordon was pushing his way through the crowd in the drugstore. None could mistake that flaming red necktie, the bright carnation, the broad-brimmed army hat cocked over one eye.

Wildcat Gordon appeared to be in somewhat of a hurry. He pushed his way to the door and abruptly waved his hand at the traffic policeman at the corner. The traffic man came over.

Wildcat spoke in a carrying voice. From the tail of his eye, he was watching the two men beside the display window, fixing their features in his mind. He talked for them to hear.

"You'll have to snap down faster on the light changes!" said Wildcat to the traffic man. "I've been standing in there for more than half an hour checking up! We've had complaints about this intersection! Now see that you cut them quicker on the red! You can take this to refresh your memory!"

WILDCAT HANDED a folded slip to the traffic officer. Then he straightened his shoulders, pulled his army hat at a cockier angle and went clumping away along the street. But he saw the traffic policeman slowly reading the slip of paper. Wildcat had written:

Drop everything—trail that green taxi and that maroon roadster behind it—pick up first detectives you see—you must not lose any of those three men—don't let them get wise—they'll be there a few minutes. I want their address.

The two shadows by the display window were there for several minutes. So was the taxicab. The surprised traffic policeman had seen two plainclothesmen by that time. When the two mystified shadows came out of the drugstore, swearing at each other, two of the department's best detectives were on their heels, with orders to stick there.

In the meantime, Wildcat Gordon went directly to Trigger's penthouse. He was wondering if the men who had been at the bank believed they were trailing The Whisperer? Also, he had in mind the threatening note sent to Jack Thurston.

The note had been signed "The Whisperer." That might mean anything or nothing. It was a chronic habit of criminals to attempt to put responsibility for their activities upon others, preferably someone well-known, already accused and hunted.

Had it been because The Whisperer had been in Duke Dolano's place when the first murder call was put through?

CHAPTER X
A SCARED SHOE-SHINER

"NOW HERE'S THE SETUP, Trigger," said Wildcat Gordon. "These blueprints apparently reveal the secret of the Black Mountain Power Co.'s dynamos. We've got them, and I've got Thurston where the dogs can't bite him. I'm holding him for his own protection, see?"

They were in Trigger's penthouse. The old retired deputy shook his head.

"I guess I'm not doing so good, Wildcat," said the old man. "I don't quite follow your drift."

"Thurston is the only man apparently who can finish the dynamos and operate them," said Wildcat. "All right. J. Grover Jones has been threatened in some manner. He won't spill anything. Even his girl being in jail hasn't shaken him. The girl won't talk. And this Ranny Howard has buttoned up."

"And so, Wildcat, you've got in mind keeping Thurston permanently out of the way and using these plans as a club to crack old J. Grover Jones?"

"That's the idea," grinned Wildcat.

"But by cracky, Wildcat! Ain't you getting just a mite close to blackmail yourself?" Old Trigger scratched his bald head. "This is only the second day, and you've piled up more trouble than any commissioner they've ever had! Son, I hate to tell you, but old Judge Wharson's on your trail about that Duke Dolano jam! There's been court deputies all over the place!"

Wildcat's Texas eyes looked over Trigger's head.

"Yeah," he drawled. "I dodged two of them coming in. You hang onto these plans. I'm calling Thorsen at headquarters and instructing him to tell everyone I'll be back tomorrow. Trigger, I'll be home when these phone call murders are busted wide open!"

It was very apparent that Wildcat Gordon again evaded court deputies on his way out from Trigger's penthouse. For less than half an hour later, The Whisperer was slowly sipping a soda in a drugstore.

Now in daylight, The Whisperer, in his gray suit, his gray tie and his absence of any distinguishing feature was an inconspicuous figure. He consumed his soda slowly. He was listening to two of the best detectives in the department giving the store clerks a stiff grilling.

Using the voice of the commissioner, The Whisperer had ordered this final check on the Travis phone call murder from Van Buren Avenue. Not for one moment had he forgotten the peculiar circumstances of these calls.

The voices saying, "I will not return—for I am dead."

Voices apparently identical with those of persons who later died, yet who could not have made the calls. There was no doubt but this was a clever trick of some sort, a scheme designed to inspire maximum terror.

And knowing the cold nerve of a man like J. Grover Jones, in all this somewhere was an element that had inspired the power magnate with the deepest fear. The Whisperer's detectives would have been amazed to know their commissioner was within a few feet of them as they questioned the clerks.

They would have been more surprised if they had known this inoffensive citizen in the gray clothes was himself The Whisperer.

The new checkup brought out nothing new on the Travis phone call. The Whisperer had not expected it would. He finished his drink and strolled out on Van Buren Avenue. Several shoe shiners were industriously plying their trade.

ONE OF THESE, The Whisperer noted, was the deaf-mute, Johnny Clatori. The Whisperer saw that he could use a shine. He hadn't seen Johnny since the blow-off in Duke Dolano's gambling house.

The night The Whisperer had visited Dolano's place, Johnny Clatori had been shining Dolano's shoes. When the lights went out and the shooting broke, Johnny had taken refuge in one of the bookmaker's booths.

The Whisperer walked close to Johnny now. The industrious little fellow was working on a customer. He had one of the man's shoes glistening.

Sometimes The Whisperer forgot his own role. The odd sound his voice made. Anyway, it should have made no difference with the deaf-and-dumb Johnny Clatori. In all the time The Whisperer, or Wildcat Gordon, had known the bootblack, he had never known him to hear or speak.

But as The Whisperer stood behind Johnny Clatori, waiting, a friendly dog crossed the sidewalk.

"Hello, old fellow!" whispered The Whisperer, patting the dog on the head. "Lost your master, boy?"

Johnny Clatori's head snapped around. He might have been a deaf-mute, but somehow that sibilant, hissing voice of The Whisperer must have penetrated his auditory senses. It did more than that.

Johnny Clatori emitted the odd gobbling sound of a deaf-mute in fear. He turned, as if to run away, whirled back and snatched one of his shoeshining boxes from under the stand on which his customer was sitting, then darted swiftly into the crowd.

"Well, I'll be damned!" ejaculated The Whisperer. "Now what do you suppose is biting him?"

The customer on the sidewalk stand used worse profanity. He had one shoe shined and the other one still muddy. Johnny Clatori only looked once over his shoulder. This seemed to add speed to his feet.

The Whisperer added two and two quickly. Then he smiled.

To be sure, Johnny Clatori had been scared at Dolano's place by The Whisperer. And now he had heard him again. No! Johnny was a deaf-mute! How could he have heard The Whisperer?

Or was it that Johnny Clatori had glimpsed The Whisperer's face in Dolano's, and now had seen it again?

The Whisperer passed that up. No. Johnny Clatori had heard him just now speaking to the dog. He had given all the evidence of a person hearing perfectly. Could it be that the quality of the penetrating whisper reached the deaf-mute's senses where an ordinary voice would have been unheard?

But wait! Though he had been badly frightened, apparently, Johnny Clatori had turned back to grab one of his shoeshining boxes. Not the box he had been using.

The Whisperer made an instant decision. It was his capacity for such decisive action that had put him where he was, in the chair of the police commissioner.

TWO MINUTES LATER, he was on a telephone. He removed his dental plates. The voice of Commissioner Gordon went over the wire.

It issued the order, "Pick up Johnny Clatori, shoe shiner, a deaf-mute, on suspicion of vagrancy! Hold him for personal examination by myself! If he is carrying a shoe-shining box, have it put away and held!"

Following the order, the new deputy, Thorsen, got on the wire.

"The court has served Mayor Van Royston with a writ for the release of Duke Dolano, Commissioner Gordon," said Thorsen without expression. "The mayor has the suspended Henry Bolton looking for Jack Thurston, the engineer in an effort to discharge him."

The Whisperer replied quietly, "That will keep the mayor busy for a while. Henry Bolton also will be fairly well occupied finding Jack Thurston. That will be all, Thorsen. Carry on."

"That I will, sir!" snapped the voice of Thorsen.

When Wildcat Gordon emerged from the telephone booth, he had restored the dental plates. He was again The Whisperer. In this role, he took a taxicab. The police roadster would have been too conspicuous for the part he was playing.

The Whisperer's next stop was a part of the city where even the toughest detectives traveled in pairs. That shady underworld section was one of the pet abominations of Wildcat Gordon. As a police officer, he had often thought a good fire would have been exceedingly effective and on the side of the law.

Yet The Whisperer maintained rooms in perhaps the worst block of all this unsavory neigborhood. The visit he now made to these rooms, situated over a saloon brothel frequented by the lowest order of criminals, was for a purpose that seemed to have no connection with the business in hand.

At the top of the stairway, when he reached it, there was a frantic scratching on the door, and a whining voice. A scotty dog on short legs and with gleaning fangs slammed into The Whisperer's body.

"Quiet, Brian Boru, old boy!" said The Whisperer. "Little late for your breakfast! Think I'd forgotten you?"

The fierce, little scotty watched The Whisperer with worshiping eyes as meat was unwrapped. Though he was hungry, the scotty did not move toward the meat until he was commanded. The dog showed giant disappointment when his master started out, leaving him there.

"Perhaps the next time, Brian," said The Whisperer, addressing the dog as if he were human. "I've some other business. Maybe I'll be needing you later."

Scotty held his black head cocked on one side. His black eyes gleaned with intelligence He seemed to understand what would be wanted if he happened to be needed. His red tongue licked across his white fangs.

BEFORE THE WHISPERER left this shady retreat, he again used a telephone. This instrument had a private, concealed wire. It could not have been tapped. No one could ever listen in on it.

Out came the dental plates and The Whisperer was Wildcat Gordon speaking. He asked a question and received an O. K. answer. This was added to by the party at the other end.

"He's doing all right, Commissioner, but we nay have to use the straps. He's been showing signs of wanting to put up an argument."

"Use the straps only if necessary," stated Wildcat Gordon. "It may be some time tonight before I see him. I can't relieve you, boys, but you'll get an extra day apiece for sticking."

Resuming his dental plates, The Whisperer stepped again into the street. That last call had been to a private rooming house. A man had been taken there by ambulance. Two stalwart patrolmen were guarding his room.

The mysterious patient was Jack Thurston, the engineer. The Whisperer had made very sure that Thurston would not be discovered by the suspended Henry Bolton or any other person at one of the precinct stations.

"He asked for protection," murmured The Whisperer with a grin. "He'll have it to the best of my ability to give it!"

By this time the afternoon was well along. The Whisperer had been unable to get a report from the detectives shadowing the men who had trailed him in the taxicab earlier in the day.

He decided to remain in this underworld neigborhood until he got that report. For The Whisperer was sure the men interested in Thurston's dynamo plans would have an address somewhere in this vicinity.

He was equally sure these men either were the direct blackmailers of J. Grover Jones, or were being used in a strong-arm capacity. It was this last thought that had impelled him to have their address discovered.

For, if they were merely being used, which was likely, The Whisperer desired very much to lay a finger on the brain engineering the whole plot. He was convinced more than bullet heads and strong arms was involved.

Elimination of J. Grover Jones's chief engineer, the terrifying telephone murders, the silencing of Jones himself—all of this pointed to some man who must be one of the cleverest of criminals. Perhaps these strong-arm boys could be used to lead the way to the mastermind?

The Whisperer was awaiting only the needed address before carrying out his idea of using the dynamo plans to compel J. Grover Jones to talk. He had left the parchment plans in the care of old Trigger, feeling sure they would be safe enough there. For, as The Whisperer, he had not at any time been connected up with the identity of Wildcat Gordon.

THE WHISPERER would have taken different action, if he could have seen old Quick Trigger late that afternoon. Old Trigger had been closely studying the dynamo plans.

Now the retired deputy commissioner itched for action. For a great many years, he had wanted to try out the effectiveness of some of his amateur disguises. Old Trigger looked at the plans and chuckled.

Then he swiftly made a rough copy, in pencil, of part of the plans, just enough to indicate he might know the rest of them. And a few minutes later, he emerged from his penthouse, carrying a roll of paper under one arm.

Old Trigger had all the appearance of an elderly professional man. A dark wig, a few bits of wax, and old Trigger was sure none would have taken him for other than a lawyer, or a doctor, or perhaps an engineer.

Indeed, old Trigger had all the earmarks of an engineer when he handed a jolt to the servant answering the button at the home of J. Grover Jones in Belvidere. He would not have been admitted if he had not sent up word to the power magnate that he had come with some information concerning the plans for his new dynamos.

"That'll fetch the old boy," muttered Trigger, as he waited. "And unless I'm badly mistaken, it'll bring some of them rats out from undercover!"

For old Trigger had formed a theory that he believed would help Wildcat Gordon break this case. He was sure the men threatening J. Grover Jones would be keeping their eyes and their ears upon him.

Then, reasoned old Trigger, if someone suddenly appeared with an apparent knowledge of the dynamo plans, it would bring the blackmailing rats from their holes.

Perhaps Trigger was reasoning more from his own love of a good fight than from a point of common sense. For he was convinced that when he got to J. Grover Jones and imparted his knowledge, he would immediately become a marked man. As such, reasoned Trigger, an attempt would be made to discover what he really knew.

For all of this possible outcome of his visit, Trigger was sure he was well prepared. He carried two heavy police positives. He had not been called Quick Trigger for nothing. The old man was sure he was still faster than a streak with those guns.

In a way, old Trigger judged Wildcat Gordon was in considerable of a jam. He wanted Wildcat to hold that commissioner's job. And he was not so sure that Wildcat was going to break this J. Grover Jones case in time to save his scalp from Mayor Van Royston.

Then, not only might he trap the blackmailers, but J. Grover Jones might be induced to loosen up if he were convinced others really knew of the dynamo plans.

So old Trigger was very sure of himself as he was ushered into the library of J. Grover Jones. Trigger had judged correctly in one respect. The millionaire was eager attention when Trigger said he had been an old friend of Homer Rand.

Then when Trigger stated the dead engineer had entrusted a separate copy of the dynamo plans to his keeping, J. Grover Jones broke entirely through his crust.

"You say you're a retired electrical engineer, Mr. Buckingham?" exclaimed Jones. Buckingham was the name Trigger had given him. "And you believe you could construct and operate these dynamos from the plans Rand trusted with you?"

"Sure of it!" boasted Trigger confidently. "I thought you might be having some trouble, Rand being dead, and your man Thurston being hurt! I'm ready to help you out! When you want me, you call this number and ask for me—or just say Dick; that's my first name!"

J. GROVER JONES was excited. His one good eye gleamed. Trigger had shown him enough of the dynamo sketches, in pencil, to prove he did know considerable of the secret. Perhaps Jones imagined here was a way out of his tough problem if something happened to Jack Thurston.

"You'll tell no one of this, Mr. Buckingham," he advised. "I'll see you're well paid for your time, whether or not I am compelled to use your plans and services. Let no one know you have visited me. I'll call you within a few hours."

Old Trigger left the residence of J. Grover Jones with what he believed to be extreme caution. During every minute of the visit, he had been on the alert. Watchful for some person in the house who might be listening. Even the aged manservant got a share of Trigger's attention.

Trigger was somewhat disappointed. Jones had neither talked too much, nor had there been any evidence of any other person knowing of his visit. The late afternoon was bright and sunny. Trigger could see over every foot of the J. Grover Jones estate.

A Negro gardener was the only person in sight. Trigger walked all the way around the house. From the position of the library windows, he was sure no person could have listened or observed from the outside.

Instead of becoming bait for a blackmailers' trap, Trigger felt he had only done something that might later handicap Wildcat Gordon in using the dynamo plans to make Jones talk.

"Guess I didn't do so good," Trigger muttered, climbing into his small car. "Maybe they knew what they were doing when they put an old fool like me on a pension."

Trigger drove from the Jones grounds completely relaxed. The heavy police positives were now only irksome. No one had watched. None had followed him. He had not even gotten around to where he could have asked J. Grover Jones a direct question about this blackmail plot, and the murders.

Trigger pulled off his revolvers and pushed them into the pockets of the car.

Trigger would have been much more on his guard could he had known that two men, more than half a mile from the home of J. Grover Jones, had heard every word of the conversation in the Jones library.

These two men had been in another house on Belvidere Drive. They were listening over a wire from a dictograph that had been in J. Grover Jones's library for many days.

CHAPTER XI
THE TRAPPING OF TRIGGER

THOROUGHLY disgusted with his effort to enact a slick role, old Quick Trigger drove out of the J. Grover Jones estate. The much-traveled boulevard wound along the lake shore. Traffic was heavy. There was somewhat of a jam at a point perhaps a quarter of a mile from the Jones residence.

It was late afternoon and hundreds were cooling themselves at an outdoor bathing pool. The car parking space was crowded. A traffic policeman was watching out for pedestrians crossing the boulevard.

Quick Trigger had no idea whatever that he was being tricked. A man walked suddenly from between two parked cars. Though Trigger was driving slowly and stopped instantly, his front fender seemed to hit the man.

This man cried out, threw up his hands and fell into the roadway. As always, the persons near by surged to the scene. The traffic man blew his whistle, but he was ineffective in keeping the crowd back.

Groaning over this misfortune, Quick Trigger climbed from his roadster. He forgot all about the revolvers in the pockets of the car. He went forward, trying to push through the crowd to ascertain how badly the victim was hurt.

Then he saw the man was sitting up, rubbing his head. Someone helped the fellow to his feet. At that instant, Trigger moved to avoid what he thought was an elbow in his ribs. But it was not an elbow.

A low voice said into Trigger's ear, "Walk right ahead to that green sedan outside this crowd. The cop will think you beat it after you struck that fellow."

Trigger started to whip around. Another hard object pushed against his side from the opposite direction. Trigger looked from under his bushy eyebrows and saw the faces of two men.

"Long Luke—Raddy Davens!" grunted old Trigger. "So you're the rats in—"

"Now you know, that'll cost you plenty," said one of the men. "Get moving! Knowing us, you won't make any mistake!"

All this was happening in the milling of the crowd. The words were low-spoken. Too well, the police brain of Quick Trigger knew this "Long" Luke and Raddy Davens. Knew them well enough to be sure the rods against his ribs were no idle threats.

That pair would let him have it right there in the crowd and get away with it. And Quick Trigger realized, instantly, that this J. Grover Jones murder and blackmail scheme was being handled by one of the slickest, most dangerous, and least-known mobs operating in the city.

Trigger walked out of the crowd. His captors walked casually beside him. Behind them, the traffic copper was shouting over the disappearance of the driver of Trigger's roadster. The man who had been knocked down had been demanding satisfaction.

Strangely enough, while the traffic policeman was seeking the driver who apparently had run away, the man who had been hit also disappeared. This fellow skirted the edges of the crowd. He got into the rear of the green sedan as it moved away.

It was not the first time Quick Trigger had been in a tight spot. But it was the first time he had ever been gagged and bound. While one man drove, the other two made a very efficient job of tying up the old man.

Trigger was blindfolded with tape; but he knew the noises of the street as well as if they had been a map of his location. He was aware he was being taken into the city's underworld locale. He could almost identify the street the green sedan was in, before it was driven into a basement garage.

ONLY THE THREE MEN were present when Quick Trigger was put on the floor in an upstairs room. Long Luke, Raddy Davens, and the third man they called "Smoky."

From the conversation, Trigger got the idea this was all there was to the mob threatening J. Grover Jones. He heard them mention a "smart guy," but no other name was spoken.

Trigger was yanked to his feet. Tape stripped from his eyes. Some of his bushy eyebrows came with it and brought a groan.

"That ain't anything!" snapped Long Luke. "We'll pull off more than your eyebrows if you don't come clean on them dynamo plans! Think you're smart, not having them on you, but that won't get you far! Well, holy hell!"

Long Luke had plucked off Quick Trigger's loose wig. He saw the bald pate of the retired deputy commissioner. Raddy Davens let out a squawk.

"Fellows, it's old Quick Trigger, and that means this damned Wildcat Gordon, the new commissioner, is hot on this thing! Having them dynamo plans is all a bluff! We know damn well who took the plans out've the bank!"

Long Luke swung a flat hand that brought blood from Trigger's nose.

"Yes, we think we know!" he barked. "Well, this is a setup! Now I savvy why we've had dicks trailing us ever since Wildcat Gordon walked out've that drugstore! And what a helluva time we had shaking 'em off! So that's where the plans went!"

Quick Trigger had his jaws set. He knew what was coming. And it came, with all of the fiendish imagination of his three captors. Trigger lost all of his eyebrows. He lost two thumbnails.

"You've seen the dynamo plans!" Long Luke kept repeating. "We're going to have those plans! Where have you put them?"

Old Trigger passed out several times. Cold water brought him around. But his torturers could have gotten as much information out of a granite statue.

"The plans are where you'll never get your filthy hands on them!" he gritted whenever he was able to speak. "You can pull me to bits, but I don't even know where the plans were taken! I was only given that pencil copy, that's all!"

Old Trigger was knocked down with a smashing blow from Long Luke's fist. The old man closed his eyes and passed out.

"I've got it!" yelled Long Luke. "This Whisperer we trailed from the bank must be playing in with the cops! Remember, he was on the job the night they nailed Duke Dolano when that Rand murder call went through. Now I know the way to make old Quick Trigger spill everything he knows! He's got a granddaughter!"

QUICK TRIGGER'S granddaughter was working in the penthouse. She was humming softly to herself. Her piquant face was wreathed in smiles.

If this funny Dunk Smith would only tell Wildcat Gordon what she had said about loads of women calling him up. That would make Wildcat really wild. Tiny pouted her pretty mouth. Would she ever be able to make Wildcat see she was no longer a child?

The telephone rang. Tiny flew into the corridor. Perhaps it was Wildcat calling. She hoped he would come home for dinner. She wondered where Quick Trigger had been for so long. It now was growing dark outside.

"Hello!" she said into the phone. "Yes. What? My grandfather? Oh, you're sure? It couldn't be! He's a good driver—he—"

Tiny was silent half a minute, listening to the other voice. "Then I'll come—right away!" she cried. "Yes, I have the number! Just as soon as I can get there! Please do everything for him you can! I'll be there as soon as I can get a taxi!"

Tears rolled down Tiny Traeger's cheeks. She had just been told that old Quick Trigger had met with a serious accident. He had been so badly hurt he could not be taken to the hospital. The "doctor" had called. The "doctor" had requested her to come at once, and he had said they also had sent for Wildcat Gordon.

The tiny girl fairly flew from the penthouse. She grabbed the first taxicab. The address she gave caused the driver to glance at her sharply. But he shrugged his shoulders. If the pretty little dame wanted to go down into that neighborhood, well, she was just another fare to him.

ABOUT THE TIME Tiny Traeger got into the taxicab, the strange, gray Whisperer moved slowly along a cluttered tenement street. All of his carefully laid plans for trapping the blackmailers of J. Grover Jones had in some manner gone into reverse.

First of all, communications from the detectives gave the regrettable report that the three men who had attempted to trap The Whisperer earlier in the day had disappeared. The detectives were sure they had bottled them up, only to discover, after a long wait, that their three suspects had vanished into thin air.

The detectives had been waiting two hours to make this report. It was now too late to do anything about it. The Whisperer's hope of getting an address had faded. His own knowledge had not enabled him to identify the men, as had that of Quick Trigger's.

For Quick Trigger never forgot the face of a crook.

The Whisperer walked along slowly, considering his next move. How could he force J. Grover Jones to talk? Would mere possession of the dynamo plans do it? Apparently the millionaire had little concern for the plight of his daughter.

Perhaps the continued absence of Jack Thurston might have some effect upon the millionaire. The Whisperer had still to question Johnny Clatori over his queer actions, but he regarded this as a minor matter.

The Whisperer slid into a small barroom phone booth. In the voice of the commissioner, he called Deputy Thorsen. His new deputy spoke without a trace of excitement. What he said was important.

"Commissioner, one of the boys left a memorandum! He says the three men they trailed this afternoon are Long Luke, Raddy Davens and Smoky Krause, and this is the first time they've been playing around for a long time!"

Well, that was something. But without an address, it wasn't enough for The Whisperer's immediate purpose. Deputy Thorsen had the added report that Duke Dolano was still being held on the shore of Grass Lake, and court deputies were trailing Mayor Van Royston, hoping to catch up with Wildcat Gordon.

The Whisperer grinned over that, as he replaced his dental plates and moved again into the street. But as he emerged from the barroom, he became aware something was wrong. Whatever it was, it seemed to affect The Whisperer himself.

Formerly those passing had given no heed to the inconspicuous gray figure. The Whisperer had been only one of the crowd. In this underworld street, it was well to stay one of the crowd. When the crowd moved away from you, it was best to remove yourself as quickly and quietly as possible from that vicinity.

The Whisperer suddenly discovered he was walking alone. Men glanced at him furtively, then crossed to the opposite sidewalk. Some vanished silently into doorways. This had begun to happen immediately after The Whisperer had come from the small barroom.

The Whisperer was thinking fast. There had been a black cat in the small bar. It had jumped on a table. He had stroked it. Yes, he remembered, he had spoken to it in his hissing whisper. That whisper had a strange attraction for all animals.

Anyway, now The Whisperer was walking alone. The sidewalk suddenly cleared ahead of him. The street was narrow. Many persons were slipping into convenient doorways.

The Whisperer did not appear to do so, but he shot a glance over his shoulder. Yes, that was it. Two men were coming swiftly along the walls of the brick buildings. They were stalking him, as quietly as possible.

The Whisperer shot a glance across the street. One other man walked there, apparently attempting to pass from shadow to shadow without being observed. And, coming slowly along, close to the curb, a closed car was being held down to its minimum speed.

There came a whispering chuckle in The Whisperer's throat. A chuckle that shook all of his body.

BACK THERE in the barroom, when he had spoken to that black cat, he had been identified. And while he had been in the telephone booth a trap had been set. The Whisperer was being ambushed. The trap was about to close.

And this was a police trap. The two men following were dicks of the department. The man across the street, ducking from shadow to shadow, was none other than the recently suspended Henry Bolton.

Henry Bolton was without doubt intent on making good his boast he would get The Whisperer. By some unlucky chance, for The Whisperer, some one in that barroom had called the police while he was in the phone booth.

The closed car slowly following The Whisperer carried two squad men. Enough reason in this troubled neighborhood for the street to be cleared. But a clear street was far from what The Whisperer now needed or desired. Had there been a crowd, there might have been a chance. Now there appeared to be none.

CHAPTER XII
A FACE IN A WINDOW

THE WHISPERER was too closely pressed to change his identity. The keen eyes upon him did not permit any sudden switch to the person of Wildcat Gordon. Of course, if they got him, that would undoubtedly come out. But they hadn't got him as yet.

Not by any move or sign had The Whisperer indicated he was aware the police trap was being closed in. He was less than twenty yards from the next street intersection. He judged his dicks and Bolton were waiting until he reached that cleared corner.

If there was shooting, they would attempt to keep bullets from smashing through windows of the lower tenements. And there would be shooting. Henry Bolton was a man to shoot first and ask questions afterward.

Only fear of The Whisperer had held up Henry Bolton to this time. The Whisperer's sidelong glance showed that Bolton already had a revolver butt snuggled in his hand.

The two detectives following him were among the best. Both were first grade boys. It would not do them any harm to be in on the capture of The Whisperer. At this moment there was no other automobile parked or moving in the block.

The Whisperer thought grimly this might as well be one of those dusty Western streets where a duel was about to be fought. Like some he had seen when in the army.

Still The Whisperer walked ahead unhurriedly.

Now it had been a black cat that had got him into this trap. By sheerest coincidence, it was another black cat across his path that pointed the barest possible way out.

The little animal crossed the street. It ran across The Whisperer's path and suddenly vanished. It had not reached the wall. The cat had scurried into a displaced grating over a sidewalk basement. Possibly the space underneath was used for coal.

The Whisperer did not change his pace. The police car was less than ten yards behind him. The Whisperer flicked a cigarette into his hand, cupped a match and lighted the tobacco. And, just as it flared, he took one step forward, pulled in his arms and shot, feetforemost, through the open grating.

YELLS, SHOTS, the high whining of bullets off the iron rim over his head informed the Whisperer that had the trap been sprung as intended, he would have been filled with slugs. Feet pounded the cement of the sidewalk over him.

The Whisperer had no desire whatever to injure anyone. But he had to have time. He used his own police gun, shooting its cylinder empty as he pointed it upward through the grating. His extra, silenced, hissing guns were useless for the purpose of creating the noise he wanted.

That emptying of his gun, he was sure, would hold back Henry Bolton and the other coppers for a few seconds. But already he could hear them hammering at the low door of the tenement to which this coal cellar was attached.

A revolver was pushed over the edge of the grating and it exploded almost in The Whisperer's face. A bony wrist was behind the weapon. The Whisperer saw there was only a narrow passageway leading from this coal cellar to the tenement house.

Henry Bolton himself it was, who was shooting through the open grating. The Whisperer got one glimpse of the tightly held small mouth, of the sloping forehead. Bolton must have believed The Whisperer had gotten out of the coal cellar, for he pulled out a flashlight and stuck one long arm down into the hole.

The Whisperer shot his body upward from his toes. Both his hands fastened firmly, one on each wrist of his suspended deputy. A squawking cry came from Henry Bolton's small mouth as he was jerked bodily downward.

If it had been any other copper on the force, The Whisperer would not have hit him as hard as he did Henry Bolton. In a matter of seconds, he had Bolton's revolver and his own. He pushed the groggy Henry Bolton into the passageway leading to the tenement.

From inside, could be heard women's voices screaming. The police were breaking in. The two detectives from the sidewalk and one man from the squad car were crowding a doorway that led from the street. Their guns were in their hands.

The Whisperer was almost invisible to these three coppers. For they saw the dazed Henry Bolton staggering from the coal cellar passageway. On each side of Bolton, under his arms projected

. . . a black cat . . . jumped on a table. . . .

two revolvers.

Three women, one old and the others young, were running around in the basement room.

"You dames get out of the way!" one of the detectives was shouting. "Over to one side! He can't get out of that trap, boys! We'll rush him!"

Then that hissing, sibilant whisper filled the room. Somehow, that carrying whisper seemed to convey death in every word. It was a hideously mocking, a laughing whisper.

"All will get out now—or this one dies—"

Henry Bolton's round lips writhed. But while he had no liking for Wildcat Gordon, Bolton was after all a copper.

"Blast him!" gasped Bolton. "Don't mind me! Let 'im have it!"

The Whisperer liked Henry Bolton much more for that little speech. But he knew the three coppers would disobey the command. Now the fourth

He stroked it . . . spoke to it in a hissing whisper . . .

policeman showed behind the other three. The Whisperer let go with one revolver.

There was the one incandescent bulb in the small room. The bulb exploded with the first bullet. The Whisperer rapped Bolton sharply over the back of the head and hurled him forward. Then he threw one revolver smashing into the opposite wall of the small room, where there seemed to be a doorway leading to a stairs.

Bolton groaned and fell. In the darkness, his fellow coppers heard what they believed to be The Whisperer hitting the door across the room. Perhaps they were fearful of hitting either Bolton or the screaming women. The four policemen plunged toward the spot where the thrown revolver had hit.

But The Whisperer already was back in the coal cellar. He took one look up at the open grating hole and sprang from his toes. He was gambling on one circumstance. There had been no time to summon

more policemen than those who had been in the neighborhood.

Residents of the street were smartly keeping away from the hot spot. The Whisperer pulled himself up, hit the sidewalk with the agility of an alley cat. In both directions he could see gathering crowds. Beyond these a siren was screaming for a pathway.

THE WHISPERER bounded across the cement and into the driver's seat of the deserted police car. He could hear shots being fired inside the tenement he had just left. The squad man had left his motor running.

With the siren screaming, The Whisperer shot the police car straight at the nearest line of the street crowd. The mob broke, parted, and the car went through. The Whisperer careened around the first corner.

He did not make the mistake of continuing in the car. With a rueful grin for damaged property, he slid out and let the car hook its radiator over a lamppost. Then he ducked into the first entrance to an alley.

Less than three minutes later, Commissioner Wildcat Gordon walked from the other end of that same alley. His army hat slouched cockily over one eye. His vivid red necktie was new and unspotted. A fresh carnation looked like a headlight in his buttonhole.

Luckily there had been no coal in that basement under the sidewalk. One of several squad cars being rushed to the scene was coming down the street. Wildcat stepped out and waved it down. He climbed into the seat beside the driver.

"What the hell and all's going on?" demanded Wildcat. "I was riding on the 'el' and heard shooting. I had to go two blocks to a station before I could get off."

"It's The Whisperer, Commissioner!" said the squad car driver. "They put in a riot call! They've got him cornered!"

"Step on it!" snapped Wildcat. "That's one pinch I'd like to be in on personally!"

The squad car whipped around the next corner. Other cars were converging on the spot. Wildcat saw his driver slew over for a passing taxicab. The driver swore at a dumb hackie.

Wildcat was looking at the taxicab. The fenders of the two cars barely grazed. The taxicab skidded toward the curb, but its driver was quick enough to straighten it out.

Then Wildcat gripped the arm of the police car driver.

"Hold it, boy!" he rapped out. "Come around! Follow that taxi! To hell with The Whisperer! You hear me!"

The squad car driver was dumbfounded. But he attempted to obey the order. The street was narrow for a quick turn. The left front wheel snapped into the curbstone. There was a cracking of metal. The squad car rolled partly over, the wheel sheered off at the hub.

Wildcat swore and sprang from the seat. There was no other car moving nearby. The taxicab had whipped out of sight around a corner. The amazed squad men saw Wildcat run in that direction.

He had seen the face of Tiny Traeger in the taxicab's window.

CHAPTER XIII
THE TRAIL OF DEATH

POURING from their wrecked car, the squad men followed Commissioner Wildcat Gordon. There were four of these coppers. Another car came into the block, its driver saw the trouble, and this shot in pursuit.

Wildcat rounded the first corner. Already the taxicab had made another turn. With his puzzled men pounding behind him, Wildcat put on a burst of speed. The other coppers imagined the commissioner had seen The Whisperer in that taxicab. They did not know about the girl

Wildcat ran three blocks, turned a corner into the fourth. He was checked by a knot of curious persons crowding around an iron lamppost. When Wildcat pushed through, he saw the green taxicab. One side of the car was smashed. It had been overturned.

The driver of the taxi never would talk. He lay with his head and shoulders protruding from his window. His forehead was split. The man's eyes were open and apparently they had seen death coming.

Rubber skid marks showed where another car had crowded the taxicab to the curbing, overturned it. Wildcat pushed a man to the building wall and started asking questions. He received various replies from this man and others.

"Two men in a black sedan were responsible." "They were in a blue coupé." "It was a yellow roadster." "There were three men." "There was only one man." "The other car had turned east, west and south."

This was the summing up of the information pouring in upon Wildcat Gordon. It was the usually incompetent eyewitness manner of seeing things. Wildcat glanced at the towering tenements of the surrounding blocks.

Back of these tenements was a river. Warehouses loomed dark and silent along the waterfront. Wildcat knew there were thousands of spots where the men he sought might be hiding out. An army of police could accomplish nothing here. Two cars of his men now awaited his orders.

WHEN HIS COMMAND came, the other coppers grunted and looked amazed. They had expected to see the commissioner direct all the men he could get to surround the district. They expected the usual stake out. Police lines should have been spread, so that none within them could make a getaway.

Wildcat Gordon was thinking of the position of Tiny Traeger. He was as yet unaware as to why she had been seized. But he suspected the dynamo plans would be mixed up in this. Now he spoke.

"All of you get after The Whisperer! I want every available man to get into that hunt! We must have him! In the meantime, I do not want an extra man to move in this district! A girl's life, or more than that, is at stake!"

Wildcat saw the impossibility of trailing the men who had wrecked the taxicab. Having got his men away, he went to a telephone. Three minutes later, he had learned all that Deputy Thorsen could tell him.

Old Quick Trigger had been abducted near the J. Grover Jones residence in Belvidere. His car had been found there with the revolvers in the pockets. Again Thorsen named Long Luke, Raddy Davens and Smoky Krause as the three men who had shaken off the detectives. Still there was no information as to the address of these men.

Wildcat's veins became filled with blood that was as chilling as icy slush. He had no doubt but that Tiny Traeger had fallen into the hands of Luke, Davens and Krause.

There could be only one reason for that. Old Quick Trigger had attempted to use the dynamo plans in some manner. He had failed.

His captors now were seeking those plans. Tiny Traeger had been tricked into their hands. Finding the three conspirators in the jumble of thousands of tenements would take hours, days, if it could be accomplished.

Wildcat could picture Tiny Traeger's position. No doubt old Trigger had been tortured. And he would die by inches before he would give up anything that would betray Wildcat. So they had sent for the girl.

It was with effort that Wildcat controlled his raging fear. It was almost impossible to think clearly. Deputy Thorsen was talking into his ear. Something about Mayor Van Royston and court deputies still pursuing him.

Wildcat suddenly swept all this aside. He was in a public telephone booth. But he started issuing crisp orders. These must have amazed Deputy Thorsen, the former police sergeant of the wooden face.

But if they did, all he said was, "Yes, sir! It will be done at once, sir! I will do it personally! Yes, sir! I will put all three in a car and drive them to the J. Grover Jones place!"

Wildcat issued another order.

"No, sir!" said Deputy Thorsen. "Not even Mayor Van Royston will find it out! I'll have them there in half an hour if I have to conk all of them! I'll make sure the car is not seen! Now I'll give you the other connection!"

Wildcat Gordon was acting on what amounted to a split-second decision. He had given Deputy Thorsen a strange order. It was to have Ranny Howard, Nellie Jones and Johnny Clatori, the deaf-mute shoe shiner, removed from their cells and driven at once to the home of J. Grover Jones.

Next, Wildcat talked to two police guards staying by Jack Thurston, the slightly wounded engineer, still confined in a private rooming house. He surprised these guards more than he had Deputy Thorsen. He ordered the immediate discharge of Jack Thurston.

"Yes, Commissioner!" assented one of the replying guards. "But you mean we're to escort him somewhere? He's been getting pretty tough! Says he wanted protection, but it wasn't necessary to make him a prisoner to do it!"

Wildcat smiled grimly to himself.

"You're not to escort Thurston when he leaves!" he snapped. "Hand him his clothes, then leave him! Neither of you is to even stay in the neighborhood! Let him find his own way out! If Thurston thinks he can protect himself, now is his chance!"

"Yes, sir!" gulped the surprised guard. "We'll give him his clothes and beat it! Do we go home?"

"You go home, and take tomorrow off," instructed Wildcat. "Report personally to me at headquarters the day after. That is all."

WILDCAT REPLACED the phone receiver. He emerged from the store in which the booth was located. Two patrolmen at the corner saluted the commissioner. If they smiled a little over his glowing red carnation, his scarlet necktie and his cockily placed army hat, they were careful not to let Wildcat see the smiles.

"Have they got The Whisperer?" said Wildcat.

"No, sir," replied one of the patrolmen. "He got away in one of our own cars, sir. It was found wrecked. Henry Bolton is having all of that district staked in."

"That's a good idea," said Wildcat. "Keep your eyes open for him, boys. I'm afraid The Whisperer is a killer."

One minute later, Wildcat Gordon walked from the street into an alley. He did not break his stride through to the next street. He had parked a coupé there more than an hour before. That hour had been fast and furious.

But it was not Wildcat Gordon who slid behind the wheel of the coupé. It was the strange figure in unattractive gray, with the colorless blur of hair brushed straight back, the thrusting chin and the peculiarly long upper lip.

The Whisperer.

He drove the coupé directly, swiftly, across town. All this time, he had been estimating time and distance, the amount of time required for a slightly wounded man to get into his clothes and out of a house. In less than five minutes, the coupé slid into the black shadows where ancient trees lined the sidewalks in front of a row of rooming houses.

The street was deserted, even at this early hour. No cars were moving. One lone pedestrian was in the block. He was whistling a mournful tune. This pedestrian did not see the inconspicuous gray figure that slipped from the coupé and blended with the shadows of the trees.

The door of a rooming house in the middle of the block opened. The inside light shone for a few seconds on a man's bare head. The hair was sleek and black. The man coming out glanced up and down the street. He could hear the pedestrian whistling. But the pedestrian was going away.

The man was Jack Thurston. His right arm was in a bandage. He closed the rooming house door and came down the steps into the street. For part of a minute, he seemed undecided which direction he should take.

The lights of the coupé were turned off. A parked car in this neighborhood was not such as to attract attention. Jack Thurston started off briskly. Possibly, he was intending to pick up the first taxicab that came along.

Jack Thurston was under the big trees near the coupé. He heard a rustling movement, and he halted, pivoting. Perhaps he had only a glimpse of the gray figure in the shadows. The next instant a wide sack, like a great hood, was whipped over his head and shoulders.

Jack Thurston swore, heaved, and kicked out violently. A hissing whisper said, "Be quiet and you won't be hurt!"

Thurston stiffened.

"You?" came Thurston's muffled voice. "I'll—"

He attempted to kick again. The Whisperer eluded him easily. Then he jerked the smothering sack tighter and hit Thurston over the head. The engineer ceased to struggle. The Whisperer lifted him bodily and jammed him into the seat of the coupé.

All of this had been accomplished in less than half a minute. Jack Thurston's freedom, after his discharge at the order of Wildcat Gordon, had been brief indeed. The coupé tore out of the dark street and headed back across town.

"If I can only make it in time!" said The Whisperer in his strange hissing voice. "Trigger—Tiny—here's hoping!"

The coupé was driven at high speed. It followed streets that carried little traffic. None noticed that a hooded sack was slumped beside the driver.

THE WHISPERER did not drive all the way to the residence of J. Grover Jones. He pulled the coupé into a dark side street some distance from the Jones estate. A strip of woods joined with the wall surrounding the Jones garden.

Jack Thurston was a bigger man than The Whisperer. That did not prevent The Whisperer swinging him over a shoulder, much as if he were an empty sack. He went over the garden wall with this burden.

A short distance from the Jones residence another car had been parked away from the boulevard. From this car four persons had emerged. Three of these were an odd trio. For they were handcuffed together.

The fourth was Deputy Thorsen. His wooden face showed no emotion as he walked behind his three prisoners. His only reply to all questions from two of his prisoners had been stony silence. The third prisoner asked no questions. He was Johnny Clatori, the deaf-mute.

CHAPTER XIV
TINY TRAEGER'S TRICK

LESS than an hour had elapsed from the time Wildcat Gordon had seen Tiny Traeger's face in the taxicab until the moment The Whisperer was carrying the hooded Jack Thurston through the garden of J. Grover Jones. During most of that hour, Tiny Traeger had delayed the unpleasant intentions of three cursing men.

Long Luke, Raddy Davens and Smoky Krause were her captors. The diminutive, attractive girl had been taken to the same barren room where old Quick Trigger was being held. No doubt it had been the intention of the three unholy crooks to immediately apply pressure upon old Trigger by their own sweet system of torture.

Tiny Traeger balked this temporarily. Her head had been bruised when the taxicab had been crowded to the curb and wrecked. The tiny girl had instantly taken advantage of this. She had heard of this trick being one of the best.

With a blue bump oozing blood from her forehead, the girl immediately feigned unconsciousness. Water slapped in her face, liquor forced between her lips, various other devices had no effect.

Tiny Traeger played her role desperately for time. For her own eyes had been as sharp as those of Wildcat Gordon. She had seen his face in the police car whirling past the taxicab. She would have stopped, turned back, but anxiety to reach her supposedly injured grandfather decided her against the delay.

Up in the barren room, Long Luke was the spokesman, the leader of the others. He greeted

Quick Trigger's groaning oaths at the arrival of Tiny with "You might as well come clean on where those dynamo plans have been hidden! If you don't, this pretty little grandchild of yours won't leave here the same as she came in!"

"You'll burn for this!" shouted Quick Trigger. "If a hair of that child's head is harmed, you'll be hunted to hell! And you won't die quickly in any hot squat either!"

LONG LUKE and the others laughed harshly. They set about reviving the apparently unconscious girl. Minutes were wasted. Old Trigger swore continuously and strained to free himself. But he was holding out on telling about the dynamo plans as long as possible.

The old retired deputy commissioner was thinking desperately of some ruse he might employ to get them out of this. It came to him that the straight truth probably would be the best, if he could make these crooks believe it.

He would tell them The Whisperer had stolen the plans. That he, Quick Trigger, was playing in with The Whisperer. Anything to save Tiny and at the same time prevent this unholy trio from tying up Commissioner Wildcat Gordon with The Whisperer.

Then it was the slow twisting of a little finger that caused Tiny Traeger to abandon her effort to appear insensible. She was forced to cry out with the burning pain that shot along her arm.

"I thought so!" grated Long Luke. "Now, Trigger, come across! You've got one chance! She's a nice little girl! I'll bet she's a good little girl, too! You wouldn't want all that changed, being her grandfather!"

Long Luke deliberately tore the girl's dress from her shoulders. Tiny looked at her grandfather.

"Whatever it is, Grandpa," she said, "don't you talk! Don't you ever tell them! Don't let them make you—"

Her brave words ended in a scream. Long Luke's fingers were hard and pinching. He was twisting a bit of the soft, white skin of the girl's throat, just enough to cause a scarlet trickle to appear under his fingernails.

The girl's scream sent old Trigger heaving against the cords, and he shouted hoarsely.

"Stop it! Stop it! I'll tell you—I'll tell—"

"No, Grandpa! No! Don't you tell them—"

Old Trigger disregarded Tiny's words.

"Yes, yes!" he yelled. "I—we tried to cut in! I guess I went crooked! I know The Whisperer! He—he stole the dynamo plans! I thought I could get in—we could—"

"Why, you old—"

Long Luke's hard hand drove old Trigger's head back ruthlessly. He was slapping him with his hard knuckles.

"Now, where are those plans? That's all we want. And where's this Whisperer, whoever he is? We'll show that cheap crook!"

"The plans—yes, the plans," mumbled Quick Trigger. "Well, I was to meet The Whisperer tonight. I hid the plans so—"

"And you thought you could cut in on this deal, huh?" snapped Long Luke. "Did you show the plans to Jones? Tell the truth."

"No! No! That wouldn't have been smart!" shouted Trigger. "I just told him I knew about them; so if you'll let me go, I'll—"

A wall telephone at one side of the room rang sharply. Long Luke clapped his hand over Trigger's mouth. He glanced at his companions.

"Take it, Raddy!" he ordered. "Be careful! I think we're in the clear! Maybe the boss is wanting us!"

Raddy Davens took down the receiver. He turned almost instantly.

"Luke! It's old Jones himself!" he said, hoarsely.

THAT CALL to the three torturers came from J. Grover Jones.

Perhaps five to seven minutes before he made that call, J. Grover Jones was seated before his desk in his isolated library. He had heard no noise downstairs. He believed his one manservant was in attendance if anyone should appear at this hour.

J. Grover Jones appeared to be in a thoughtful, a desperate mood. His unwounded hand slowly twisted at the bandage around the fingers where he had been shot. His one good eye was bloodshot; he looked as if he needed sleep badly, but could get none.

He had carefully locked his library door. He had also secured bars across the windows. Tonight, he was about to come to a decision. Several times, he reached toward the telephone on his desk, but each time he withdrew his hand.

"No," he muttered, "I can't do it! But if I don't, they'll get us—they'll get her!"

He was touching the telephone again. Apparently his decision involved making a call. It might have been he intended to do something about having his daughter released from jail.

This time, his hand did not reach the telephone. He had not heard the instrument turning the lock of his library door. Now he did not see anyone, for the lights suddenly went out.

J. Grover Jones started from his chair, a gasp of fear coming from his lips. His nerves had been raw-edged for hours.

Before he could speak or move from the desk, the darkened library was filled with a ghostly, sibilant whispering. This did not seem to come from any particular spot. It was everywhere, a penetrating voice without a hard tone, but as commanding as a gun would have been, put at a man's head.

"Sit down, Jones—do not move until you are told—you have visitors—the rest of you stand where you are!"

There was then the movement of several figures. A little exclamation seemed to come from a woman's throat. It appeared that a man was trying to repress an audible oath. Still another voice had the low babbling such as an idiot might have made.

"Be silent, all of you!" came that hissing whisper. "Jones—I have no time to waste! We have decided the time has come! You have the money ready?"

"No! Daddy, don't—"

This was the voice of Nellie Jones. It ended on a cry. The hard hand of The Whisperer had choked back the girl's words.

"Now you know she is here, Jones!" again came that awe-inspiring whisper. "Others are here! Jack Thurston, your only engineer! Tell him you're here, Thurston!"

J. Grover Jones was springing from his chair. The Whisperer seemed to be everywhere in the room. Hands of steel gripped the power magnate and slammed him back into the seat. The muffled voice of Thurston came from what appeared to be a black bundle thrown to the floor in the darkness.

"Pay them J. G.—it's The Whisperer—he'll kill all of us, J. G. if—"

Nellie Jones tried to speak again. Her words went into a low-gurgling moan. Handcuffs clinked in the darkness. The man beside her, Ranny Howard, cursed loudly and tried to strike out. One hand of The Whisperer had slapped a damp cloth over the mouth of Nellie Jones.

THE ROOM FILLED with a sweetish odor. The girl did not speak again. She had inhaled chloroform. That idiotic babble came again as Ranny Howard attempted to strike The Whisperer. For the man was handcuffed to Nellie Jones on one side and the deaf-mute, Johnny Clatori, on the other.

Now The Whisperer said with sibilant hissing, "Jones—your daughter will die— Thurston will be removed—you will go last if you do not call the others now and tell them the money is here—call them now—understand!"

J. Grover Jones started to say, "I'll never—"

His words trailed off, and he said, "Nellie! Please, Nellie! My little girl! Yes, I'll call!"

It was Thurston's muffled voice speaking suddenly.

"Don't, J. G.! Don't! It's a trick—it's a—oh, my—"

Jack Thurston must have reared to his feet. Now J. Grover Jones heard his hooded body pitch to the floor. There had been swift death agony in his final words. The room filled with a hissing sound that was not the voice of The Whisperer. It was like air being slowly expelled from a cylinder.

The Whisperer was holding one of his strangely silenced pistols in his hand. He had fired the bullet that had cut off Thurston's speech. When he pulled the trigger, he was trying to keep from his mind the picture of what might be happening to Tiny Traeger, to old Quick Trigger.

J. Grover Jones had to be forced to make that call. The Whisperer had shot Thurston. He did not intend to kill him. But the bullet had silenced the engineer effectively.

The deaf-mute's idiot babbling shaped into words. Words that could be understood. He did not utter many of these. The Whisperer struck with a weapon held in his left hand. It was a soft, thudding blow. The deaf-mute dropped into silence.

The raging Ranny Howard found himself trapped. Each wrist was handcuffed to an inert body. The blond young man was more handicapped, because one of his wrists was linked to the soft flesh of Nellie Jones.

"Make that call!" commanded The Whisperer. "Tell them the money is ready! I have the plans of your dynamos here, Jones! And Thurston may live! If you don't call, I'll tear up these plans, and the girl will be the next to go!"

A pencil flashlight flicked from The Whisperer's hand. It showed the blueprinted dynamo plans he held.

J. Grover Jones picked up the telephone slowly.

CHAPTER XV
INTO THE POLICE TRAP

WHEN RADDY DAVENS took the telephone call from J. Grover Jones, Long Luke sprang to the instrument.

"I can do nothing else," came the heavy voice of J. Grover Jones. "Yes, I have the money ready, and I will pay at once. You must assure me my daughter will not be harmed. That Thurston, my engineer, will be permitted to carry on the work. Come now, so we may settle this and my girl can be liberated."

A gloating smile of triumph played over Long Luke's face.

"We'll be there," he said, "but if this is a trick, you won't live another day. We'll get the girl, wherever she is. Now wait."

Long Luke was smart, or he imagined he was. He cut off the phone connection.

"Get the old man and this girl out the back way and tie them in the car!" he ordered. "If this pans out O. K., we'll maybe dump them on the way out of town! Now we'll see!"

Long Luke pulled off the phone receiver. He called back the number of J. Grover Jones. The power magnate's heavy voice replied, "Yes—who is it? I'm busy!"

"Listen, Jones!" snapped Long Luke. "At this moment there is a man in your house! He has his orders! If there is anything suspicious outside, or we are stopped, you are going to die suddenly and very unpleasantly!"

J. Grover Jones assured him wearily, calmly, that nothing would interfere. He said he himself would be at the door when the blackmailers' car arrived.

In less than five minutes, a closed sedan was speeding across town toward the suburb of Belvidere. In the rear, Quick Trigger and Tiny were securely bound.

AND AT THIS SAME TIME, a little light had come on in the library of J. Grover Jones. The aged power magnate himself sat bound and gagged in his big chair. The hooded bundle of Jack Thurston lay in the middle of the floor. The hood over his head had become damp with blood.

The blond Ranny Howard was desperately trying to revive the unconscious Nellie Jones. Now, strangely enough, his wrists had been freed from the handcuffs. The girl and the deaf-mute shoe shiner were still senseless.

J. Grover Jones glared with his one good eye at the figure queerly hunched near the one little light that had been turned on. This was the illumination for a typewriter desk. The figure seated there was The Whisperer. Only his back showed, with the blur of colorless hair.

The Whisperer pecked at the typewriter keys with two fingers. For some inexplicable reason, Ranny Howard seemed no longer filled with anger. His eyes turned on The Whisperer with something like awed admiration.

For The Whisperer had spoken quickly, quietly, to Ranny Howard as soon as J. Grover Jones had made the call summoning his blackmailers. What The Whisperer had said had acted like some powerful, soothing drug on Ranny Howard's nerves.

Now The Whisperer stopped pecking on the typewriter. He flicked out the little light, again putting the library into darkness.

He was gliding from the room when his sibilant hissing filled the place.

"It will happen to all who double-cross The Whisperer!"

Then The Whisperer was gone from the room that for minutes had been filled with terror. A terror that had been only increased by one dead man with a black hood over his head. As he might have died had he been a murderer and met his fate on a gallows.

J. Grover Jones still sat, bound and gagged. The telephone he might then have used was beyond his reach.

Downstairs, The Whisperer paused at another instrument. It was an extension to the library telephone. The dental plates were removed. It was Commissioner Wildcat Gordon now speaking. His call did not go to police headquarters. It reached the wooden-faced Deputy Thorsen at a precinct station closest to Belvidere.

Around that precinct station, by his authority as the new deputy commissioner, Thorsen had assembled a score of men.

"All set, Thorsen!" snapped the voice of Wildcat Gordon. "Remember, no car within two blocks of the Jones place! Come in over that back wall, through the garden and the rear door! It has been opened for you! Don't leave a single man outside! If three men come in, jump them before they can pull rods!"

"Yes, sir!" said Deputy Thorsen.

"But if there are only two men," said Wildcat, "there will le a third in their car, wherever they leave it! There may be two prisoners in that car; look out for them! You have less than twelve minutes, if they are driving fast, and they will be!"

"Yes, sir!" said Deputy Thorsen.

THE WHISPERER departed from the estate of J Grover Jones, as he had come, over the back garden wall. His little car rocketed toward the downtown section. At the moment Deputy Thorsen and his men were receiving three visitors at the home of J. Grover Jones, Commissioner Wildcat Gordon walked jauntily into his office.

Mayor Van Royston came out of a chair so fast his silk hat almost toppled off. At one side of the office the suspended Henry Bolton was glowering oddly through one open eye. The other eye had been temporarily closed.

A young man who could have been none other than a court deputy started waving a paper.

Mayor Van Royston seemed stricken speechless by the freshness of the elusive Commissioner Gordon. No commissioner had ever been more debonair, appeared more carefree.

Wildcat's carnation was brighter than ever. His tie looked as if it had been carefully knotted within the past few minutes. As a matter of fact, it had. His army hat was cocked at just the right angle.

"This summons says you've got to produce Duke Dolano—"

The court deputy was first to speak, thrusting the paper at Wildcat.

"Where have you been, Commissioner Gordon?" snapped Mayor Van Royston. "They tell me you could have helped get The Whisperer tonight, but it seems you had some other business suddenly! There's a murdered taxicab driver, too, that you know about! Bolton, here, distinguished himself—"

The telephone on the desk started ringing. Wildcat waved his hand and picked it up. He said, "Yes? Oh, Mayor Van Royston? He is right here!"

Wildcat's Texas eyes flickered a little, but his expression did not change. He had instantly recognized the excited voice of J. Grover Jones. So the police trap had been sprung. Wildcat passed the instrument to the raging mayor.

"Now, that summons," said Wildcat to the court deputy. "I have Duke Dolano on his way here from a little trip up in the country. He will be produced in the morning. Along with him will be the murder headlight taken off his car, which matches the glass in our detective division.

"Sure, we'll produce Duke Dolano, but by then the charge will be murder in the first degree. You can pass the word along to Attorney Hempel and Judge Wharson."

MAYOR VAN ROYSTON was putting the telephone down on Wildcat's desk. The mayor's eyes were trying to pop out. He pulled off his silk hat and rubbed his retreating chin.

"More murder!" he gulped. "The Whisperer again! Right under your nose! That Thurston, the engineer, is dead! J. Grover Jones and his daughter were threatened! Your new deputy, that Thorsen, had just happened along, moving some prisoners, and arrested three men who were breaking into the Jones home after The Whisperer had terrorized my friend!"

Henry Bolton's small mouth was screwed into a knot. He was swearing.

"The Whisperer!"

Wildcat caressed the carnation in his buttonhole.

"I was having the Jones girl, that Howard and another prisoner moved over to the Belvidere precinct," he said, quietly. "I had an idea something might happen to them down here. You know, Mayor, J. Grover Jones isn't altogether in the clear on the Rand and Travis murders. There's something decidedly funny there."

Mayor Van Royston climbed upon his dignity.

"You have been the choice of the reformers for commissioner, Gordon," he stated primly. "But tomorrow, I shall demand a change. We must have someone in this office who can get results! Perhaps you can't get The Whisperer, but I demand these telephone murders be cleared up!"

Wildcat smiled quietly. Deputy Thorsen was coming along the corridor. Wildcat saw he was bringing Johnny Clatori, the shoe shiner. Fear jumped from the eyes of the bootblack.

"You know, Mayor Van Royston," said Wildcat,

calmly, "I believe we have the answer to the telephone murders. And here he comes. Little Johnny Clatori, we have so long known as the deaf-mute shoe shiner."

Mayor Van Royston looked as if the statement was too much. He sat down heavily in a chair, staring at Wildcat Gordon.

The mayor had every reason to look at Wildcat Gordon as if he believed the commissioner had lost his senses, if he ever had any.

"You're telling me, Gordon, a deaf-mute telephoned? Used the voices of two different men? Played a trick of saying he was dead? Gordon, I'm afraid it comes to more than a mere demand for your removal at the meeting tomorrow!"

Wildcat heard Henry Bolton's muttered words.

"Crazy—just plain crazy—"

Deputy Thorsen's wooden face showed no emotion. He seated Johnny Clatori, snapping one handcuff to a radiator. Then he extended a paper to Wildcat Gordon.

"I have to report, Commissioner, the arrest of three men known as Long Luke, Raddy Davens and Smoky Krause," said Thorsen. "We caught them, apparently trying to break into the residence of J. Grover Jones. Unfortunately, there had been another visitor. We discovered Mr. Jones tied up, and that fellow Jack Thurston dead. This letter was in the Jones typewriter."

Wildcat perused the closely written note slowly.

"You are correct, Mayor," he said after a minute. "J. Grover Jones must have entertained The Whisperer. But as for the murders of Homer Rand and Charles Travis, I have suspected from the first we had the very dead Mr. Thurston to thank for that. The Whisperer seems to want us to be sure of it."

Wildcat passed the typewritten paper to Mayor Van Royston.

MAYOR VAN ROYSTON read aloud, slowly, as if the words were choking him:

TO JAMES GORDON,
Commissioner of Police:

You may find a dead man here. I have warned you to have your police here to trap three others. They are the telephone murderers and the black-mailers of J. Grover Jones, the Black Mountain Power Co. Jack Thurston, a former actor and ventriloquist, was behind the plot. I was to have shared in the blackmail money, but they double-crossed me. Thurston was behind the murder phone calls. He knew the pet names Homer Rand and Charles Travis called the wife and the daughter.

Thurston could imitate voices perfectly, so he built himself a perfect alibi. Once he was with

J. Grover Jones and once in the police commissioner's office when the murder calls were made. Johny Clatori made those calls. He never was a deaf-mute. It was a fake game to get more tips.

Thurston found this out and used Johnny. He dictated the Rand and Travis messages to a specially constructed dictaphone. This was concealed in one of Johnny's shoe-shining boxes. Johnny made the call to Mrs. Rand from Duke Dolano's place. All he did was call, wait for an answer, then turn on Rand's voice with the dictaphone. He repeated this with the voice of Travis from that drugstore on Van Buren Avenue.

Thurston connected up the high-powered wire that killed Travis. He hired the taxi and truck drivers to kill Rand, his superior. Long Luke, Raddy Davens and Smoky Krause were associated with Thurston in an effort to blackmail Jones out of twelve millions. The Whisperer, was to be in on the cleanup. They froze me out. But Thurston and his three confederates did not trust each other.

The plans of the new dynamos were placed by them jointly in a safety deposit box. I robbed that box. The plans are now in the mails, addressed to J. Grover Jones. Nellie Jones and Ranny Howard knew some of the plot. They suspected Thurston, but were afraid to go to the police. So Howard tried to remove Thurston.

I regret to say I beat him to that little job, and saved the State some expense. You may give my regards to the coppers who gave me a bad half hour tonight and almost prevented my social call upon J. Grover Jones.

THE WHISPERER.

MAYOR VAN ROYSTON'S mouth was slack. His eyes went back over The Whisperer's note. Suddenly he seemed to get something for the first time.

"Great Scott, Gordon!" he shouted. "You knew about this! This murdering scoundrel says here he called you—you set a police trap—you, why, you compounded a felony, if there ever was such a thing!"

"'Confounded,' I think is the word, your honor," grinned Wildcat. "Too bad I didn't get my boys there in time to nab The Whisperer himself; but, then, we've got the phone murders nicely cleaned up, and the J. Grover Jones blackmailers on the spot, and apparently Miss Nellie Jones all reconciled with her father, or she should be. Well, Mayor, we can't have everything."

"Everything! Everything!" shouted Mayor Van Royston. "Why, when I put this before the Citizens, Committee tomorrow—"

But Wildcat Gordon was not listening. His telephone had given a buzz. The slow, meek voice of old Quick Trigger came over the wire.

"You all right, Wildcat? I guess maybe I didn't do so good, but I'll know better next time. Tiny's staying up, keeping your coffee hot."

THE END

INTERLUDE by Will Murray

In the Fall of 1936, with the U.S. economy seemingly emerging from the depths of the Great Depression, the Street & Smith pulp publishing company launched a new magazine dedicated to a different kind of hero—*The Whisperer!*

It's not hard to guess what motivated S&S. Ever since *The Shadow Magazine* rocked the pulp industry in 1931, rival publishers had rushed into print sundry and assorted imitations of *The Shadow*. *The Phantom Detective* in 1933. The Spider later that same year. *Secret Agent X* the following year. By 1936, less successful knockoffs had already bitten the dust.

Street & Smith had not done well with their revival of the old dime-novel detective, Nick Carter, nor their new Western hero, Pistol Pete Rice. So after quietly folding those valiant attempts, they cast about for something new.

One can imagine editor John L. Nanovic saying to General Manager Henry W. Ralston, "Well, if everybody and his brother can imitate The Shadow and make money, I don't see why we can't."

Puffing thoughtfully on a trademark cigar in his golden oak office, Ralston must have concurred. The Shadow was still selling surprisingly well after more than three years at a twice-a-month frequency. Plans to shift *Doc Savage Magazine* to the same incredible schedule had been initiated for the Autumn of 1935—using writer Laurence Donovan to supplement Lester Dent's regular output—had been called off when Ralston realized that *Doc Savage* would probably make more money in the long run as a monthly.

Out of this changed reality emerged the idea of an alternate version of The Shadow, but pitched to a slightly different audience. For *The Whisperer* was nothing less than Street & Smith's answer to *The Spider*. In its third year, the Popular Publications magazine written by Norvell W. Page as "Grant Stockbridge" had earned a fevered following thanks to the intense portrayal of a beleaguered crimebuster caught between the ferocious forces of the law and a savage underworld, both of which wanted him dead. Realistic and uncompromising, *The Spider* offered an alternative to pulp readers who wanted more red meat in their melodrama. Since Laurence Donovan had proven that he could produce exciting novels every thirty days like clockwork, he was probably the first—if not the only—choice to write the new series.

In fact, since the beginning of 1936, Donovan had been pounding out monthly yarns in S&S's new seagoing superhero series, *The Skipper*. It was scheduled for a Fall release. But in the Spring, Donovan was abruptly put on *The Whisperer*, which was rushed into production and ultimately released two months before *The Skipper*. Why? Perhaps with all the *Shadow* takeoffs proliferating, it was deemed more urgent to fight back on that newsstand front.

The usual procedure was for Ralston and Nanovic to brainstorm concepts before bringing in the writer to add his creative input. No doubt that was the case here, in Spring of 1936.

Some of the ideas were simply variations on The Shadow. The Dark Avenger wore black, so the new character would dress in gray. The Shadow had his trademark laugh, while The Whisperer often vented a ghostly chuckle when not speaking in the chilling whisper that became his eerie signature. Ever since Lamont Cranston began hobnobbing with the New York police commissioner, it had become an unshakable pulp cliché that his imitators do the same.

For a fresh twist, this unorthodox crimefighter was in real life the commissioner of police! Like Weston and so many other police department heads in fiction—as well as in real life back in the gangster era—he was an ex-Army officer, brought in to crush crime through military methods.

Thus was born the colorful James "Wildcat" Gordon—his name a play on the fact that the untamable Arabian wildcat is known as Gordon's cat.

This may have led to another twist. Both The Shadow and Doc Savage were headquartered in Manhattan. While Doc never encountered Commissioner

The Whisperer

Weston, there was little to suggest that Weston wasn't part of that same fictional reality.

But if The Whisperer in reality headed the police, relocating his adventures outside of New York City would be advisable. Street & Smith's Manhattan was already pretty crowded. Nick Carter also lived there. Bill Barnes had a private airfield over in Long Island. How many heroes did one metropolis really need?

The city where The Whisperer stories are laid is never explicitly named. Clues point in different directions. It appears to be a city of hills. The Ponto Hills. Society Hill. And others. Could this be Boston? Or is this often fog-shrouded metropolis really San Francisco? Donovan never reveals. But the nearby lake and suburb of Lakeside point to crime-ridden Chicago. And the presence of the "El" severely limits the possibilities. Only Boston, New York, Philadelphia and Chicago boasted elevated subway systems back in the 1930s. Almost certainly, Commissioner Gordon watched over a city as corrupt as Chicago. But the Illinois capital was not alone in owning that reputation. Described as a "big city of iron and steel" by the rivers, it brings to mind Philadelphia or Boston, both bounded by rivers.

Yet in some novels, the city is on a bay and boasts a complex cable-car system, which can only fit San Francisco, where Donovan resided in the early 1930s. In all likelihood, Donovan meant The Whisperer's grim and gritty hunting grounds to be read as a fictional Everycity, deliberately evoking New York, Chicago, Philadelphia, San Francisco,

and other major metropolises. The political cast made that approach mandatory. For example, New York City's colorful Jazz Age mayor, Jimmy Walker, may have inspired its dandified Mayor Van Royston.

The Whisperer cast is largely established in the debut novel. Richard Traeger and his daughter Tiny will be Wildcat's staunch allies for the duration of the series. Detective Sergeant Tom Thorsen remains Wildcat's good right hand—even if Donovan soon forgot his first name. Political adversaries Mayor Van Royston and his toady, Deputy Commissioner Henry Bolton, will be thorns in Wildcat's side—or is it the other way around?—as long as Donovan is penning the series. And Brian Boru is certainly the strangest sidekick any pulp crimefighter ever owned. A couple of semi-recurring characters will show up later, but the core cast is firmly in place by the end of *The Dead Who Talked*. Another important early ally, Judge Patrick Kyley, first appears on the second novel, *The Death Roses*. He will surface often in the coming months. But continuity didn't matter much in the pages of *The Whisperer*. Donovan skipped over the origin story, and it's clear that the strange gray supercrook known only as The Whisperer had been operating for months prior to the events in *The Dead Who Talked*.

This is a more realistic world than that depicted in the pages of *The Shadow* and *Doc Savage Magazine*. It's a world of tough Irish cops, police brutality, brutal Italian mobsters, swanky nightclubs, brothels and sudden death. It might have been culled from the Warner Bros. movies of that period, with Jimmy Cagney playing Wildcat Gordon. Tom Lovell had been doing the interior art for *The Shadow* since 1931. For Popular Publications, he executed numerous striking cover paintings for *Dime Mystery Stories* and *Detective Tales*. His work graced *The Whisperer* covers beginning with the first issue. To give these covers a different look, each one included a newspaper headline crying a piece of the plot. This no doubt to

Tom Lovell

suggest that the stories were torn from the headlines, which they almost certainly were. The motif of The Whisperer looking down over a crime scene is one borrowed from *The Phantom Detective*. The overall effect is deliberately muted, as befits a series pitched to a more mature audience.

After three unusual covers, Lovell was gone.

To replace him S&S took a page from Popular Publications, which when it launched *The Spider* and *Operator #5,* borrowed Walter M. Baumhofer and Jerome Rozen. John Newton Howitt had been painting the covers for both series since their second issues. Now he was lured into painting *The Whisperer* covers for Street & Smith.

The selection of Howitt seems to have been part of the S&S strategy to carve out a chunk of the market share The Spider had captured at The Shadow's expense. Both characters took a harsh punishment-first approach to crimebusting. And in the eyes of the law, both were considered outlaws to be hunted down without mercy. Other than the interesting fact that both characters inserted artificial teeth into their mouths in order to become their alter ego, The Spider and The Whisperer were otherwise poles apart. The Spider wore a Shadow-style cape and slouch hat, lanky fright wig and plastic vampire fangs as the chief elements of his disguise.

Longtime Doc Savage interior artist Paul Orban was assigned the interior art chores. He executed some of the sharpest work of his entire career illustrating *The Whisperer.*

This is a crime suspense series, as hard-boiled as anything found in the pages of *Black Mask.* No costumed supervillains. No superscientific menaces. Just the saga of a two-fisted tough-as-nails cop who chooses to combat crime from both sides of the law, playing a dangerous double game in which he dodges death and disgrace at every deadly turn.

Where The Shadow blasted bad guys with his thundering .45 automatics, and Doc Savage devised his supermachine pistol to contend with the Thompson submachine gun, The Whisperer blazed away with his unique supersilenced automatics. They may hiss like serpents, but he used them with deadly efficiency. For despite his nebulous alter ego, The Whisperer is a born killer—as Donovan constantly reminds us when describing his hero's cold Texas eyes.

In a curious way, it's really Wildcat Gordon who is the star of this series. Bold and two-fisted, Gordon carries as much series weight as does his spectral alter ego. For what Laurence Donovan has done is to turn the old secret identity convention on its head. Going back to the Scarlet Pimpernel, and down through Zorro, Superman, Batman and all the rest, the hero pretended to be lazy, or weak, or ineffectual in his civilian identity, so that after he transformed into his colorful alias to combat crime, no one would ever dream, for example that Don Diego de la Vega was really the swashbuckling Zorro.

Here, "Fighting Wildcat" Gordon—as he was sometimes known—was the dynamic one. When he transformed, it was into a creature so colorless he was virtually invisible. The Whisperer often walked down the street in broad daylight and was not recognized for who he truly was—unless he happened to speak. Then that weirdly penetrating whisper gave him dead away.

Often the covers played up the name Wildcat Gordon instead of The Whisperer. It was as if they really were two people. In practice, The Whisperer was a creature of Wildcat's imagination, and an extension of his unorthodox war on crime.

Wildcat was a character that must have made a profound impression on Batman creators Bob Kane and Bill Finger, both avid readers of Street & Smith pulp magazines. When they "adapted" the 1936 Shadow novel *Partners of Peril* for the debut Batman adventure in 1939, it also introduced Police Commissioner Gordon. For a long time, Finger avoided mentioning Gordon's first name. "I felt it wise to just give Commissioner Gordon an official title," he once explained. "There was the chance that Batman might reveal his own secret identity by referring to the Commissioner by his first name. And besides, it lent that much more of an official tone to the storyline by not having Batman on familiar terms with Commissioner Gordon."

Not until the early 1950s was Gordon given a full name. It was James W. Gordon. This could scarcely be a coincidence. Otherwise, the two characters are not physically similar. It's certainly intriguing that *Partners of Peril* and the first issue of *The Whisperer* were released within weeks of each other in the Autumn of 1936. "Batman was written originally in the style of the pulps," Finger once admitted.

"I was very much influenced by The Shadow and Doc Savage, The Phantom, things of that sort. But Bill had it down pat," acknowledged Bob Kane. "He was a pulp reader. As a matter of fact, I read all the pulps that Bill Finger read. He'd give me his magazines and I did read them. I was influenced by Doc Savage and the pulps, to some extent."

Add to that The Whisperer. "I patterned my style of writing after The Shadow," recalled Finger, who once freely admitted that his first Batman script was a takeoff of a Shadow novel. "Also after Warner Bros. movies, the gangster movies with Jimmy Cagney, George Raft, Bogart. I always liked that kind of point of view. It was completely pulp style."

That same grim point of view, so different from the world of The Shadow, which seemed to consist of high society on one hand and the underworld below it, reverberates like a chattering tommy-gun all through the Whisperer saga. If you compare the early episodes of Batman with The Whisperer, you'll discover that same Warner Bros. ambience and human-interest storytelling which was a marked departure from the idealized Street & Smith worldview. And you might also notice that like

The Whisperer, Batman dressed largely in subtle gray . . .

True to his pulp roots, Finger sometimes dipped into back issues of *The Whisperer* for inspiration. *The Red Hatchets, School for Murder* and *Kill Them First!* provided the springboards for early Batman stories—although Finger invariably gave them his own spin to fit the Batman mythos. One issue featured Shadow ghostwriter Theodore Tinsley's novelette, "The Grim Joker," whose white-masked villain might well have been one of the pulp seeds from which The Joker sprang.

The heroic name "Wildcat" also made a distinct impression on Finger. When he was trying to come up with a suitable name for Batman's new kid side-kick in 1940, Finger listed numerous possibilities—among them Dusty, Scamp and Tiger—before deciding upon Robin. Also high on that list was "Wildcat."

In 1941, Finger created a new superhero for *Sensation Comics,* a former boxer turned crimebuster. He called him "Wildcat"! Dressed in a black catsuit, Wildcat was a fighting fury worthy of his name.

Perhaps Superman creators Jerry Siegel and Joe Shuster also read *The Whisperer.* Not until the advent of comic book superheroes did any pulp hero execute so many lightning changes between his dual identities as did Wildcat Gordon. And his favorite place to do so? A public phone booth! Of course back in those Depression days, phone booths were wooden closets affording considerable privacy.

For the record, Siegel once admitted that in his youth, "I read enormous quantities of eerie-hero oriented magazines like *The Shadow.*" Certainly *The Whisperer* was among the eeriest.

And strangely enough, when writer Jerry Siegel lifted a pulp plot for the early Superman, as often as not it was from one of Laurence Donovan's Doc Savage novels.

We've chosen for our second novel one of "Clifford Goodrich's" most brutal and violent Whisperer novels, *The Red Hatchets.* Mysteries set in Chinatown were a longstanding tradition in *The Shadow Magazine.* That tradition was transferred effectively to *The Whisperer.* But in the name-less metropolis of Wildcat Gordon, it's not called Chinatown, but "China Hill."

By the time this novel was printed in the April, 1937 issue of *The Whisperer,* Donovan had sharpened his depictions of the colorful cast surrounding Wildcat Gordon over six stories. And it shows. Now, prepare to enter the fog-shrouded summit of China Hill as the dreaded Whisperer confronts the bloody reign of—*The Red Hatchets!* •

The Dark Avenger follows a bizarre murder trail that leads to the walking dead, a living skeleton and the **MASTER OF DEATH** and The Shadow and his agents struggle to protect Manhattan from an underworld war conducted by **THE RACKETS KING.**

Bonus: **THE PURPLE GIRASOL,** a previously-unpublished 1931 short story by Walter B. Gibson!

Ask your bookseller to order your copies today!

What is the strange connection between a snowstorm in July and the death of a woman transformed into a shadow? Doc and Pat Savage journey to the Syrian Desert to unravel the strange secret of the **MURDER MIRAGE** in a novel that inspired a 1940 Superman story by Jerry Siegel. Then, a mysterious animal pelt leads Doc and his aides through a crack in the Earth to the prehistoric dangers of **THE OTHER WORLD.**

Plus: a tribute to the late Doc Savage writer Philip José Farmer.

The Whisperer

In the pages of this magazine you will become acquainted with a new character—a vigorous, fascinating, unusual individual who dares to do what others have thought of doing; what others have felt ought to be done.

There is nothing strange about this character. He is just a good, hard-hitting American cop who sees that the Law is often made helpless by rules and regulations, and who has decided to sweep aside red tape when he deems it necessary. He metes out justice as he sees it. If the evidence points to the crook as guilty, the crook gets his just punishment, even if the evidence is not the type that would stand up in court.

In other words, this man's method is refreshingly American; real, true, sincere and honest. His job is to uphold the law, and uphold it he does, despite all the silly, routine difficulties that might be in the way. He fits, we believe, the real American ideal of the individual who gets things done; the one who gets his man, regardless of obstacles in the way. We sincerely hope he will catch your fancy and hold it!

THE EDITOR.

THE RED HATCHETS
by Clifford Goodrich

They carve a crimson trail of murder from China Hill to the drive of the wealthy—a trail for The Whisperer to follow and wipe clean!

CHAPTER I
EIGHTEEN SHARP HATCHETS

"STRINGER" DURKIN and "Opium" Peters would not have believed they were walking straight to their deaths. Durkin and Peters were too contemptuous of the shuffling residents of Mall Street and all the other narrow streets of Chinatown to imagine any danger could threaten them.

Opium Peters, especially, was scornful of the yellow-faced men who moved silently past with their hands thrust into the sleeves of their blouses for protection against the raw night fog off the bay.

For Opium Peters, as his moniker signified, had had some dealings with one of the lower orders of the Orientals. So Opium Peters was firmly convinced he knew all there was to know about the intricacies of the Chinese mind.

"The slant-eyed mugs'll double-cross each other, but they ain't got the nerve to make a pass at a white man," Opium Peters told Stringer Durkin. "Besides that, Stringer, this Wildcat Gordon can't touch Dollar Martino, an' the cops is takin' off their hats to all us boys."

This remark classified Peters and Durkin as "Dollar" Martino's men. Chinatown, with its straggling, narrow streets on the hill, and its hidden passages behind darkly fronted shops, held no sinister mysteries for this pair.

The leaning, gorgeous buildings with pagoda-shaped roofs housed only a few more "joints" whereby Peters and Durkin imagined Dollar Martino was beginning to collect on a new racket.

Packages of firecrackers were snapping, for it was the week of the Chinese New Year. Strings of paper lanterns ornamented with lurid dragons swayed in the fog over Mall Street. But the yellow-faced men, as usual, seemed to slink on soft feet from one dark doorway to another.

"Dollar ain't cracked the crust of the rake-off on them dinky curio shops," stated Opium Peters. "When we get goin' down here, I'll wise him up to this fan-tan an' some other games that'll make the numbers racket look cheap."

"Sure!" grunted Stringer Durkin. "The Chinks oughta be layin' it on the line. They're a pushover when it comes to collectin'. I guess this Lo Sing rake-off is Dollar's way of beginnin'. Maybe he's payin' off for all of 'em as a starter."

DOLLAR MARTINO'S sleek, loudly dressed henchmen, swung along over the uneven sidewalk which was laid on only one side of the cobblestone roadway of Mall Street.

They felt themselves flashily important, indeed, among the shuffling Orientals who seemed never to glance at them from their slanting, black eyes.

Opium Peters and Stringer Durkin might well have reason for their feeling of superiority and security. What if both of these nice boys did rate a little walk up the thirteen steps of the gallows across the bay?

Didn't Dollar Martino have half the big town in his pocket for a long time? Didn't most of the cops, on the side, take off their hats to Dollar Martino? Hadn't Dollar Martino easily fixed several "raps" for both these boys, which might have led to the thirteen steps?

As for "Wildcat" Gordon, the police commissioner who had put the clamps on some of the lesser eggs, he hadn't shown any stuff when it came to a big guy like Dollar Martino. And Dollar Martino had the "protective bug" pulling the dollars that gave him his name, all the way from the fish markets on the waterfront to the casino outfits spotted on the hills.

Now Dollar Martino was branching out. No other gentleman in the rackets had ever figured the hidden profits of Mall Street, or the many shops with their perpetually dusty windows.

But this was the third time that Stringer Durkin and Opium Peters had been sent on the seventeenth of the month to pick up a "protective payment" from the fat, unsmiling Lo Sing, who sat like a yellowed, imperturbable idol in the luxurious den back of his importing house on Mall Street.

Durkin and Peters knew nothing beyond their sweet little assignment of picking up Lo Sing's "contribution." For all they had been informed, the bland Lo Sing himself might be in league with their boss, the invincible Dollar Martino—the one biggest racketeer who could give Wildcat Gordon's coppers the runaround and make them like it.

The collectors were also triggermen. That is, their guns reposed snugly in their side pockets, though it had been some time since their itching fingers had been employed.

Durkin and Peters certainly expected no use for those same death-dealers in Chinatown where, according to their view, the Orientals stepped softly with respect for them.

Durkin and Peters were walking up Mall Street because the cobblestones were slippery with fog. Their newest sedan was left on one of the broader streets below China Hill.

They had been told to make their monthly visit to Lo Sing unobtrusive, as it would not be well for them to be seen driving up to the house in their big car.

Stringer Durkin and Opium Peters would have been less, much less, sneeringly confident of their boss's supremacy and the respect of the softly moving Chinese about them, if they could have looked behind the pagoda-curved front of the tall shop which had only the small sign, "Lo Sing—Importer," and under it a replica in Chinese characters.

Indeed, could Dollar Martino's crooked-mouthed triggermen have seen into the den where the fat Lo Sing sat, they would have hastily gripped their guns and hurried back down the steep hill of Mall Street.

LO SING did not sit alone. But his great, carved chair might have been some sort of dais, and his

visitors squatted in a half circle on the soft, thick rug. Curtains hung in motionless folds on three sides of the den, which was a big room to have been hollowed out from the stone of the hill back of the importing house.

These costly draperies suggested they might conceal anything, from rare treasure to tunnel entrances. There were doors opening into the

When The Whisperer and Quick Trigger entered the opulent, draperied den of old Lo Sing, the Chinaman seemed to be sleeping in a thin, sweet vapor of incense. His drooping lids opened only a trifle over the black pools of his eyes.

hill, for some of the visitors who squatted in silence on the thick rug had emerged from them.

Lo Sing was so fat as to be almost shapeless. His face was impassive, wrinkled and wise. The slanted eyes never seemed to be more than half opened. His thick hands were folded over his enormous stomach, and the inches of protected fingernails indicated it had been many years since those same hands had

been active.

From little polished brass pots a thin, sweet vapor of incense curled in blue threads about Lo Sing's big head. Lo Sing himself might have been one of the strange gods to whom the sweet incense was being burned.

Eighteen men sat in the half circle on the rug. It might have been seen that none was a young man.

Though not so fat, all were about the age of Lo Sing himself. Their faces were nearly as wrinkled and fully as expressionless as his own.

When Lo Sing spoke, he did not employ the language of his fathers, but used English, without a trace of an accent.

"It is again the seventeenth day of the white man's calendar," said Lo Sing.

"It is the seventeenth day, so we have come," stated one of the eighteen solemn men before him.

The trace of a smile appeared across Lo Sing's thick lips, or it might have been merely a thought passing through his mind. A musical gong with six separate notes struck an hour.

"The two of the loud-speaking tongues approach," stated Lo Sing. "He who is best prepared walks the longest road of life."

The words appeared to have an obscure meaning, and there was in the Chinaman's tone the suggestion that those who might not be prepared would be walking the shortest road to death.

At this, the eighteen solemn Chinese spoke as one man, as if reciting a chant:

"We have come prepared, Lo Sing. The measure of our own passing suns has become short. By this we hope to become more worthy to join our ancestors."

The hands of the eighteen wrinkled men had been idly held within the voluminous sleeves of their loose blouses. Now eighteen right hands came into view, uplifted. Held in each hand was a shining, sharpened hatchet, so polished it might have been silver.

The hatchets were upheld on short handles, newly painted with the color of human blood. The eyes of all eighteen men were fixed upon Lo Sing.

"I pledge myself," said Lo Sing, "that whatever befalls each or all of you, that same fate shall come upon my own house.

"We pledge ourselves," chanted the eighteen men, "that what overtakes one of us shall overtake all."

Pair by pair, the blades of the hatchets touched and grated.

The musical gong striking the hour had lost its last echo. Another bell tinkled more sharply. Lo Sing slowly waved one hand in a gesture of dismissal. The eighteen wrinkled men arose and vanished through parting draperies that stirred for their passage, then again hung in motionless folds.

There could be no doubt now of tunneled passages under China Hill, for none of the bearers of the red-handled hatchets moved toward the front of the Lo Sing building.

Hardly had the curtains ceased to move when a younger Chinaman came through a door from the front. He was bowing his sleek, black head before the two men who followed, as if they might have been honored guests.

THE PALE EYES of Stringer Durkin and Opium Peters took in the heavy opulence of the room, and Durkin wrinkled his nose at the sweet odor of the burning incense.

"Hell!" grunted Stringer Durkin. "Lo Sing, this dopey joint o' yours gives me the creeps! I had to send my clothes to the cleaners the last time to get the smell out o' 'em!"

"I have been expecting you, and you are punctual," stated Lo Sing, without any expression on his yellow face. "The god of the last sun must be appeased."

"Heathen junk," said Opium Peters, out of one corner of his mouth to Stringer Durkin. "You'll get to know these Chinks better as Dollar Martino works in a little deeper."

If there was any resentment on the part of Lo Sing over the blatantly insulting speeches, his impassive face gave no visible sign. One hand gestured dismissal, and the young Chinaman glided from the room.

"You're ready to lay it on the line, huh?" grunted Stringer Durkin.

Lo Sing did not speak, but one pointed fingernail was held protectively outward as his hand went into the voluminous folds of the richly decorated robe draped over his huge shoulders. In his hand appeared a flat packet of banknotes enclosed by a rubber band.

Opium Peters took the money and roughly flicked a finger over the ends of the bills.

"Two grand, an' all jake!"

"You're there, Lo Sing, when it comes to layin' it on the line," said Stringer Durkin. "Wish some of the other eggs on our route had the same idea. You'd be surprised at how some of 'em want to stall for time. But maybe you an' Dollar's got this thing all fixed up between yuh?"

"Can it, Stringer," growled Opium Peters. "You'll want to find out too much someday, an' Dollar don't take to that stuff. An' when you get to know these Chinks better, you'll find out they don't talk. How about it, Lo Sing?"

Opium Peters closed one pale eye in what he considered an understanding wink at the fat Lo Sing. The half-closed eyes of the wrinkled Chinaman might have been black slits for all the emotion they showed.

"That concludes our business until another seventeenth," he stated, without any change in the monotone of his voice.

The dignity of Lo Sing seemed to keep his ears closed to the words of his no doubt unwelcome guests. His fat hands clapped softly together, the sacred inches of fingernails being held carefully so they would not strike each other.

"O.K.! O.K.!" grated Stringer Durkin. "If you won't spill nothin', you won't! Well, we'll be seein' you, big belly, on another seventeenth, an' be sure you have it to lay on the line!"

"You will come this way," spoke the low voice of the young Chinaman from the doorway through which Dollar Martino's henchmen had entered.

Lo Sing's fat hands were again folded in the silken robe, and his eyelids had dropped until his eyes appeared to be closed in sleep or weariness.

"These Chinks now would like you better if you didn't talk so damn' much, Stringer," said Opium Peters, as they entered the narrow passageway leading back to Mall Street. "It scares 'em off an' they button up when you go spillin' questions."

Stringer Durkin started to growl a fitting reply, but he halted suddenly and laid a hand on Opium Peters's right arm.

"Where'd that little Chink go, Opium?" he grated. "Say—this ain't the way we come in! Wait a minute! This alley don't lead no place!"

Opium Peters swung around at Stringer Durkin's touch.

"That's damn' funny!" he gritted. "What the devil? There ain't no door out this way!"

DOLLAR MARTINO'S collectors turned slowly in the narrow passage. There were no curtains on these walls. The passage was only a tunnel cut through wet, oozing rock. It was similar to the one through which they had entered Lo Sing's luxurious den.

But it was not the same passage. There was no door, only a blank wall ahead. And as the two suddenly bewildered triggermen turned, two lights between them and Lo Sing's den winked out. There was but little light now, and it came from a concealed bulb which they could not see.

The young Chinese guide had vanished, where or by what means the puzzled pair did not know. Stringer Durkin let loose a choice brand of oaths and started back in the direction they had come.

The silence got on the nerves of both men, and they pulled their pistols from their side pockets.

"You don't think that yellow devil's pullin' somethin', do you?" asked Stringer Durkin.

"Naw!" replied Opium Peters.

The gleaming hatchets flashed from the darkness into which they were walking.

"Keep your shirt on! Why, Dollar Martino would take China Hill apart and—"

The faith of Opium Peters in the supreme rule of Dollar Martino did not save him. Neither did the automatic pistol in his hand, nor the one in the hand of Stringer Durkin. Neither gun was ever fired.

Two gleaming hatchets flashed from the darkness into which they were walking. The sharpened blades split the triggermen's skulls exactly where their hair would have been parted in the middle if they had worn it that way.

The none-too-smart brains of Stringer Durkin and Opium Peters flowed out with their blood on the stone floor of the passage. No voice spoke, but yellow hands lifted the still-warm bodies and bore them along the tunnel to where a door had now appeared as if by magic.

Back in the incense-filled den of Lo Sing, the draperies parted and fell. Two wrinkled Chinese, who had a short time before been squatted on the

rug, came in with their hands empty. Each stretched his right hand toward Lo Sing.

"We have other hatchets prepared, and may our measure of suns be sufficient," one man stated, without emotion.

The other man extended to Lo Sing a packet of money held by a rubber band.

"The souls of the Hop Jo walk again," stated Lo Sing. "There will be no more of the seventeenth on the calendar of days."

Placing the returned money in his robe, Lo Sing held his long fingernails at a careful angle as he tore off a sheet from his calendar of days, which he had placed close beside his carved chair.

About this time, a lone patrolman saw a sight that pulled him across the street on the run and swearing. Two dead men, with red-handled hatchets buried in their heads, were sitting in the front seat of a new sedan.

CHAPTER II
MARK OF THE HOP JO TONG

"STRINGER DURKIN and Opium Peters?" said the clipped voice of the gaudily dressed man who was seated with bright yellow shoes resting beside two red-handled hatchets upon his desk. "Now that's what I call coöperation with the police. Too bad Dollar Martino wasn't one of them."

The speaker pulled the brim of an army hat lower over one eye, flicked a petal from a red carnation in his coat lapel and slanted his gaze at a silk-hatted, gray-spatted man who was nervously pacing the office.

James Wildcat Gordon was deliberately inviting the outburst he knew would be coming from Mayor Van Royston, who had been summoned to headquarters from a midnight dinner when the hatchet killings broke.

Mayor Van Royston's slightly retreating chin moved as his mouth tightened.

"Murder's murder, Commissioner Gordon!" he rasped. "I don't like to hear the head of the department speaking as if he approved brutal killings! All citizens are entitled to protection of the law and the police!"

"Perhaps I should send a couple of squads down to the Iola Club to see that some of the Chinese don't take a notion to smack a hatchet in Dollar Martino's own hair?" grinned Wildcat Gordon. "Stringer Durkin and Opium Peters would have had their necks cracked instead of their skulls, if Martino hadn't been able to provide his own law protection."

Wildcat Gordon gently moved one of the bloody hatchets with one yellowshod foot. They had become exhibit A in the passing of Martino's pair of triggermen.

"What do you make of the hatchet angle, Sergeant Thorsen?" said Wildcat Gordon. "You wouldn't imagine Dollar Martino playing dumb enough to try muscling in on China Hill."

The detective sergeant addressed as Thorsen had a square face, about as full of expression as wood taken from some old battleship. Since his coming into the commissioner's office a few months before, Sergeant Thorsen had been Wildcat Gordon's right-hand man.

"It's been several years since we've had a tong war on China Hill, Chief," stated Sergeant Thorsen. "I remember, in the last flare-up, it was believed the Hop Jo tong was wiped out. But them red handles are the mark of the Hop Jo. If it means anything, then old Lo Sing could talk if he would."

"Lo Sing, huh?" snapped a hard voice. "I say there ain't any yellow mug that's got a right to keep himself locked up in a hill where the place ain't open to police inspection!"

THE SPEAKER had a hooked nose that overhung a small, round mouth. This, with a low forehead, gave him an odd appearance and made most of his words unpleasant. He was Deputy Commissioner Henry Bolton, and his disposition was as unpleasant as his voice.

Deputy Bolton's amiability had not been increased any since Wildcat Gordon had been commissioner. Deputy Bolton had wanted that desk, and Mayor Van Royston was his backer.

Unfortunately, for his ambition, the reform party that had elected Mayor Van Royston also had specified the appointment of James Wildcat Gordon who had gained the name of "Wildcat" as a fighting inspector.

Deputy Bolton now added: "I'd say the thing to do is show this old Lo Sing a trick or two, and if you say the word, Mayor Van Royston, I'll have the boys bring him in."

"Certainly! Certainly!" agreed Mayor Van Royston instantly. "Commissioner Gordon, since you applied the tactics of your army career to the police force, it might be well to close down right now on these Chinese! When they start killing white men with hatchets, there is no telling where it will end!"

Wildcat Gordon's broad mouth took on a crooked grin. His cold eyes, or rather the one visible under his cocked army hat, rested upon Deputy Henry Bolton.

"When Lo Sing is interviewed," he said, "I'll attend to it personally. I agree with you, Mayor Van Royston, about killing white men. Thus far only two of Dollar Martino's thugs have been rubbed out.

"If this is a demonstration of the use of hatchets, I'd suggest, Henry, you order a few hundred

red-handled hatchets at once for the soft-handed police force. In the meantime, I'll be having a little talk with Dollar Martino as to why his pair of rats were exterminated."

Wildcat Gordon's yellow shoes slapped to the floor. When he stood up, he was shorter than many men, being only five feet five inches tall.

But the commissioner was a former army officer, and his eyes—neither blue nor gray, but almost colorless—were the kind most often seen among the old and strong breed of Texas eyes.

"But Commissioner Gordon," said Mayor Van Royston, "aren't you putting out squads for a roundup on China Hill?"

"For the present," snapped Wildcat, "we'll stay off of China Hill, in the hope that some more of Martino's nice little boys wander up that way!"

The door banged behind his striding figure. Deputy Bolton ran a finger over his long nose.

Mayor Van Royston said, "Henry, I'm afraid we're in for another outbreak of lawlessness. I can see it coming when Commissioner Gordon acts like that. As if we haven't had enough trouble with The Whisperer since he came into office, now he actually seems pleased at this outbreak of the Chinese."

If Mayor Van Royston could have followed Wildcat Gordon, he would have been even more convinced that his unwanted commissioner was about to step over the fringe of the law, in the interest of justice.

FIVE MINUTES after he left his office, Wildcat Gordon was driving furiously along the broad main street that ran down to the bay and the ferry buildings. Seated beside him was an oldish man whose bared head was bald, except for a gray fringe above his ears.

This older man was Dick Traeger, a retired deputy commissioner of police, known because of his former prowess as "Quick Trigger." At this moment, old Quick Trigger was protesting.

"But Wildcat, everytime The Whisperer gets on the job, we get into a jam," he argued. "One of these times will be the last, and you'll be all washed up as commissioner. Danged if I don't wish I'd never monkeyed with those crazy dental plates."

The police coupé was dashing along the streetcar tracks at high speed. Wildcat Gordon smiled at the older man. Quick Trigger had been almost a father to him, and he lived with the retired deputy in his penthouse on top of a waterfront loft building.

"Sometime, Quick Trigger, has to be the last time," said Wildcat. "But this time, it happens that old Lo Sing is a very close friend of The Whisperer, and as soon as I've had a little talk with Dollar Martino, The Whisperer will see what Lo Sing may have hidden behind his yellow wrinkles."

"I don't like it, Wildcat," reiterated Quick Trigger. "You've given Mayor Van Royston and the others time to almost forget The Whisperer, and now you're off again."

This conversation was mysterious, or would have been to all others but Wildcat Gordon and old Quick Trigger. For The Whisperer had become a notorious figure in the city, continually baffling the police, a terror to the worst elements of the underworld.

A plain, gray little man, who had never been positively identified, The Whisperer usually appeared mysteriously, struck at the lowest and the highest of criminals, and vanished in an equal cloak of mystery.

Wildcat Gordon had said The Whisperer was a close friend of the wily old Chinaman, Lo Sing. None would know of that better than Wildcat, for he himself was The Whisperer. The gray little man, so inconspicuous he had never been positively identified.

Old Quick Trigger had made the odd dental plates that could instantly change Wildcat into The Whisperer. It accomplished more than that, for The Whisperer could speak with these dental plates in only a commanding, penetrating whisper that had given him his name.

Old Quick Trigger was still arguing when Wildcat swung the coupé into the circle before the brilliantly lighted Iola Club. Here, overlooking the bay, was the gambling resort conducted by Dollar Martino, whose criminal cleverness and political influence had apparently made him immune to the law.

Though it was now after midnight, the rooms of the club resounded with activity. Seemingly, the hatchet murder of two of Dollar Martino's henchmen was having no effect upon the night's play.

A tall man in correct evening clothes appeared almost instantly at a side door of the club building when Wildcat Gordon and Quick Trigger approached.

This man himself might have been one of the wealthy playboys enjoying the dubious hospitality of Martino's Iola Club, but he opened the door before Wildcat's thumb had pushed the button.

"So I was expected, Breezy?" said Wildcat. "You were waiting up for me?"

"Dollar's been expecting you," said "Breezy" Taro, known to the police as Dollar Martino's right-hand man and personal bodyguard. "He said to bring you right up when you came. He didn't say anything about anybody else, but I guess it's all right."

"It's all right, Breezy, if I had decided to bring along a squad!" snapped Wildcat. "I wouldn't be surprised if you boys would be expecting us to keep the hatchets out of your hair!"

Breezy Taro uttered a short, harsh laugh.

"I wouldn't worry too much, Commissioner," he sneered. "Dollar's smart enough to look after his own hatchets and get in your hair besides."

Quick Trigger dropped back and said into Wildcat's ear, "Did you see anything funny as we came in the door?"

"I saw the two Chinese walking past the cars, if that's what you mean," said Wildcat, in a low tone. "But we'll see what Dollar Martino has to offer."

Breezy Taro missed this quick exchange as he strode ahead of Wildcat and Quick Trigger up one short flight of stairs. He opened a door at the end of a short second-floor hallway.

DOLLAR MARTINO did not arise from behind his wide, polished desk. His black eyes and his voice held insolent confidence. He was a big man, with an overstuffed body and a head that looked too small on his broad shoulders. He merely wagged his chin in the direction of two chairs.

"Nice to see you up here, Commissioner Gordon," he smiled suavely. "First time you've ever been worried about my friends, and I'm sorry to have you troubled at this late hour."

"It's a pleasure, Martino," stated Wildcat. "Too bad I have to stay up late when there were only two of them. You're not thinking of sending some more of your friends over on China Hill by any chance?"

Breezy Taro was lingering just inside the door. Dollar Martino said, "Shut it as you go out, Breezy, and see that nobody comes up to interrupt our little chat."

He clipped off the tip of a cigar and shoved a box across the desk. Wildcat Gordon shook his head and stuffed tobacco into his stubby pipe.

"I thought you'd be getting wrong ideas, Commissioner," said Martino. "That's the trouble with Stringer Durkin and Opium Peters right now. They got the wrong ideas. That usually causes trouble."

"So you hired a couple of hatchets instead of the usual torpedoes, Martino? Is that what you mean?"

Dollar Martino bubbled with laughter and spread out his hands.

"Why, Commissioner, you wouldn't be kidding me?" he sneered. "Anyway, I might as well give you the low-down. I haven't the faintest idea myself how Durkin and Peters happened to get themselves bumped off. I'm smart enough to run my little club and keep out of other things. Maybe they got themselves mixed up in some kind of dope deal on China Hill."

Wildcat Gordon prodded the tobacco down into his pipe and grinned a little.

"So that's the way it's to be, is it, Martino? You think your two boys strayed off and perhaps were putting something over on you, is that it?"

"Exactly, Commissioner. China Hill's one place my friends should know enough to stay away from. But Opium Peters has been mixed up over there before and—"

"And you're just a plain liar, Martino!" rapped out Wildcat. "And a damn' poor one! I didn't come up here to listen to any greasy talk! I want the truth! What were Durkin and Peters doing on China Hill?"

The oily smile slipped from Dollar Martino's insolent face. His heels moved on the rug under his chair.

"You may be the Commissioner, but there ain't any copper calling me a liar!"

"I'm calling you a liar, Martino," repeated Wildcat quietly. "More than that, you're trying to walk into Chinatown; but you're going to find it isn't collecting protection from fish dealers and vegetable peddlers over there. You're running into a new kind of hell, and all I'm going to do about it is help push you and the rest of your scurvy rats into it if I get the chance."

DOLLAR MARTINO reared his big body from the chair and stood at one corner of his desk. When he was on his feet, his head looked more than ever like a misplaced bullet.

"Well, Commissioner Gordon, you seem to want a showdown, and I've been expecting it!" he said insolently. "You've been getting yourself a great reputation as 'Fighting Wildcat Gordon,' but you've just now crossed it out!

"Ever since a bunch of nitwits imagined a broken-down has-been of an army officer could run their police department, you've been walking all over the toes of the best people! Now we'll take steps to have that changed!"

Old Quick Trigger was sitting with clenched fists. Wildcat Gordon had not moved from his chair. Wildcat dumped the burning ashes from his pipe on the thick rug and said calmly, "You're still a liar, Martino. Why did you send Durkin and Peters to China Hill?" Dollar Martino's suddenly calm, mocking tone matched Wildcat's own.

"We've had our say, Commissioner," he said. "Now I'll have Breezy show you out, in case some of the boys might have overheard our conversation and got the idea we're not friends. If you take my tip, we could still be friends."

Dollar Martino stuck out his hand with a derisive movement. Wildcat's movement from his chair was so fast that Dollar Martino's derisive hand was still sticking out when a fist splattered his lips over his teeth. His bullet head jerked back on his shoulders, and Wildcat shot a driving left into his bulging stomach.

"Great gravy!" exploded old Quick Trigger. "Now you've done it, Wildcat! This is going to start a lot of trouble!"

Dollar Martino was at the moment in no position to make the trouble immediate. His bulletlike head struck and bounced off an edge of his desk and he rolled, groaning, onto his back, mouth gaping open in an effort to get back some of the wind that had been knocked out of him.

"Maybe you've killed him," said Quick Trigger, as blood oozed from Martino's mouth over his white shirtfront.

"No such good luck!" snapped Wildcat. "Breezy Taro doesn't seem to answer, so we'll show ourselves out!"

Quick Trigger turned the knob of the door, which swung inward. Wildcat Gordon had halted, one hand dipping to the automatic he carried in a side pocket. After all, it was likely that some immediate trouble might develop when Breezy Taro saw what had happened.

Breezy Taro, Martino's right-hand man, did come in suddenly with the opening of that door. But Breezy Taro was not starting trouble on his own account, nor was he likely to summon help from the gambling rooms beyond the second-floor hallway.

For Breezy Taro had been sitting upright, with his back against the door and a red-handled hatchet buried in his skull. The blade had split his forehead to the middle of his nose. The blood was still flowing and spread in a wide stain on the rug inside.

Behind Wildcat and Quick Trigger came a gasp from Dollar Martino. Though he had been nearly out, the racketeer rolled his body to one side, pulling himself up by the desk.

"Gordon!" gulped Dollar Martino. "Gordon! They're after me! You've got to get me out of here!"

Martino's insolence had been erased. His black eyes contracted with fear, as he seemed unable to take his gaze from the red hatchet sticking in Breezy Taro's skull.

WILDCAT COULD SEE the length of the short hallway to the stairs leading downward. There was no evidence anyone had been there. From the gambling rooms came the usual humming of voices. Perhaps Martino had kept only Breezy Taro on guard, uncertain as to what his interview with the police commissioner might develop.

Old Quick Trigger stepped over the bleeding corpse and went to the head of the stairway. He turned, shaking his head. There was no one down there.

Dollar Martino was sick, and he slumped into his chair at the desk.

"So now I've got to get you out of here?" said Wildcat Gordon. "You haven't any idea what your rats were doing on China Hill? I guess then this may be just the old Chinese double cross. What's the answer Martino?"

The racketeer wiped blood from his lips and continued to stare at the body of Breezy Taro. Having seen there was no one outside, some of his panic was leaving him.

"Never mind," muttered Martino thickly. "I'm taking care of it. I don't know what it's all about, but I'll find out."

"That makes two of us, Martino!" rapped Wildcat. "Don't be touching that body until some of the boys come along to pick it up. I'll put in a call, and here's hoping they come all the way in the next time."

"But Wildcat," said Quick Trigger, in the hallway, "hadn't we better stick around until a squad gets here?"

"Call a squad downstairs," directed Wildcat. "You and me have got sudden business over on China Hill."

CHAPTER III
LO SING'S COMPLACENCY

ONCE MORE in the speeding coupé, Quick Trigger said, "We're not doin' so good, Wildcat. I've never seen a copper yet that could make a Chinaman talk."

"Right, Quick Trigger. And if old Lo Sing had the faintest notion The Whisperer was the police commissioner, we would never find out what is behind that wrinkled, yellow face of his."

The police coupé swung wide to miss a rattling cable car coming down the hill. Wildcat drove the little car into an alleyway and parked it close to a billboard.

Less than five minutes later, two odd figures emerged from the alleyway on the edge of the section that was almost as Chinese in architecture as the heart of Hong Kong.

Old Quick Trigger had made a hobby of disguise since retiring from the force. Strangely enough, he never had employed one when an active copper.

Now he was a bent, bearded old man, wearing colored glasses and thumping the sidewalk with a cane. One hand held onto an arm of Wildcat Gordon. But a queer transformation had taken place.

Wildcat was now The Whisperer. His red necktie, flashy clothes and yellow shoes had been swiftly replaced by a sober gray from head to foot. The odd dental plates slipped into his mouth had changed the whole contour of his square-jawed face. Now his chin was pointed, and his upper lip was lengthened.

A round hat with a round brim had replaced the cocky army headgear. Where his hair had been a brownish-red, it was now only a whitish blur under the round hat.

The Whisperer was only one of many thousands of inconspicuous men with no outstanding feature to be remembered. And as such he was known among many in Chinatown by the name of "Dunk" Smith. Lo Sing, the venerable exporter, was one he numbered as a friend.

AS THE WHISPERER and Quick Trigger came to the steep hill of Mall Street, with its one sidewalk and fog-slick cobblestones, not a single figure moved. Down below the hill there was still the occasional snapping of a package of firecrackers.

In some of the hidden banquet halls the Chinese celebrants of their New Year season would be consuming vast quantities of chop suey, chow mein and other Oriental delicacies.

At the New Year they gorged themselves, as if the remainder of the year might produce a famine.

The Whisperer said, in his low, husky tone, "There may be a hundred pairs of eyes upon us, but it is unusual that no one is abroad in the streets even at this hour. Notice that the Chinese have become scarcer as we have neared Lo Sing's place?"

"Reckon they know where the Hop Jo tong stuff would start," said Quick Trigger. "You think Lo Sing will talk to you, Wildcat?"

The Whisperer emitted a ghostly chuckle, the only laugh he could manage with the dental plates in his jaws.

"The venerable Lo Sing will gladly speak with his friend, Dunk Smith. Since I've had one of my hideouts in China Hill, I have been able to do Lo Sing a number of favors. A Chinaman may lie to you, and no doubt Lo Sing will lie to me, but nevertheless, he never forgets a favor."

Quick Trigger grunted that he did not see where this would gain any information for the police, if Lo Sing refused to tell the truth.

"You forget," stated The Whisperer, "that in this guise I am looked upon as a crook myself. But a crook that would not double-cross his friends."

The curving corners of the pagodalike roof of Lo Sing's house reared high in the gray fog. The front of the place showed no light, and the street lamps in narrow Mall Street were but white blurs in the mist, giving almost no ground illumination.

Near the importing house, The Whisperer glided abruptly to one side, entering a narrow passage between Lo Sing's building and the next.

Quick Trigger, in his role as the aged blind man, stumbled here and swore a little. There was room between the wall for perhaps four men to walk abreast, but an automobile could not have been driven through.

"It's one of several ways to reach the old yellow idol," stated The Whisperer. "Any one of these sunken places in the wall might open into one of the old tunnels. These remained after the big fire of years ago."

The Whisperer referred to a fire that had destroyed a major portion of the city nearly two score years before. Prior to that time, China Hill had been even more of a mystery than at this moment, for in those days trade in contraband goods had run high.

"Lo Sing's own entrance is at the end of this—"

The Whisperer was saying this to Quick Trigger when he ceased speaking and drew the older man close to one wall with silent hands. He hissed into an ear, "Be quiet! We are not alone! Perhaps we are just in time!"

The Whisperer's Texas eyes were almost colorless, but they were keen enough to pierce the fog. He saw three dark shadows, gliding along the wall near the Lo Sing entrance. This was a heavy wooden door set back in the stone.

THE WHISPERER'S prompt action prevented their being detected. The big wooden door creaked a little as it swung open. A light from inside showed a short, squat Chinaman who stepped into the passage and looked both ways.

The Chinese uttered some guttural words in his own language. He had one hand stuck into the loose sleeve of his blouse, apparently prepared for trouble, but perhaps thought he had been mistaken in the summons.

The Chinaman's turn to reenter the doorway was a grave mistake. One of the three shadows that had slunk to one side now leaped across the passage, his uplifted hand bearing a weapon that struck downward with terrific force. Old Quick Trigger grunted as the skull of the Chinaman crunched.

Beside Quick Trigger came a sudden, hissing sound, as if the escape valve of a compressed-air tank had been released. It was a high, whistling noise that filled the fog with a sound of death.

Even as the mobster's arm was flashing down and his weapon was making its impact with the Chinaman's head, The Whisperer had used one of his strangely silenced automatics. This was a weapon with a silencer so advanced that it gave forth no cracking whatever.

The man who had struck the Chinaman down whirled on his heels, an oath of pain filling the passageway. The hand with which he had hit the Oriental was shattered and bleeding. The wounded man followed his oath with a yell.

"They got me! Duck for cover! Look out for the hatchets!"

The Whisperer chuckled and sent more bullets deliberately high along one wall causing them to scream in that narrow space with the venomous threat of quick death. The man's words had indicated he and his companions feared the red hatchets of the Chinese more than any other weapon.

It is not a nice thought to imagine one's brains being spilled through a hole in the skull.

The three gunmen were uncertain for a few seconds from which direction the attack of the silenced automatic was coming. The Chinese who had been struck down had retained consciousness. In that interval of indecision, he scrambled to his feet and the heavy wooden door thudded shut.

The gunmen got their guns into action. Slugs split and whined upon the walls of stone. Old Quick Trigger produced a huge revolver, a relic of his active police days, and its booming caused echoes to resound.

The Whisperer gripped his arm and hissed, "Shoot over them! I don't want them hit! They must get out of here alive!"

"Great gravy!" exploded Quick Trigger. "You crazy, Wildcat?"

The Whisperer had a definite purpose.

At this instant, a hidden door opened softly in the niche where they had sheltered themselves from the flying bullets.

The three gunmen, one with an arm dangling, were cursing and seeking a position to rout out their mysterious attackers. Perhaps they believed they were Chinese. Suddenly the trio of mobsters halted as if gripped by an unseen giant hand.

Weird and high—penetrating to their ears though it was only a whispering voice—The Whisperer's warning filled the narrow passageway.

"Go back, you fools! Go back to Dollar Martino! Tell him his time has come! The Whisperer speaks!"

PERHAPS FIVE SECONDS of silence bound the three gunmen. One exclaimed, "The Whisperer! I'm getting out of here!"

His companions did not speak, but already they were reversing their movement, making for the other end of the passage.

Quick Trigger groaned, "Now you've done it, Wildcat! Why in time do you want to hook The Whisperer up with these heathen Chinese?"

The Whisperer's eerie chuckle of humor came with his reply.

"I hope to make this more interesting for Dollar Martino, and there's my friend, Henry Bolton. It may divert his mind from old Lo Sing and the red hatchets."

The door which had opened in the nitch behind Wildcat and Quick Trigger revealed a low, musty tunnel. Two solemn-faced Orientals stood under a vague light. Both inclined their heads to the quiet, gray man, but their sharp, black eyes scrutinized old Quick Trigger searchingly.

When The Whisperer employed a low voice, his weird whispering became husky words, as if he suffered from some affection of the throat.

"He is my friend," he said, indicating Quick Trigger. "His eyes do not see, and his ears hear nothing. You will conduct us to Lo Sing at once. I have important news for him."

When The Whisperer and Quick Trigger entered the opulent, draperied den of old Lo Sing, the Chinaman seemed to be sleeping in a thin, sweet vapor of incense. His drooping lids opened only a trifle over the black pools of his eyes.

"My good friend, Dunk Smith, this humble one has been expecting your coming," stated Lo Sing, dismissing the other Chinese with a wave of his long fingernails. "I have been grieved to learn that human blood again stains the cobblestones of Mall Street. Does my honorable friend know of these strange murders?"

"They are of little concern to me, Lo Sing," said The Whisperer, in his husky tone. "I cannot say I am displeased, for those who have died have long invited violent justice. I have been alarmed to discover the trail of blood seems to lead to the door of your peaceful house."

The complacent Lo Sing received this statement by the solemn folding of his hands.

"Perhaps there is one known as Dollar Martino who would have reason to shame the face of Lo Sing and cause suspicion to fall upon his house," he said blandly. "It might be the framing up of disgrace, but of that I have no fear. You have come, my friend Dunk Smith, and I alone in all China Hill know you are The Whisperer."

Old Quick Trigger did not like this. He would have liked very much to speak, but being blind and deaf, he made no sound.

"You are burning the incense to the last sun," stated The Whisperer suddenly. "Surely it could not be for the death of those commanded by Dollar Martino?"

"My friend is great and wise, and The Whisperer can do me a favor even tonight which only his extraordinary courage could accomplish," said Lo Sing.

"The incense to the last sun burns for death, but the greatest of knowledge cannot point truly where death will strike. As for these murders of the red hatchet, they seem to be the mark of the spirit of the Hop Jo, but I know nothing of their meaning."

The Whisperer was fully aware that old Lo Sing was lying. He was equally aware that Lo Sing knew he was not deceived. But that was one mark of their friendship, that the truth should be employed as one willed.

"This favor? Whatever it is, if it is within my power, it shall be done," pledged The Whisperer.

NEITHER THE WHISPERER nor Quick Trigger expected the bolt about to be exploded. The next words of old Lo Sing were to carry this case of the red hatchets into a sphere far removed from either China Hill or the Dollar Martino underworld mob.

"A good and respected friend has been marked by Dollar Martino, in what manner and for what purpose I do not know," said Lo Sing. "But within the hour there will be emissaries of Dollar Martino in the house of Andrew Lundin on the great hill. Perhaps they go there to rob the strongbox of my respected friend. Only the quickest of action may prevent this outrage."

Old Quick Trigger's grunted oath gave plain evidence he was not a deaf man. Old Lo Sing apparently gave this no attention. The wily Chinaman with his masklike yellow face probably had not been deceived in the least about either Quick Trigger's sight or hearing.

The Whisperer did not speak for several seconds. The name "Andrew Lundin" was one that carried great weight. A millionaire owner of coastal ships, a civic leader and a highly respected citizen, it still was not remarkable that Lo Sing should count him as a friend.

Andrew Lundin, The Whisperer recalled, traded in a variety of imports and exports of the character that would pass through this Lo Sing house on China Hill.

Neither was it amazing that Andrew Lundin's house should have been marked for a robbery, if indeed a robbery was being planned. The henchmen of Dollar Martino might be expected to attempt such a theft, though the racketeer's mobsters for the most part followed the simpler methods of extorting money by their own rackets.

The Whisperer did not quite swallow all that Lo Sing had said. Even when Lo Sing added his direct reason for this knowledge, it did not quite make sense.

"My son, Lo Wun, has the honor of being houseboy in the home of Andrew Lundin," stated Lo Sing. "From him I have learned that this visit will be made by the emissaries of Dollar Martino. Perhaps the police should be informed, my friend, but I would not keep face if the word seemed to come from me."

Quick Trigger was thinking, the crafty, old scoundrel. He is too smart to make any direct contact with the police. The Whisperer may have been thinking along the same line. For he had not for a minute imagined but that Lo Sing knew all about the red hatchet murders.

One of the last resorts of any Chinese, especially this wise Lo Sing, would be to appeal to the police. Then there must be some reason why Lo Sing wished the police to visit the home of Andrew Lundin.

Lo Sing might be the friend of Andrew Lundin, as he claimed, or in his oblique way he might be Lundin's deadly enemy.

CHAPTER IV
A MILLIONAIRE'S SECRET

LO SING had said that within the hour, and it was now well after midnight, Dollar Martino's men might be expected to rob the home of the respected millionaire, Andrew Lundin. But this was considerably more important to Police Commissioner Wildcat Gordon than the hatchet extinction of any of Martino's thugs.

Also, the unexpected, oblique tip-off coming from the smart old Lo Sing undoubtedly had complications kept secret behind the yellow, wrinkled face of the Chinese exporter. Nevertheless, Lo Sing knew nothing of Dunk Smith's, of The Whisperer's, double identity.

At least, The Whisperer hoped Lo Sing did not suspect the truth; but he admitted to himself that to be sure of that any man would have to know much more of the Chinese mind than he ever hoped to learn. The important move at this moment was to follow out Lo Sing's tip as if he believed the Chinaman implicitly.

The Whisperer wasted no time reaching the foggy darkness of Mall Street, with Quick Trigger grumbling beside him.

"I tell you, Wildcat, you're just playing some game that wrinkled yellow devil wants you to play," he protested. "It's bad enough getting mixed up as The Whisperer with this China Hill feud, whatever it is, but when it comes to roping in a citizen of importance like Andrew Lundin, I'd think twice."

"I've thought more than twice," stated The Whisperer. "I'll have a police stakeout around the Lundin estate within ten minutes, if Sergeant Thorsen is still on the job. You will go on home, and tell Tiny not to keep the coffee hot for me."

"Tiny" was Tiny Traeger, the pretty granddaughter of Quick Trigger. A doll-like girl, who had only recently grown up, she was very much in love with the hard-boiled Wildcat Gordon. This affection may have been all on one side, but nevertheless, Tiny Traeger always waited up for Wildcat, and kept a pot of coffee on the stove.

Tiny knew nothing of Wildcat's exploits as The Whisperer, whom she regarded as a dangerous crook. She did, however, know the gray little man called Dunk Smith, believing him to be a friend of her grandfather and Wildcat.

Quick Trigger left The Whisperer in a lower street of China Hill. The Whisperer drove swiftly out of the Chinese district, wishing his call to headquarters to go out from some other than the Chinese exchange. If Henry Bolton happened to get that call, a tip-off of trouble at the Andrew Lundin home, it would promptly be traced to China Hill.

The Whisperer entered a downtown drugstore and slipped into a telephone booth. He observed it was now after two o'clock in the morning. If Lo Sing's information were correct, perhaps it was already too late to prepare a stakeout at the Andrew Lundin home.

Inside the phone booth, The Whisperer's voice became that of Wildcat Gordon by the simple expedient of removing the odd dental plates from his mouth.

Wildcat swore under his breath when he got direct contact with Deputy Henry Bolton, but he had been informed Sergeant Thorsen was out with a squad on the hatchet murder of Breezy Taro. There was no time for delay.

"Get a four-squad stakeout on the home of Andrew Lundin!" ordered Wildcat, crisply. "Don't ask fool questions, Henry! Ease your men into the neighborhood and don't arrive blowing the sirens! I have been informed Andrew Lundin may have visitors, and I want them trapped in the act of breaking into the house! So hide your men!"

Deputy Henry Bolton disliked taking direct orders from Wildcat Gordon. His unpleasant voice started to argue.

"Shut up!" snapped Wildcat. "Get going! I'll be watching!"

He did not inform Henry Bolton it would be The Whisperer and not Wildcat Gordon in person watching at the Lundin residence.

A FEW MINUTES later, The Whisperer parked the coupé under the hill on which was located the wall-enclosed estate of the millionaire, Andrew Lundin.

Deputy Bolton might have employed the greatest of care in placing his stakeout, but The Whisperer knew his methods too well to blunder into any of the four squads of coppers.

The great house of Andrew Lundin appeared to be dark, as a house should be at that foggy hour in the morning. But The Whisperer moved through his own police lines so silently and cautiously that he went over the wall and into the grounds within a few yards of two of his own best detectives.

From inside, it could be seen that two big windows back of a second-floor balcony had lights burning behind them. The shades of these windows had been drawn, but it was evident that someone was waiting up or the lights had been forgotten.

The Whisperer glided noiselessly through the shrubbery, gaining a position where he had a view of two car entrances and the front of the house. His own silenced guns were ready. He would have liked nothing better than to have come upon any of Dollar Martino's men in the act of direct robbery.

"It doesn't sound reasonable," said The Whisperer to himself. "Martino's much too smart to have housebreaking or the cracking of a safe pinned on any of his mob. Lo Sing's got something up that embroidered sleeve of his, or he wouldn't want the police called into this thing."

The Whisperer could hear some of his stakeout policemen moving restlessly. They had established a perfect trap, however, and none but The Whisperer himself could ever have gained his position close to the house.

Lo Sing had said Andrew Lundin's residence would be visited within the hour. The Whisperer noted that the hour had almost passed.

From what direction would Dollar Martino's men approach? Most certainly they might be expected to come over the high wall at some spot away from the front entrance, which was brightly illuminated by two electric globes.

The Whisperer, as Henry Bolton and all of His coppers must have been, was amazed at what then happened. A big, new car came up the hill directly to the front driveway of the Andrew Lundin place. It was driven in through the gate and swung along the circle of the driveway to the front door of the residence.

Two men alighted from the car, both smoking cigars and making no pretense whatever of lowering their voices or otherwise acting in a furtive manner. Both men walked up the front steps, and The Whisperer could hear the strident buzzer sounding inside the house.

The staked-out coppers very apparently were mystified. The Whisperer could hear some of them moving through the grounds, converging upon the big car in the driveway. There was no doubt of the identity of these visitors.

"PORKY" GRATH and Joe Hilton were known as the leading aides of Dollar Martino. In off moments, they acted as dealers in his Iola Club. Their chief business was the same as that of the murdered Stringer Durkin and Opium Peters, racket collectors and triggermen.

Grath and Hilton, however, had a little more polish of manner and attire than either Durkin or Peters had possessed.

Nevertheless, they were mobsters of the most dangerous order and henchmen of the owner of the Iola Club. Despite this, even as the staked-out police swung to hedge in the car in the driveway, the Andrew Lunclin front door was opened by a tall butler.

This butler was fully clothed, and there could be no doubt but that he was awaiting these visitors.

"The master is expecting you, gentlemen," came the butler's greeting.

"Sure! Sure!" growled one of Martino's men. "You don't have to tell us!"

The dignified butler made no reply, but the door closed upon the strange early morning guests.

"Now what the hell an' all do you think of that?" grated the voice of Deputy Henry Bolton from the shrubbery nearby. "Just one more time Wildcat Gordon's putting something over on us! Where is he, an' what's the gag? Well, this time, I'm going to know what's what!"

The Whisperer did not hear all of this, for he was gliding silently toward the mass of heavy vines under the balcony where the two windows showed lights. He was climbing toward the balcony, hand-over-hand, when Henry Bolton reached the car Martino's men had left in the driveway.

The car contained no extra driver. Deputy Bolton snapped out an order to half a dozen of the nearest coppers.

"It looks all right, but anytime Dollar Martino's mugs walk into a millionaire's home, I'm finding out more about it! Come on! We're going in!"

The butler was quick to answer the second summons to the door, but his welcome was not the same as it had been for Martino's men. He made a quick attempt to close the door against Bolton and the detectives following him.

Deputy Bolton jammed the door open, one lanky hand grabbing the butler's collar.

"Now, you conduct us right along up where them other mugs went!" he rapped out. "Maybe you're in on this, an' it's a damn' clever setup to walk off with the family jewels! But you ain't foolin' Henry Bolton for a minute!"

The shaking butler walked ahead with Bolton's hand still fastened in his collar. From the door of a room upstairs a man's voice said, "What is it, Parsons? You haven't let anyone else come in?"

"He didn't let us, but we're in!" snapped Henry Bolton. "Maybe you don't know who you're entertainin' right now—"

THE WHISPERER had reached the balcony of the double, lighted windows before Deputy Bolton and his men had gained entrance. Though the shades were drawn, there was a crack through which the interior of a library room could be fully observed.

The Whisperer identified Andrew Lundin sitting at his desk. The millionaire was a small man, slight of figure, with thin, blue-veined hands. It seemed that his hair must have been prematurely gray, for Andrew Lundin was not an old man and he had been for several years a most forceful figure in civic affairs.

Now The Whisperer noticed that Lundin's tapering fingers were drumming upon his desk and he was looking at the door as Porky Grath and Joe Hilton appeared. Moreover, the millionaire spoke and nodded with every indication he had been expecting these strange visitors.

Porky Grath's first words filtered to The Whisperer.

"You all ready, big shot? It's a helluva an hour to have to be callin'!"

"I'm ready, of course," came the reply of Andrew Lundin, and The Whisperer knew the words were short and clipped, as if there was something the millionaire shipping man wanted to get over with.

There was a packet lying on the desk that might have contained money or something else. The fellow Joe Hilton started to say something, when Andrew Lundin raised one hand. Deputy Bolton had nailed the butler at the downstairs door.

Lundin arose quickly from his desk and went through the door.

Joe Hilton growled after him: "Now what the hell? Whatever it is, Lundin, watch what you say!"

Deputy Henry Bolton came pounding up the stairs, shoved the butler into the library and strode inside. Two detectives stood at the door.

"Damned if it ain't the cops!" grated Porky Grath. "So you've—"

Andrew Lundin was standing in the middle of the library, staring at the detectives. He interrupted Grath's speech quickly and angrily.

"I'll handle this, Grath!"

The millionaire faced Deputy Henry Bolton. He did not need an introduction.

"Suppose you tell me, Mr. Bolton, to what I'm indebted for this intrusion in my home?"

Deputy Bolton's Adam's apple jumped up and down in his scrawny throat.

"Why—say, Mr. Lundin! You couldn't be knowin' who these men are! We had a tip-off—that is, I had an order from Wildcat Gordon to come up here and—"

The Whisperer was listening intently. He saw an angry red fade from Andrew Lundin's thin face, but the millionaire's attitude was unchanged.

"Wildcat Gordon, eh?" rapped out Lundin. "Well, Wildcat Gordon or no other person has any right to intrude on my own private affairs! What is it you want? Certainly I know these men, and they are here on business which doesn't concern the police department in the least!"

The Whisperer saw a quick glance pass between Grath and Hilton.

Grath said, "You tell them, big shot, and we'll be easin' along! I'll take the stuff with me! So Wildcat Gordon sent you, copper? He'll be sendin' his little tin soldiers into the wrong business conference someday and they'll get all their solder burned off 'em—"

"Never mind it, Grath and Hilton," interrupted Andrew Lundin. "We'll discuss the matter some other time. This intrusion will have my whole family awake."

AS Grath and Hilton threw leering grins at the amazed Deputy Bolton and went out, Bolton said, "Maybe we're in the wrong, Mr. Lundin, but when Dollar Martino's mugs go visiting, it's a good idea to know why they pick on a millionaire's home."

Andrew Lundin put up both hands in an amazed attitude.

"Dollar Martino?" he exclaimed. "You must be mistaken, Mr. Bolton! Why, my business with these men couldn't in any way indicate they've ever had any connection with Martino! There's a big mistake somewhere!

"Anyway, I don't want to discuss the subject at this hour, so if you gentlemen will take my word for it, my private business is no affair of the police!"

"I wish you'd tell that to Wildcat Gordon," grunted Deputy Bolton.

"I shall do just that," promised Andrew Lundin. "Dollar Martino's men? That couldn't be possible!"

The Whisperer waited to hear no more. He heard the car carrying Grath and Joe Hilton crunching gravel as it swung from Andrew Lundin's grounds.

There was no time to speculate upon the fantastic affair, or the motive the crafty Lo Sing might have had in causing a police descent upon the supposedly law-abiding civic leader at a time when he was entertaining a pair of the city's best-known public enemies.

The Whisperer had decided there was about to be an automobile collision. He knew that if Deputy Bolton had been smart enough, he might have figured there could be something in the package taken from Andrew Lundin's desk which would interest the police.

CHAPTER V
ANOTHER LAST RIDE

THE WHISPERER had decided to get that package. It was difficult to believe that the respectable Andrew Lundin could be involved with the rackets of Dollar Martino. Yet stranger collusions had been uncovered in these days when anyone from a judge on the bench to a banker in his office might suddenly be summoned before a rackets grand jury.

No better pose could be adopted by any nefarious citizen than that of a leader on the side of civic virtue. But as Wildcat Gordon, The Whisperer had always regarded Andrew Lundin as one of the best. Perhaps the contents of that package in the hands of Martino's aides might supply some explanations.

Henry Bolton was withdrawing his stakeout, and his language was hardly printable. The Whisperer glided noiselessly along the wall, making for a spot where it would be easy to cross and reach his coupé. He judged Grath and Hilton would be driving directly to the Iola Club to see Dollar Martino.

Things would begin to pop when Martino learned Wildcat Gordon had sent a police squad on a futile raid at the Lundin home. The Whisperer caught the edge of the wall and started pulling himself over. He could see his coupé where he had parked it and he eluded the stakeout coppers and made his way toward it.

Having gained the coupé undetected, The Whisperer planned to cut down a cable-car street to the waterfront and intercept Grath and Hilton. His hand was on the door of his car when half a dozen shadowy figures seemed to arise from the ground.

The Whisperer saw that all were Chinese, and that all had half-wrinkled faces; proving they were not young men. He started to lash out at the nearest Chinaman with one fist, but the man eluded him swiftly; the others closed in so rapidly, he realized the uselessness of fighting now.

The Chinese displayed no weapons, but long cords suddenly appeared in their hands and were whipped from man to man. Before The Whisperer could move aside, he was being tightly bound in the queerest form of attack he had ever experienced.

"If Lo Sing sent you, you'd better drop it!" he hissed, in his eerie, penetrating whisper.

The Chinaman who spoke was as calm as Lo Sing himself might have been.

"Be quiet, and you will not be harmed," he stated. "It will be only for a little while."

The cords had been wound around The Whisperer's arms, binding them to his sides. A saturated cloth now was thrown over his head and drawn around his throat. He realized instantly there was little sense in delaying his breathing.

The sweetish odor of the damp cloth quickly did its work. The Whisperer then ceased to know what was happening or where he was being taken. But his last conscious thought was that he had been played for a sucker by the wily Lo Sing.

THE WHISPERER had no means of knowing whether it had been minutes or an hour or more that he had been sitting unconscious in his small coupé. The little car was no longer parked close to the wall of the Andrew Lundin estate, but had been driven into an alley lower down on the hill.

In a minute, The Whisperer knew nothing but his removal from the vicinity of the Lundin home had happened. His silenced automatics were in place and nothing about his clothing or the coupé had been molested.

**Before The Whisperer could move aside, he was being tightly bound
in the queerest form of attack he had ever experienced.**

"Maybe I'm lucky not to be wearing a red hatchet in my hair," he grinned to himself. "But now Lo Sing is going to talk plenty."

His foot pressed the starter. At that instant the scream of a police siren cut into the early morning darkness. It was quickly followed by a second and a third. That meant some sort of general alarm.

The Whisperer backed the little car from the alley. He saw then that he had not been taken many blocks from Andrew Lundin's residence. The hillside streets here were narrow and crooked, following original lines mapped out back in horse-and-buggy days.

The police sirens indicated the squad cars were converging at a point no more than two blocks distant. The Whisperer knew it was too late to take up the pursuit of Grath and Hilton with their mysterious package.

He swept off his round-brimmed hat, moved zippers on his shoes and clothes. His army hat came out, and the whitish effect left his hair. A carnation came from a car pocket and with it a red necktie.

In one minute, Police Commissioner Wildcat Gordon was sending his coupé shooting toward the scene of the latest alarm. He drove the little car through a knot of citizens and policemen, sprang out and pushed his way to the sedan that had split its hood around a fireplug, causing a flood of water to pour down the street.

But the coppers were not engaged with the fireplug breakage. Two men sitting in the front seat of the wrecked sedan were stiff corpses. Their hair had been neatly parted in the middle, but this treatment was permanent.

Two red-handled hatchets were sticking in the skulls of Porky Grath and Joe Hilton. Another pair of Dollar Martino's nice boys had joined what had become a grisly funeral procession.

In a minute, Wildcat Gordon knew the police had not found the package taken from the Andrew Lundin home.

He had not expected they would. He was fully aware now why half a dozen wrinkled Chinamen had gathered him in and put him temporarily out of the way.

MAYOR VAN ROYSTON himself had arrived on the scene. He confronted Wildcat, his silk topper slightly out of line. The mayor was in an excited state that was bad for his blood pressure Also, he was a little sick after looking into the open, bugging eyes of Porky Grath and Joe Hilton.

"Deputy Bolton informs me, Commissioner Gordon, that you caused him to insult one of our leading citizens and party supporters!" said the irate mayor. "What is all this about raiding Andrew Lundin's home without authority, and causing the men of your department to be humiliated? What have these—these men in the car got to do with that wild order of yours?"

Wildcat flicked a petal off his red carnation and pulled his army hat over one cold eye.

"You might ask the men in the car, Mayor Van Royston," Wildcat suggested ironically. "If Henry had been a little smarter, he could have nabbed these Martino thugs outside and frisked them. In that case, though, they wouldn't have had their hair parted, so I'm glad Henry's no smarter than he ought to be."

Deputy Henry Bolton blurted out, "This is what I'm compelled to take, Mayor Van Royston! Gordon knows all about these men, or he wouldn't have sent us to the Lundin home! I demand to know why he made a fool out of me!"

"I agree, Deputy Bolton!" said Mayor Van Royston, in a firm tone. "Commissioner Gordon, I demand to now why you made a fool out of—"

"That goes much farther back than my acquaintance with Henry," interrupted Wildcat quietly. "I would suggest that you clean up this mess and add these little red hatchets to your collection. I know just as much about this as you do, Mayor Van Royston, but I'm on my way to find out some more."

"But—but—"

Mayor Van Royston was sputtering at the disappearing back of his hardboiled police commissioner. Wildcat was sliding into his coupé, and the little car roared away around a side street.

Wildcat was doing a juggling act with his thoughts and with his personal appearance. As swiftly as he had become the commissioner, he again was the gray Whisperer.

His juggled thoughts tossed up Lo Sing, Dollar Martino, Andrew Lundin and a few red hatchet Chinamen. But any way he juggled them and let them fall back into place, there seemed to be but one logical conclusion:

The wily Lo Sing had deliberately played his friend, The Whisperer, for a sucker. There must be a bitter feud between the Chinaman in his China Hill den and the millionaire shipping magnate in his park-surrounded home high above the bay.

That feud in some manner involved Dollar Martino and his crowd, and Lo Sing must have hoped to have the police trap Andrew Lundin in conference with the now very dead racketeer's triggermen.

Still, that did not altogether make sense, in view of a certain confidence The Whisperer had come to place in the wrinkled Chinese exporter. Plainly enough, The Whisperer had been safeguarded against his will from running into the latest red-hatchet murders.

The Whisperer considered grimly that Porky Grath and Joe Hilton would never inform Dollar Martino of the strange raid of the coppers at the Lundin home. But possibly that fact already had been communicated to Martino by Lundin himself.

Well, that was a little matter that came up as the first order of business.

The Whisperer was on his way to find out more about Andrew Lundin. His coupé turned a corner under the Lundin wall.

Yes, the lights still glowed behind the windows of the millionaire's library. In the final hour before dawn, The Whisperer glided into the grounds and, five minutes later, was pulling himself onto the balcony outside the library windows.

Excited voices were coming through the ventilating screen in the window. The clear but intense tone of a woman was distinct.

"But what in the world was it, Andrew? Why must these men come here in the night? What was it those policemen were saying? You may think I don't know those terribly vulgar men have been here before, but I have heard them and said nothing."

THE WHISPERER could see a stately, beautiful woman whose hair was only slightly touched with gray. The wife of Andrew Lundin appeared much younger than he, as though she had led a sheltered existence.

Beside Mrs. Andrew Lundin was a willowy, graceful girl whose brown hair and brown eyes gave her a beauty that must have been like that of her mother twenty years before. The Whisperer knew this was Nellie Lundin, whose advent into society had recently been in the society pages.

"Please, father?" came the girl's vibrant voice. "Mother and I were listening, and you know if you are in some trouble we want to help you."

Andrew Lundin was seated at his desk. It seemed to The Whisperer that the millionaire tried to put an angry note into his tone, but it did not serve to cover the fear behind his words.

"I'm sorry, my dear, very sorry you have been disturbed," he said heavily. "But it really was nothing. I've always had trouble with the seamen's union, you'll remember, and these men have been working for me to get it fixed up. The police made a mistake."

The Whisperer had to admit to himself it was a good explanation, whether true or untrue. Andrew Lundin was the head of shipping interests that employed many men.

The Dollar Martino angle could enter into labor trouble, for the Iola Club racketeer was not one to overlook any bet where promised "protection" would get him a few dollars more.

"But what were the police saying about that infamous Dollar Martino, Andrew?" insisted his wife. "I know little about your business, but I cannot think of any reason why you should become entangled in any way with a man the newspapers say is one of our worst public enemies."

"I tell you, my dear!" came the sudden shouting voice of Andrew Lundin, "that I know nothing of any connection with Dollar Martino and these men! Mr. Grath and Mr. Hilton are influential with the seamen's organization and I have had to use them to keep my ships moving!"

"Why, Andrew! You're excited! You've never spoken to me like that before!"

Mrs. Andrew Lundin stared at her husband as if she hardly believed he had been shouting at her.

The Whisperer's gaze suddenly crossed the lighted library and picked out the half-opened door. The smooth, yellow face of a youthful Chinaman had appeared there, the light catching his black, shining eyes.

The Whisperer was aware this must be Lo Wun, the houseboy, and the son of old Lo Sing. Lo Sing had told him he had his information about the visit of the Dollar Martino men from this houseboy. At this moment, Lo Wun was plainly eavesdropping at the door.

Andrew Lundin said, "Forgive me," to his wife, and added: "Now, I think all of us should get some sleep. Nellie, you don't look well for the party you are giving tomorrow; no, it's already today."

The millionaire's modulated tone did not deceive The Whisperer. There was the hint of deepest fear in his voice, and it was noticeable enough to cause his stately wife to continue staring at him.

At that moment the telephone on the library desk rang sharply. Andrew Lundin picked up the instrument.

"What? What?" he exclaimed. "Grath and Hilton? You must be mistaken, Mayor Van Royston! That's terrible! Just a minute, Mayor Van Royston!"

Lundin's blanched face was turned toward his wife and daughter. "Please go to your rooms," he said, in a stricken voice. "There's been—well, the men who were here have been robbed and—and hurt."

UNDER THIS STRESS, Mrs. Lundin put an arm about her daughter and they left the library. The Whisperer knew that Mayor Van Royston himself had called Andrew Lundin concerning the murders of Grath and Hilton. The mayor would prevent, if possible, any police questioning of the millionaire.

This was just as well for the time, The Whisperer decided. As the shaken man was getting more details from the solicitous Mayor Van Royston, and Mrs. Lundin and the suddenly trembling girl were leaving the library, the yellow face of Lo Wun faded from the doorway.

The Whisperer would have listened to more of Lundin's conversation, but a few seconds after Lo Wun vanished, a light flashed on in a room on the first floor at the back of the house. It was apparent that this downstairs section must house the servants.

The Whisperer climbed noiselessly down the vines. He glided on his softsoled shoes along the house wall toward the room that had just been illuminated. Crouching beside a window, he could see under a shade.

The spying houseboy, Lo Wun, had picked up a telephone at the far side of the room and was dialing a number. The Whisperer saw a wire coming down close to the window. He whipped a compact instrument from one pocket.

This was like a lineman's telephone, with steel clips. The clips bit through the insulation of the phone wires and The Whisperer clamped the earpieces to his head.

CHAPTER VI
LO SING'S STRANGE PLOT

THE WHISPERER'S telephone tapping device brought the soft, slow voice of the houseboy, Lo Wun, the young son of Lo Sing, clearly to his ears! Lo Wun was in his own small room. He had carefully closed the door behind him.

"I have received the package, honorable father," said Lo Wun, in meticulous English. "Tonight the time has come. Because of the happenings I have seen and heard in the house of Andrew Lundin, we can delay no longer."

The Whisperer heard the reply in the calm, unemotional voice of old So Ling. He could picture the Chinaman with his wrinkled, yellow face sitting calmly in all his fat in the carved chair that looked like a dais.

"Perhaps it is the time, my son," stated Lo Sing. "But this humble one must first consult with the most worthy eighteen. Remain close by, Lo Wun, for my instructions. You must be careful in all that you do not to draw down the suspicion of the police. Especially, my son, you must avoid my friend, Dunk Smith. The Whisperer is a most wise person."

Lo Wun's reply implied full obedience to his father's wishes.

"I shall await the word of the most worthy eighteen," he said. "I am prepared for what may come, but it is a time, honorable father, when delay may cost us much."

The Whisperer unclipped his wiretapping device. The strange conversation he had just heard might mean almost anything. Plainly enough, Lo Wun was nothing more than a spy for his wily father in the house of the millionaire.

But who were the "most worthy eighteen"?

The Whisperer's thoughts went instantly to the red-hatchet murders. The worthy eighteen? In the past among those considered the most worthy by their fellow Orientals were the tong wielders of the hatchets.

The red-handled hatchets were the mark of the supposedly disbanded Hop Jo tong. The men who had so strangely attacked The Whisperer with binding cords and their stupefying cloth over his head had been old men with wrinkled faces.

Could it be possible these were aged survivors of the once-dreaded Hop Jo tong? A worthy eighteen?

Thus far, the red hatchets had struck only at the men of Dollar Martino. But clearly there was some mysterious association of Martino and the well-known civic leader, Andrew Lundin.

Lo Sing now became The Whisperer's goal. If the aged Chinaman was about to consult with his "most worthy eighteen," he wanted very much to find out more about that meeting.

THE LIGHTS in Andrew Lundin's library had snapped out. Now the houseboy, Lo Wun, darkened his room. The Whisperer would have been much less sure of himself if he had seen Lo Wun's window softly raised.

The Chinese houseboy's slim yellow hand moved along the edge of the window. His fingers touched the telephone wires, feeling of the punctures where The Whisperer's tapping steel clippers had penetrated. Lo Wun softly closed his window and his room remained in darkness.

The Whisperer was gliding swiftly toward the wall around the estate. In spite of Mayor Van Royston's call, he considered it likely that Andrew Lundin might still receive a visit from the police.

Deputy Henry Bolton was an efficient copper, in his unpleasant way. He might decide to have a little talk of his own with the millionaire about these latest murders.

The Whisperer came to a space on the wall where vines grew thickly. His steel-wire hands gripped the climbers and he started to climb. He neither saw nor heard any one move, but a numbing blow rapped his head.

The attacker missed in the darkness, but some blunt instrument came down sharply on one of the Whisperer's shoulders, loosening his hold on the vines and bringing him to the ground.

The Whisperer continued falling as if his brain had been numbed. But his body turned and he landed on his hands and toes. The bulk of his assailant was outlined as The Whisperer snapped all of his weight upward.

One exploding fist caught the man whose face was invisible, and this fellow smashed into the wall and slid to the ground. Because of thick trees near by, the space was too dark for The Whisperer to determine whether his attacker was white or yellow.

He was bending over the fallen man, getting out his flashlight, when the crushing weight of another man came from the top of the wall. The new arrival's knees thudded into The Whisperer's back high up, close to the joining of the spine with his neck. A spine of less tough seasoning would have snapped.

As it was, The Whisperer pitched forward, the top of his head crashing against the stone wall. He fell unconscious across the figure of the first man he had knocked out. For all he had been able to see before blackness enfolded him, his assailants might have been either white men or Chinese.

SHORTLY AFTER The Whisperer was temporarily removed from consciousness in the darkness of the hour before dawn, the brown-eyed Nellie Lundin kissed her mother and went to her room farther along the second-floor corridor. Being youthful, the girl was less worried than Mrs. Lundin over the mysterious visits to her father.

Later today, Miss Nellie Lundin was to be hostess at a party. She needed what little sleep she might manage during the early morning hours. Having gone to her father's library with a fleecy negligee pulled over her nightdress, the girl closed her door softly and walked directly to the canopied bed.

She did not trouble to snap on the lights, a glance assuring her that the window was lifted against its screen the proper distance for good ventilation.

If she had employed the lights or even looked more closely, she would have seen that the open window was in the position she had left it earlier in the night, but that there now was no screen.

By failing to touch the light switch, Nellie Lundin possibly saved herself from a knockout blow. For as she moved toward her bed, the raised arm of a figure standing inside her door was slowly lowered. The uplifted hand had gripped a blackjack, prepared for a stunning attack.

As it was, the motionless figure stayed close by the wall as the girl drew the covers of the bed to her chin and closed her eyes. She would not have dropped so quickly to sleep if she had known of the intruder, or of two other shadows flattened against the wall close under the window balcony.

Though daylight was not faraway, these waiting men had the wisdom of patience. A girl awake would scream. But sleeping, her cries may be so swiftly smothered as to create no alarm.

Nellie Lundin did not scream, or hardly more than sigh deeply and struggle for the brief part of a minute when a strong hand clamped a moist cloth over her face, and its companion hand used a soft pillow to further throttle any possible outcry.

In less than a full minute, the millionaire's daughter was tightly wrapped in covers from her own bed and was being silently lowered from her window balcony into the hands of men waiting below. Except for the disturbed bed and the removed window screen, there was no evidence of the girl's room having been disturbed.

THE FIRST STREAKS of dawn were coming over the hills above the bay, and the night fog was breaking up. A heavy, closed car rounded a corner at high speed, narrowly missing one of the small, hill-climbing cable cars. The street was roughly paved with cobblestones, and the big car jolted and swayed.

The Whisperer was brought back to his senses by the thumping of the car's floor against the back of his head. His first discovery was that his body was jammed down back of the front seat and the feet of two men were resting roughly upon him.

With infinite caution The Whisperer moved his hands as soon as the blinding pain of his head had cleared a bit. But he found that his silenced automatics had been removed. Apparently he had been tossed quickly into the car after being knocked out by the Andrew Lundin wall.

He knew he could not have been unconscious for many minutes, for that would have given his captors time to have reached whatever destination they were seeking. But now The Whisperer could hear muttering voices, though the words were indistinct.

He felt the sickening skid of the big car as it swung on squealing tires around another corner, and that instant came the cutting, shrill scream of a police siren. The Whisperer thought whimsically this must be his night for getting himself knocked out and being awakened by the calls of his own squad cars.

The siren's scream might have been a block or two away and was behind the big car. Suddenly a second siren cut in, coming from one side. Another and another joined in. A hard voice of a man in the rear seat spoke to the driver.

"This is a helluva time to make a mistake, Pete! I told you we should cut straight down to the bay! Now you're headin' right into a trap! Hey! There's a red headlight coming into the block up there!"

At this instant, The Whisperer was thankful for the warning red light of the police car. Ordinarily, he opposed this warning light along with the screaming sirens, which he declared advertised the coming of police to all the crooks in any neighborhood. But at this time, he did not in the least desire to have his captors trapped by his own police with himself a prisoner in the car.

He now had no opportunity to transform himself into Wildcat Gordon, and being dragged out by the coppers as The Whisperer was not a pleasant thought.

One of the men moved his feet from his body, but at the same time he jammed what undoubtedly was the snout of a pistol into his back.

"We'd better give him the works!" this man growled. "We don't know who the damn' mug is, but he must know somethin' or he wouldn't have been prowlin' around the big shot's hangout!"

The Whisperer was helpless. Nothing he could do would have saved him from the prodding automatic. But the driver who had been called Pete seemed to have a more level head.

"Hell, no!" he snapped back at his companions.

"Lay offa the rod, you sap! Want us to get messed up in a murder rap? We're leaving him as he is! Get set, I'm smackin' 'er!"

None of at least three squad cars could have been more than a block away. It was apparent the police were looking for someone, possibly this big car. Or, at least, the driver seemed to think they were marked.

THE BIG CAR jumped a sidewalk curb, skidding on the morning dampness of a lawn and came to rest with a hard thud against a tree. The driver, Pete, was the first out.

"C'mon, you mugs!" he rapped out. "Haul that egg out of there an' dump him over behind that hedge!"

The Whisperer closed his eyes and remained limp. Hard hands pulled him outside. He could tell now there were four men in the party. Pete took command, and The Whisperer's body was carried for a few yards, then tossed behind a low hedge.

Pete ordered, "Lam across lots! There's a phony number on the bus! Anyway, we've pulled the cops off the trail!"

Two squad cars shot headlight beams across the lawn and picked up the abandoned car beside the tree. The coppers poured across the sidewalk, shouting, but the men who had been in the big car had faded out between the houses.

The Whisperer lay behind the hedge where he had been thrown. He had got an unexpected break and he was playing it. Deputy Henry Bolton was in a third squad car that squawled to a stop, and the deputy's unpleasant voice spoke:

"What you fellows got here? Smacked-up car, huh? Maybe, some joyriders! Didn't you pick up the radio calls?"

The occupants of the other cars admitted they had not received any radio calls, one driver explaining they had spotted the abandoned car speeding and that they were still on the lookout for the mysterious hatchet murderers.

"Hatchets, the devil!" shouted Deputy Bolton. "There's a general alarm out! Headquarters just got a call from Andrew Lundin's house! Mrs. Lundin has reported their daughter has been snatched right out of her own bedroom! We're on the way up there, an' all of you get out and block every car movin' on this side of town!"

The swift examination of the abandoned car revealed nothing. The Whisperer did not move as his coppers poured back into their machines. He was remembering the conversation of Lo Wun and Lo Sing.

Nellie Lundin had been abducted. There seemed to be only one answer to that. The worthy eighteen must have spoken.

CHAPTER VII
THE SILENT MILLIONAIRE

LESS THAN half an hour after he was roughly tossed over the low hedge beside an abandoned car, The Whisperer had removed his dental plates and transformed himself into Police Commissioner Wildcat Gordon. He had worked so swiftly, that his startling blue suit, his new red necktie and glowing carnation all had the evidence of fresh morning dress.

Wildcat climbed from his police coupé and threaded his way through several squad cars to the front entrance of the Andrew Lundin home. The tall butler, called Parsons; was firmly barring the doorway against a dozen clamoring newspaper reporters and photographers.

Wildcat Gordon pushed the newspapermen aside, giving them a cheerful, "Good morning, boys; I'll see what I can do."

Wildcat always promised the reporters he would see what he could do when they were on the trail of a hot story. But when it came to getting information from the police commissioner, he was about as useful to the headlines as the proverbial clam.

The police commissioner went up the stairs to Andrew Lundin's library. He saw Mrs. Lundin sitting, white-faced, in a side room, with several women comforting her. Through the closed library door came Deputy Bolton's harsh voice.

"You'll play ball with us, Lundin, whether you want to or not! I ain't for coverin' up on any snatch racket! I want to know who you suspect and all about it! It looks like an inside job to me! So you'd better loosen up!"

Wildcat halted, listening a moment.

"I'm not opposing the police," Andrew Lundin stated. "It isn't that! But I'm going to handle this in my own way! It's my daughter, and whatever is demanded, I'll give my last cent to have her back unharmed! Flatly, I'll have nothing to do with the police in this!"

"That's what you think, Lundin!" snapped Deputy Bolton. "Why were we called in then? It's all hooked up with them murders! I'll bet you know more than you're spilling!"

"I didn't call the police and I wouldn't have," stated Lundin. "My wife was the first to discover Nellie was missing. She was in a panic and called before she found me. Police interference has caused too many killings in these kidnappings. I'll tell you nothing, understand, and I want you and your men to get away from my place!"

WILDCAT GORDON, his army hat cocked over one eye, opened the library door and walked in. Deputy Bolton and half a dozen detectives were confronting the slight, thin-faced millionaire. Wildcat saw that Lundin's blue-veined hands were drumming nervously on his desk.

"I'm glad you got here, Commissioner Gordon," said Lundin. "I don't know what your order last night could have meant, but I'm telling Deputy Bolton your police will only bring about my daughter's death, or possibly worse, Can't you see my point of view, Gordon?"

"I can see your argument clearly, Mr. Lundin," said Wildcat, not missing the look of disgust on Deputy Bolton's face. "But first I would like to have a word with your Chinese houseboy, Lo Wun. Will you have him called?"

The blue-veined hands of the millionaire flattened on his desk. Any man could have read the stark fear that had caused his eyes to sink deep in their sockets. Andrew Lundin's face took on the color of gray chalk.

"Lo Wun, yes," he said, hoarsely. "I, well—he was sent out on an errand some time ago, and he hasn't come back. As soon as he returns, you can talk with him."

Andrew Lundin could not have told Wildcat Gordon more plainly if he had spoken the words, that Lo Wun, the houseboy, was missing.

Lo Wun had said over the telephone to his father that the time had come. Lo Sing had cautioned him not to act until he had consulted with the mysterious "most worthy eighteen."

Wildcat Gordon did not believe for an instant this was merely a kidnapping for ransom. In some manner, he knew the disappearance of the girl must be involved with the red-hatchet murders on China Hill. The attacks had been directed at Dollar Martino's henchmen.

Two of Martino's men had been in "conference" with Andrew Lundin, and they had had their hair permanently parted by red hatchets before they could return to their chief. A package taken from Lundin's own desk was missing.

Lo Sing had, for some obscure purpose of his own, caused his friend, The Whisperer, to spring a police trap while Martino's men were visiting Andrew Lundin.

These were the facts Wildcat Gordon was swiftly reviewing as he faced the millionaire and heard his stubborn refusal to cooperate with the police. Wildcat came to the instant conclusion that whatever sinister mystery lay behind these happenings, Andrew Lundin's daughter was in danger of death, and the millionaire knew it.

"It's one helluva note, Gordon!" then complained Deputy Bolton. "You got us into this thing last night, and I guess you know all about why Dollar Martino's men were here! Maybe you know more than the rest of us about this snatch?"

"Perhaps I do, and perhaps I don't!" rapped Wildcat Gordon, arriving at a swift decision. "However, we still respect Mr. Lundin's wishes for the present! Henry, you will order all men out of this neighborhood and give Mr. Lundin a chance to make contact with these kidnappers! Is that what you want, Mr. Lundin?"

"That's all I want, Commissioner Gordon," replied Lundin, his nervous hands rubbing across his desk. "That'll be a favor I won't forget, and I'm sorry that I cannot in any way cooperate with the police."

Wildcat Gordon was the last to leave the library. As he went out the door, he turned and said quietly, "I only ask you get in touch with me directly when your houseboy, Lo Wun, returns. Otherwise, I promise you the police will not interfere with anything you may want to do in the next twenty-four hours."

A POLICE COMMISSIONER with less knowledge of the Chinese mind and the mysteries of China Hill would possibly have directed an immediate police descent upon the house of Lo Sing. Wildcat Gordon realized that twice his army of coppers could not at this moment have turned up a single clue on China Hill.

Deputy Henry Bolton was raging, and Mayor Van Royston, who had slept not at all during the night, was backing him up. Wildcat Gordon only listened for some little time.

"We ought to throw out all the reserves and take China Hill apart!" declared Deputy Bolton. "Mayor Van Royston, there's only one way to find these hatchet killers: And that is to descend upon the Chinks in force! We haven't got an extra man on either China Hill or on Dollar Martino's Iola Club!"

Wildcat Gordon inspected his yellow shoes with colorless eyes. Several hours had passed since the abduction of Nellie Lundin, and not a single emergency order had emanated from the commissioner. Outside his office, newspaper reporters were demanding of the wooden-faced Sergeant Thorsen to know what the police were doing.

"I agree with Deputy Bolton, Gordon!" said the harassed Mayor Van Royston. "It's afternoon now, and not a thing has been done toward rounding up these hatchet murderers or helping Andrew Lundin get some word from his daughter's kidnappers! The newspapers are taking the hide off of us!"

"I gave Andrew Lundin a specific promise the police would not interfere with anything he might want to do to get his daughter back," said Wildcat quietly. "As for the newspapers, none of the editors is running my cops, anymore than are you or Henry Bolton. They may take your hide off, but mine's tough enough to take along home and get some sleep. I have my own reason for waiting, and I happen to be commissioner of police."

Whereupon Wildcat's yellow shoes came from his desk, and he walked out of his office. He did not need to glance at newspaper headlines to know what was being said concerning the inactivity of the police.

And up in his penthouse, old Quick Trigger had these same newspaper headlines spread out on a table. As Wildcat Gordon came into the kitchen, a doll-like girl with clustering black curls and dark-blue eyes, in which little devils danced, walked from the stove and thumped a steaming coffee pot before the commissioner.

"I suppose you know I've been up all night, waiting!" snapped Tiny Traeger. "I don't know why I continue to stay in a house with a cop who doesn't seem to think anyone ever wants to sleep!"

Wildcat only grinned, reared back a chair and erected his feet to the corner of the table. On most occasions like this, old Quick Trigger would have unobtrusively withdrawn from the kitchen. For the retired deputy was well aware of Tiny's fondness for the tough Wildcat, and he had the furtive hope that someday the hard-boiled former army officer would discover the truth.

Just now, though, Quick Trigger's eyebrows were drawn into a scowl. He punched a forefinger at the accusing headlines.

"What's holding up the works, Wildcat? These red-hatchet murders are some devil of a mess, and how come Andrew Lundin won't play with the police?"

"I wish I knew the answer to that last one," stated Wildcat, folding the front page of a newspaper in and running his eyes over the classified column. "As for holding up the works, it's become a habit. I wonder if they would use the personal columns?"

"Great gravy, Wildcat!" exploded Quick Trigger. "Why don't you put the pinch on this yellow devil Lo Sing?"

"Nellie Lundin's a sweet little girl, and I wouldn't want to sign her death warrant," said Wildcat calmly, his fingers following the personal column.

THERE WAS NOTHING there that might have been a message from either Andrew Lundin or those who had abducted his daughter. Wildcat had not much expected there would be. His eyes roved across the page. Suddenly his feet slapped to the floor.

"Tiny, how would you like to have a job?"

The girl's blue eyes surveyed Wildcat from his yellow shoes to his cocked army hat.

"You think I haven't enough of a job?" she said, in a dangerously purring tone. "From what I see in the newspapers, it will be you that's looking for a job, Wildcat."

Wildcat grinned at her broadly.

"Perhaps we'll all be looking for jobs if the China Hill boys keep on sticking their little red hatchets in other people's heads," he said. "But I mean it this time, Tiny. I see here where a lady up on the big hill is looking for a personal maid. You may not be quite as refined as the job calls for, but I think you'd do."

Tiny's curving mouth popped open.

"Refined?" she squealed. "I'll show you who's refined! You with your red neckties and race-track clothes! I'll show—"

"All right, Tiny," interrupted Wildcat. "But I'm serious. It happens that the lady who wants the maid is the mother of Nellie Lundin. There are several things that could be learned by a real smart girl in the Lundin house, and sometimes you're not so dumb."

Wildcat's implied insult to her intelligence was instantly passed over by a Tiny Traeger, whose eyes started sparkling. Many times, she had proved her nerve and smartness by becoming involved in the toughest police cases with her grandfather and Wildcat Gordon. But this was the first time Wildcat had invited her help. All the other times had been of her own free will, and against his wishes.

Tiny's vivid, pretty face was eager, but she tried to conceal it. Wildcat had a habit of changing his mind quickly.

"Anything would be better than staying forever in a house full of coppers with bad manners," she stated.

"It's a go then, Tiny," stated Wildcat; "I'm giving you no instructions, but I can frame some references that may land you the job as Mrs. Andrew Lundin's personal maid. If you get it, I'll tell you what I want and when I want it."

Tiny was already slipping off her apron. Quick Trigger frowned, but whether he approved or not, there was no stopping the impulsive girl.

The kitchen extension of the telephone in Wildcat's rooms buzzed insistently. It was the highly excited voice of Mayor Van Royston.

"While you've been sleeping, Henry Bolton has been on the job, Commissioner Gordon!" he stated. "If you had done a little more inquiring this morning, you could have discovered something worthwhile!"

Mayor Van Royston was fairly shouting. Wildcat eased the phone away from his ear.

"I take it that Henry has gone right out and cracked the Lundin case wide open, is that it, Mayor Van Royston?"

"If he hasn't, he soon will, Gordon!" rapped the mayor. "You'd never guess what has come up, and all because Henry has been working on the quiet!"

"So," drawled Wildcat, "our Henry has found out that the Lundin houseboy, Lo Wun, has been missing since Nellie Lundin was abducted?"

Mayor Van Royston sounded as if he were choking.

"How did you know that? When did you find it out? What do you mean, keeping—"

"Take it easy, Mayor," cut in Wildcat Gordon. "Now that he has got that far, you might inform our Henry that hell is due to break loose in China Hill any minute now."

"You're wrong there, Gordon!" rasped Mayor Van Royston. "I have personally ordered Deputy Bolton to stake out all China Hill! There are two dozen squads already in Chinatown, and Deputy Bolton will find Nellie Lundin if he has to take the hill apart! I am ready to—"

Something more than Wildcat's sudden oath interrupted Mayor Van Royston. Wildcat could hear the voice of the wooden-faced Sergeant Thorsen speaking abruptly. The detective sergeant's words came clearly over the phone.

"Mayor Van Royston, we've got a report that hell has broken loose on China Hill!"

Wildcat Gordon snapped the instrument back into place, a grim smile across his broad mouth.

"That's the move I expected next," he said mysteriously to old Quick Trigger. "You couldn't expect Dollar Martino's boys to keep on forever getting their hair parted. But we'll let Henry pick up the pieces on China Hill. This whole thing will have to cook a bit more, and in the meantime I'm having the sleep I came home to get."

Mayor Van Royston

IN the meantime, Deputy Henry Bolton was picking up the pieces on China Hill. Few cars were ever driven along the steep cobblestone ascent of narrow Mall Street with its one sidewalk.

At about the time Deputy Bolton was assigning squad cars on Mayor Van Royston's authority, then vaguely guessing where it would be best to start in on the silent, dusty shops of China Hill, a small, sightseeing bus appeared at the top of Mall Street on China Hill.

Several women were among the apparent tourists aboard the bus. The passengers stared at the pagoda-like tops of the buildings in colorful Chinatown.

Firecrackers snapped merrily in many of the narrow streets. If the stolid, shuffling Chinese were in the least perturbed over the red-hatchet murders, the seeming renewed life of the historic Hop Jo tong, it did not interfere with the continued celebration of the New Year period.

A few of the smart Chinese merchants usually prolonged that New Year celebration, for it brought more white visitors and more business for the scores of dusty-windowed curio shops. The tourists aboard the yellow bus coming down Mall Street jabbered and pointed.

There was plenty to be pointed out in China Hill. The driver of the yellow bus held squealing brakes against the rough, steep descent of Mall Street. High above other buildings loomed the pagodalike towers of Lo Sing's exporting house.

The windows of Lo Sing's place had little light behind them. The carved pieces and curios on display in these windows could be only dimly seen. The yellow bus was seen by policemen in one of Deputy Bolton's squad cars.

Deputy Bolton fortunately—or unfortunately—lacked the information that the Chinese houseboy from the Andrew Lundin home was no other than the son of old Lo Sing. That was one of the reasons why Deputy Bolton was at a loss to know where to start taking China Hill apart.

Several thousand visible Chinamen shuffled along about their business, as if wholly unconcerned with the sudden advent of the numerous police cars. The yellow bus carrying the tourists certainly was not a vehicle to draw police suspicion.

The squad car below passed Mall Street. It had reached the middle of the next block when from up on China Hill came the tearing, splintering crash of a double explosion.

The driver of the squad car backed onto the sidewalk before he could turn in the narrow street. As he got the police car back to the intersection of Mall Street, the yellow tourist bus was careening down.

ABOARD THE BUS half a dozen women were screaming. The bus driver, with a cap pulled over his eyes, sped up the hill. The police car jolted on the steep cobblestone ascent, making toward the rising cloud of smoke and debris dust near the top.

Coppers poured from the squad car and from another one that arrived shortly afterward. They saw that the whole front of Lo Sing's exporting house had been shattered. The windows had crashed inward. One of the pagoda towers had toppled. The police pushed into the choking dust.

They came first upon the bodies of two Chinese who had been mangled and torn by the explosion. Other Chinese were inside the store portion of the Lo Sing establishment. Old Lo Sing himself, yellow and imperturbable as ever, was seated behind a huge desk.

The first policemen to arrive got nowhere with their questions. Lo Sing kept his fat hands folded and said, "It is hard for one who had no enemies to understand. The police are wise to the ways of those who offer to protect their neighbors."

Lo Sing himself pointed the way to open some of his great doors. The coppers were not even denied admittance to his draperied den. But in there they found nothing, no solution of the explosion. They found no Chinaman who admitted seeing anyone throw those pineapples.

Several blocks from Chinatown, the excited tourists alighted from the yellow sightseeing bus. To the last woman who alighted, the bus driver said from a corner of his mouth, "Dollar Martino will settle with all of you tonight. Be at the Iola Club at eleven o'clock."

The yellow bus then rumbled away into a side street. The driver was carefully handling one unused pineapple in one side pocket.

CHAPTER VIII
TINY IS ALSO A "WILDCAT"

DEPUTY HENRY BOLTON threw an army of coppers into China Hill. His net result was the arrest of a few Chinamen with oblique eyes and the general denial that any one of then spoke English. Even when an interpreter was produced, Henry Bolton elicited nothing. He could not be sure the interpreter was telling the truth.

China Hill remained closely picketed by squad cars and policemen on foot. In the face of raging demands from Mayor Van Royston that he do something, Commissioner Wildcat Gordon did little more than keep cold and amused eyes upon the fruitless efforts of Deputy Bolton.

Wildcat was biding his time, convinced of one thing. They might take China Hill apart, stone by stone, but they would not find the missing Nellie Lundin. In fact, Wildcat was beginning to suspect that the millionaire's daughter was not in the hands of Lo Wun, his father Lo Sing, or the "most worthy eighteen."

If they were holding the girl, the Chinese were much too smart to have her where the police might stumble upon her.

So Wildcat Gordon merely waited and watched Deputy Bolton's maneuvering of police details. He was well aware that the newspapers were headlining demands that the police do something. The editors were demanding everything from the blowing up of Chinatown to the immediate arrest of Dollar Martino.

"What kind of a car carried the pineapples?" demanded Wildcat of Deputy Bolton.

"There wasn't any car in Mall Street at the time," admitted the deputy. "Some of the boys saw a sightseeing bus with a bunch of scared women that just missed getting trapped in the blast, but that old yellow devil Lo Sing ain't foolin' me. I'll bet he blew up his own place to throw us off the track!"

"A sightseeing bus?" said Wildcat, in a musing tone. "It was closest to the explosion. So, of course, you detained its occupants and the driver as witnesses, Henry?"

Deputy Bolton's round mouth screwed into a knot. He had been expecting that question.

"The boys were in too big a hurry to get into Mall Street to fool around with a lot of hysterical rubberneckers," he grunted.

"Sure, I know," said Wildcat. "And since then I've checked up on all of the bus companies, and none knows of any sightseeing tour into China Hill at that hour. Also, Henry, that's the first time on record a tourist bus ever skidded down that steep grade of Mall Street."

Mayor Van Royston then insisted it was high time Commissioner Gordon took some direct action.

"I'm taking more direct action than you think, Mayor Van Royston," stated Wildcat. "I'm waiting for a little message from the inside of this mix-up."

Wildcat Gordon had in fact been waiting all day and part of the evening for a message. Tiny Traeger was at the moment employed in the capacity of personal maid to Mrs. Andrew Lundin.

LATE IN THE EVENING, Mrs. Lundin, griefstricken and weary, accepted a sedative from her physician and retired. Besides the new and dainty personal maid, the doctor had installed a nurse to look after the mother who was close to the breaking point.

The nurse said to Tiny, "Mrs. Lundin will sleep a few hours. You go to your room, and if I want you, I'll call."

Tiny Traeger went softly to her room on the lower floor. The girl's dark-blue eyes had made a careful study of everyone in the house. She was aware that the tall, solemn butler, Parsons, had been keeping a close eye upon all of her movements.

Andrew Lundin had remained most of the day in his library and apparently was waiting for some word from the missing girl's abductors. So far as Tiny could determine, no word had been received.

The Lundin house had settled into a midnight silence. Tiny had gone to her room. She had been there long enough for Parsons, the butler, to believe she was asleep.

When she was sure of this, Tiny pulled a light cloak around her small figure and slipped quietly into the dimly lighted hallway.

The gritty granddaughter of old Quick Trigger was acting upon a part of Wildcat Gordon's instructions. Now would be her opportunity to visit the library of Andrew Lundin. She was sure that by this time the millionaire would have retired.

Tiny's doll-like form, shrouded in the light-gray cloak, was easily hidden. It was well that this protected her. She had planned to take the backstairs to the second floor and reach the library.

Tiny was at the top of these stairs when the front-door buzzer startled her, sounding loud in the night's silence. Tiny knew then that Parsons, the butler, must have been waiting for that summons, for his footsteps sounded immediately along the lower hall.

Tiny hurriedly concealed herself in an alcove of the upper hallway not far from the library door. She discovered she was in a recess which also had a door giving access to the library.

Voices muttered downstairs; then someone was coming up with the butler. Tiny peered around the corner and saw a bulky man with diamonds flashing on his fingers. His bulletlike head looked like an unimportant knob on his broad shoulders.

"Dollar Martino!" whispered Tiny to herself.

The racketeer's face had been in the newspapers too often for anyone who could read not to know him instantly. Parsons conducted him to the library door, but before he could rap light streamed into the hallway.

Andrew Lundin's strained voice said, "I've been expecting you, Martino, but you shouldn't have come here. The police may be watching in spite of the commissioner's promise."

"To hell with Wildcat Gordon and the police!" growled Dollar Martino. "I'm going to settle with Gordon personally, but that hasn't anything to do with us! You know why I'm here!"

THE LIBRARY DOOR closed. Tiny could tell that Parsons stood there for a minute, then moved back toward the stairs. Lundin's and Martino's voices murmured, and a few words came to her when she pressed an ear to the door in the recess.

"Lundin, it's a showdown, and you know it," came from Dollar Martino.

"Either you stop these Chinks and this hatchet stuff, or our agreement is off. And that ain't all. If you don't pass the word to China Hill, you'll never see your daughter alive. She'll be sent back to you, a piece at a time!"

Tiny applied one eye to the keyhole of the door. It framed the gray face of Andrew Lundin. His blue-veined, skinny hands were drumming on his desk. His eyes were deeply sunken, but they burned as he looked at Dollar Martino.

"Send my daughter home, Martino, and I'll stop the Chinese," he said heavily.

"That's what you say, Lundin!" grated Martino. "You'll stop the Chinese, then we'll have one final settlement; and after that we'll see about sending back the girl in one piece!"

Shivers like little pieces of ice slid down Tiny's spine. She was hearing the inside of some diabolical plot, about which she knew nothing. She was keenly aware that this respectable millionaire and civic leader was definitely linked up with Dollar Martino. There could be no doubt of that.

But it seemed that Andrew Lundin had his limit. The gruesome threat of Dollar Martino had hardly been spilled from Dollar Martino's insolent tongue before Andrew Lundin was on his feet.

The millionaire's slight figure swayed, but one of his blue-veined hands held an automatic steadily upon his visitor. For the first time, the millionaire's tone was edged, and fear seemed to have gone out of it.

"There can be only one final settlement between us! This will be it, Martino!"

Tiny's whole body grew tense. Her ears were set for the shock of the pistol's explosion. She had never actually seen a man killed, and now the big town's biggest public enemy was about to die, with her and Andrew Lundin as the only witnesses.

But Dollar Martino did not die. His sneering lips twisted, and his voice held mocking scorn.

"Shoot and be damned to you, Lundin! If anything happens to me, the boys have their instructions! It wouldn't change a thing that would happen to you!"

If Dollar Martino had sent a bullet from some concealed weapon racketing into Andrew Lundin's heart, it could not have been more effective. The millionaire's automatic dropped from his nerveless hand. His slight figure fell back into his chair.

"Leave me alone, Martino," he said. "Yes, I'll see what I can do for you on China Hill."

"Now that's more like it!" Dollar Martino's voice was changed and hearty. He added: "I'll be waiting, Lundin," and strode toward the door.

Tiny heard Parsons letting the racketeer out a minute later. She crouched in the recess, again watching Andrew Lundin. Slowly, he picked up the automatic pistol. The man's face was a gray mask under his white hair.

He thumbed the safety catch of the weapon and lifted the muzzle to his left temple. Tiny wanted to scream, but she could not make a sound. Her chilled senses refused to operate her vocal cords or move her body.

Tiny could almost see Andrew Lundin's hand tightening on the trigger that would blast forever the fearful, secret fear in his brain.

The other door of the library burst open. Parsons, the tall butler, said, "Don't do it, Andrew! There are Margaret and Nellie to think about! Put it down, Andrew!"

Strange words, indeed, coming from a butler to his master. It added one more obscure angle to the already tangled puzzle of the millionaire's relations. Tiny's breath fluttered back to her constricted lungs as Andrew Lundin slowly nodded and laid the pistol on his desk.

Parsons placed the automatic in a pocket, took Andrew Lundin's arm and led him from the library. Tiny heard the butler say: "You're taking a sedative now, Andrew, and when you awaken we must go to China Hill."

Their slow steps receded and presently a door closed softly. The library light had been extinguished. Tiny glided swiftly to the other door. It had not been locked, and her hope of trying out her expertness at picking the tumblers was not realized.

TINY CROSSED the library in the darkness. She produced a little flashlight from under her cloak and began opening the drawers of Andrew Lundin's desk. There were many papers, and she opened some of them, but replaced them.

One small drawer of the desk was tightly locked. Tiny's wire instruments started feeling around inside the brass aperture. It was lucky for her the desk was of an old pattern. The drawer opened so easily it surprised her.

Now she had a few more papers, some old and yellowed, and with them half a dozen photographs. Her flashlight showed these pictures to be of Andrew Lundin and his family. Old snapshots of many years before. Tiny drew in her breath sharply as she looked at one photograph.

She slipped this snapshot into the bosom of her dress.

Brilliant light suddenly flooded the library. With her thick hair streaming about her face, Mrs. Andrew Lundin stood in the doorway. The face of a worried nurse appeared at her shoulder.

"You! So it's you!" screamed Mrs. Lundin, who apparently had been too hysterical to sleep. "I thought you were such a sweet, lovely little person, and you're a thief!"

Mrs. Lundin screamed again, calling Parsons the butler. The solemn servant who had addressed the millionaire with such familiarity only a short time before had no expression as he crossed the library and his hand gripped Tiny's arm.

"What shall I do, madam?" he said.

"Do?" said Mrs. Lundin. "I'll call the police, the same as for any other thief! Perhaps she is one of them, a part of the kidnappers and they sent her here!"

Parsons pulled Tiny to one side, and then over by the library window. Tiny had time to think even then that Andrew Lundin must have taken a sedative and was sleeping. The young nurse showed no sympathy for a personal maid caught in the act of thievery.

None knew that one of the millionaire's snapshots was still hidden in Tiny's dress. Mrs. Lundin got police headquarters. But as the woman made her report, Tiny's hand came from under her gray cloak.

"Open that window and be quick about it, Parsons, if you want to keep healthy!" snapped the doll-like girl. "I mean it, and I'd shoot you as quickly as Dollar Maritino!"

Tiny was jamming a small automatic into the amazed butler's ribs. Mrs. Lundin saw this, dropped the telephone in the midst of her report to the police, and screamed.

Parsons had one look into the suddenly cold blue eyes of this pretty but remarkable child. Then he turned and started to lift the library window.

Tiny kept her pistol in Parsons's ribs until she was on the balcony outside; then she directed, "Stay right there, Parsons, until I'm down, or I'll still let you have it!"

The girl was not as expert a climber as The Whisperer had been. She fell part of the way to the ground and the breath was fairly knocked out of her, but she got up and ran gasping in the direction of the first car entrance.

The report to the police worried Tiny. If Wildcat did not happen to be at headquarters, she feared her encounter would involve him in difficult explanations.

FIVE MINUTES LATER, Tiny had reached a telephone booth. She exclaimed with relief when Wildcat's edged voice finally replied. Tiny quickly told him what had happened, but for once Wildcat said, "Good girl! It couldn't have been better! Now, describe that photograph!"

Two minutes later, after he had directed Tiny to go home at once, Wildcat pounded from his office and intercepted an excited Deputy Henry Bolton.

"Now we're getting somewhere!" said Bolton. "We've just got a call that a maid at the Lundin home has been trapped robbing a library desk! Maybe we'll find out some other things now!"

"You will countermand your order, Henry," said Wildcat quietly. "This department is interfering in no way in the affairs of Andrew Lundin!"

Henry Bolton sputtered, but Wildcat was not listening. The commissioner was already leaving headquarters. Tiny's telephone message had brought to a head the things he had believed to be cooking. She had told him of the visit of Dollar Martino to Andrew Lundin and of their conversation.

CHAPTER IX
THE DEN OF A MOBSTER

WILDCAT GORDON'S suspicion had been confirmed. Nellie Lundin was in the hands of Dollar Martino. The vanishing of Lo Wun had made it appear that the Chinese houseboy had been responsible for the girl's disappearance.

Tiny's excellent work had added as much to the maze of the red-hatchet murders as it had cleared up.

The conversation of Dollar Martino and Andrew Lundin had disclosed a direct fear of the racketeer on the part of the millionaire. At the same time, it had been made apparent Martino believed Andrew Lundin had the power to influence the Chinese and stop the red-hatchet murders.

Tiny had heard the millionaire admit he might be able to end the war on China Hill. And the faded snapshot Tiny had stolen from Andrew Lundin's desk had been strange indeed.

For it showed Andrew Lundin years before, standing beside a Chinaman who, also, was young. The faded writing at the bottom of the photograph read:

TO MY GOOD FRIEND ANDREW FROM LO SING. WE SHALL STAND TOGETHER.

This was all very mysterious. In some manner the now leading citizen and millionaire had been closely associated with the wily old Lo Sing. Had something happened recently, whereby they had failed to stand together?

It had become apparent to Wildcat Gordon this must be true.

There was the indisputable fact of Lo Sing's warfare upon Dollar Martino. There was the equally indisputable circumstance of Andrew Lundin being involved with the Martino crowd.

Because of these facts, and the certainty Nellie Lundin must be in the hands of Dollar Martino, that Wildcat for the first time was able to map a straight course of action. So his small coupé whirled down the hill from headquarters toward the bay. In only a few minutes it was parked in a side street not far from the Iola Club.

IT WAS SHORTLY after midnight and several hundred persons had been making the night's play against Dollar Martino's doubtful games. Many were now streaming from the Iola Club, so none noticed the unobtrusive entrance of the little man clad all in gray, whose oddly pointed chin and whitish hair marked him for perhaps an old-timer at the games.

The Whisperer was walking directly into Dollar Martino's well-known web. His knowledge enabled him to produce the proper card and to identify himself in a husky whisper, which was all right with the man behind the little slot of a gaming room on the second floor.

The Whisperer had chosen this room of the dice games because he knew it was adjacent to Martino's own office. There were still two score persons playing at the crap tables, and none paid attention to the inconspicuous gray man who slipped onto a stool.

The Whisperer was hoping that Dollar Martino had not returned directly to the Iola Club after his visit to Andrew Lundin. He desired very much to get into Martino's office, unobserved, and discover what rooms lay behind it in the wing of the building that jutted over the water of the bay.

The hour being late, play was slackening at the tables. Only half a dozen players, with the same number of dealers and watchful guards, were in the room.

As others left his table, The Whisperer ignored his stack of chips and moved with them toward a washroom and the door that he was sure opened into Martino's office.

So quickly and quietly that none noticed, or it appeared they had not, The Whisperer glided from the room of the dice games.

The door from the dice room did not give directly into the office of the racket boss. The Whisperer discovered himself in a short hallway, with another door at the end. He flattened himself against a wall for a moment, but saw no one, so moved along toward the door.

His confidence in his easy access to Martino's stronghold would have been shaken if he could have heard two of the guards talking as he left the dice table.

"Sit tight, but map that egg in the gray clothes," said one guard, from a corner of his mouth. "What do you think, Pete?"

Pete, none other than the driver of the car that had been abandoned the night before when The Whisperer had been dropped behind a convenient hedge, swore softly and nodded.

"The same mug, sure as hell," he said. "Well, let him play along and see what happens. The boss ain't back, so we'll wait and spot him outside."

The smart Pete had not moved when The Whisperer had gone through the door into the hallway.

The Whisperer quickly negotiated the lock of Dollar Martino's office and closed the door behind him. He moved silently in the darkness, hand touching the wall until he encountered another door behind Martino's big desk. One hand slipped down, and he discovered the lock was strong and complicated.

Dropping to his knees, The Whisperer went swiftly to work with a variety of curved steel instruments. He heard the tumblers click and was turning the knob, when he suddenly became aware he was not alone.

There was no sound of movement, but there was the slow, regular breathing of some other person in the office room. The door from the hallway could not have been opened without light being detected. So someone had entered some other way, or had been concealed in the room.

Listening intently, The Whisperer became aware at least two persons were breathing close by. He let himself down slowly, flattened against the wall and got a flashlight into one hand. His other hand already held one of his deadly silenced pistols.

A thumb flicked the button and the flashlight sprayed illumination directly upon two men. Each held an automatic in one hand, and in the light The Whisperer identified the face of Pete from the night before.

The two automatics centered on the flashlight, but Pete still was a smart mobster.

"So we meet up again, mug!" he rasped. "I wouldn't make any bad play, smart guy, for you can't get both of us, and we'll let you have it! Stand up!"

PETE'S ASSURANCE was his mistake. The flashlight blinked out at the same instant The Whisperer rolled lithely to one side. Two guns spat blue flame and slugs pounded into the wall. No flame showed from the silenced pistol in The Whisperer's hand. It only hissed with the slow release of its compressed explosion.

One of Martino's men croaked hoarsely and his body thumped to the floor. Pete alone was left standing, so accurately had The Whisperer placed that single shot.

"Stay where you are!" came the eerie, penetrating whisper that seemed to bring an icy chill into the closed office. "You may live, Pete, if you don't move!"

Pete's awed voice said, "The Whisperer! And we had you and let you go!"

"Stand where you are, Pete!" again commanded that weird whispering voice. "We will go into this other locked room together! Now walk slowly toward the door!"

The Whisperer pushed himself up against the wall, changed his position with the lightning stealth of a jungle animal. Pete continued to prove he was smart.

"I'm walking," he said, calmly. "But you won't get away with it."

The Whisperer glided toward the mobster, his back to the door he had been attempting to open. He did not know what happened or how. The closed door might have opened noiselessly in the darkness. Another man might have been creeping steadily toward him.

A blinding flash and blackness came together. A blackjack or the butt of a gun had crashed on The Whisperer's head.

AS THE WHISPERER struggled back to consciousness through a fog of pain, he first became aware he must have gained the room behind Dollar Martino's office. Not that it would do him any good, for he had been rigidly wrapped with yards of adhesive tape that made his body as stiff as that of a mummy.

The tape had been wound over his face and across his mouth. He was lying in a window alcove of a big room, and he could hear the slapping of waves on the piling that supported the building. So he realized he must still be in the Iola Club.

The Whisperer had only a partial view of the room, due to the dimness of a single light bulb. Perhaps Dollar Martino wished to avoid having too much light shining on the windows.

Once having heard the insolent mockery of Dollar Martino's voice, none could ever mistake it. The bulky body of the boss, with his bulletlike head cocked on one side, was erect before a chair in which the lovely, brown-eyed Nellie Lundin was bound.

The Whisperer saw that the girl's mouth was tightly taped so she could not scream. Four other men lounged about the room, their avid eyes upon Dollar Martino and the girl.

"Maybe you wouldn't happen to know anything about this guy they call The Whisperer?" said Dollar Martino. "You saw him just now. He has been to your house to see your father, hasn't he? Your father sent him here?"

The beautiful Nellie Lundin stared at Martino with her terror-filled brown eyes. She shook her head slowly, unable to speak, indicating she had never before seen The Whisperer.

Dollar Martino stepped forward and slapped his loose fingers across the girl's cheek, leaving marks that reddened on the whiteness of her skin.

"O.K.! O.K., then! But you're lyin', baby! Anyway, your old man ain't half as smart as he thinks he is! So before he decides to put a finger on the wrong guy,

**A thumb flicked the button and the flashlight sprayed illumination directly upon
two men. Each held an automatic in one hand, and in the light The Whisperer
identified the face of Pete from the night before.**

we'll be sending him a little finger that will make him
think! Pete, bring that red hatchet!"

"Aw, boss!" protested the mobster Pete. "You
got it wrong! This Whisperer egg is hooked up with
Lo Sing! Didn't the boys hear him when he sliced
Corky's arm with one of them damn guns of his up
on Mall Street?"

Dollar Martino's thick lips twisted, and his

bulletlike head wagged.

"Goin' soft, Pete?" he said, in a low, mocking
voice. "I don't like boys that go soft. Now you will
have the chance to use that red hatchet, or I'll let
Angel do it."

Pete said, "I ain't gone soft, but it's down Angel's
alley, not mine."

One of the mobsters grinned, and his nostrils

twitched, It was a matter of guessing how he got his name. "Angel" was anything but that.

"O.K., boss!" said Angel, and the tip of his tongue ran along his lips. "It's the same hatchet that split Breezy's head! I copped it before the police got here!"

The Whisperer could only lie helpless and listen. He could neither move nor make a sound.

Now The Whisperer had looked upon varied horrors and many brutalities in his dual role as police commissioner and a defender of justice, but nothing had ever equaled what he now saw.

DOLLAR MARTINO deliberately pulled one of Nellie Lundin's slender white hands loose from the cords that had bound her wrists. His strong fingers slowly turned the hand over, until the cracking strain on the bones of the girl's arm brought what would have been a scream of pain, but was only a gurgling behind the tape over her mouth.

Dollar Martino held the shapely hand over the hard edge of the chair, separating the fingers and forcing one across the wood alone. Nellie Lundin's brown eyes were pools of pain and sheer horror.

"This one, Angel," said Martino, softly. "It's a nice little finger, but it ain't wearin' no diamond yet, so it never will. Be careful, Angel, and make it clean, and we'll send it back to Papa Lundin, all wrapped up with the little red hatchet that cut it off. I think—yes, I'm sure he can stop the Chinks when he gets this."

Nellie Lundin's curved figure fought against the tape holding her. But she was helpless to withdraw the hand and the single finger laid for the hatchet across the edge of the chair

The Whisperer could see Angel's twitching nostrils, his ugly mouth and the tongue licking along it.

"All right, Angel, what's holding you back?" said Dollar Martino.

The hatchet with its red handle was lifted. Every mobster in the room was watching the hatchet—fascinated. Dollar Martino's piggish eyes held a mocking smile. None saw the door swing open.

A hatchet hissed through the air, but it was not the one in the hand of Angel. For Angel fell down, and a red handle the color of human blood stuck from between his ears.

CHAPTER X
MOBBING THE MOBSTERS

THAT FLYING red-handled hatchet had come like a bolt from a clear sky. Its keen blade, polished to the brightness of silver, cleft the skull of Angel, who had fallen down. His blood and brains spilled out together, as Dollar Martino and the other were struck motionless for five or ten seconds.

One of the mobsters got an automatic into one hand and it spouted fire toward the door. But it fell to the floor when a gleam of red and steel whizzed through the air. The gunman went down with his forehead split, and one of the others, perhaps the smart Pete, then had the good sense to jump to the light switch.

As the bulb blinked out, Dollar Martino yelled, "The red hatchets! They've come! This way!"

There must have been a secret exit, for as gabbling Chinese poured into the room, Dollar Martino and his remaining men were fading out of it. The Whisperer could see only two wrinkled, old yellow faces just before the light went out.

In the room for the moment there was silence, but from the opened door came the tearing screams of men in fear and pain. The Whisperer could hear the smashing of tables in the nearby gambling room and the hoarse agony of some who were dying.

For in the dice room, and in two other rooms where the night's patrons had recently departed, a dozen or more Chinese were wielding their red-handled hatchets. So swiftly had the massed attack come, that the men at the doors were lying on the floors with cracks in their skulls.

Guns started cracking. There were perhaps a score of dealers and guards in the gaming rooms when the hatchet attack began. Of these, it became apparent later that only nine had escaped. Eleven men, besides the two in the room with The Whisperer, had their sleek hair permanently parted.

THOUGH HE STRAINED desperately, The Whisperer was unable to free himself as the sounds of the murderous massed attack arose, then slowly died out. Chinese hatchetmen, all wrinkled and old, were vanishing from the Iola Club as swiftly as they had come.

The Whisperer started rolling his taped body slowly in the direction of Nellie Lundin's chair. He knew the girl was still there, and had not been moved.

Apparently the raiding Chinese had all departed, and The Whisperer realized that if Dollar Martino and his remaining men returned quickly enough, the girl's life would be snuffed out in reprisal.

Then, as he rolled, The Whisperer became aware that men had again entered the room. He could hear them approaching the bound girl. The Whisperer's desperate straining at the tape accomplished nothing. He could tell the girl was being lifted and borne from the room.

Feet padded from the place. No word had been spoken. Then The Whisperer became aware he had not been left alone. Someone was bending over him.

That red-handled hatchet had come like a bolt from a clear sky.

He could feel the razorlike edge of a knife slicing along the tape around his body. His numbed arms were being freed.

A voice, a Chinese voice, spoke softly in his ear.

"You are the friend of Lo Sing. You will leave quickly before the police arrive. The girl will be safe for the present."

The knife separated the tape around The Whisperer's legs. He could not move quickly because of his numbed limbs, but he threw himself toward the voice in the darkness. There was a low, vague laugh and the door of the room closed.

His mysterious liberator had vanished. There were only the moaning cries of men in other rooms of the Iola Club. Sirens screamed on police cars coming down toward the bay.

NEVER IN THE previous history of the city had there been such a bloody massacre as confronted the thronging coppers. In three gambling rooms lay eleven of Dollar Martino's dealers and aides. In each case a red-handled hatchet was either still in the skull or lying beside a body.

Thirteen dead men in all. For there were the

Its keen blade, polished to the brightness of silver, cleft the skull of Angel.

two in the room where Nellie Lundin had been imprisoned. Deputy Henry Bolton gaped at the body of Angel especially. He could not understand how Angel happened to be gripping a red-handled hatchet in his own hand.

There was nothing to indicate the abducted girl had ever been in this room.

Deputy Bolton shouted, "Round up every damn' Chink in the neighborhood! Bring them all in!"

Detective Sergeant Thorsen, of the wooden face, said, "We have rounded up all that were to be found. One Chinaman, with a bullet in one leg."

Deputy Bolton raged. He learned that the Chinaman they had caught, the lone one of all that mass attack, had been found leaving. And he had been armed only with a knife, with which he had made no defense.

"Bring the yellow devil in here!" directed Deputy Bolton. "I'll sweat the truth out of him or I'll send him to the hospital!"

Two squad men brought in a wrinkled Chinaman who was limping, with blood running from one knee. One of the coppers held a knife, which he said the Chinaman had been carrying in his hand.

"Lee Tow's his name," said a detective. "Runs

a shop on China Hill. I think we're getting somewhere now. I seem to remember having heard him mentioned once as having been of the old Hop Jo tong."

"I'll crack it out of him, or I'll bust his—"

Deputy Bolton's dire threat was interrupted by the cold voice of Wildcat Gordon.

"You'll take Lee Tow to headquarters, Henry! You'd better get your men busy rounding up Dollar Martino! It would be too bad if the Chinamen got him and dumped him in the bay!"

Wildcat appeared in fresh, sartorial splendor, his cocked army hat concealing the bruised cut between his ears. He had made a swift transformation. He was aware he had arrived in the nick of time to save his own rescuer, old Lee Tow, from the rough methods of Deputy Bolton.

Wildcat was sure Lee Tow had been caught only because he had lingered to release The Whisperer and got a bullet in his leg. He certainly owed the ancient Chinaman a big debt, for otherwise he would again have been trapped by his own police.

And Wildcat alone knew that Nellie Lundin had been a prisoner in the hands of Dollar Martino, and now was in the hands of the Chinese hatchet men. He decided to say nothing of this. Perhaps the girl would be returned to her home.

But Wildcat believed she would not. Dollar Martino and many of his mobsters were still at large. They had escaped the massacre and, temporarily at least, they had fled from the Iola Club. Probably within a few hours, Dollar Martino himself would be demanding that the police protect him from the hatchet men.

Like all other racketeers, he would be quick enough to seek the aid of the law when he discovered he was getting the worst of it.

Wildcat Gordon pushed his way through the thousands jamming the waterfront streets around the Iola Club, leaving the scene of death behind. He got to the first convenient telephone. In a minute he was talking with old Quick Trigger.

"Tiny got home all right, Wildcat," said the older man. "She is staying up to keep the coffee hot."

"Tell her to hang onto that photograph," instructed Wildcat. "Quick Trigger, I'm going to headquarters. Mayor Van Royston and Henry will soon be bumping their heads together. I want you to get into the blind man's outfit and jump over to Andrew Lundin's place."

"I'm practically on my way, Wildcat," said Quick Trigger. "But the radio is screaming that Iola Club stuff. Where's all this going to end?"

"I wouldn't be surprised but that it will keep up until Dollar Martino's mob is as extinct as the dodo, Quick Trigger. But here's the lay: I imagine Andrew Lundin will be leaving his place for an early morning call. Stay near him, and you'll probably find yourself on Mall Street. I think the time has come for Lundin to have a little talk-talk with old Lo Sing."

WILDCAT GORDON did not explain why he knew Andrew Lundin would be going to see Lo Sing. Having started Quick Trigger on his way, Wildcat appeared half an hour later in the little bedlam of his own office.

Mayor Van Royston and Deputy Henry Bolton were literally going around and around, and neither seemed to know where he was coming out.

"So you're back again, Mr. Commissioner!" greeted the mayor. "How many murders will it take to wake you up to the responsibilities of this office, Gordon?"

Wildcat pushed through a group of citizens who had accompanied Mayor Van Royston to the office. He cocked his hat over one eye and put his yellow shoes up on a corner of the desk.

Sighting across the toes, he said cheerfully, "I don't remember when I've had such a pleasant evening, your honor. But I'm somewhat disappointed. I didn't see Dollar Martino anywhere with a hatchet sticking between his eyes. It rather spoiled the party for me."

The half a dozen leading citizens who had accompanied Mayor Van Royston to police headquarters had been guests at one of the receptions the mayor was always attending. They were good, law-abiding citizens. All were readers of the newspapers, and they believed what they read.

One man said, "We have what amounts to a massacre on our hands, and our police commissioner speaks as if he approved these brutal killings. I would say it is the duty of the police to bring in this Dollar Martino, without the employment of brutality."

"Yes, yes, yes!" agreed Mayor Van Royston, halting before Wildcat's desk. "You should detain Dollar Martino, Gordon. Perhaps he could be persuaded to name some of the Chinese. I know he is listed as a public enemy, but under the circumstances no doubt he would be willing to talk."

Wildcat stuffed some tobacco into his smelly old pipe, lighted it and looked at his visitors through an odorous cloud of smoke.

"Yes," he said, quietly. "If I had Dollar Martino here at this moment, he could be persuaded to talk. I would like nothing better than to get Martino right now. I would derive the utmost pleasure in taking one of those little red hatchets and shaving off both his ears, then if he refused to talk, I'd enjoy chopping off a few of his fingers."

"In Heaven's name!" came from Mayor Van Royston. "Gentlemen, you can see what I'm up against!"

The assembled gentlemen stared at the grimly

smiling Wildcat Gordon. What they saw in his eyes was evidence he was not indulging in a mere pleasantry. Nor was he.

For Wildcat was remembering that interval when Dollar Martino had pulled Nellie Lundin's white hand across a chair and directed one of his mobsters to chop off a finger. These citizens could judge him on what they read in the newspapers, but Wildcat Gordon was judging Dollar Martino and his murderous rats on the brutal horror he had witnessed.

Wildcat Gordon knew that the daughter of Andrew Lundin might be returned to her home unharmed, but that she would carry through life the terrible dreams of an experience which would stay always in her memory. For the present, Wildcat made no mention of his theory concerning the possible position of the abducted girl.

Mayor Van Royston cracked it when he said, "Now we can be sure the Chinese have Nellie Lundin. Gordon, you've had all the time we can give you to get at the truth of this kidnapping and these murders."

"I'M GETTING AT the truth of it!" rasped the unpleasant voice of Deputy Henry Bolton, a finger rubbing his long nose as he played for the approval of the mayor and his friends. "I have arrested a Chinaman known as Lee Tow, one of the hatchet killers, and I am going now to sweat the truth out of him."

"That's the thing to do!" chorused the visitors, Mayor Van Royston adding: "Deputy Bolton, have this yellow killer brought in! I thoroughly approve of the third degree under some circumstances, and you should have witnesses!"

Deputy Bolton made a move toward the door. Wildcat's yellow shoes remained on his desk. But his crisp, cold voice wrapped around Henry Bolton's ears.

"The minute you pass through that door, Henry, you cease to have any authority as a deputy commissioner. In fact, Henry, you will no longer be a policeman. If there is any sweating of Lee Tow to be done, I'll do it personally."

Deputy Bolton's muttered oath and his outspread hands appealed to Mayor Van Royston. The mayor started to speak. Wildcat was touching a button on his desk.

"Have Lee Tow brought to my office," said Wildcat, into one of his phones. He added: "Mayor Van Royston, this Lee Tow is an old man, and he will speak as he pleases. All the third degrees in the world could not produce one more word than he desires to utter."

"You've become impossible, Gordon!" exploded the mayor. "In one minute you speak of torture for a white man, and the next you seem to want to protect one of these heathen."

"If you're speaking of Dollar Martino as a white man, your honor, I'll take this so-called heathen for mine every time."

A jailer from the headquarters detention cells came pounding along the corridor, swinging the door open suddenly. He was a veteran of the department, and Irish. His normally red face had gone a bit white.

"I can't bring you Lee Tow, chief!" he announced. "Unless it's on a stretcher! He'll never talk! The old Chink was searched from head to foot, but nobody thought about the long nails on his little fingers!"

"You're telling us that Lee Tow is now with the spirits of his father, is that it?" asked Wildcat.

"I wouldn't be knowin' where he is, chief, but he slit his jugular vein with a knife blade hidden under one of them fingernails!" said the jailer. "So he won't talk!"

"No, he won't talk," agreed Wildcat. "I was afraid of that. Now, Mayor Van Royston, and gentlemen, you can bring in all of the Chinese you might suspect, and you'll get just as much out of them."

Deputy Bolton said, "The commissioner wouldn't let me sweat him when I had Lee Tow alive."

Wildcat ignored this. His feet slapped to the floor. Mayor Van Royston and his friends were talking to each other.

"All right, Henry!" rapped out Wildcat. "You have no doubt got all of China Hill now hedged in by extra squads?"

"I most certainly have, an' that's the only way to—"

"You will withdraw all squads from China Hill at once, Henry! I want China Hill left wide open for the remainder of tonight and all day tomorrow. Issue the order instantly!"

MAYOR VAN ROYSTON planted his silk-topped figure in front of Wildcat.

"You can't do that! I won't stand for it, Gordon! The citizens are demanding we wipe out China Hill! For once, I am ready to go the limit!"

"Henry, get busy!" snapped Wildcat. "Leave China Hill wide open! Mayor, up to a certain point these heathens, as you call them, have done a mighty fine job. We could save the taxpayers a lot of expense if this police department started using red hatchets on a few of our slick murderers and torturers!

"Now, if I find one extra man of my own department on China Hill half an hour from now, he will be suspended along with the officer who put him there!"

Mayor Van Royston's mouth popped open, and his guests looked to him for an explosion that would possibly blast this insolent commissioner off the map. But experience had taught his honor when it was dangerous to explode.

Anyway, the bell saved him in that round. It was the telephone on Wildcat's desk. Wildcat heard the slow voice of old Quick Trigger.

"Andrew Lundin left his home, walking, and he was followed by his butler to Mall Street, Wildcat. I have trailed both to Lo Sing's place, but the butler is keeping watch outside. Wildcat, I've got another trouble, too."

"What's the other trouble?"

"Only five minutes ago I saw a little Chinese girl, only I don't believe she's Chinese. I'm thinkin' it's Tiny all dolled up, an' I'll bet she's up to some of her tricks."

"Stay where you are!" directed Wildcat Gordon.

CHAPTER XI
TWO GIRLS IN A TRAP

MAYOR VAN ROYSTON was saying, "Your action is unthinkable, Commissioner Gordon! The public won't stand for it!"

"Any public that has stood for Dollar Martino and his rackets will stand for anything!" rapped out Wildcat Gordon. "I'm taking over the China Hill patrol in my own way! I hope to save the life of at least one innocent girl! I advise all of you to go home and get some sleep!"

Deputy Henry Bolton knew when he was licked. Temporarily at least, he could either withdraw the China Hill squads or his own name from the police rolls.

Wildcat Gordon paused only a moment beside the desk of Detective Sergeant Thorsen, then left Mayor Van Royston and his friends stranded in their own bewildered conversation.

Wildcat hesitated only to call Quick Trigger's penthouse. He received no reply. Quick Trigger had been correct: The adventurous Tiny had embarked upon a mission of her own.

Wildcat was recalling that Tiny had heard Andrew Lundin and his butler say they were going to Mall Street this morning. Tiny fancied herself to be a smart little sleuth. She had learned many tricks from her grandfather. One of these was makeup.

So, at the moment, while Wildcat Gordon was pouring the gas to one of his coupés, driving recklessly toward China Hill, a diminutive Chinese girl in silken pantaloons and a hand-worked blouse was tripping lightly over the foggy sidewalk of Mall Street.

The girl's black curls had been smoothed and rolled over a set of golden pins. Makeup shadows made her eyes appear to be slanted, and none came close enough to observe they were a dark, Irish blue rather than an Oriental black.

Tiny Traeger had shadowed her grandfather. Now she imagined she might in some way add to the valuable assistance she had given Wildcat. Tiny knew all about the murders at the Iola club and was convinced Wildcat had more on his hands than following up the Lundin case.

Like all the others, including Quick Trigger, Tiny did not know that Wildcat believed Nellie Lundin to be in the hands of Lo Sing.

TINY ATTRACTED little attention from the Chinese who shuffled past. Strangely enough, in Chinatown, a little Chinese girl is much safer on the street at a odd night hour than any white girl would have been in the American section of the city.

Tiny kept to the shadowing fog along the peaked and pagodaed buildings of Mall Street. She had seen Andrew Lundin's slight figure pass, accompanied by Parsons, the tall butler. They had apparently walked into some doorway near the wrecked front of the Lo Sing establishment.

Tiny was not certain as to what steps she could take to overhear a conversation between Andrew Lundin and old Lo Sing. The doll-like girl was wholly unacquainted with the mysteries and intricacies of China Hill. If she had expected some residence where she might gain entrance by a window, she was greatly disappointed.

Soft-footed Chinese seemed to emerge and disappear from what might have been solid walls. Only because she appeared so perfectly Chinese did Tiny escape the police of Henry Bolton planted in every block.

Tiny did not see the concealed figure of Quick Trigger in an entrance across from Lo Sing's house. Nor did she observe that Parsons, the tall butler, had not entered Lo Sing's house with Andrew Lundin.

Tiny tripped lightly along in the shadows, coming near the wrecked front of the Chinese exporting house. If there were only some means by which she could follow Andrew Lundin.

Tiny halted, shrinking her doll-like figure into a recess of the wall. A tall, somber shadow was gliding toward her. The girl realized it was that of Parsons, the butler.

He had seen her, but Tiny was sure he could not have recognized her as the little maid who had so expertly pushed a pistol into his ribs at the Lundin home.

Parsons, the butler, was sharper-eyed than Tiny imagined. He had, of course, noted the Chinese costume the girl was wearing. But the fog was in Tiny's throat, and as she neared Parsons she had given a little cough.

Parsons instantly decided he had heard that same little cough before. There was a certain quickness and lift to Tiny's walk that was utterly different from the softly shuffling steps of a Chinese girl.

Parsons intended to investigate. In fact, he had remained outside Lo Sing's for the purpose of conveying a warning to Andrew Lundin if any danger threatened. Parsons cautiously approached the stone-walled niche into which Tiny had darted.

In half a minute, the butler was growling out oaths. He imagined he had been tricked. The recess into which Tiny had stepped was empty. It was only a small space, backed by a door so solid that it appeared to be made of great beams.

Still swearing, Parsons retraced his steps to the front of Lo Sing's place. He kept from betraying his presence as a squad car passed, toiling up the Mall Street hill.

TINY HAD DISAPPEARED, though that had not been her intention. She had been pressing her small body against the big door of the wooden beams when the whole wall seemed to move.

Before Tiny could dart away or cry out, strong hands closed about her head, shutting off her yell and pulling her quickly into the opening.

Tiny employed her fingernails, even her teeth, but she was held with hands of inexorable strength. One man was carrying her. The passage along which he walked had a musty smell, relieved somewhat by the thin, sweet odor of incense and spices.

A big door opened and closed, and Tiny was deposited upon a thick rug. One small hand had slipped inside the silken Chinese blouse and was gripping her automatic pistol, but a wrinkled Chinaman caught her wrist and removed the weapon so deftly that Tiny was helpless.

Tiny raged and cried out. She was no longer a dumb, little Chinese girl as several caustic Americanisms fell upon the unheeding ears of the old Chinaman. His face was inscrutable as he left her, a great door concealed by swaying curtains closing upon the room.

Then Tiny saw the other girl staring at her. This other girl was rising from a silken couch, and her brown eyes were wide. Tiny knew she was Nellie Lundin, could be no other. Unwilling to reveal her own identity, Tiny forgot that her Americanisms had been heard.

But before either girl had a chance to talk, another curtain swayed. A youthful, smooth-faced Chinese came in. He was followed by a grotesquely fat, waddling figure.

"Lo Wun?" cried out Nellie Lundin, to the young Chinese. "You are here? Oh, now everything will be all right! My father sent you, Lo Wun?"

The houseboy from the Lundin home smiled and inclined his head, but he did not speak. Behind him stood the fat, older man. His hands were folded across his capacious stomach.

"Inform her, my son," he stated.

"This is my father, Miss Lundin, Lo Sing," said Lo Wun simply.

"Oh, now I'm all right!" the girl cried delightedly. "It is you who had me rescued from that terrible place! You will send me home at once? Lo Wun, you have called my mother?"

LO SING'S pudgy, yellow hands moved and his protected fingernails waved. Lo Wun bowed obediently and went out.

"The fair daughter of Andrew Lundin will not be harmed, but for the present it is best that you remain as the guest of my humble house," he stated, the words coming from lips that scarcely seemed to move in his yellow, masklike face. "I have a settlement to make with your father, and after that—"

"But you can't!" cried Nellie Lundin. "Lo Wun is our friend! My father will pay anything you want, only take me home! Send for my father! I demand it!"

"My time grows short," stated Lo Sing calmly. "You would not know of the debt which I must settle. Andrew Lundin will never pay for the freedom of his beautiful daughter. For the present, you are the guest of my house.

"This other one, who so foolishly believed she could deceive those of China Hill with her poor pretense, apparently is very dumb. But she shall remain to keep you company, Miss Lundin."

"Why, you old, slant-eyed—"

Tiny was bristling, slapping the words at the imperturbable Lo Sing. She paused only because Lo Sing was no longer there. He had bowed his head and backed through an opening and closing door.

Tiny rushed at that beamed door, vainly seeking some knob or latch. She pounded on it with her small fists until Nellie Lundin said, "Whoever you are, it will do no good. I tried. I don't understand any of this, but I believe we are in the hands of enemies of my father."

Tiny had a temper that quickly subsided. In a moment she had her arms around the other girl. She wanted to tell her that Wildcat Gordon could be counted upon to find them, but felt she must not reveal her identity. Her foolish attempt to solve some of the Andrew Lundin and China Hill mystery had only got her into this trap.

That would mean trouble for Wildcat, and the police commissioner had multiple troubles already.

IN FACT, at this time, Wildcat Gordon was unaware how greatly his troubles had multiplied. At the moment his little coupé was skidding around fog-wet corners on narrow cable car hills, in his urge to reach Quick Trigger on China Hill, and something had happened which completely upset his order for the vacating of Chinatown by the police squads.

Hardly had Wildcat Gordon left a cursing Henry Bolton and the discomfited Mayor Van Royston and his friends at headquarters, than the commissioner's telephone buzzed. Henry Bolton took the call.

The expression of Henry Bolton's face was a puzzle.

For it was none other than the hard, mocking voice of Dollar Martino himself, first demanding to talk to Wildcat Gordon. Bolton managed to convey this information to the mayor and his friends as he listened to Martino.

"Well, if your smart commissioner ain't there," went on Dollar Martino, "I've got some information to pass along to him. You can tell the big mug for me that he won't get any of these damned hatchet men until he finds The Whisperer."

Deputy Bolton gasped, then said to Mayor Van Royston, "Dollar Martino says these hatchet men are commanded by The Whisperer!"

Dollar Martino was telling more. There was no doubt but that the big shot racketeer was pushed to the wall. The latest murdering raid of the red hatchets had completely shaken his nerve, besides leaving him with only about half his regular force of mobsters.

He spilled all that he knew, from the report of his men that The Whisperer had shot one of his men near Lo Sing's place, down to the final capture of the mysterious, whispering menace in his own Iola Club.

"And for once," snarled Dollar Marino, "us boys were all set to do Wildcat Gordon a favor. We had The Whisperer all wrapped up and ready to deliver to the police, when his yellow devils landed in the club with their hatchets. That makes it a cinch that the Chinese and The Whisperer are hooked up."

Henry Bolton's eyes were bulging. Next to replacing Wildcat Gordon as commissioner, his greatest ambition had long been to get The Whisperer. Many times, he had been close to that scourge of the underworld and the despair of the police, only to have The Whisperer make monkeys out of him and all of his men.

Deputy Henry Bolton replaced the telephone.

"There isn't a damned man coming off China Hill, if it costs me my job!" he declared. "I knew all the time it must be The Whisperer behind these murders! There isn't any Chinaman smart enough to plan the hatchet murders!

"One thing is sure: Wildcat Gordon can't stop me now! The Whisperer is holed up somewhere on China Hill, and I'll bet he's the one who engineered the kidnapping of the Lundin girl!"

Mayor Van Royston was only too glad to agree to all of this. Seldom did the mayor go completely contrary to the commissioner's orders, but here was an emergency. Wildcat Gordon was absent.

"You've got a description of The Whisperer from Dollar Martino," stated Mayor Van Royston. "Deputy Bolton, I give you authority to take China Hill apart, if necessary, to find him."

Thus it happened that Wildcat Gordon was walking directly into a new trap of which he was wholly uninformed. Just above Mall Street, Wildcat inserted his odd dental plates. His flashy clothing and army hat were replaced by the gray apparel of the inconspicuous Dunk Smith, The Whisperer.

CHAPTER XII
HENRY BOLTON'S MISTAKE

THE WHISPERER moved with the speed and same slithering shuffle as the Chinese of Mall Street. His gray-clad figure merged with the patches of after-midnight fog drifting up to China Hill from the bay. His thoughts were upon what the action of the next few hours might develop.

Well enough The Whisperer knew that under the hill upon which he was walking were myriad tunnels, concealed rooms, mysterious passages, hollowed out of the rock in the earlier days when the Chinese had first arrived.

There had been one historic day in the city when the Chinese had been hunted by white men for gold they might have concealed. At a later period, nearly every Oriental trade of an illicit character had been carried on in those same carved tunnels under the hill.

Once there had been opium dens and other places of evil. The Whisperer knew that even now a few such places still existed. None, though, not even The Whisperer, could say which of the Chinese might be conducting these unlawful enterprises.

Perhaps old Lo Sing was one of these. Certainly

the front of the exporting house was only a cover-up for what might be his real business. Lo Sing was a crafty man—one who could fool The Whisperer if need be.

So The Whisperer knew that the Chinese must be outsmarted, if the hiding place of Nellie Lundin were to be discovered. An army of police would only prevent the strategy that might trap Lo Sing. There was Andrew Lundin to think of, who was connected in some strange manner with the Dollar Martino crowd. Right now he was visiting Lo Sing.

Years before Andrew Lundin's face had appeared beside Lo Sing's on the faded snapshot which read: "We shall stand together."

It was for this reason, based on his own deeper knowledge of the Chinese, that The Whisperer had caused the police squads to be ordered from China Hill. He had expected Henry Bolton to obey that order.

Now The Whisperer shuffled close along the buildings, coming slowly down the hill of Mall Street. He could see the pagodalike towers of the Lo Sing house jutting into the murky sky. Only a few Chinese shuffled into view, then shuffled from sight, as if they were denizens of the night, hoping to escape observation.

THE WHISPERER was at the end of the block housing Lo Sing's place when he paused suddenly, then merged his figure with the nearest wall. A whispering oath came to his lips. He had become aware that his order to remove the police from China Hill had been disregarded.

Instead, moving from shelter to shelter, shadows in pairs were right now converging upon the block he had entered. He knew they were detectives from headquarters, for their movements were much more abrupt and more easily followed than those of the Orientals.

If it had not seemed too fantastic, The Whisperer would have believed the augmented patrol on the hill was closing in upon him. Then, suddenly, The Whisperer did believe it. For he heard an exclamation from one of his own detectives.

"If it is The Whisperer, Bill, don't give him a chance! They say he is as fast as greased lightning with his funny rods!"

The Whisperer remained a part of the fog and the wall. Slowly turning his head, he could see other detectives in a side street. Then he saw two big cars moving slowly in opposite directions.

He knew instantly they were not police cars. And he was aware that he had noticed these same cars twice before as he had driven in his coupé to China Hill. One car passed close by, and a voice rasped out, "Dammit, Pete, it's a funny lay, workin' with

the cops! But they want The Whisperer worse than they want the Chinks! You think you saw him at the top of the hill?"

The fog was cold, and that did not account for the sweat that broke out on The Whisperer's forehead. At the moment when he had hoped to personally break the hatchet-murder cases and penetrate to the possible hiding place of Nellie Lundin, he was being hunted directly by his own police and the remnants of the Dollar Martino mob!

A funny combination, indeed, and The Whisperer could only make a vague guess as to how it had happened. But he did not have to guess to know that Dollar Martino had something else up his sleeve besides pretended cooperation with the coppers.

That could be no less than a final, desperate attempt to regain possession of Nellie Lundin, to root out the Chinese who had disrupted the Iola Club and wiped out many of Martino's mob.

The Whisperer eluded the nearest detectives and reached a point where he could spot an old man walking slowly along the Mall Street sidewalk. The old man was thumping the stones with a cane and had all the appearance of being blind.

Old Quick Trigger must be tipped off, kept out of this for the time being. The Whisperer figured he had only one out. He must make a lightning change into the person of Wildcat Gordon and get these coppers off the hill.

Quick Trigger was only a few yards away, when The Whisperer took his chance. His eerie, penetrating whisper lay for a moment like a ghostly echo in Mall Street.

"Keep out of it, Quick Trigger! Slip out of sight! Wait for me!"

Old Quick Trigger thumped along with his cane as if he had not heard. But at the nearest opening between the buildings, he turned abruptly and disappeared. No doubt the ex-deputy had been as quick as The Whisperer to detect the double forces of the police and the Dollar Martino mobsters hemming in the block.

The Whisperer had swiftly mapped out his immediate action. He would whip into one of the convenient recesses, transform himself into Wildcat Gordon, then confront his own men. He glided along the sidewalk, welcoming the yawning mouth of an opening in the wall.

With a breath of relief, The Whisperer already had his hand to his mouth to remove his dental plates and was stepping into the opening, when a hard voice rapped out, "Not so fast, buddy! Get them hands up, an' keep 'em there or I'm borin' you!"

THE WHISPERER put up his hands, thankful he had not got the dental plates from their position. For the detective grinding the snout of a revolver into his stomach was "Chuck" Rafferty, and he was one dick who never fooled about it when he got out his gun.

Another detective, The Whisperer identified as Dillon, equally tough, slapped hard hands on his shoulders. At this moment The Whisperer saw this pair had set their squad car back in the darkness off Mall Street. No doubt they had been waiting there to trap him.

Detective Dillon's hands played rapidly over The Whisperer's body. The dick triumphantly produced two strangely shaped pistols, the deadly, hissing guns. He reached up and caught The Whisperer's left wrist and snapped it down, at the same time encircling it with the cold steel of a handcuff.

"Great stuff, Chuck!" he grunted to Rafferty. "It's him, all right, an' we've got 'im nailed to the cross! Here, hold your wrist over!"

The Whisperer did not attempt to speak or move. There were too many coppers within the immediate vicinity. He was waiting for the instant when Dillon or Rafferty might blow a whistle; then he would be forced to go into fast and rough action if he expected to escape.

The handcuff on his wrist was pulled over by Dillon, and the companion cuff went around the thick wrist of Chuck Rafferty.

"Deputy Bolton's up in the next block," stated Dillon. "Push the mug into the car, and we won't tip off the others. This is our pinch, and what a pinch!"

The Whisperer said nothing. Here was a break. The pair of dicks wanted to be sure they alone got all the credit for his capture. He made no resistance as Chuck Rafferty kept the gun in his stomach and pushed him into the seat of the hidden car.

"Don't give him a chance, Chuck," advised Dillon. "He's poison with a capital 'P.' Keep your gat in his ribs and look out for the Chinks while I get Bolton."

The Whisperer had hoped that this would be his chance. Dillon clumped rapidly up the narrow street, looking for Deputy Bolton. No doubt the hard-bitten dick was having visions of exchanging his good first-grade rating for an inspectorship.

Chuck Rafferty was nobody's fool when it came to keeping the clamps on a hard egg. He pulled The Whisperer down into the seat of the car in the darkness, hooked their handcuffed wrists over the steering wheel and prodded his revolver into his prisoner's ribs.

"Don't think I wouldn't be puttin' a tunnel into your stomach," he warned. "Dead or alive, you're a big feather in the caps o' Rafferty an' Dillon!"

The Whisperer had tensed his muscles, still hoping he might have a chance to shoot a wicked fist to Rafferty's jaw. He could have done it, but a man suddenly smacked on the chin is quite likely to tighten down on his trigger finger. The Whisperer's ribs were hardly bulletproof.

Chuck Rafferty kept hard eyes upon The Whisperer, being too smart to even glance sidewise to follow the progress of Detective Dillon. Rafferty was not muffing his great chance for glory.

The Whisperer knew the arrest had been accomplished so swiftly that old Quick Trigger could not have detected it. He was glad of this, for it would have been like Quick Trigger to have attempted a rescue, even if it earned him nothing but one of Rafferty's bullets.

From up the street, above the Lo Sing block, came the hooting of a police car. It was followed immediately by the sound of quick shots. Or the shots could have been Chinese firecrackers suddenly letting go.

The Whisperer heard Rafferty's, "Now what the hell?" But the stalwart dick did not so much as shift his eyes from his prisoner or move his gun. A few more shots, then shouting indicated that trouble of some kind had broken out.

"I'll bet it's them damn' Chinks you've been murderin' with!" grunted Rafferty. "Well, they've started in the wrong place this time and—"

Chuck Rafferty was wrong to the extent of failing to see the swiftly creeping figures alongside the parked car. The revolver exploded in his hand, and some solid instrument clunked onto his head at the same instant.

THE WHISPERER'S side and back were scored by the powder of the shot, but he had seen that striking hand just in time to squirm forward and miss the bullet that buried itself in the seat cushion behind him.

Detective Chuck Rafferty groaned hollowly and his chin struck the steering post. Chinese—old men with wrinkled faces—were swarming about the police car. They quickly saw that The Whisperer was handcuffed to the unconscious detective.

Low words were uttered in Chinese gutturals. The disturbance farther up Mall Street was still in progress. The Whisperer needed no second guess to know that it must be merely a diversion to distract attention from this particular spot.

The rescuing old Chinamen wasted no time to attempt to break or find the key to the handcuffs holding The Whisperer to the detective. Their skinny old hands pulled both men from the car and bore them swiftly toward the place in the wall where The Whisperer had been trapped.

"Who are you?" hissed The Whisperer, but his question was given no reply.

The Chinese now found the key to the handcuffs, unlocked them quickly, and as quickly shuffled away in the darkness. The Whisperer did not attempt to follow, for a heavy door had closed in his face.

From up the street still came the sounds of trouble, and then the harsh voice of Deputy Henry Bolton was heard shouting somewhere in the street.

"Where the hell, Dillon? You ought've known better than to leave him with one man!"

The Whisperer looked down at the unconscious Chuck Rafferty. He whipped the odd dental plates from his mouth. His hands went over his clothes. The gray became a vivid brown. His shoes turned yellow and his cocky army hat replaced the round-brimmed one of The Whisperer.

There followed a strange ten seconds.

The transformed Wildcat Gordon lifted his fist and smashed it into his own nose. Only the cold nerve instilled in the army could have enabled him to do that. He tore his collar loose above a new red necktie, then he let out a hoarse shout and started shooting into the solid door with Chuck Rafferty's gun.

CHAPTER XIII
INTO LO SING'S DEN

BLOOD TRICKLED from Wildcat Gordon's nose over his grimly set mouth as he backed his way into Mall Street. One hand was gripped into the collar of Detective Chuck Rafferty's coat. Rafferty was still out cold and his head bobbed on a limp neck.

Wildcat Gordon let the detective slip to the sidewalk and pivoted. Deputy Henry Bolton stood there beside Detective Dillon, and they were competing to see which one could open his mouth the widest.

"What the—Wildcat Gordon—"

Henry Bolton managed to get out these few words before Wildcat's knuckles smashed into the end of his long nose.

"That's for what I just collected saving Chuck Rafferty from your damned disobedience!" roared Wildcat. "You're suspended from duty, Henry, and Dillon, you pass the word to the rest of the details to get the hell off China Hill! When I give an order, I mean it!"

Henry Bolton was swearing, gulping. He backed off from the raging Wildcat.

"This'll be the end of you, Gordon!" he got out. "Maybe you don't know we got The Whisperer, an' it came on a tip-off from Dollar Martino himself! Why, Dollar had his own boys up here hunting for him, and Dillon and Rafferty—"

"Shut up!" rapped Wildcat. "Sure, you and Dollar Martino just about got Rafferty rubbed out! If I hadn't got here in time, he might have been hatchet meat for the Chinks! So you got The Whisperer? Well, Rafferty was here with him until the smart Chinese started working on him! If I had been two seconds later, Rafferty would be back under that hill somewhere!"

"But we had him, chief!" exclaimed Dillon.

"Maybe I oughtn't have left him alone with Rafferty! I told Chuck to look out for the Chinks when I went to get Deputy Bolton and—"

"Sure!" interrupted Wildcat. "As for you and Rafferty, Dillon, you will both get citations for bravery! It was good work, but it didn't fit in with my plans! You pass the word along to all of the boys to clear off China Hill! And, Henry, you get going before I get mad again!"

The unconscious Chuck Rafferty was placed in the car, and Detective Dillon drove off, muttering to himself over his partner's dumbness. Deputy Henry Bolton faded out, and within a minute or two the police squads were moving off the hill.

Wildcat Gordon retained his identity and pounded along Mall Street. He looked for old Quick Trigger, but the ex-deputy still was under cover somewhere. In a Chinese drugstore, Wildcat contacted headquarters. He got Detective Sergeant Thorsen.

"Deputy Bolton is rolling off China Hill with all of his men, Sergeant Thorsen," said Wildcat. "Get together five picked squads and start moving. Within the next few minutes, Dollar Martino will learn his effort to get a police cover-up for a move of his own has been blocked, and then we're going to have some real hell."

WILDCAT'S INSTRUCTIONS for the next minute were fast and explicit. In the first alleyway after he came out of the drugstore, Wildcat inserted his odd dental plates. Never had he been forced to make so many swift changes. But he knew that it would be only as The Whisperer, Lo Sing's friend, Dunk Smith, that he would be able to gain entrance to the Mall Street house.

Next, he planned to pick up Quick Trigger. In this he was balked unexpectedly. Old Quick Trigger had already been picked up. The Andrew Lundin butler, Parsons, was responsible for this.

Quick Trigger at this minute was half throttled and unconscious.

Parsons was without a doubt much more than a butler. His attitude of protectiveness toward Andrew Lundin placed him in the role of loyalty more intense than that to be expected of a servant.

When Andrew Lundin entered Lo Sing's house, Parsons maintained his watch outside. Whatever his millionaire master's association with the notorious Dollar Martino or the apparently sinister figure of old Lo Sing, it was clear that the butler believed Lundin's life to be in grave danger.

Whether he feared the Dollar Martino mob, the Chinese hatchet men, or the police could not be decided by old Quick Trigger, who had been observing the tall man across Mall Street. Quick Trigger had heard The Whisperer's instructions to fade out of the picture and he had obeyed temporarily.

Quick Trigger missed the attack upon The Whisperer and the following rescue by the hatchet men. The crafty Chinese fooled Quick Trigger as well as the police when they created a diversion farther up Mall Street.

Quick Trigger, disguised as a blind man, had thumped his way in that direction. He had observed that what had seemed to be shooting was the explosion of Chinese firecrackers around two squad cars. Swearing softly at being taken in by this deception, Quick Trigger thumped his way back toward Lo Sing's wrecked house.

In this movement, he had been observed by Parsons, the butler. Quick Trigger made a mistake that no blind man would have made. He halted in the fog and glanced quickly up and down the street through his colored glasses.

Parsons instantly judged here was a spy. The butler was shy of everyone since the strange and violent conduct of Tiny Traeger, the pretty personal maid to Mrs. Andrew Lundin. Whether Quick Trigger was of the Dollar Martino crowd or representing someone else, Parsons did not wait to ascertain.

The tall butler stepped from the shadows and his long arms shot out. Strong fingers gripped Quick Trigger's throat, cutting off his breath. The ex-deputy, though in his sixties, was a remarkably vigorous fighter.

One gnarled fist came up with smacking impact against Parsons's chin. It rocked the butler's head, and his hands loosened temporarily. If Quick Trigger had been content to hit him again at that moment, he would have put him out.

But the ex-deputy attempted to get his revolver. The butler's fingers fastened on his nose and a thumb pushed under one ear. The punishing hold certainly was not according to any American ethics. But it was highly effective.

Old Quick Trigger groaned and fell down. Something happened to the great nerves, for he could neither see nor feel now. The butler pulled him into the passage leading to Lo Sing's private entrance and left him there. He again took up his station, watching the street.

Parsons was doubtless amazed when he saw the police patrols were vanishing from Mall Street. He, too, had missed witnessing the encounter of The Whisperer with the detectives and his rescue by the Chinese hatchet men.

FOR THE SPACE of many minutes an uncanny silence brooded over narrow Mall Street. No Chinese were shuffling along. The police cars and those of Dollar Martino had disappeared. Twice Parsons

turned toward the Lo Sing door as if he would enter, but returned each time to watch the street.

At this time, the two Dollar Martino cars that had been seen by The Whisperer had disgorged a dozen heavily armed mobsters. These were the survivors of the Iola Club racketeers. Half of these men had produced machine guns.

The bulky Dollar Martino himself was directing the movement.

"If I only knew what the hell's become of Wildcat Gordon!" grunted Dollar Martino. "Some way he butted into things when them Chinks got The Whisperer away from the dicks! He made it mighty sweet and nice for us, clearing the cops off the hill, but where'd he go then?"

"I wouldn't know, boss," said the mobster called Pete. "But if you're going to blast that Lo Sing dump and rout out them hatchet killers, I'd say now's the time. Maybe Wildcat Gordon's planning a trap, and maybe we've got this break because he got into a jam with Deputy Bolton. They don't like each other much."

"O.K.!" rapped Dollar Martino, his bulletlike head nodding. "Scatter out, and I'll show you a new way into Lo Sing's dump! Don't stop burnin' with them choppers as long as there's a Chink in sight, an' be sure and rub out that old devil Lo Sing! But I don't want Andrew Lundin hurt! Get that? He's too valuable!"

It was because Dollar Martino's men were moving toward this new way Martino said he had found into Lo Sing's, that Parsons, the butler, saw no one moving in Mall Street. Martino and his triggermen were descending upon the Lo Sing house from another direction.

It was for this same reason that The Whisperer halted in the foggy silence near Lo Sing's house in Mall Street and could detect no movement. He had vainly tried to make contact with Quick Trigger, and now he was aware he must delay no longer. It was imperative that he get into Lo Sing's curtained den before Andrew Lundin had departed, or Dollar Martino's men had struck.

For The Whisperer was convinced the smart Martino had duped Henry Bolton and the police into a cover-up chase while the racketeer prepared for a reprisal attack upon the Chinese. Andrew Lundin's position in all of this was still most mysterious.

The Whisperer even considered the theory that Lundin himself was working with Martino's crowd and might be tricking Lo Sing in some manner. It was clear that the millionaire was closely associated in some way with both Martino and Lo Sing.

Which was Andrew Lundin's enemy and which was his friend?

Before he reached the wrecked front of Lo Sing's place, The Whisperer had made every effort to find

Quick Trigger. He thought then of Tiny Traeger being in the neighborhood in the guise of a Chinese girl. Perhaps her grandfather had caught the venturesome Tiny and was removing her from China Hill.

The Whisperer hoped this last guess might be true. And in another few minutes he expected to know more of the inside of the relations of Andrew Lundin and Lo Sing. His gray-clad figure glided directly into the usual passageway by which he had often entered Lo Sing's den as a friend.

Parsons, the butler, may have considered himself a crafty fighter. He watched the little gray man cross Mall Street and enter the mouth of the walled passage. Then he acted quickly and quietly.

In the same manner he had seized Quick Trigger from the shadows, the butler descended upon The Whisperer. But The Whisperer was not a man in his sixties, and his senses were keen. He had seen the tall butler's first movement, though it was as noiseless as a tall shadow coming along the wall.

The Whisperer's back bowed into one mighty heave. The butler's own weight drove his skull hard upon the stone paving.

THE WHISPERER did not turn. He maintained his own shuffling forward stride. The butler's long arms shot forward, the fingers hooked to grasp the neck of the little gray man.

Two hands snapped back over The Whisperer's shoulders. The locking of his fingers was like the closing of two steel vises. Parsons was given no time to change his method of attack or to retreat. The steel-wire hands jerked his wrists forward, and The Whisperer's back bowed into one mighty heave.

The butler's own weight drove his skull hard upon the stone paving. Only the toughness of the bone saved his life. But his long body quivered and he rolled inertly to one side.

At this instant, old Quick Trigger was beginning to revive, and he uttered a hollow groan. The Whisperer saw that he was not badly hurt, and he talked fast.

"You find Tiny, Quick Trigger."

"The yellow devils got her, I think," groaned the older man. "I couldn't be sure, but she seemed to disappear into the wall below here."

"I've just put the Lundin butler out of business," said The Whisperer. "It looks as if Lundin has been hooked up with Martino in some of his crookedness. That means that old Lo Sing was not out to rescue Nellie Lundin, but wanted her only as a hostage. The Chinese are holding the girl to compel Andrew Lundin to see things their way. And Lundin's also been connected with Lo Sing in the past."

"If we can only find Tiny, Wildcat," murmured Quick Trigger. "If anything happens to her, it's all because I'm an old fool and thought I was smart. We ain't doin' so good, and I wish I'd never made those dental plates."

The Whisperer was gliding toward Lo Sing's passage door. He thrust Quick Trigger to one side. His knuckles rapped a signal that would be understood by the Chinese on guard. The beamed door opened a few inches and a yellow face was in the aperture.

The Chinese guard's head nodded when he saw the face of The Whisperer, and he swung the door wider. It seemed that whatever had inspired Lo Sing's mysterious use of his friend, Dunk Smith, the welcome of the old Chinaman's house was still the same.

The Whisperer spoke calmly.

"I would speak with Lo Sing at once."

The young Chinaman's countenance was inscrutable, but his black eyes darted along the tunneled passage toward the door that opened into Lo Sing's den. Nevertheless, he did not betray what The Whisperer knew he was thinking.

Perhaps it would not be best to admit the little gray man during the presence of another visitor. The Chinaman turned to close the outside door. The Whisperer regretted the necessity of smashing a fist under the young fellow's ear. There was no alternative, if he hoped to reach Lo Sing's den while the millionaire was still present.

The Whisperer pulled the young Chinaman's inert figure to one side, gestured to Quick Trigger and the passage door was closed.

The pair moved swiftly along the narrow tunnel. There were no other Chinese in evidence when The Whisperer manipulated the inside door that gave entrance directly into the draperied den of Lo Sing.

ONE OF THE swaying curtains hung before this door on the inside. As the space widened, The Whisperer touched Quick Trigger's arm. The monotone of old Lo Sing's voice could be heard. It showed no emotion whatever.

"It is only wisdom that your daughter shall remain a guest in the house of Lo Sing until all that is written for the worthy eighteen has been finished."

"No! No!" came the pleading voice of Andrew Lundin. "Haven't we suffered enough, Lo Sing! You have become mad! My daughter must be freed at once, or I shall go to—"

Never before had The Whisperer heard old Lo Sing speak with other than the greatest deliberation. Never before had the imperturbable Chinaman, so much like a wrinkled, fat idol, been heard to interrupt the speech of another. For Lo Sing would have considered that an insult to any guest within his house.

"The game has come to its end, Andrew!" came Lo Sing's voice. "Watch yourself in the darkness! This way!"

The Whisperer snapped out, "Come on, Quick Trigger!"

But even as he slapped the heavy curtain to one side, the racketing scream of a machine gun filled Lo Sing's den. The Whisperer had only a second's glimpse of smoky fire laid across the room of the draperies, and the fantastic view of two red-handled hatchets whizzing across the space toward the spouting weapon.

Then the lights were cut off. The strange interview between Andrew Lundin and Lo Sing was ended in a sudden bedlam, equaling that which The Whisperer had heard at the Iola Club massacre.

Slugs from newly exploding guns whispered venomously into the heavy curtain where The Whisperer and Quick Trigger were standing. The Whisperer dived, one hand pulling the older man to the floor and the other producing one of his own silenced pistols.

In an interval between the shooting and the dying screams of men, Dollar Martino's voice arose above the din.

"Protect Andrew Lundin! Take him alive! Rub out Lo Sing! Get all the Chinks!"

Perhaps it had been the wise Lo Sing who had caused those lights to go out. Above and around The Whisperer and Quick Trigger, white men and Chinese were surging together in a fierce battle of hatchets and bullets.

The Whisperer identified the voice of Pete.

"Quit shootin'! Stop it, mugs!" yelled Martino's aide. "You damn' fools, we're blastin' each other!"

The Whisperer pulled Quick Trigger under curtains toward a wall. Curses of the mobsters mingled with hissing voices of the Chinese. This was one time when hatchets with red handles were more effective than bullets. The Martino triggermen had rushed the den from three sides; the cutting off of the lights had placed them in the line of fire from their own guns.

The Whisperer could tell that the Chinese with their hatchets must have outguessed the mob raiders. Dollar Martino had announced his discovery of a new way to enter Lo Sing's stronghold. No doubt the racketeer had been tricked. Whenever a white man finds out such a secret, it would be intended that he discover it.

THERE WERE perhaps ten seconds of silence from the guns after Pete had cried out his warning. Into that came the agonized voice of Andrew Lundin.

"Martino! Stop them! My girl is in here! Stop them! I'll settle it all!"

Then the voice of Lo Sing, sharp and unusual:

"Quiet, Andrew! Come! You fool, you'll never settle!"

Whatever this may have meant, Martino's voice yelled a command, and there was apparently a new surging of his men toward these voices. Then came the instant thud-thudding of hatchets into bone, the gurgling screams of white men whose split brains possibly had only time to signal one short cry of death.

The pale luminance of a square door showed abruptly, then it was cut off. Lo Sing and Andrew Lundin must have passed through that opening and closing door. Martino's surviving mobsters were heard to slam bodily into the wall where the two men had vanished.

"Lie still, Quick Trigger," said The Whisperer. "Don't move. I shall follow Lo Sing. The Chinese are having the best of it. Sergeant Thorsen will be coming along."

The Whisperer was sickeningly aware that Sergeant Thorsen and the picked squads he had ordered had not been given time to reach China

The racketing scream of a machine gun filled Lo Sing's den.

Hill. Guns were cracking again, in the mob's desperate stand against the hatchets slicing down their numbers from concealed advantage.

The Whisperer slipped along the wall. He believed he knew another door through which the twisting maze of tunnels under the hills back of the Lo Sing house could be reached. His groping hand touched the rough wood of the door. It would have opened, and The Whisperer was turning to summon Quick Trigger to his side, when a thrown hatchet flashed through the darkness.

Perhaps the hatchet man had been aware of The Whisperer's movement. No doubt he had mistaken him for one of the mobsters. The Whisperer had the sensation of feeling his own warm blood bathing the sides of his neck. Still he heard another thudding blow and the deep groan of old Quick Trigger as his own senses faded out.

CHAPTER XIV
RED HATCHET DOOM

AT PRECISELY the moment The Whisperer was struck down, a door to a cavelike room far back under China Hill swung open.

Tiny Traeger and Nellie Lundin were sitting beside each other on a luxurious couch. For long minutes that had seemed like hours, the two frightened girls had clung to each other.

They could read only a sinister threat in the acts of the Chinese and the words Lo Sing had uttered. No one had entered the imprisoning room after the departure of Lo Sing himself.

The place was as soundless as a tomb. Tiny could only guess what might be happening outside in Mall Street. She regretted the rashness that had brought her here, and yet she was thankful she had come.

For she had been able to comfort the terrified Nellie Lundin. There was something in the other girl's fear, a horror in the brown eyes, that Tiny could not fathom. Nor could the daughter of the millionaire bring herself to speak of the terrible experience in the room at the Iola Club.

Tiny did not know why the other girl put up her slim white hand again and again, staring at it. Perhaps Nellie Lundin shuddered and closed her eyes often because she could still see the lifted red hatchet in the hand of the dead Angel.

Thus they had waited, talking little, until this door opened suddenly. Nellie Lundin instantly clamped the back of her hand to her teeth and screamed. Tiny caught her trembling figure and pulled her into her arms.

Four wrinkled Chinamen walked into the room without speaking. A red-handled hatchet with a gleaming, sharpened blade was in the right hand of each old man. Their yellow bodies were bared from their waists. From the shrunken shoulder of one man a slow rivulet of blood had poured from a bullet wound, leaving a scarlet track over his breast.

"The red hatchets! They've come! That is it! That is it!"

Nellie Lundin screamed out the words, then Tiny knew she had fainted in her arms. Tiny's nerve was badly shaken, but she placed the other girl gently on the couch and whipped to her feet.

"What do you want?" she cried out. "You wouldn't dare touch us!"

The four hatchet men were as silent as yellow automatons. They turned, facing the door through which they had entered. They had left it swinging open, and beyond the room was only the black, yawning mouth of a tunnel.

Tiny then perceived it was not the purpose of the Chinese to commit immediate murder, as Nellie Lundin had seemed to believe. Tiny was relieved, and then terror gripped her heart.

SOMEWHERE along that black tunnel another door must have opened. Screaming shouts of men penetrated to the inner room. Shots crackled, and curses echoed through the passage. Tiny did not need to be told that some of the screaming came from dying men.

Now she believed she could understand the silent attitude of the four Chinese with the hatchets. They took up their positions, one pair at either side of the opened door. Certainly the light from the room could be seen by the battling men farther up the tunnel.

This could be no other than an ambush, perhaps a last stand of the Chinese. Tiny hoped Wildcat Gordon had broken in with his police. Then she was sickeningly aware from the oaths she heard that the raiders could not be the police.

Suddenly another figure glided from the tunnel. The smooth face of Lo Wun, the son of Lo Sing, appeared. His dark eyes took in the motionless figure of Nellie Lundin on the couch.

"It is well the young miss sleeps," said Lo Wun.

"Sleeps, you fool?" cried Tiny. "She's scared stiff! What is it? Have the police come?"

"Lo Wun regrets the police have not come," stated the young Chinese. "Have no fear of the red hatchets. You will not be harmed. The men of Dollar Martino walk to their death."

"Dollar Martino?" gasped Tiny.

But Lo Wun was speaking rapidly in Chinese to the four hatchet men. One of these old men stepped forward and spoke in English.

"This humble one will serve," he stated simply. "The honorable son of Lo Sing has a long measure of suns, and my own are short."

Tiny heard the soft creaking of another door. She turned in amazement to see the fat, shapeless Lo Sing standing beside Andrew Lundin. The white-faced millionaire pulled his arm free from the Chinaman's grip. He crossed the room, falling on his knees and pulling the unconscious girl on the couch into his arms.

Lo Sing's emotionless voice seemed to reply to the wrinkled Chinese who was arguing with Lo Wun.

"The house of Lo Sing must keep face. Lo Wun, my son, you will go. May fortune bring you back."

From up the tunnel came the hard voice of Dollar Martino.

"Down this way! Bring that chopper! There's a light and a door! Blast it first!"

Tiny felt herself whirled suddenly from her feet. She was aware that the hands of Lo Wun had caught and thrown her to one side. Bullets streamed through the doorway, hitting the sides, screaming into the room. The four hatchet men were crouched out of line with the bullets.

"Go, my son!"

Again it was the voice of old Lo Sing. Tiny was looking at the opened door; then she could see nothing. The lights in the room had been clicked off. At that, the machine gun ceased racketing and the feet of men could be heard pounding along.

"Take it easy!" came a command from up the tunnel. "Lundin himself may be down there! Get moving!"

Tiny crawled across the floor. She could hear Nellie Lundin sobbing. The girl had recovered consciousness in her father's arms.

"Hold my hand, oh, hold my hand," the millionaire's daughter was crying out. "Don't let them —"

Andrew Lundin said, "You're all right, honey, all right now."

Tiny heard the door where the four hatchet men stood close suddenly. Old Lo Sing was muttering in Chinese. His words sounded to Tiny like a prayer.

That machine gun exploded again, but it came with a muffled thudding from the tunnel. Old Lo Sing's words ceased. Tiny wondered if Lo Wun had gone out there. She wanted to know and she called out, "Lo Wun!"

SHE COULD NOT have heard a reply, if there had been one, for the room under China Hill suddenly rocked and its wooden doors shook in their fastenings. It was a heavy detonation, and the door that had blocked the black tunnel was ripped from its hinges and cracked into the room.

Nellie Lundin screamed, and Andrew Lundin shouted, "Lo Sing, your son! You couldn't have done that!"

Lo Sing did not reply. The fat Chinaman was standing by the wall, and one of his long-nailed hands moved a switch. The light flashed on and pungent blue smoke drifted in from the tunnel.

There were no oaths now, no cries, no sound of anything as the blue smoke threaded above the four wrinkled Chinese who were still crouching with their hatchets in their hands. Lo Sing folded his hands across his capacious stomach, and his yellowed idol face was impassive.

"Tonight you will burn the incense to the last sun for the house of Lo Sing," he said, calmly. "All has been finished as was written for the worthy eighteen."

Tiny stared at the four aged Chinamen as they bowed and solemnly laid their four red-handled hatchets on the rug at the feet of Lo Sing. The four then passed out through the door that had admitted Lo Sing and Andrew Lundin.

"We will wait, Andrew, and perhaps The Whisperer will come," stated Lo Sing.

CHAPTER XV
DOLLAR MARTINO'S END

THE JOLT of the rocking explosion under China Hill brought The Whisperer to aching consciousness.

One hand felt the wet blood over one ear and at one side of his neck. He was living, but he was not so sure a red hatchet hadn't split his head.

But a groping hand found the hatchet that had hit him and he was sitting up, so he judged his skull must still be intact. There was still a rolling echo that came from a broad, opened door nearby. Almost at once thin threads of blue powder smoke assailed his nostrils.

Old Quick Trigger had also been knocked out, but now he was crawling around on his hands and knees. Abruptly the light in Lo Sing's draperied den flashed on. The Whisperer and Quick Trigger looked at each other.

"You still alive, Wildcat?" groaned Quick Trigger. "You don't look human!"

The Whisperer pulled himself to his feet, staring at the door where the blue smoke thickened. The floor of Lo Sing's den was a bloody shambles. Six dead Chinese and as many more white men with hatchets stuck in their skulls lay grotesquely about.

But around The Whisperer and Quick Trigger for the moment was an appalling silence as the echoes died. Then both heard the quick sound of feet coming from the tunnel in which the explosion had taken place.

The running feet were those of Dollar Martino. Shrewdly looking out for his own hide to the last, he had suspected a trap down that tunnel and as the last of his mobsters had rushed toward the room in which were Tiny Traeger, Lo Sing and the others, Dollar Martino had dropped back and waited.

He heard the final, awful screams of his men as shattered, falling rock crushed their bodies. Martino knew then that the last of his mob had gone to their deaths. He had saved himself by his own smartness.

Now he had the fear that perhaps some of the hatchet men were between him and the street. So he caught up a dropped machine gun and carried it as he ran. The light of Lo Sing's den flashed on almost in his face.

Dollar Martino crooked the "chopper" across one arm. He could see two living men in the room of death. Then he was facing the little gray man he knew as The Whisperer, and another older man with a bald pate and fringe of gray hair.

THE WHISPERER and Martino saw each other at the same instant. Martino's head bobbed on his huge body. He could see The Whisperer's hands were empty. The Whisperer had lost his silenced pistols, and he was unarmed.

Martino's dark eyes flashed to Quick Trigger. He recognized him as the former police deputy, the close companion of Commissioner Wildcat Gordon.

A great truth dawned upon the mobster.

"Get them hands up!" he yelped. "So that's it! The Whisperer, huh? Wildcat Gordon! If I'd had any brains, I'd have got it sooner!"

The snout of the machine gun was lined across both men. The Whisperer said, "Up with them, Quick Trigger?"

Dollar Martino laughed shortly, mockingly.

"And so, I'll be the only guy to walk out of this jam! By all the devils in hell, but that's a good one! And before your cops come poppin' in, Wildcat Gordon, I'll have the pleasure of stretchin' The Whisperer! Won't that let me out clean!"

The Whisperer's own hands were up. He was listening intently, in the hope that Sergeant Thorsen's squads would be breaking in. There was no sound. There was not one chance in a million that Dollar Martino would hesitate to use the deadly chopper.

In fact, the racketeer had to use it, if he wanted to leave this China Hill massacre with an alibi. He would hardly dare risk the chance of Wildcat Gordon or Quick Trigger talking. He could murder them in cold blood, and five minutes later Dollar Martino would be all in the clear.

"This'll make a hero out of me!" sneered the mobster. "A public hero number one! Ain't that a good one! And before you go, Wildcat Gordon, it's a pleasure to tell you how close you were to cracking something really big, and then missed out on it because I was too smart for you!"

"Yes?" said The Whisperer, playing for time.

Dollar Martino held all the cards of death. Behind him, he knew the tunnel was blocked with his own dead men. Between him and Mall Street there was no one but Wildcat Gordon and Quick Trigger.

So Dollar Martino boasted. His words mocked the helplessness of his prisoners while one finger played with the trigger of the "chopper." He told them all about Andrew Lundin.

He said, "And Andrew Lundin is still alive and will keep on paying so long as he lives. In fact, he'll put up a cold million after tonight. He's in there somewhere and after a while he'll come crawling out. Now you know why he'll pay, why Lo Sing paid for years until he got wise to himself. So, Wildcat Gordon, that's all!"

He pulled the machine gun slowly into position.

"It's the finish of The Whisperer, and Wildcat Gordon," he snarled, the killer light coming into his black eyes.

"The finish!" he repeated, delaying the final few seconds to enjoy his moment, to feed his murder lust.

Then Dollar Martino's bulletlike head split as mushily as a ripe tomato under the red-handled hatchet that came down, wielded by a fat, yellow hand with long fingernails. The machine gun fell to the floor unexploded, and the crooked brains of Dollar Martino stained the weapon.

"The finish," spoke the colorless voice of old Lo Sing. "It had to be the finish."

THE SHAPELESS Chinaman was staring at the hand with which he had wielded the deadly hatchet. The long, curving nail of the little finger had been broken in that effort, a sacred fingernail to old Lo Sing, that had been protected for many years.

Lo Sing's eyelids drooped as he looked at The Whisperer.

"It is good," he said. "You are the great commissioner, the Wildcat Gordon. You were my friend, and now you know about my other lifelong friend, Andrew Lundin."

The Whisperer heard the distant hammering at a door. He began the fast transformation from The Whisperer to Wildcat Gordon as old Lo Sing watched.

When his odd dental plates came out, he said, "Wildcat Gordon, also, is your friend, Lo Sing, and the friend of Andrew Lundin. And as a friend, the police commissioner is uninformed of the tribute you have been paying this ruthless racketeer at your feet. If years ago, you and Andrew Lundin and John Parsons, a butler, came into the United States illegally, it is forgotten."

"Andrew has been my friend," stated Lo Sing. "We entered together on a ship, but we did not then know of the law. Andrew has helped my house become honorable and rich. This Dollar Martino has collected from us for years, threatening to expose us, drive Andrew Lundin from the country, from his family who know nothing of all this."

"And for Andrew Lundin's sake you called together the old Hop Jo, the worthy eighteen, to clean up the record, is that it, Lo Sing?"

"That is it, my friend," said Lo Sing. "And now, they come."

From the side tunnel through which Lo Sing had come upon Dollar Martino came Andrew Lundin, his daughter, and Tiny Traeger. From the Mall Street entrance the police of Sergeant Thorsen could be heard coming toward the big door.

"The record will remain clean, Lo Sing," pledged Wildcat Gordon, so that Andrew Lundin might hear. "Your worthy eighteen, some are dead, others have gone."

Old Lo Sing stared at his broken fingernail. His wrinkled face held no expression.

"The worthy son of the humble house of Lo Sing gave his life in the explosion," he stated. "So I, too, would join my ancestors. Long life and happiness, my friend, Andrew—"

"No! No, Lo Sing!" shouted Andrew Lundin,

attempting to get to the man with the face of a yellow idol.

But the poison the wily Lo Sing had concealed under that broken fingernail was instant in its effect. His death smile was like that of some benevolent god carved in stone.

MAYOR VAN ROYSTON accompanied Henry Bolton, trailing behind the first of Sergeant Thorsen's coppers. Mayor Van Royston gulped and was very white. Andrew Lundin and Quick Trigger were leading their daughter and their granddaughter from the bloody room.

"It's a sweet cleanup, Mayor Van Royston," stated Wildcat calmly. "It seems that Dollar Martino tried to put the racket bug on Lo Sing. There's Dollar himself with his hair parted, and the rest of his boys are buried back under China Hill. If there are any of Lo Sing's Hop Jo left alive with their hatchets, I'd like to round them up. What a racket squad they would make!"

THE END

Coming soon from Sanctum Books—

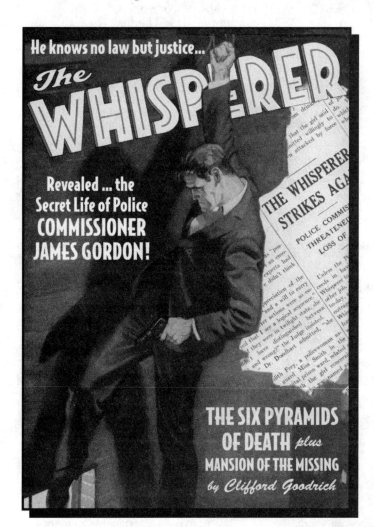

One by one,
the possessors of
THE SIX PYRAMIDS
OF DEATH fall victim
to a silent killer.
Can
The Whisperer
solve this
deadly riddle?

• • • • •

When the home
of a prominent
judge is turned into a
house of horror,
Wildcat Gordon realizes
The Whisperer must
return from the dead
to haunt the
MANSION OF THE
MISSING.

• • • • •

BONUS: a NORGIL THE MAGICIAN story by The Shadow's Walter Gibson writing as "Maxwell Grant"

Don't miss the excitement in THE WHISPERER #2

EVIL EYE
by Clifford Goodrich

THE FIRST WOMAN who saw the wispy figure grabbed her child and ran into the tenement.

The second one pointed her finger at him. She said, "E-e-e-!" Then she fainted.

A group of children scattered into various doorways on the squalid street. It was very peculiar.

The little figure in gray turned a pointed chin to the spot the children had vacated. He hissed an eerie whispering warning and glided down the street. Eyes looked furtively out of windows. The shades were drawn tight and housewives shuddered within the privacy of their dwellings.

A tall, gaunt man who happened to turn the corner

When The Whisperer bumped into *himself* on the street, all hell broke loose!

at that moment, stopped suddenly. He pushed a hat back on his bald head and scratched the space between the two tufts of grizzled hair at the sides. His eyes seemed to squint in surprise.

Swiftly, he overtook the gray-clad figure.

"Dammit all," he began, "You're—"

The gray figure whirled. The lips above the oddly pointed chin twisted into a whispering snarl.

Two guns leaped into his hands. There was the dull *pffffft-plop* of silenced weapons. Lead screamed past the gaunt man.

"What in hades!" the gaunt man yelled. Then he dropped flat on the pavement. More lead whipped the air above him. There was amazement on the gaunt man's face.

The gray figure scuttled around a corner. Retired deputy Richard Traeger, better known as old "Quick Trigger," scrambled to his feet. What had happened seemed impossible! Quick Trigger didn't like it at all.

Old Quick was the only man alive who knew that The Whisperer, dreaded "supercrook" nemesis of the underworld, was really Police Commissioner James "Wildcat" Gordon. Old Quick had practically raised Wildcat.

A master at disguise, he had made the queer dental plates that gave The Whisperer his chilling huskiness of speech. It was a masterpiece that Quick Trigger frequently regretted.

Quick Trigger started to pursue the fleeing gray man. Then he stopped. If The Whisperer had fired those shots in earnest, he would not have missed. The Whisperer seldom did.

For some reason, it seemed, The Whisperer did not wish even his closest friend to follow him. That probably meant the danger was great.

It turned out that it was.

The retired deputy started back toward police headquarters. He had come to this squalid section because he had heard that The Whisperer had reappeared here. Quick had been hunting for him for more than an hour. Wildcat was needed at headquarters.

A tip there warned that a murderous extortion racket was about to close in on the trucking industry of the city.

As he pulled up in front of headquarters, Quick Trigger wondered what there could be in that poverty-stricken section that tied up to a major racket. But he knew The Whisperer was usually far ahead of underworld tips that reached the police.

The first person Quick Trigger saw when he clumped into the building was a chunky, red-haired human dynamo with a jaw like granite. He was clad in a suit that would have been the envy of a sideshow barker. It could also have been used for a checkerboard.

Loud yellow shoes, a bright, button-hole carnation and a necktie to match, topped off the suit.

"Henry," Wildcat Gordon shouted, "you've been howling for months for The Whisperer's neck! Now I'm beginning to agree with you, and you don't like it!"

Wildcat strode through a door and faced a tall, long-nosed individual. He had a mouth like a fish. He used it now to protest. The man was Deputy Henry Bolton.

Normally, Bolton had two overpowering ambitions. One was to replace Wildcat as commissioner. The other was to have The Whisperer caught— preferably by somebody else.

"B-b-but, here's a racket threatening some of our most influential citizens," Bolton argued. "I've been telling you that for half an hour!"

Quick Trigger's jaw dropped open. His recent encounter with The Whisperer had been less than ten minutes before!

The retired deputy started to speak. He was interrupted by a high-pitched scream from outside. Staccato bursts of shots ripped out from the street.

Wildcat Gordon dived across the floor, made the hall in a single jump. Two Police Positives leaped into his hands.

Br-r-r-r-r-rt! came from the street.

A smallish, shriveled man stumbled down the hallway. He was so excited he fell flat on his face. He sat up and began wiping his forehead with a handkerchief.

"Th-th-they'll get me yet!" he stammered.

Wildcat rushed past him, to the outside steps. Another burst of shots parted his reddish hair. A second figure lay sprawled below him. The man scrambled to his feet, then looked calmly at a speeding sedan that disappeared down the block.

"Close," he said. "But it could have been closer."

Wildcat's cold gray eyes surveyed the second man. He was a tall, bushy-haired individual with snapping black eyes. His name was Terrington Small. But he was better known as Terry "Silk." He was a trial lawyer who boasted he had never "fixed" a jury.

Many persons did not believe the boast. They doubted that his silky, persuasive voice and knowledge of legal gymnastics made it unnecessary to fix a jury, as he claimed.

Terrington Small always insisted his client was innocent. Few persons believed that, either. Much to old Quick Trigger's snorted disgust, Terry Silk had the temerity to consider running for district attorney.

Wildcat Gordon looked coldly now at the lawyer.

"If it was really you they were after, they had a good chance," he said, flatly.

Terry Silk looked quickly at Wildcat.

"I rolled behind the concrete side of the steps," he explained. "I was out of line."

The voice of the man inside interrupted him. The small man had gotten to his feet and was screaming for help.

Wildcat knew him. His name was George "Rocky" Crangle. He was in both the trucking and bonding business. His boyhood pals had dubbed him "Rocky" because he was about as hard as a pound of butter in the summer. Crangle was notoriously afraid of his shadow. He never played anything but a safe bet, if he could help it.

He was demanding plenty of safety as Wildcat, with the lawyer, came back into the headquarters building.

"I've been threatened, and now they're trying to kill me!" he shouted. "It's the biggest trucking racket that ever broke!"

He paused and looked a moment at Wildcat. His eyes were wide. When he got no response, he went on.

"Knuckles Werner is behind it," he insisted. "I'd be the first one he'd go after. He forced me to bail him, and he knows I'd cancel it the first chance I got."

Wildcat's expression did not change. He knew that "Knuckles" Werner had bragged of forcing Crangle to bail him a robbery charge. And he probably wouldn't beat the charge. Unless he skipped the bail.

Wildcat Gordon also knew that Terrington Small was attorney of record for Knuckles Werner! There had been reports that the two had quarreled. But that often happens, when a lawyer names a stiff fee for a case that is tough.

Quick Trigger cleared his throat.

"You were talkin' about The Whisperer," he said. "I saw him on Cleary Street, ten minutes ago! He got away." Quick Trigger stressed the ten minutes.

Wildcat Gordon whirled. In the same motion, he reached for his army hat, pulled it down over one blue-gray eye.

"I'm going to get him," he snapped. "Personally! And now!"

Wildcat stamped out of headquarters, Quick Trigger at his heels. Halfway down the steps, they almost ran into a human projectile in the form of a girl. Her hair was a tawny mane about the color of a lioness. She was Sarah, the daughter of Terrington Small.

"I must see my father," she cried. "I know he's inside!"

Wildcat merely nodded. He stepped to the curb, climbed into a police car with Quick Trigger.

"This impostor's been raising hell in the foreign district," Wildcat clipped. "I just found out he's got the section scared to death with a petty extortion racket. And I've got a hunch it's a lot more than that."

Wildcat was too busy talking to notice a second car falling in behind him. Had he looked in the rearview mirror, he might have recognized the scarred features of Knuckles Werner. Knuckles was just as murderous as his reputation indicated.

Had Wildcat looked a second time, he might have seen the muzzle of a submachine gun creeping out of the right-hand window of the pursuing machine. But Wildcat Gordon was thinking of The Whisperer.

Even when he was considered a crook and hunted by cops, or when he was a superclub in the hands of a ruthless justice that made its own rules, The Whisperer was the friend of children and dogs alike.

The impostor had been chiseling in petty ways. He had convinced the ignorant dwellers of the squalid tenements that possessed the evil eye. Thousands of ignorant people believed in that power, paid tribute to it.

Women fear for their children, and the children themselves are made afraid. Cases of it pop up in magistrates' courts every year.

Wildcat was thinking of that, instead of a car that might be behind him. He didn't want The Whisperer's usefulness ruined.

The pursuing machine caught up with the police car a block from Cleary Street. The muzzle of the tommy gun came all the way out and began to talk. It talked in short, jerky bursts of lead and flame.

Wildcat didn't even look at the machine. The bulletproof glass of the squad car began to split. It wasn't built for quite that kind of leaden hurricane.

Wildcat twisted the wheel sharply. The police car tilted up, almost capsized. Then it slammed into a light pole, burst into flames.

Wildcat Gordon was out of the car in an instant. He rolled under it, leaped to a crouch on the other side.

Quick Trigger was already leaning behind the blazing hood. An amazing brace of revolvers roared in his hands. They were big enough to belong to the old Wild West, and they sounded like army field guns.

Wildcat's Police Positives began to speak with authority. He stood well out from the burning machine. The blaze created an effective smoke screen. A tire on the mobsters' car burst with a plop. Knuckles Werner stepped on the gas and the car pounded around a corner.

By the time Wildcat got there, it had turned into some alley, disappeared. It might have gone into any hidden garage in that neighborhood. It would be useless to make inquiry. People who lived on Cleary Street didn't talk. They preferred to live.

Wildcat turned to old Quick Trigger.

"First move in the trucking racket," he snapped; "Werner must have known a tip came to headquarters."

Quick Trigger didn't answer. Instead, he pointed a finger toward the corner.

A scrawny, threadbare man was racing toward them. There was no mistaking the fear in his eyes. That kind of fear could not be simulated without great acting ability.

He ran jerkily, rabbitlike. At first, he didn't see Wildcat and Quick Trigger. When he did, he tried to dodge. Wildcat seized him by the shoulder.

"What's on your mind, Smoky?" he demanded. "Better come clean."

"Smoky" was a drug addict, who was always trying to quit but didn't have the stamina. He turned wild, dilated eyes at Wildcat. His jaws worked strangely; then his eyes gleamed.

"The Whisperer!" he squealed. "He's got the evil eye! At Roundman's Saloon!"

Smoky twisted suddenly, eluded Wildcat's grip. The commissioner let him scamper up the street, noted the direction he took. Then Wildcat's jaw set in a hard, straight line.

"I think we're getting somewhere," he ripped. "Let's go!"

Roundman's Saloon was one of those places where anything can happen—and frequently does. The window was smeared with soap so pedestrians could not see what went on within. There was also a lookout to tip off customers who did not wish visits from the police.

Wildcat Gordon didn't go in. He saw what he was after before he got there. But what he was after saw him just an instant before that.

A slight, gray figure burst out of the saloon. He wore a quaint round-brimmed hat. He looked just as The Whisperer should. Before Wildcat could bring up his police guns, that flat *pfffft-plop* of a silenced gun split the air.

Quick Trigger suddenly realized that the note was sharper than that of The Whisperer's super-silenced pistols. And he knew he should have recognized the difference earlier in the night.

This time, the impostor's aim was better. A slug struck Wildcat in the shoulder, spun him around.

Under any other circumstances, Quick Trigger's portable cannons would have boomed immediately. But Quick did not know how badly hurt Wildcat was. And Wildcat Gordon was Quick Trigger's main weakness.

Instinctively, he leaned over the fallen man. In that instant, the fake Whisperer got away.

Wildcat struggled to his feet.

"Flesh wound," he snapped. "Now we've lost the guy!"

Quick Trigger stuttered an apology. But he ripped Wildcat's coat back, hauled him into a nearby drugstore. He knew Wildcat wouldn't stop going; so he refused to take any chances on infection. He probed out the slug and applied disinfectant.

Then he scratched his bald head in puzzlement.

"Dammitall, Wildcat, what do you make of this?"

Wildcat took the proffered slug. It was a lead bullet, but around the lead was a hard resinous substance. Wildcat Gordon whistled softly.

"They're making cartridges and casings now of synthetic resins," he said slowly. "It's a new invention. Probably it gave somebody this idea. Look at it closely."

Quick Trigger looked at the slug. The heat of Wildcat's body had so softened the resinous surface of the bullet that no rifling marks remained.

"He's not taking any chances on identification," Quick Trigger observed.

Wildcat stood suddenly erect. He thought he saw a lot of things. Things that connected, and which he didn't like.

"I don't think that's the idea," he snapped. "It goes deeper than that. And it's no petty racket."

Outside the drugstore, Wildcat unfolded his plan. Quick Trigger protested volubly, but Wildcat insisted.

Wildcat Gordon was alone when he approached a disreputable looking rooming house, a few minutes later. It was a place where a queer, elusive fellow known as D. Smith had rooms.

D. Smith was The Whisperer. Wildcat had decided to use his Whisperer guise to get the impostor. He had suddenly realized that this was a most important step to be taken.

At the foot of the stairs, he stopped suddenly. A body was sprawled in the vestibule. It lay in a spreading pool of blood. Wildcat turned the man over. A few moments before it had been Smoky, the drug addict. Now, it was nothing.

A low growl came from Wildcat's throat as he carried the undernourished body upstairs. Smoky had never harmed anyone but himself. Many times, The Whisperer had tried to straighten him out. Smoky's constitutional distrust of law might have prevented his telling the truth to Commissioner Gordon.

But Smoky had obviously been on his way with information he considered important. And he had intended to tell it to the gray man he knew stood for a justice that even Smoky could understand.

In the rooms above, a furry black ball of canine dynamite leaped upon Wildcat. The dog whined in a frenzy of excitement. He lived only for The Whisperer. He was a scotty as black as the ace of spades.

The nose of a dog could not be fooled. He knew Wildcat Gordon was his gray-clad master, The Whisperer.

"Quiet, Brian Boru," Wildcat said. "You can't go this time."

Wildcat was busy for several minutes. Rapidly, he became The Whisperer. The loud checked suit disappeared. Gray spats went over the shoes. The insertion of false teeth made by old Quick Trigger gave the jaw its oddly pointed appearance.

The Whisperer went out. But he was wrong about one thing. Brian Boru was quick in the dimness. The dog went out, too.

Ten minutes later, The Whisperer tooled his shabby gray coupé down the street. His whitish, powdery hair showed dimly as he passed a street light. An eerie, whispering chuckle drifted from the car's open window. The chuckle did not contain mirth.

The Whisperer stopped near Roundman's Saloon. He locked the doors of his little coupé and drifted toward the doorway. The lookout suddenly snapped erect, darted inside.

The gray figure with the oddly pointed chin glided through the door. He walked up to the bar and ordered a beer. The chilling voice made the bartender turn.

He dropped the glass he was drying. Shakily, he reached for another and filled it with beer. Apparently, he knew this was not an impostor.

The Whisperer picked up his glass and turned toward the room. His colorless eyes gave no indication that he recognized the hulking form of Knuckles Werner sprawled in a chair by a table.

Werner's hands crept slowly into his pockets. The Whisperer knew those two hands held death-dealing guns. Other ugly-faced mobsters moved slowly along the bar.

The gray man raised his glass slowly and drained it. Then, without another glance at the thugs, he glided silently toward the street. At the door, he almost ran into a bundle of fury. The fury was the tawny-haired daughter of Terry Silk, the great trial lawyer.

The girl's blue eyes narrowed to slits. She whipped out a gun, squeezed the trigger. The gun blatted and the window of Roundman's Saloon crashed into fragments.

The Whisperer thought idly, as he twisted away, that he was missing a chance to learn if she were using bullets coated with resin. But that shot had told him something.

He became a blurry, indefinite figure in the gloom. The door of his coupé slammed and The Whisperer drove down the street. He pulled to a halt in the shadows of an abandoned warehouse. He thought that he would soon have visitors. He hadn't, however, believed they'd come as quickly as they did.

His speculation was rudely interrupted by their arrival. The coupé had scarcely stopped when a black delivery truck screeched to a halt. Machine guns let loose with a ragged roar and a barrage of lead.

The little gray car rocked under the impact. Lead screamed through it. The windows were open. The figure in the car slumped forward, jolted as lead plowed into it.

Knuckles Werner piled out of the truck. He ripped open the door of the coupé, snapped on a flashlight. Then he hauled the body out into the street.

"Easy!" he gloated. "Now we take care of the body!"

Harsh voices laughed as he hauled the gray form into the truck. Then the truck rumbled off.

The delivery wagon stopped before a house in a distant part of the city. Considerable activity went on within the place. Feet could be heard shuffling about in the cellar.

Then the big form of Knuckles Werner appeared in the room at the front. In the shadows, near him, sat a second figure. The second man was masked. Knuckles seemed highly elated.

"We're almost set, now," he growled. "There's just one more thing I got to do."

Werner crumpled up a paper and threw it into a fireplace. Then he and his companion sauntered out of the room. As the door closed behind them, another opened. It was the one they had come through, from the cellar.

A gray figure stood motionless for a moment in the center of the room. It drifted toward the fireplace, looked quickly at the burning embers.

The flames were consuming a crumpled letter. Most of it was then a feathery ash. As the gray figure looked, the flames crept over the engraved letterhead. They ate up the name, "Terrington Small, Attorney at Law!" The letter became ash in a final burst of flame. A gust of a draft sent it soaring up the chimney.

The gray figure straightened and chuckled. The chuckle was an eerie, triumphant whisper. Then the man turned, glided back to the door that led to the cellar. Silently, he crept down the stairs.

There was a strong smell of ozone, as if highly charged electricity had been passed through the air. As the gray figure passed over the floor, a key clicked in the lock of the door above him.

The gray figure chuckled again. He knew that ozone would preserve a body. It would prevent decomposition. The body could be produced, later; it would seem it had been a dead man only a very short time. Even months later.

And The Whisperer knew that the resin-coated bullets were not being used to prevent identification of the killer's gun. Their lack of rifling marks would indicate that they could have been fired by The Whisperer's super-silenced pistols! That was part of the plot.

But the gray man had his own pistols, as he crept out of a cellar window that was open.

The gray man darted quickly down a darkened street. His silent footsteps took him through a business and industrial district. He had to pass one of the major trucking depots of the city.

Dozens of great vans were drawn up at the curb and in the loading yard. The gray figure was not thinking of the trucks, right then. He knew that the fake Whisperer and the truck extortion racket were closely bound together. But he was thinking of another job he had to do, before that racket could be taken care of.

He hardly noticed the surly drivers of the trucks. But they noticed him. One of them yelled in sudden fright.

"The Whisperer!" he screamed. "We've been warned. Here he comes!"

Huge, two-fisted drivers piled out of truck cabs. It seemed ludicrous that so many hard-boiled battlers would flee before such an insignificant figure. But such was the reputation of The Whisperer.

It turned out that it was well they did run. The gray figure was in the center of the trucking area when the first time bomb went off.

There was a roar, as if a bombing plane had dropped its deadly cargo. A ten-ton truck seemed to disintegrate. Burly men were knocked to the ground. Flying bits of metal struck others.

Then a second truck was demolished by a bomb.

The slight figure of The Whisperer was picked up literally by the force of the blast. His small body hurtled across the street, slapped against the areaway of a cellar window.

The explosion seemed to excite the truckers out of their first fear. They cursed The Whisperer, started menacingly across the street.

The only thing that saved The Whisperer was the force with which he had struck the cellar window grating. It was old and rusty. The Whisperer fell through. Dimly conscious, he broke the glass of the window, eased himself into the cellar.

The back door yielded to his touch and the gray man raced out into the alley at the rear. He knew he had no time to lose. He was pretty sure what would happen next, but he wanted confirmation.

He knew the extortion mob had struck their first major blow. What had happened to those behemoths of the road would serve as a warning to every other truck owner in the city. They would pay whatever tribute the gang demanded. They would pay and keep their mouths shut. The police would be entirely helpless. And The Whisperer would be blamed for the terror.

The gray man reached the back door of a tall office building. A sharp tool jimmied the spring lock and the dim figure mounted the emergency fire stairs. On the fifth floor, he went silently to a door marked "Terrington Small, Attorney."

A ring of skeleton keys jingled briefly. Then The Whisperer was inside.

Quick hands went through the file marked "Correspondence." The pale, colorless eyes examined every carbon duplicate in the file. Finally, The Whisperer found one addressed to Knuckles Werner.

He scanned it briefly. It was the one he wanted. A ghostly, whispering chuckle sounded as he switched off the light.

Blam!

A gun roared and the lead tugged at The Whisperer's coat sleeve. A girl's voice rapped out, "I'll get you before you get my father! I know you plan to get him!"

The gun roared twice more in quick succession. Slugs tore through the spot where The Whisperer had stood. But the gray man was moving, weaving in an uncertain pattern. Before the girl could fire again, a strong hand clamped over her automatic. One finger slid quickly behind the trigger.

The Whisperer ripped a telephone from the wall. He used the cord to bind the girl. He tied a gag in her mouth. Not too tightly, but secure enough that she would be a while getting rid of it. The Whisperer had no intention of letting Terry Silk's daughter interfere with plans he had made. And he knew he had no time to lose.

He padded to the street by way of the stairs. The night watchman dozed in the main entrance. He had a vague impression of a gray shape flitting quickly by him. The front door slammed and he jerked awake. He decided it must have been the wind.

A newsboy was hawking papers on the street. The gray man bought one and looked at the headlines. The headline screamed that The Whisperer had been killed on Cleary Street. Then his body had been hauled away. There was also a last-minute bulletin of a mysterious explosion in the trucking depot.

The Whisperer hailed a cab. The driver looked nervously at the nondescript fare he had picked up. The man looked something like descriptions he had heard of The Whisperer. But then, he knew The Whisperer was dead. He had seen the papers.

The little man did not give him an address. He merely gave directions.

The driver looked around after he had traversed a tree-lined street, to find out where to go from there. Then he swallowed twice. The cab was empty, but a five-dollar bill fluttered in the crack of one of the doors.

The Whisperer crept up the driveway of a house set well back in a carefully gardened lawn. It was a house that had taken plenty of cash to build. It belonged to Terrington Small.

Like a human fly, the little figure climbed the side of the house. The structure was built of ornamental brick. The unevenness of the contour gave beauty to the building. It also gave The Whisperer a foothold.

There was silence within the house for many minutes. Then a car hesitated on the street outside. A door below seemed to click.

Suddenly, the lights flashed on in the bedroom of the lawyer. Terrington Small jerked erect in his bed. His bushy hair was awry from sleeping.

Before him crouched a slight gray figure. Two automatics were in his hands. They were snubbed with big silencers. The little man snarled through thin lips.

"You are going to die, mouthpiece!" he hissed. "You're going out slowly, with a bullet in your guts!"

Terrington Small suddenly thought he was going crazy. Before he could protest, an eerie, whispering chuckle came from another side of the room. A second figure, that looked at first glance to be a duplicate of the first, stepped from behind the window drapes.

The second figure in gray was The Whisperer. He, too, held a brace of automatics; but they didn't look like the others. They weren't. The husky tones that came from his lips were filled with a chilling deadliness.

"You wanted him to die slowly, rat," The Whisperer grated. "You wanted him to live long enough to tell the cops that I was the one who shot him."

There was a sudden roar of an unsilenced gun. One of The Whisperer's automatics ripped from his hand. Blood spread over his fingers.

"He'll die quickly enough, now," the harsh voice of Knuckles Werner rasped. "And you'll die with him! Maybe it'll look like you just shot each other!"

A gun jabbed sharply into the back of The Whisperer.

Another gun waved in the direction of the lawyer on the bed. There was the ominous click of a safety catch. The Whisperer impostor had raised one of his own silenced guns, pointed it at Terrington Small.

"I'll shoot you with these," he snarled. "We'll leave them with The Whisperer. It will be perfect!"

Sarah Small suddenly screamed in the doorway. Apparently, she had gotten the gag out of her mouth, had fled from her father's office. Her scream may have saved her father's life. At any rate, it gave The Whisperer a chance to whirl on Knuckles Werner.

The mobster's gun boomed. But the slug thudded harmlessly into the wall.

The Whisperer's one good fist slammed into his jaw. The fist drew back like the lash of a whip. The fingers straightened, plunged stiffly into the throat of Knuckles Werner.

The killer gurgled once, fell to the floor. He stabbed out convulsively with a gun, aimed it at The Whisperer. The gray man's queer guns hissed like highly compressed air released from a tank. Werner lay still.

The fake Whisperer's guns were spitting lead. But he had a target that was hard to hit. A small, angry bundle of black fur was hanging to the seat of his pants.

No impostor could fool Brian Boru, The Whisperer's dog. He had followed his master, sneaked into the house when Sarah Small came in.

The Whisperer stepped quickly toward the other man in gray. In that instant, the final strength that sometimes comes to a dying man came to Knuckles Werner. His face writhed with pain and hate. He staggered to his knees. His eyes were wide and dazed. But the gun was steady.

He fired.

As the gray figure dropped, Werner sank back.

"Anyway," he babbled, "I got the rat!"

But Knuckles Werner's dying eyes had played him a trick. The figures looked too much alike. Knuckles shot the wrong figure in gray.

As the stricken impostor rolled on the floor, The Whisperer ripped the disguise from his face. It was Rocky Crangle, truck owner and bail bondsman. "You never liked to take a chance," the Whisperer said. "And you didn't want to undertake a major racket until The Whisperer was out of the way. That was Werner's assignment. You acted as a decoy, to lure the real Whisperer to Cleary Street for the killing. You knew your petty racketeering on kids and women would bring me in to find out what was going on."

Sirens whined suddenly in the street below. Half a dozen squad cars screamed into the driveway.

"Surround the place!" came the voice of Quick Trigger. "Shoot The Whisperer on sight! I'll take the front driveway!"

Sarah Small gasped.

"O-o-oh!" she cried. "I thought the real Whisperer had threatened dad. I called the police when I got free at the office. I wish I hadn't!"

The Whisperer didn't answer. He stooped quickly over the body of Rocky Crangle; scrawled rapidly on a sheet of paper, pinned it to the dead bondman's coat. Heavy footsteps pounded up the stairs.

With a hoarse triumphant chuckle, The Whisperer glided to the open window. Brian Boru was in his arms. The dog licked confidently at The Whisperer's chin. Then the gray man disappeared.

In the driveway below, Quick Trigger paced angrily. He had seen the story that The Whisperer had been killed. And Wildcat Gordon had told him he was going to drive down Cleary Street in the gray coupé. Quick Trigger believed the paper; believed Wildcat had at last overstepped himself. And he was very nearly right.

As the gray figure of The Whisperer crept silently through the shrubbery, Quick Trigger's squinted, peering eyes saw what perhaps no other cop had the eyesight to perceive. He saw The Whisperer.

With a roar, Quick Trigger plunged through the gloom. His cannonlike guns began to boom. And Quick Trigger's aim was far too accurate.

Then the retired deputy suddenly cursed. He wanted to bite off his arm. He saw the furry form of Brian Boru bounding ahead of the gray man. Quick Trigger began to shoot at the trees. Then he went into the house.

He knew the dog's devotion to The Whisperer, and he knew the dog could not be fooled.

Inside the lawyer's bedroom, Deputy Bolton was examining the two bodies. His first impulse had been one of elation.

"Now Mr. Crangle will be safe," he opined.

Then his small mouth dropped open with a gulp. He saw that the face of the man in gray was that of Rocky Crangle. The note pinned to the coat startled him even more.

"I was so sure no intelligent lawyer would write an incriminating letter on his own stationery," the scrawled handwriting at the top stated. "This proves he didn't."

The letter was the carbon The Whisperer had rifled from Terrington Small's office.

"I know you are guilty and, therefore, I cannot defend your case," it read. "You know I never do. Furthermore, I expect to run for prosecutor. If I am elected, I will see that you are convicted."

Quick Trigger was leaning over Bolton's shoulder.

"What's the rest of the scrawled handwriting?" he demanded. "What's that about The Whisperer?"

Bolton gulped and read it aloud:

"'If you will go to the cellar of 43 King Street, you will find another Whisperer.' Signed, 'The Whisperer'."

"Well," roared the voice of Wildcat Gordon, "why don't you find him!"

Wildcat strode briskly into the room. He was his loudly immaculate self, save for the fact that he carried his left hand in the pocket of his coat.

The cops did find another Whisperer. And in his hand was a note.

"My name was Smoky," it said. "I was dead anyway, and I didn't mind helping The Whisperer. He was a friend. He got away through the floor boards of his car."

Quick Trigger squinted at it.

"Sometimes," he mumbled in disgust, "I'm going to be sorry my aim wasn't better tonight."

THE END.

MASTER OF PRESTIDIGITECTION

by Anthony Tollin

"MAGIC AND MYSTERY are so closely interwoven that it is hard to tell where one leaves off and the other begins, or vice versa," Walter Gibson observed. "From the literary standpoint, this makes it very difficult to blend the two, without favoring one at the expense of the other."

Walter Gibson knew that better than anyone, having worked as a professional magician before becoming America's premier author of books on prestidigitation and the biographer and ghost writer for such legendary magicians as Houdini, Thurston, Dunninger and Blackstone.

"I knew Houdini quite well, up to the time he died," Walter recalled. "I used to travel with his show as his press agent and ghosted several of his books on magic and the occult." After writing books for the legendary escape artist, Gibson was given unprecedented access to Houdini's private notes, leading to the publication of *Houdini's Escapes.*

By 1930, Walter was determined to move into fiction writing with a hero inspired by the world's greatest illusionists. "For that, I needed an outstanding character and I had been thinking of one who would be a mystery in himself, moving into the affairs of lesser folk much to their amazement. By combining Houdini's penchant for escapes with the hypnotic power of Tibetan mystics, plus the knowledge shared by Thurston and Blackstone in the creation of illusions, such a character would have unlimited scope when confronted with surprise situations, yet all could be brought within the range of credibility."

A chance visit to the Street & Smith offices resulted in his being assigned to bring the nebulous host of CBS' *Detective Story Program* to literary life, allowing Gibson to incorporate his earlier ideas into a character that quickly grew into an American icon. Originally intended for quarterly publication, *The Shadow Magazine* became a monthly with its third issue, and eleven months later moved to a twice-monthly schedule.

Walter concocted his famous "Maxwell Grant" pen name by combining the names of two popular magic dealers, U. F. Grant and Maxwell Holden. "The choice was apt, for Max Holden specialized in Hand Shadows, casting lifelike silhouettes on

Blindfolded, Walter Gibson performs his "twenty card" trick in 1946.

screens or walls, while Gen Grant, as we called him, was the inventor of 'Walking Away from a Shadow,' a baffling illusion performed by the great Blackstone," Gibson explained. "Since these were both devices that I intended to attribute to The Shadow as a means of baffling or intimidating crooks, I felt that the pen name of Maxwell Grant would be appropriate; so I appropriated it, with due respects to Maxwell Holden and U. F. Grant."

Gibson pounded out Shadow novels twice a month for a dozen years, a magical act in itself. As if that wasn't enough, in 1937 he launched a second series for a new monthly pulp magazine—with another sleuth inspired by real-life magicians.

"Gibson . . . had the newspaperman's knack for giving you enough facts so you wanted to read on to the next paragraph, and enough of the magician's flare to flash things before you long enough to intrigue you, but not to give his point away."

—Crime Busters editor John Nanovic

MASTER OF PRESTIDIGITECTION   115

"The magazine *Crime Busters* was my idea," Gibson related to pulp historian Bernard Drew. "I suggested it to them one time. I was talking to [Street & Smith general manager] Ralston about more character magazines. And I was thinking myself of a magician detective, though I didn't know how it would go. He said, 'Well, it's costly to start a character magazine, and if it flops . . .'

"So I suggested that they put out one with three characters in it. And then whichever one went well, that would be it. They went ahead, but they put in five or six characters."

Crime Busters debuted in the Fall of 1937. The first issue introduced a number of new recurring characters including Ted Tinsley's distaff sleuth Carrie Cashin, private eye Dick Barrett (by *Spider* scribe Norvell Page), Lester Dent's Click Rush (the "Gadget Man"), postal inspectors Joe Bimbo and Howdy Hawks by *The Whisperer's* "Clifford Goodrich" (Laurence Donovan) and Walter Gibson's Norgil, the master of "prestidigitection."

"I was called on for a magician story for the first issue," Gibson recalled in 1977, "so I gave my character the name of Norgil, which he formed by juggling the letters of his actual name, which was Loring. He could also change it to Ling Ro, a title which he used when called upon to perform

Walter Gibson (right) discusses a comic script with Bill Neff, whose *Madhouse of Mystery* inspired Norgil's spook shows.

Courtesy William V. Rauscher / Pleasant Nightmares

wizardry in Chinese costume. Since The Shadow's popularity was at a peak and Street & Smith had earlier contracted to take my entire output of mystery fiction, I used my pen name of 'Maxwell Grant' with the Norgil stories as well, partly on the assumption that it would help the sale of *Crime Busters,* which it may have, for the new magazine sold well from the start."

Gibson drew heavily upon his friends in the world of stage magic in developing the new series. "Norgil was modeled somewhat on an earlier Harry Blackstone, typical of the vaudeville acts. Miriam Laymond was a typical leading lady of the show."

Walter often traveled with the Blackstone show, serving as press agent and even performing the show when the magician was ill or had multiple commitments. (Some observers claimed that he performed

Real-life magicians who inspired Norgil included (from left) Dr. Harlan Tarbell, mentalist Joseph Dunninger, Dai Vernon and John Calvert.

Rajah Raboid and Johnny Eck (of Freaks and sideshow fame) perform their unique version of "sawing a man in half."

Dr. Neff teaches Jimmy Stewart the "linking rings" trick.

the show as well as Blackstone himself.) "Part of the reason I went with Blackstone on tour was because *The Shadow Magazine* had a new policy of localizing the stories. The editors wanted to put The Shadow in action around the country, and I was collecting 'local color' for those stories." Gibson would join the Blackstone show full time in 1946, during an extended contract dispute with Street & Smith.

"Norgil, himself, had so many prototypes that many of the stories suggested themselves automatically. Like Blackstone or Calvert, both headliners at the time, he could switch from fifty-minute shows in movie houses to a full evening extravaganza, with an enlarged company."

John Calvert, who also starred as The Falcon in three Hollywood films, is still touring today at age 97. "There is no question that John Calvert has lived his magic," Gibson noted. "He is reminiscent of the legendary Scottish magician, Professor Anderson. . . . John Calvert will be remembered as one of the great and unique magicians of history."

Norgil "also had a counterpart in Russell Swann, who played deluxe hotels in New York, Washington, San Francisco, and even London. That put him into society circles and lecture circuits like Dunninger, the mind reader, and Dr. Harlan Tarbell, author of a famous magic course.

"Norgil's occasional switch to the character of Ling Ro was inspired by George Reuschling, who did a Chinese act under the name of 'Rush Ling Toy' and also doubled in a quick-change act—often on the same program!—as Lafollette, the Man of Many Faces."

Reuschling was a major vaudeville performer during Walter's early years in the magic fraternity. He appeared in Asian makeup on and off

Magician George Reuschling (left) performed as "Rush Ling Toy" (center) and also in a quick-change act as "Lafollette, the Man of Many Faces."

"I applied much that I had learned about a magician's technique when I came to devise situations in mystery fiction. I think every writer can work a hobby or adapt specialized knowledge to fiction uses."   **—Walter Gibson**

stage, providing a real-life prototype for several of Gibson's Chinese villains who were ultimately revealed to be Caucasians masquerading in Asian makeup. Reuschling also performed as "Lafollette, the Man of Many Faces," displaying a mastery of quick changes that rivaled The Shadow's own.

"Nor was Norgil averse to donning Hindu robes and appearing as a Hindu mystic like Rajah Raboid; and when occasion demanded he could stage a midnight spook show, rivaling the real-life Doctor Neff, whose *Madhouse of Mystery* teemed with ghosts galore." Neff had launched his act in his Indiana, Pennsylvania hometown, initially assisted by his childhood friend, future Hollywood star Jimmy Stewart (who'd helped Neff construct much of his original magical apparatus).

"Bill Neff's company had two men, himself and three girls. I traveled with him briefly. He put on a popular midnight spook show. In his regular act, he'd do 30 or 40 minutes of magic, with some weird stuff such as burying a girl alive. He'd put her in a coffin-like thing and set it afire, and her arm would flop out. He'd put it back in. At the end, there was a skeleton in there, and its arm flopped out." During the 1950s, screen legend Bela Lugosi (whose 1927 Broadway performance in *Dracula* helped inspire The Shadow) costarred in Dr. Neff's *Madhouse of Mystery.*

Gibson produced 23 magical Norgil stories for *Crime Busters* and its successor, *Street & Smith's Mystery Magazine.* Though Norgil soon bowed out with from the pages of *Mystery,* he briefly reappeared in a handful of Gibson-scripted adventures in *Shadow Comics* and *Doc Savage Comics.*

Walter Gibson was not finished with magician-detectives; he recast his friend Harry Blackstone as a "prestidigitective" in *Super Magician Comics* and the *Blackstone, the Magic Detective* radio series, and also scripted four color adventures of Dr. Bill Neff for S&S's *Red Dragon Comics* and *Ghost Breakers,* and later for Charlton's *Racket Squad in Action.*

We're pleased to present the first Norgil story by Walter Gibson (writing as "Maxwell Grant"), reprinted from the premier issue of *Crime Busters.* We plan to showcase Norgil adventures regularly in future volumes of *The Whisperer.* •

Harry Blackstone performs his famous "dancing handkerchief" illusion for Walter Gibson (left) and magic enthusiasts Will Lindhorst and George Karger.

NORGIL— MAGICIAN

by Maxwell Grant

CHAPTER I
THE GHOST THAT WASN'T

THE ORCHESTRA finished with a crash, as the girl stepped from the front of the huge, framed glass. Brisk assistants, in natty uniforms, were folding the screen that had covered her mysterious passage through the solid crystal. Norgil, the magician, bowed to the applause that billowed in from the audience.

He was a superb showman, Norgil; suave to the tips of the pointed mustache that adorned his sophisticated, oval-chinned face. His wealth of jet-black hair showed at best as he took another bow.

He displayed the ease of a dancing master when he sent the girl on a pirouette toward the wings.

Norgil followed, bowing himself off the stage. New notes from the orchestra crept into the applause. Hand claps finished as ears were haunted by the strains of spooky music. That melody was the prelude to Norgil's next mystery, his famous spirit cabinet.

In the wings, Norgil stopped by a large trunk where a uniformed assistant was peeling off his monkey suit. Norgil soft-toned:

"All set for it, Fritz?"

Fritz raised his head. Norgil saw his face in the back-stage light. He gave an approving nod; moved

The hand is quicker
than the eye—but Norgil
must fight the speed of
steel-jacketed bullets.

swiftly away. Fritz remained beside the trunk, finishing his preparation for a coming task.

The glass penetration had been performed "in one"—in theatrical parlance, before a curtain styled a "front drop." The spirit act called for a full-stage set; and the lights were dimming as the curtain slicked upward on its wires. A hush had gripped the audience; the darkened theater was stilled throughout.

Norgil felt that silence. It always came before the spirit cabinet trick. Music lulled until its weird strains were scarcely audible. These were the moments that brought the spectators to the edges of their chairs. On the bare stage they saw a skeleton cabinet, its chromium posts and cross bars reflecting the subdued light.

There was a floor to that cabinet. It was thin, and raised above the stage. There were curtains hanging at the corners but their sheen showed that they were too thin to hide concealed assistants. The only object in the cabinet was a chair, where Norgil was to seat himself.

Yet, once the magician drew those curtains, ghosts would materialize within the cabinet Norgil never claimed his spooks to be real, but there were credulous persons who considered them as such. Even doubters became tense when the spirit act was on. The trick was Norgil's masterpiece.

THERE WAS A figure coming on the stage. It was Norgil. His steps were dramatic in their slowness. He reached the cabinet; closed every curtain except the front one. The audience saw Norgil seat himself. His face was solemn, almost mystic. Like a man in a trance, he stretched his hand; he drew the front curtain shut.

Music had ceased. A dozen seconds passed, while tense viewers waited for weird, glowing faces to press aside the curtains. There were whispers in the audience, mild gasps of strained expectancy. Most of those sounds were lost. There was one, however, loud enough for some to hear.

That was a hissing sigh that came from a lower box. Timed to that odd tone, the curtain of the cabinet quivered. That motion held the audience. Their eyes fixed toward the stage, those who had heard the sigh forgot it.

Only an expert could have identified that sound, and linked it with the curtain's stir. The sigh wasn't a human one, nor a ghostly manifestation. It was the suppressed hiss of a rifle, equipped with a silencer. The motion of the cabinet's curtain marked the winging passage of a bullet, aimed straight for the heart of the hidden magician.

The marksman had chosen a perfect post for his sniper's job. Box seats were never sold for Norgil's show, except when the theater had a capacity audience. The house wasn't full tonight. It had been easy for the sniper to sneak into one of the empty boxes, unnoticed.

That lone shot fired, the marksman slid to the side aisle, packing; his portable rifle beneath his coat. He wanted to get out of the theater before people wondered why the act didn't continue. From the darkness of the aisle, the satisfied murderer looked over his shoulder. He noted the gloomy cabinet, its front curtain motionless.

An instant later, the scene changed. The orchestra, taking a special cue, shrieked lively music. The stage flooded with light. Assistants bounded from the wings, whipped the curtains from the skeleton cabinet.

It was empty, except for the chair. Norgil was gone. He had changed his spook routine into a vanishing act.

Before the foiled marksman moved a step, he was treated to a second surprise, which he alone of all the audience could appreciate. Crouched in the darkness of the aisle, the gunner felt rounded steel freeze his neck.

With the revolver muzzle came the undertone:

"I'll take that toy. Turn around; keep moving, with your hands high!"

The captured crook was thrust through a passage leading from the aisle, past the boxes. A fire-proof door slid open; the unsuccessful killer was back stage. The revolver muzzle prodded him toward

a dressing room, where a half-opened door bore a star. Stumbling down the steps, the surly prisoner turned about at a new command.

His captor was Norgil!

Five seconds later, Norgil was using the revolver with which he had cowed the would-be murderer. He was firing it at a tub of water, from which dripping ducks appeared in quick succession, flopping to the stage in accompaniment to the blank shots from the magician's gun.

Norgil had handed the portable gun to Fritz, who was now beside him. As Norgil lowered the revolver, the crook sprang up the steps, only to meet a swift uppercut from Norgil's free fists. Sprawling back downward in the dressing room, the crook lay stunned while Norgil told Fritz: "Watch him while I work the first act. We'll quiz him later."

Fritz made a bad mistake during the duck act. He left the unconscious prisoner, to stow the fellow's gun in a trunk. While there, Fritz changed to his uniform. When he came back to the dressing room, the lights were out. Before Fritz could click the switch, the crook piled upon him.

He was tough, that crook. His quick recovery from Norgil's punch proved it, and Fritz couldn't pack the wallop that Norgil could. That fight in the dark produced a quick result. The prisoner slung Fritz across the dressing room; the assistant did a sprawl beside the wall.

Fritz rallied, too late. The door slammed; a key turned in the outside lock. By the time Fritz's pounding brought a stage hand to unlock him, the prisoner was gone. He had ducked out through the stage door, gunless, but free.

Norgil learned that when the show was over. Seated in his dressing room, the magician took pad and pencil. He produced a portrait, as accurate as it was speedy.

"Remember the lightning sketches I used to do at Coney?" asked Norgil. "Years ago, Fritz, but I haven't lost the touch. There's the ape that tried to wing you. Find out who he is."

Fritz left with the ex-prisoner's picture. Norgil smeared his face with cold cream; toweled away his makeup. Someone rapped at the door. Norgil tied the sash of his dressing gown and called for the visitor to enter.

It was Rickenbury, the theater owner, a big, bull-dozing man, whose tuxedo was as paunchy as his jowlish cheeks. Rickenbury had a squawk to make. He delivered it in booming tone.

"What went sour with the spook stuff, Norgil? That vanish wasn't in your regular act."

"I know it." Norgil eyed the theater owner in the dressing table mirror. "Sometimes I make changes. No reason for you to object. I've bought the house."

Rickenbury's boom dwindled to a grumble. A wince came with it. Rickenbury had made a bad bet, leasing the theater outright to Norgil for two thousand dollars. He was wishing that he had played the magician on a percentage, instead. Business had been building everyday; Norgil was likely to gross eight thousand for the week.

"Mayor Davison was here," explained Rickenbury. "He wanted to see the spook show. You disappointed him. Joland Frew was in the house, too. You know how important he is?"

Norgil nodded. Joland Frew was the biggest real estate promoter in the city. Public rumor rippled that Frew owned half the town.

"They'd like to meet you, Norgil—"

"All right, Rickenbury." Norgil came to his feet. "Show them in."

MAYOR DAVISON proved a withery old fossil. His handshake was crablike; his laugh a cackle. Frew was middle-aged, square-built and genial. He didn't have much to say, for Mayor Davison took the floor.

"I wanted to see a ghost," cackled the mayor. "But there wasn't any. Why not, Mr. Norgil?"

Norgil gave a nonchalant smile. If he had gone through with his usual cabinet act, there would have been a ghost: his own. He didn't tell that to the mayor. Instead, Norgil simply replied:

"I wasn't in a psychic mood."

His honor didn't know how to take that explanation. He fancied that Norgil was jesting; but wasn't sure. Norgil's face sobered; he picked a sheet of paper from an inside pocket of his dress suit.

"This worried me," admitted Norgil. "Tell me what you make of it, Mr. Mayor."

The paper was a printed billhead that bore the title: "Theatrical Protective Association." It called for payment of twelve hundred dollars. The bill was made out to Norgil. At the bottom was the typewritten reminder: "Overdue. Remit before 10 p. m."

Mayor Davison showed a rankled expression. The city was in the grip of a racket ring that took its toll from many businesses. The mayor had promised to curb that crookery. But he hadn't. In fact, the cogwheels of the racket game had spun even more merrily since Davison had taken office.

To cover his embarrassment, his honor turned to Rickenbury. Plaintively, the mayor announced:

"This is a new one on me, Rickenbury. Have you known about it?"

The theater owner gave a reluctant nod.

"Why didn't you report it?"

"What was the use?" grumbled Rickenbury. "That outfit's got me stopped. They call for fifteen percent on what they think the house is going to gross. I've paid it, to avoid trouble. This week, Norgil bought

the house; so they passed the buck to him."

"Who are they?"

Rickenbury shrugged. He didn't know; apparently, he wasn't anxious to find out. The mayor questoned Norgil.

"I've been getting phone calls," stated the magician. "Always some fellow with a faked voice. Always the same argument. If I'm ready to pay up, he'll tell me how. A stagehand answered the last of those calls at quarter of ten tonight, just before I went on with the penetration illusion. I said I couldn't be bothered."

Frew was studying the billhead. In caustic tone, the promoter expressed his indignation. Some of his own enterprises had been hit by the racketeers, but they hadn't yet come after him in a big way. Frew was beginning to think it wouldn't be long before they did. He was therefore interested in Norgil's case. Frew asked the magician what he intended to do about it.

"I'm carrying twelve hundred here," replied Norgil, spreading his dressing gown, to show a money belt, "just in case they want the money bad enough to come after it. Otherwise, I don't pay up."

THE LISTENERS liked Norgil's stand. Mayor Davison, in particular, approved it, especially when his honor saw a chance to change the touchy subject. The mayor suggested that they have some drinks and a midnight supper at the club. Norgil accepted the invitation, then remembered something.

"I'll meet you later," he said, as he donned his street clothes. "I have to take Daphne over to the hotel, first." His tie adjusted, Norgil opened the door and called: "Fritz! Bring Daphne!"

Mayor Davison tilted his head and gave a withery smile. He was anxious to see which one of the pretty girls Daphne was. There were plenty of good-lookers in Norgil's troupe; probably Daphne was the damsel who had walked through the plate glass. His honor was hoping that she would arrive in the same scanty costume that she had worn during that illusion.

The mayor's face drooped when Fritz arrived and handed Daphne to Norgil. Daphne was a wire-haired fox terrier, scarcely more than a pup. Norgil was amused by the mayor's change of expression. So was Frew, who also noted it.

Once outside the stage door, Norgil bundled Daphne under his dark overcoat. His long, easy paces took him swiftly from the alley. He darted quick, expert looks as he crossed the backstreet. He was sure that no one was watching him. The same was true all along the back route to the hotel. Norgil was unobserved when he entered a sheltered rear doorway, to take a little-used stairway to the third floor.

Corridors were empty. Norgil's room was unwatched. The magician wore his suave smile as he neatly unlocked the room door. Inside the room, Norgil purred to Daphne:

"We're going to stay in the dark a while. You're used to it, pup, since I've been putting you in that place where you can't chew shoes. We won't have long to wait, though."

CHAPTER II
THE RIGHT HUNCH

NORGIL EXPECTED strategy with the coming thrust. There might be a bluff to throw him off his guard. If such came, it would only prove a boomerang to those who tried it. Bluff was part of Norgil's own technique; he could recognize it.

He was fooled, though.

The telephone bell jangled. Norgil suppressed the summons almost instantly. The telephone was on a table right beside him. As he gripped it, he lifted the receiver from the hook.

That ring could be a signal for someone who had sneaked into the third-floor corridor. That was why Norgil's mind was intent on the door, while his lips purred a "hello" into the telephone's mouthpiece.

The voice that answered made Norgil forget the door. It was Fritz, giving eager news. Fritz had shown Norgil's sketch to a friendly cashier in an all-night hash house. He had identified the ugly face as belonging to "Toughey" Eward, one of the town's reputed gunmen.

"A local cowboy," mused Norgil, voicing his thoughts softly across the wire. "Good work, Fritz. Find out some more about him. I still want to talk to him."

Norgil's own tone was to cause him trouble. It prevented him from hearing the turn of the door handle. Norgil had left the door unlocked; he was counting on hearing it if it opened. He was depending, too, on the corridor lights. But they had been extinguished.

Norgil hung up the receiver. Before he could sense that someone had entered the room, the arrival announced himself. There was the snap of a light switch by the door. Norgil bounded from his chair, too late. The room was filled with light from ceiling sockets. He was covered by a steady revolver, gripped by a hand below a bandanna-masked face.

The stocky, ill-dressed intruder meant business. He wasn't a sneaky marksman like Toughey Eward. The fellow had the way of a professional stickup artist. He nudged Norgil toward a corner; then showed a long chin, as he growled:

"I'm here to get that dough, lug. Peel off that money belt—an, go easy when you do it. None of that sleight-o'-hand baloney."

NORGIL KEPT HIS right hand raised, while he dipped his left fingers to the bottom of his vest, where the clasp of the money belt was. The masked crook watched those fingers closely, particularly one that wore a two-headed snake ring, gold with jeweled eyes.

Norgil made his move openly, carefully. He could guess that the crook's revolver had a hair trigger. The fellow had him, hands down, thanks to Fritz's ill-timed phone call. Luck had put Norgil on the spot. He didn't like it. Not because of the twelve hundred dollars that he was going to lose, but on account of the stupid way he had to hand it over.

Norgil would have paid twice the twelve hundred for a way out of this dilemma. Suddenly, he saw one. It was his turn for a lucky gift, but he needed nerve to back it.

What Norgil saw was a quiver of a closet door, only five feet from the masked thug's left shoulder. Norgil happened to know the symptoms of that door. It trembled again; another shake like that, and it would be loose. The thought steeled the magician.

Norgil let his left hand come up like his right. That brought a savage threat from the masked crook; with it, a gun nudge.

"Hey, you—don't try no stall—"

"There's no stall about it," interposed Norgil. "You're hooked, fellow, that's all. You were a sap to walk into it."

The crook's eyes glared doubt through the slits of the bandanna. He didn't like the shrewd smile that Norgil seemed trying to restrain.

"The house dick's got you covered," added Norgil. "That's why I brought him up here. I had a hunch you'd be due, because—"

Norgil did not complete the reason. There was no need for it. The closet door had started a swing, although the masked gunman didn't hear its groan. Turning his head toward the door, Norgil kept on talking. That, likewise, was something the crook didn't guess. Norgil's lips had fixed. His words were a deep-throated tone; gruff, delivered in a ventriloquist's pitch:

"I gotcha, guy! Hoist those dukes. Hurry it!"

No lip motion was needed in any of those syllables. The illusion was perfect. Though close to Norgil, the armed crook would have sworn that the words came from the closet. Wheeling, the rowdy saw the closet door swinging outward.

Norgil was right about the hair trigger. The crook pumped bullets into the darkened closet, aiming on a level of a man's chest. He thought he had beaten the imaginary house dick to the shots. He remembered Norgil, but that came too late.

THE MAGICIAN charged. His left hand nabbed the crook's gun. His right drove a hard uppercut. The crook's lucky twist saved him from that punch. As the gun went flinging across the room, the masked man came to grips.

As they thrashed on the floor, they had a witness. It was Daphne. The pup came loping from the closet. Daphne had shoved that door loose once before, when Norgil had stowed her in the closet. Norgil had remembered it when he saw the door tremble. He'd taken a long chance that it would swing loose, as it had before. Chances, though, belonged to the stage magician's game. Guessing when to take them was something that Norgil had learned through long experience. He had outwitted entire audiences when he played long odds. Here, he had needed only to fool one man.

Norgil was using more headwork against the grappling crook. The fellow gained an advantage. Norgil's quick hand offset it. He couldn't grab the crook's throat; instead, he snatched the bandanna mask and pulled it sideways. The eye slits slid to the crook's ear. The bandanna became a blindfold.

By the time the oath-fuming crook had snatched off the improvised mask, it was Norgil who had the edge. He held the crook's neck; was ready to batter the man's head against the wall, when the hall door opened to show the startled face of a house detective.

Norgil did a sudden, backward sprawl. The elated crook lunged down upon him, only to receive Norgil's feet against his chest. With propelling power, Norgil catapulted the crook across the floor. His wind knocked out, the man slumped panting at the house dick's feet.

That finished matters. Together, Norgil and the house detective marched the gasping thug downstairs and turned him over to the police. Norgil left the hotel, to have his midnight supper at the Town Club. Once there, he asked for Mayor Davison. An attendant showed him to a reserved table.

ONLY JOLAND FREW was there. Rickenbury had been detained at the theater; Mayor Davison had stopped off at the city hall. Frew had obligingly come ahead. While Frew was mentioning that, Mayor Davison arrived. Rickenbury showed up a few minutes later.

All became tense listeners when they heard Norgil's account of the hotel episode. The mayor promised speedy justice to the crook who had been captured. Frew congratulated Norgil on the effective way he had saved his twelve hundred dollars. Rickenbury expressed the hope that this would make the racketeers lay off theaters in the future; but didn't speak as though he counted on it.

Not one of the trio mentioned the idea that was paramount in Norgil's mind. They didn't seem to recall that they, alone, had known that the magician

intended to return to the hotel. It was plain to Norgil, though, that the masked collector who had visited him had come at a tip-off from one of these three.

Perhaps the big shot was ready to drop the matter. Norgil would be gone next week. The prestige of the racket ring could be restored without the collection of the magician's twelve hundred dollars—paltry change, compared to all that the big shot had at stake.

But Norgil wasn't ready to forget the racketeer. By tomorrow, if need be, he'd have new bait—the sort that any fish would swallow. His companions were discussing a special show, scheduled for tomorrow midnight. It was a convention affair, in the ballroom of the local hotel. They wanted Norgil as a headliner on the bill.

Obligingly, the magician agreed; but his smile meant more than ordinary willingness. Norgil was picturing how neatly that event could top off his plan to wreck the racket ring.

CHAPTER III
CASH DELIVERED

NEXT day, Fritz termed the matinee a "flopperoo"; and Fritz was right. Norgil wasn't himself on stage. He showed it when he fumbled the fishbowls; again, when he opened the door too soon with the Upside-Down Cabinet. The audience would have caught that one, if Fritz hadn't faked a stumble against the door, to bounce it shut.

When Norgil wasn't right, the rest of the company felt it, too. The show ended with weak applause from the audience. On the way to their dressing rooms, the assistants muttered that the wizard had the jitters. That pleased Norgil, when he overheard it. If he could fool his own company with fake nervousness, he could put it across on others.

Norgil was at dinner when a bellhop called him to the telephone. A forced voice repeated the old question: was he ready to pay up? Norgil replied in the affirmative. The voice growled instructions.

"Stick the dough in an envelope. Put it in a coat pocket and send your suit down to the tailor shop. Before eight o'clock. That's all."

Soon after dinner, Fritz found Norgil in his hotel room. The magician was pacing the floor, smoking his fifth cigarette, while Daphne chewed slippers unmolested. Norgil told the assistant what was up, then motioned toward the open closet. A suit was hanging there. Norgil ordered Fritz to take it to the tailor shop.

That brought a flash of Fritz's pluck.

"Not a chance, boss," he argued. "Say, I did the double in the spook cabinet, didn't I? You don't think I'd have gone through with that, if I'd known that you were quitting cold—"

Norgil's hand thwack interrupted. It was planted on the middle of Fritz's back.

"Good boy, Fritz." It was the steely tone that the assistant had expected. "I knew you'd be ready for another stab at it. I wouldn't be sending the money along, if I didn't like the setup. I've looked into it, though, and I like it."

Norgil penciled a diagram. It showed a pair of long, narrow connecting rooms, with only one door, at the front.

"The tailor shop," he explained. "In the basement. No windows. Only this door. What goes in there, comes out there."

Fritz nodded. He could see advantages in that.

"We've broken in that new man," recalled Norgil. "He can take your place, Fritz. You won't be needed at the theater. You'll be needed right over here."

Emphatically, Norgil dotted a diagram to indicate a spot across the street from the tailor shop, where Fritz was to watch. He added the remark:

"Whoever carries that money out will take it to the big shot, We'll risk the cash, Fritz, on the chance of a trail."

THE EVENING SHOW was finished earlier than usual, for Norgil sped the program. He found Fritz at the watchpost; and the assistant had glum news. There had been a rush of business at the tailor shop. Half a dozen bellboys had come and gone on frequent visits. Each had carried away an average of five suits, all tuxedoes

"It's the convention," explained Fritz. "And these bellhops were delivering pressed suits to rooms instead of to people. There's thirty suits to pick from, all alike. It's a cinch the money went with one of them—"

"No one else entered the shop?"

"Nobody. There was a kid stopped and handed in a kettle of coffee to the old tailor. But the old guy didn't pass anything out. He's still in there, the tailor. Been busy as a monkey, I guess, though most of those suits were pressed earlier."

"Nobody except the tailor."

Norgil's purred interjection snapped Fritz to new life. Fritz had been thinking of the bellboys; not of the tailor. It struck Fritz suddenly that the magician had expected this very result. That was why he had gambled on it. While Fritz was still bubbling his admiration of Norgil's foresight, the magician drew him across the street.

It didn't take long for Norgil to finish the lock on the shop door, while Fritz kept watch. The light in the front room was out. Norgil edged through the door and beckoned Fritz to follow. The rear part of the shop was lighted. That was where the tailor did his mending and handled the pressing machine.

The tailor was there. Fritz grinned as he saw the fellow resting with arm and head upon the mending table, sound asleep. Needles, thread and a patch of black silk lining lay beside the man's half-finished cup of coffee. He'd be due for a sudden surprise, that tailor, when Norgil woke him up.

There, Fritz guessed wrong. The surprise was to be his own.

It was Norgil who suspected the real situation. The magician placed his hands upon the sides of the tailor's head and tilted the man's face upward. He looked into bulgy, sightless eyes. The head had inert weight when Norgil let it drop.

A tool of the racket ring, the tailor had been no longer needed. He was one man who had learned too much. That problem had been settled—by a delivery of poisoned coffee. The tailor was dead.

CHAPTER IV
BLADES OF STEEL

NORGIL RECALLED what Fritz had said about the parade of bellboys to and from the tailor shop. That procession had been part of the big shot's game. It broke the trail, as Fritz had supposed; and it ruined Norgil's bet, since the tailor was dead.

Rickenbury—Davison—Frew. All would be at the hotel tonight. Each would be dressing in tuxedo. By this time, the big shot—whichever he was—had collected the listed money.

What would he do with it?

"Come along, Fritz." Norgil's tone was low. "We're going to talk with a taxi driver about a rat."

They found the right taxi in front of the hotel, where people were already arriving for the convention show. Norgil questioned the fellow about Toughey. The cabby had never heard of him.

The man was lying, but that couldn't be helped. Norgil sized him as a small-fry hoodlum in the racket ring's employ. Even a gun threat wouldn't make him tell where Toughey was. If the taxi driver spilled what he knew, he'd get bullets from his own pals later.

Fritz didn't catch that point. He was reaching for the cab door, when Norgil stopped him with a shin kick that the driver didn't see.

"Come along, Fritz," voiced the magician, smoothly. "We don't have to waste time with this bird."

That remark brought a quick look from the cabby. It seemed to have significance that applied to Toughey Eward. The cabby strained his ears as Norgil drew Fritz back from the curb. Norgil spotted the cab driver's interest, and used it.

The magician could use a stage whisper to perfection. He had a sotto voce tone that carried every word, although it seemed to be deliberately hushed.

The cabby never guessed that Norgil's whisper was intended for his benefit.

"That note the tailor left," undertoned Norgil, intervening to hide Fritz's puzzled blink from the cabby. "It named the big shot. That's all we need. Let's go to the theater and get the affidavit from the dressing room."

Fritz managed a nod. He turned in the direction of the theater. Norgil stopped him with a smile. He nudged toward the hotel coffee shop; remarked in normal tone:

"There's time for a cup of coffee first."

They'd hardly passed the revolving door before the taxi whipped away. Its driver was off with an urgent message for Toughey. Fritz expected Norgil to grab another cab and follow. Instead, the magician insisted on his coffee. Fritz ordered milk. Coffee didn't interest him, after that visit to the tailor shop.

Five minutes later, they headed for the theater. Stagehands were through with their work, but the stage door wasn't locked. Cleaners would attend to that when they were through out front. Norgil turned on a light. The stage showed dim, with the big asbestos curtain as a barrier between it and the house.

Norgil stopped Fritz before they reached the dressing room steps. They were beside the sword box, a squarish cabinet mounted on high legs. Its heavy sides and door had slits through which the swords could be thrust. The blades, big cavalry sabers, were arranged in orderly fashion upon a rack beside the wall.

There was an oddity about the sword box tonight. Usually, it was turned with its door toward the stage. At present, it had been shifted so the hinged door faced the dressing room. Norgil observed that, but Fritz didn't. That was why the magician, alone, saw the slight motion of the door.

Norgil didn't go past the front of the box. Instead, he pressed one hand to his lips; motioned with the other for Fritz to hand him a sword. Fritz was perplexed, but he obeyed, with the absolute silence that Norgil wanted. Receiving the saber, Norgil gestured for Fritz to take one, also. The assistant obliged.

Pointing his sword at one angle, then the opposite, Norgil indicated that they were to deliver similar thrusts. His nod was the final cue. Norgil shoved his sword through a side hole in the box. The point came stabbing out through the front. Simultaneously, Fritz's blade thrust into sight. The sword points almost clicked.

THERE WAS a scuffle in the box as an occupant tried to open the door. He failed; the swords had locked it. Norgil grabbed another saber, started it through the side, crosswise near the front. There

was a howl; a body floundered backward to avoid the poke of the sword.

With a few swords still remaining on the rack, Norgil and Fritz could find no further paths for them. The magician mounted the platform, lifted off the box lid and handed it to Fritz. The assistant peered over from the other side.

In the box, they saw a panting prisoner, in the person of Toughey Eward. The thug had a gun, but he could neither reach it nor use it. He'd dropped the revolver when he dodged a sword. Steel blades, thrust from varying angles, had contorted Toughey's scramble. He was twisted askew; his body was girded with the crossing sabers. So were his arms and legs. The sharp blades had them hunched in different directions.

"Keep him that way, Fritz," ordered Norgil. "If he gets too nervous, warm up some of the coffee we brought from the tailor shop. Toughey might like a drink of it."

With that last thrust, Norgil stepped from the platform. Fritz and the steel-bound prisoner heard the stage door slam as the suave magician departed, to settle his final score.

CHAPTER V
BETTER THAN RABBITS

NORGIL WAS the sparkling attraction of the midnight show at the hotel. Most of the audience had seen his stage performances; they were treated to a different Norgil, whose close work held them awed. Cards materialized at the tips of long, deft fingers; coins vanished with a similar ease.

All the while, the magician's suave smile seemed to say that greater surprises were to come. His well-chosen program showed that design. Spectators wondered if each new trick could match the one before it. Norgil never disappointed them. He was building to a climax that this audience wouldn't forget.

In various tricks, Norgil required the assistance of the audience. He remarked that his final experiment needed the help of three spectators—prominent persons well known to everyone present. He didn't have to suggest the names. People called them.

Mayor Davison was one; Joland Frew another. Norgil was inviting them to the platform, while the audience wrangled about who was to be the third. Norgil's tapering hand raised, to quiet the unsettled clamor. Since there was doubt, he would choose the third man to aid him. Norgil picked Rickenbury.

His final effect, Norgil announced, was an improvement over an older mystery. Undoubtedly, members of the audience had seen the famous Hindu Needle Trick, which had often been presented by Houdini. Norgil's version required other implements than needle and thread.

To the mayor, Norgil gave a glass of water. He handed Frew a length of fish line. For Rickenbury, he opened a package of double-edged razor blades, asking that they be examined. Rickenbury made the inspection, gingerly.

Taking the fish line from Frew, the magician coiled it into a compact wad, placed this on his tongue. He took a swallow from the glass of water. When he opened his mouth, the fish line was gone, Norgil reached for the razor blades.

There were gasps from the audience as Norgil's fingers carefully set the blades, one by one, upon his outstretched tongue. A back tilt of his head, and Norgil finished the glass of water. Amazed eyes watched the swallow that he made. Norgil grimaced as he shook his black-haired head. Coolly, he opened his mouth wide.

The razor blades had followed the fish line.

NORGIL'S SMILE met the startled gaze of those about him. The magician was thinking of other blades of steel—those swords that still incased Toughey Eward. That thought was scarcely more than a flash. Norgil's mind returned to the trick that he was now peforming.

He reached to his lips, drew forth a razor blade, with easy, but careful motion. Attached to the blade was the end of the fish line. As it paid out, Norgil reached with his fingers to slide another blade from between his lips. The rest were following, a full dozen of them, while the first blades dangled. With the last, Norgil stretched his hands apart. There was the entire line of razor blades, knotted at regular intervals.

Applause was terrific. Nonchalantly, Norgil let his helpers examine the threaded blades. Obligingly, he sliced the fish line with the edge of a blade, so that each man could inspect a different segment of the cord. An odd blade remained in Norgil's right hand. As he turned to lay it on a table, his left thumb turned the snake ring that was on the third finger.

Instead of putting the loose razor blade aside, Norgil let his right thumb jab the end between the two heads of the snake ring. The blade pressed tight in place, flat against the palm of Norgil's left hand. Neither edge quite touched his flesh.

Mayor Davison was stepping from the platform. Norgil stopped him with a right-hand gesture. Reaching to his own coat pocket, the magician produced a timepiece that dangled on its chain.

"Your watch, your honor."

The audience roared its laughter as the stupefied mayor received the watch. From that same right pocket Norgil brought a flat wallet that he tendered to Rickenbury, with the quizzical comment:

"Yours?"

Rickenbury nodded, while the laughter increased. Frew, in the center of the platform, was indulgently feeling his own pockets. He shook his head to indicate that nothing was missing. Norgil approached him.

"There's something under your coat collar, Frew—"

"A rabbit?" Frew laughed, as he raised his arms to the back of his coat. "I don't think so, Norgil. But maybe you can find one."

They were close together. Norgil was working swiftly, smoothly. Frew felt something beneath his coat, at the back. Norgil wanted him to notice it, so he would miss something else. The magician's left hand was busy, unseen by Frew and the audience. They were watching Norgil's right, as it came from the back of Frew's collar, bringing a string of silk handkerchiefs in front of the promoter's eyes.

Frew laughed; his mirth became hearty as Norgil followed with a line of baby's clothes. With another dip, he produced a whole fistful of silks that he clutched in his right hand. His left hand lowered. Its thumb flipped the razor blade loose, to fall noise-lessly on the carpeted platform.

"Very good, Norgil," laughed Frew. "Nevertheless, I'd like a rabbit."

"No rabbits." Norgil's tone had become method-ical. His left hand brought an envelope from his own inside pocket. "Here, Rickenbury, you hold the affidavit. And you, Mr Mayor—"

As Norgil looked toward the mayor, Frew did the same. The magician's left hand darted with whipped speed, inside the front of Frew's coat. From the long slit that the razor blade had sliced in the lining, Norgil whipped a compact envelope that crinkled from the currency inside it.

"Hold the money, Mr. Mayor!" added Norgil. "The bills that match the numbers in the affidavit. Meanwhile, let me present"—he was on Frew's right, gesturing his left hand toward the promoter— the big shot of this city's racket ring!"

FREW'S FACE was maddened. His clenched fists shook toward Norgil.

"A lie!" Frew's voice was a bellow. "You planted those on me, Norgil—"

"Hardly," purred Norgil. "I had to slice the lining of your coat to get the envelope."

"It wasn't in the lining—"

"Not until the tailor sewed it there. He was murdered neatly, Frew; but he left the black silk on his mending table."

That impeachment was enough for Frew. With murderous glare, the big shot sped his hand to his hip pocket. Spectators sprang for the platform, to grab him before he could pull his gun. They were too late to halt Frew's move. In his turn, Frew was tardy in seeking the revolver.

Norgil's right hand gave a flourish. The cluster of silk handkerchiefs scattered, drifted to the platform.

In Norgil's fist was a pearl-handled .32, its muzzle pointing straight for Joland Frew. The big shot recognized that weapon, as he heard Norgil's dry comment: "Yours, I believe."

A dozen hands fell on Frew. Still bellowing an innocence that no one believed, the head of the racket ring was dragged from the platform. Norgil joined Davison and Rickenbury. He added Frew's revolver to the money and the affidavit that were already exhibits on the table.

"Better than rabbits" was Norgil's smiling comment. "By the way, Mr. Mayor, there's a prisoner at the theater who will clinch the case against Frew."

Later, after Toughey Eward had joined Joland Frew in the city jail, Norgil expressed a whimsical thought. He voiced it to the mayor and the theater owner, while they sat with the magician at a table in the Town Club.

"Each year," recalled Norgil, "I give a free performance at the State penitentiary. When I see Frew there, I'll have his rabbit for him."

THE END

MASTER OF MAGIC AND MYSTERY

WALTER B. GIBSON (1897-1985) was born in Germantown, Pennsylvania. His first published feature, a puzzle titled "Enigma," appeared in *St. Nicholas Magazine* when Walter was only eight years old. In 1912, Gibson's second published piece won a literary prize, presented by former President Howard Taft who expressed the hope that this would be the beginning of a great literary career. Building upon a lifelong fascination with magic and sleight of hand, Gibson became a frequent contributor to magic magazines and worked briefly as a carnival magician. He joined the reporting staff of the *Philadelphia North American* after graduating from Colgate University in 1920, moved over to the *Philadelphia Public Ledger* the following year and was soon producing a huge volume of syndicated features for NEA and the Ledger Syndicate, while also ghosting books for magicians Houdini, Thurston, Blackstone and Dunninger.

A 1930 visit to Street & Smith's offices led to his being hired to write novels featuring The Shadow, the mysterious host of CBS' *Detective Story Program*. Originally planned as a quarterly, *The Shadow Magazine* was promoted to monthly publication when the first two issues sold out and, a year later, began the twice-a-month frequency it would enjoy for the next decade. He eventually wrote 283 Shadow novels totalling some 15 million words.

Gibson scripted the lead features for *Shadow Comics* and *Super-Magician Comics,* and organized a Philadelphia-based comic art shop utilizing former *Evening Ledger* artists. He also found time for radio, plotting and coscripting *The Return of Nick Carter, Chick Carter, The Avenger, Frank Merriwell* and *Blackstone the Magic Detective.* He wrote hundreds of true crime articles for magazines and scripted numerous commercial, industrial and political comic books, pioneering the use of comics as educational tools. In his book, *Man of Magic and Mystery: a Guide to the Work of Walter B. Gibson,* J. Randolph Cox documents more than 30 million words published in 150 books, some 500 magazine stories and articles, more than 3000 syndicated newspaper features and hundreds of radio and comic scripts. Walter also hosted ABC's *Strange* and wrote scores of books on magic and psychic phenomena, many co-authored with his wife, Litzka Raymond Gibson. He also wrote five *Biff Brewster* juvenile adventure novels for Grosset and Dunlap (as "Andy Adams"), a *Vicki Barr, Air Stewardess* book and a *Cherry Ames, Nurse* story (as "Helen Wells"), *The Twilight Zone* and such publishing staples as *Hoyle's Simplified Guide to the Popular Card Games* and *Fell's Official Guide to Knots and How to Tie Them.*

No one was happier than Walter when The Shadow staged a revival in the sixties and seventies. Walter wrote *Return of The Shadow* in 1963 and three years later selected three vintage stories to appear in a hardcover anthology entitled *The Weird Adventures of The Shadow.* Several series of paperback and hardcover reprints followed and Gibson wrote two new *Shadow* short stories, "The Riddle of the Rangoon Ruby" and "Blackmail Bay." A frequent guest at nostalgia, mystery, and comic conventions, Gibson attended the annual Pulpcon and Friends of Old-Time Radio conventions on a regular basis, always delighted to perform a few magic tricks and sign autographs as both Gibson and Grant, using his distinctive double-X signature. His last completed work of fiction, "The Batman Encounters—Gray Face," appeared as a text feature in the 500th issue of *Detective Comics.*

Walter Gibson died on December 6, 1985, a recently-begun Shadow novel sitting unfinished in his typewriter. "I always enjoyed writing the *Shadow* stories," he remarked to me a few years earlier. "There was never a time when I wasn't enjoying the story I was writing or looking forward to beginning the next one." Walter paused and then added, a touch of sadness in his voice, "I wish I was still writing the *Shadow* stories."

So do I, old friend. So do I.

—Anthony Tollin

MEET THE WRITERS by Will Murray

LAURENCE L. DONOVAN was one of the most prolific and versatile pulp fictioneers of his era. Born in Ohio, circa 1884, he worked as a copyreader and journalist for the San Francisco *Call-Bulletin* and the *Vancouver Sun*. During the latter '20s, he began contributing to myriad pulp magazines ranging from the dignified *Argosy* to the bizarre *Zeppelin Stories*. Prior to that, he appears to have toiled in Hollywood. Family legend has it that Donovan was offered the chance to script the 1925 silent screen version of *Ben Hur*, but went off on one of his infamous drinking binges, blowing the chance forever. That same year, his vignette, "The Old Copy Desk," was published in *The Saturday Evening Post*.

Donovan broke into Street & Smith in 1929 via the story "Brick Sacrifices," written for *Sport Story Magazine*. By 1933, he was writing for Street & Smith editor John L. Nanovic, contributing short stories to the back pages of *The Shadow, Doc Savage*, and *Nick Carter, Pete Rice* and others, sometimes under the house name of Walter Wayne. In the pages of S&S's *Detective Story Magazine, Clues* and *Western Story Magazine,* he inexplicably employed the byline Patrick Everett.

Donovan under his own name wrote virtually the entire first issue of Street & Smith's *Movie Action*, converting to novelettes such then-current film scripts as *Tumbling Tumbleweeds, The Crime of Dr. Crespi, Powder-Smoke Range, The Last Days of Pompeii, Drake the Pirate* and *Moonlight on the Prairie*.

In 1935, Nanovic asked him to write Doc Savage novels under the house name of "Kenneth Robeson," alternating with originating author, Lester Dent. After producing nine Docs, Donovan drew on his nautical background to create Captain John Fury for S&S's *The Skipper*. While writing The Skipper as "Wallace Brooker," he launched *The Whisperer*, also for Street & Smith. This time he was "Clifford Goodrich."

When those magazines folded in the aftermath of the October 1937 stock market crash, Donovan continued both characters in the back pages of *The Shadow* and *Doc Savage*, and began ghosting the adventures of Pete Rice in *Wild West Weekly* as "Austin Gridley." His "Boxcar" Reilly character began appearing in *Crime Busters* in 1937, as did postal inspectors "Bimbo" and "Howdy," whom he had originated for *The Feds*.

After a alcohol-induced falling out with John Nanovic in 1938, Donovan moved over to the rival Standard Magazines, where he began ghosting the adventures of The Phantom under the house name of "Robert Wallace." There he created The Phantom's teenage sidekick, Chip Dorlan. For Standard, Donovan ultimately ghosted episodes of most of their heroes, including G-Man Dan Fowler, The Masked Detective and The Black Bat. One of his 1942 Black Bat novels, *The Murder Prophet*, was a rewrite of "The Crime Prophet," an unpublished Whisperer novel.

Concrete information on Donovan's life is scanty to non-existent. His first name may have been spelled Lawrence, while his middle name was either "Louis" or "Lewis." It's not certain that Donovan was his actual birth name, however. The Shadow's Walter B. Gibson remembered that he changed it from something like "Donegal." But it might have been "O'Donovan." Donovan was married at least twice, divorcing first wife Ruth in the late 1930s, and was reported to have been a seasoned sailor. He may have belonged to the Merchant Marines in his younger days.

Donovan was living in Vancouver British Columbia, in 1927, when his son, Laurence Junior, was born. Another son, Patrick, came along a year later, while the family was living in Washington State. The family moved often, residing in Flushing, New York, Southampton, Long Island, and Old Greenwich, Connecticut, before relocating to Florida. He lived in St. Augustine and later, Miami. His other pen names included "Don Lewis," "Don Lawrence," and "Larry Dunn," by which he concealed his identity in the lurid *Spicy Detective Stories* and sister magazines like *Spicy Western* stories. His "Pa" Howdy stories ran in *Detective Fiction Weekly* and *Clues* in the 1930s, and in *G-Men Detective* a decade later. "Joe Bunt" appeared in *Popular Detective*, as did Wildcat Martin, who also ran in *Exciting Detective*. Strangely, three of his Doc Savage novels were "adapted" as early Superman comic book stories. He is also believed to have written for radio. Donovan virtually disappears from the pulps after 1949. His last known published story was "Redheads Kill Easy," for Popular Publications' *New Detective*, February 1952. It was a final "Pa" Howdy story. He is believed to have died in Miami in the early 1950s.

ALAN HATHWAY (1906-1977) was born in Chicago and grew up in Michigan. Migrating to Manhattan in the 1920s, he joined the staff of the New York *Daily News*. He began writing short stories for Street & Smith in 1936, taking over The Whisperer stories in *The Shadow Magazine* when Laurence Donovan moved on. In 1940, he ghosted four Doc Savage novels, and launched a revived *Whisperer* magazine. When it folded in 1942, he joined *Newsday* as city editor, and soon moved up to become managing editor. In his able hands, the paper won a Pulitzer Prize in 1954. •